MASK OF NIGHT

MASK

OF

NIGHT

LOIS WOLFE

DOUBLEDAY

NEW YORK LONDON TORONTO SYDNEY AUCKLAND

L O V E S W E P T ®
PUBLISHED BY DOUBLEDAY
a division of Bantam Doubleday Dell Publishing Group, Inc.
666 Fifth Avenue, New York, New York 10103

DOUBLEDAY and the portrayal of an anchor with a dolphin
and the word LOVESWEPT and the portrayal of the wave device
are trademarks of Doubleday, a division of
Bantam Doubleday Dell Publishing Group, Inc.

Library of Congress Cataloging-in-Publication Data

Wolfe, Lois.
    Mask of night / Lois Wolfe. — 1st ed.
        p.   cm.
    "Loveswept."
    ISBN 0-385-46908-X
    I. Title.
PS3573.O5234M3   1993
813'.54—dc20   92-24130
                             CIP

MASK OF NIGHT

1

December 1867

NEW YORK

She died passionately and well, plunging the dagger to her bosom and screaming, raw with pain. It was her seven hundred and sixty-third suicide and, of all, the most rewarding.

She crumpled to the floor. Long, fair hair landed in a silken stream across Romeo's doublet. Her white moiré gown billowed around them and slowly sank.

Silence. That sweet moment of stillness when a spellbound audience holds its collective breath. The moment was hers.

A small rippling of applause began and grew mighty.

She heard it in a private darkness, her eyes closed, emotionally spent and physically frozen in place. The pose was an anguished stretch of neck and torso, one arm braced on the floor to keep from crushing her brother, Edmund. She knew his lungs were frail from abuse, and she had landed awkwardly to ease her weight.

He had brought this difficult death upon both of them. Two nights the previous week the audience had watched "dead" Romeo twitch his itchy nose through the crypt scene. And the night before, dead Romeo had coughed once, then breathed so deeply the rise and fall of his chest could be seen in the highest boxes.

That was when the theater's manager, Augustin Daly, ordered Katie to die head and shoulders atop Edmund. "Smother the bastard," Daly had said. The whole cast had heard, Daly's repertory crew and the embarrassed Henslowe family players.

Above Katie, gas chandeliers burned, hot as floating hearths. A bead of sweat began at her temple. Her arm ached. Her neck was romantically crooked, too awkward to hold, but a thousand eyes watched, alert.

A cramp jerked her forearm taut. She kept her face peaceful, masking pain. "Without the mask, you are naked on stage," her father had taught her.

She needed her father now, front and center as they had planned. But he was lingering upstage to grandstand in his role of the noble Prince. "Search," he commanded his soldiers, "seek and know how this foul murder comes!"

A tremor rippled the muscles in her arm. Near collapse, she was about to let her head drop visibly when she heard her father approaching center stage.

He paused squarely in front of the two dead lovers to thunder the Prince's lines. When she felt the hem of his long robe skim her hair, she knew she was covered. She shifted her arm and relaxed her neck.

Alleyn Henslowe moved on. " 'And therewithal came he to this vault to die'," boomed the cloudy baritone of her father, British-born scion of the troupe he had grandiloquently named Populus Felicitas. Theater managers on the northeast circuit had long ago tamed the name and her father's ambitions. Henslowe's traveling troupe was known simply to all as "Poppy."

Poppy was always on her mind. Even now, with the severe strain of the pose under control, she could not relax. She remembered her answer when, as a child, a stranger asked her, Where do you live? She had thought of towns they had played, rooms where they had stayed, sometimes for a few days, sometimes for weeks or months. Finally, she had answered honestly, "We live in Poppy."

The troupe had ten members, always touring, always one step ahead of the bank agents and bill collectors. This winter, though, the situation was more than grim: Poppy was closer to insolvency than it had ever been.

Barely raising her lashes, Katie chanced a glance at her half brother, Edmund, Poppy's star. He was staring at the back wall of the stage, his heavy-lidded eyes blankly fixed in a strange, waking sleep. His face was thin and ghoulish in his white powder makeup. He rarely ate or slept anymore. New York held far too many diversions for a man of voracious appetite.

She didn't want to think about his night habits. He was nine years her senior; he should have been mature, a good manager. Instead, he caroused in gin palaces, faro houses, and darker haunts until dawn. He had shrugged off every aspect of managing a troupe —except the title. He liked the sound of actor-manager. And he liked letting Katie handle the work.

A good thing, she thought. He, like Father, was a rotten businessman. Poppy desperately needed another lucrative booking at the Daly, an extended contract. To get it, she had driven herself tirelessly every night of the run, casting off her natural reserve in her gestures, the mannered restraint in her voice, allowing sheer financial desperation to fuel the fire of her role.

As a result, Juliet had become a startling creature of heartfelt need and radiant passion. Katie had infused the naive girl with high emotion, burning a path to Juliet's core.

The audience had loved it. The house was full every night.

Unfortunately, as house manager, Augustin Daly counted more than tickets on an actor's scorecard. Daly was a stickler for stage discipline and teamwork, and Edmund was notoriously self-gratifying on the stage. He missed cues, stole scenes, and threw backstage tantrums when crossed. Daly's repertory cast was downright hostile to him.

Edmund. It was useless to admonish him. He was Father's glorious, prodigal gift to the stage. He was Poppy's star, their grandest promise, their greatest lie.

Her hand had gone numb. Thank God, the last couplet.

" 'For never was a story of more woe Than this of Juliet and her Romeo'," her father intoned, arms wide in a grand and final sweep.

The curtain drew together on the hiss of well-greased pulleys. Applause began in a generous burst, the clap of gloved hands muffled, like unshod ponies running across a field.

She rose quickly, her fingers stung by a surge of nettles as circulation returned. Edmund rolled to his knees with a grunt and got up. As she ran into the wings, she heard cries from the audience. Plaudits. For her! She smiled, trying not to be affected. Feeling light-headed, she leaned against a post backstage, allowing the sound to run over her. They loved it. They loved her.

The cast milled around her. Even her sister, Peg, came forward, prompt book held to her chest, dark braid draped across one shoulder. "Good theater, Katie," she said without emotion, jealousy hidden. Her limp as she walked away, though, was pronounced.

Katie composed herself for the curtain call and followed a line of satin doublets, striped tights, and white wimples onto the stage. Each actor took a bow to enthusiastic applause, but when Katie stepped forward, the gallery roared. Not to be outdone, the "Bravos" from the loges grew louder. Whistles burst shrill above the melee, and Katie stepped back into line, hiding her shaking hands in the satin folds of Juliet's gown. Her last night. A glorious last night.

She hurried back into the wings with the rest of the cast, one hand holding Juliet's jeweled cap to her head, her waist-length hair flicking counterpoint.

Cheers for Juliet grew wild as the manager, Augustin Daly, made his way through the cast. He took Katie by the shoulders, turned her to face the stage, and gently pushed her out for a second curtain call, alone.

Elated, she ran to center stage and curtsied deeply. Remember this, she thought. She glanced to the wings at Edmund. He was haggard and drawn. He would remember too. She had bested him that night.

His melodious voice and overblown gestures were beloved by townsfolk in village squares and rustic barn theaters. But here in a city blessed with good theater she had bested him.

4

Triumph was a wonderful feeling. She spread Juliet's skirt wide as a fan and sashayed it front and back, unable to hold still.

Triumph was a glorious feeling. She twirled with the gaiety and bold abandon she had given Juliet twelve nights running.

Spectators laughed, delighted. Stopping, she extended her hands to the audience and sank into another curtsy. The curtains closed. She faced the blank, rippling cloth wall.

The applause ended abruptly, and she rose breathless. The lights went black around her. Unsteady, she crossed the dark, empty stage.

"Well done."

"Splendid show."

She shouldered her way through well-wishers as Daly introduced her to city officials and their smiling, ermine-swathed wives. A rotund man with a gregarious smile plowed his hand forward to take hers.

Daly proudly introduced him. "Katie, may I present our distinguished congressman, Senator Bill Cahill?"

The senator had a warm, practiced smile. "My dear, you were stunning. I just wanted to thank you for a superb evening of tragedy."

Katie bowed her head. "My pleasure."

As the senator moved on, someone handed her a bouquet of red roses. The fragrance was heady and thick. She smiled as she opened the notecard nestled in the flowers.

To sweet Juliet. Until we meet,

J.G.

J.G.? she wondered. A secret admirer? A stage-door Johnny? Was he here? She glanced around, looking for the most promising gentleman, anyone covertly watching her. She noticed a tall, bearded man at the edge of the throng, but he was not well dressed and he didn't seem interested in catching her eye. He was intent on reaching the senator, who was on his way out. Katie could see the senator's face as he greeted the bearded man; he was smiling, but his expression was guarded. The bearded man led him quickly into the shadows beside the stage door.

Conspiratorial, Katie thought idly as she tucked the card back into the roses. She lost interest as more congratulants surged forward. Daly leaned close; she could smell his pomade. "I want to see you in my office before you leave," he said.

"Of course," she said, smiling. Daly wanted to talk. It was a good sign. She began to think about terms: What was the least she could accept for renewing the contract?

Her father crowded close. "Kemble Thea Henslowe." He hugged her boisterously. "I'm so proud of my K.T., my buttons are bursting." His smile faded, though, as he watched Daly move on, shrugging off accolades on the way to his office.

"Of course," her father said under his breath, "Edmund earned his moment of glory too." He shook his head. "Edmund should've gone out for a bow. Daly knew that." Alleyn reached inside his princely robes for his flask. "My boy deserved it." With practiced speed, he tipped the flask and his lower lip shot out. "Daly knew. We all knew." He skinned back his lips, gaping with the burn of cheap whiskey. "Edmund deserved more, didn't he?"

Katie's euphoria drained downward, leaving her leaden. Her father patted her arm and wandered away. She said polite goodbyes to the congratulants around her.

Cradling the roses in one arm, she woodenly joined the procession of cast members going downstairs to the dressing room. Someone jostled her, and rose thorns pressed into her arm, piercing.

At the bottom of the stairs, she elbowed her way out of the crowd and began handing out the thorny flowers. Supernumeraries who had played walk-on parts grabbed them, excited.

She gave away every rose, except one. The cast moved on, and she remained alone at the bottom of the stairs. With quiet concentration, she broke off every thorn on the lone stem. She didn't like being hurt.

A prickling unease made her stop. She wasn't alone.

A thorn held between thumb and forefinger, she stepped away from the wall and peered up the steep stairwell. All she could see was a pair of tooled leather boots and dark wool trouser legs.

She gathered her skirt, preparing to leave, but the rustle of satin prompted movement above. Unhurried, the boots came down four steps, then their owner sat on the step, laying a dusty, broad-brimmed hat beside him.

She stared a moment, recognizing him. It was the bearded man who had pulled Senator Cahill into a dark corner for conversation. She made note of the man's chestnut hair and close-trimmed russet-colored beard.

"I see you don't care for flowers," he said.

Oh God, the roses. Was he the one? She contritely pulled out the note and checked the initials. "Are you 'J.G.'?"

"'J.G.'?" He paused a long time. "No, I'm not."

Something about his answer was odd. "Then who are you?"

"Just one of Juliet's many admirers."

Assured, she thought. Everything about him was so assured. "I'm glad you enjoyed the performance," she said.

"Of course, you overplayed the girl's passion."

Not only was he a churl, he was a critic. She turned away, ready to leave. "Playing true to the passions is an art men often misunderstand in a woman, Mr. . . . ? She turned to get his name.

He had already stood, and the steps creaked as he climbed them. He was gone.

She heard his bootsoles as he crossed the backstage floor above her head. She waited for the clank of the latch that meant he'd opened the back door to the alley.

She heard no clank, no closing door. He was still up there, unless he'd left through the sidestage and front aisles. What did he want?

"Ow." She'd forgotten about the thorn she held, and had embedded the point in her finger. She took it out and walked on to her dressing room, sucking on the sore fingertip.

In the dressing room, a lantern flickered beside the mirror. Her Chinese maid, Song Lin, sat sewing, her eyes narrowed to slits in the dim light.

Lin greeted Katie, then pointed up at the low, raftered ceiling. "They stomped like cows tonight." She brushed ceiling particles

7

from the fabric she was mending. "They must have liked you very much."

"Yes." Katie put the rose with the naked stem in a jar of water.

"I see how much." Lin shook her head at the drooping flower. "One little rose. You know how that looks? A pitiful honor. Why do you give away your honor?"

Katie ignored the question and went to the makeshift bed on the dressing room bench. "How's Beth?" she asked, kneeling beside her three-year-old daughter. "She looks so pale."

"She'll be better tomorrow," Lin said, standing to hand her a damp washcloth.

Katie folded the cloth and smoothed strings of hair from her daughter's feverish forehead. Beth stirred. "Mommy?" Her voice was phlegmy and nasal.

"I'm here, sweet."

Beth held out her arms. Katie pulled her from the blankets and settled her on her lap. Beth's clothes had a penetrating odor of vinegar and peppermint camphor—Lin's chest plaster to help the child breathe. Katie knew it was only a bout of cough and catarrh, but nursery illnesses unnerved her. They made Beth seem smaller, unduly fragile.

Beth tensed between bursts of sawing coughs. "Mommy."

Katie rocked her. "I know, sweet."

"Home," Beth said.

"Yes. It's time to go home now." Katie always felt vaguely dishonest when she used that word. Home was a boarding house, and it changed with each town. "We're going on the train tomorrow," she whispered.

"Go home," Beth said.

Katie kissed her daughter's cheek. "Yes." Somewhere, home.

After Katie had tucked Beth in again, Lin handed her a note. The handwriting was large and bold. Edmund's.

You and I dine at the St. Nicholas tonight.

Poppy's new patron will meet us there.

8

New patron? Hogwash. Poppy hadn't had a benefactor in years. And the St. Nicholas? What an outrageously expensive place to eat. Poppy couldn't afford jaunts like that. In all its existence, Populus Felicitas had yet to make a profit and had broken even only during the years her mother had managed the troupe on a shoestring and a prayer. But Thea Henslowe was dead, and for four years Poppy had struggled to survive on the meager take of circuit bookings.

Tomorrow they were bound for Larsen, a little Pennsylvania milltown, for a three-night bill, alternating *Hamlet*, *Much Ado About Nothing*, and a Boucicault comedy. Then it was upriver for— What? What in God's name were they performing five days after that?

What did it matter? Katie thought as she crumpled the note. The repertory only grew larger, the time to memorize lines shorter, the performances more haphazard. And here was Edmund, boasting capture of a wealthy patron. Ridiculous. She'd had dinner with some of his prospective "patrons" before. Their hands were freer than their purse strings. No. Everything depended on Daly and a second booking there at his Fifth Avenue theater.

Thinking of Daly, she hurried to change. Lin tugged the laces of the costume's stiff stomacher until they loosened. Katie shrugged the elaborate white satin dress off her shoulders. Blue galloon embroidery covered the bodice and the moiré skirt. It was a classy piece of costuming. Daly had commissioned it for her when she had shown him her moth-eaten circuit gown.

She sat before her mirror and removed Juliet's beaded cap. Her fawn-colored hair looked dark sepia in the yellowed glass. She went to work on the stage makeup with a clean towel, wiping kohl from her eyelids. Her hazel eyes had an exotic cant, a legacy of the Genoan weavers her father told her were part of her ancestry. She didn't like the Mediterranean tilt of her eyes; it made them look too inviting. She liked her smooth, pale skin, though, and the prim oval of her face. But she didn't like her lips. They had generous width and full curves. Men liked them. Men liked looking at her. It was a relief, sometimes, to climb into her white mask of makeup for

9

a performance. Then she was free of everyone's expectations except the playwright's.

At the age of twenty, after thirteen years in theater, she felt as if Shakespeare were an old friend. Not a comfort, though. He was too didactic, too despairing, too fickle with his women to be a source of reassurance. Besides, she always heard his lines in her father's voice, that barrel-deep baritone of countless middling performances and endless pretense.

Her father was a great dreamer but an inept administrator. Each season she tried to tell herself that she was saving Poppy for her father, for Peg, for Edmund.

Each season, she knew, she saved the troupe for herself. She had no other skills. And no other haven for her daughter.

Steeling herself for negotiations with Daly, she dressed quickly in an evening gown. "Make sure Beth is bundled warmly," she told Lin.

"You have to tell me that?" Lin rebuked her. "I am not a good nurse?"

"Song Lin is good at everything," Katie said. "The better to keep her mistress humble."

Lin smiled. *"Nǐ zhēn kè-qi,"* she said. Very kind of you.

Katie suppressed a groan. A lesson. *"Nǐ zhēn kè-qi,"* she repeated in a rush on her way out. She reappeared a moment later. *"Wǒ bú huì shuō hàn-yǔ,* you know." I don't speak Chinese.

"Duì," Lin said curtly. Correct.

Upstairs, the backstage area was deserted. Katie wended past props and painted flats on her way to Daly's office. Stopping suddenly, she looked behind her at the door that led to the alley, her professional instincts alert, as if she stood on a darkened set with an actor she didn't know.

She was sure the bearded man was somewhere watching, face shadowed by his broad-brimmed hat. Not a city hat. Headgear a plainsman would wear. She was as curious about him as she was apprehensive. She began to walk toward the dark shadows by the door.

Before she could get close, though, Edmund came running up

10

the dressing room steps, buttoning his vest. "Katie!" he called excitedly. "You got my note?"

She turned reluctantly. "Yes, but—"

"Good." Edmund took his evening jacket from his valet, Song Zemin, who was Lin's cousin.

Zemin set a large wicker valise on the floor in order to help Edmund with his coat.

"I take it you're ready to go," Edmund said to Katie, twirling his top hat on one finger.

"No, I'm not. I've got a meeting with Daly. You go on and have dinner with your patron. Just make sure he pays for it. I need everyone's gate shares to help make trainfare tomorrow."

"Not mine, you don't," he said, adjusting his watch chain. "I need every receipt that's due me."

His eyes were bright, betraying the intensity of his need. He already had a place to spend the night's take, she thought, watching as he combed his hair with nervous fingers. He loved his hair. It hung chin-length, light brown, full and curly. It lacked luster now, as did his sallow skin. Her gaze strayed to the wicker valise that held the exotic tools of his habit. They were always with him in his night revels: the carrying case and the Chinese servant who could transform the contents.

Edmund cleared his throat to get her attention. "And what does that little barracuda want from you anyway?"

"It's what I want from him, Edmund. A contract."

"Whatever offer Daly makes, it won't be enough."

"How would you know how much is enough? You never involve yourself with the business of running the troupe."

"I told you," he said. "I've secured us a patron."

His confidence was false. She saw how his hand shook, how the habit called. "Yes," she said wearily. "Well, go on and meet him."

"You don't believe me. You'll see. You know I get on famously with old moneybags. God knows I deserve a more fashionable life." He tugged his coat tight across his chest. "Now, don't make a deal with Daly until you talk to Julian."

"Julian . . . ?"

"Gates. Julian Gates."

11

The J.G. who gave roses, she thought. "Until we meet," the note had said.

"He's a millionaire," Edmund went on. "A railroad builder. Quite a force in the charities too."

"Obviously, if he's considering Poppy," she said.

"I'll be waiting for you, Katie!" Edmund called after her as she walked away. "I'm waiting right here!" He stomped his foot.

She looked back toward the door, but nothing stirred in the shadows. Maybe the bearded man was gone. She gave a last sweeping glance of the backstage clutter and went on to Daly's small office.

His desk was clear, his ink set precisely centered. As she closed the door, he got up from his chair behind the desk.

"I've never seen a Juliet like you and I want you to stay," he said without preamble. "I'm going to cast *Frou-Frou* and I know you'll do well in it."

She was taken aback. "As the lead?"

He paused. "In one of the lead roles, assuredly."

She took a seat and lay her reticule on his desk. "I see. And what kind of roles would there be for Poppy's other players?"

"None. I don't want Poppy. I want you."

"Mr. Daly, I'm sure my father's told you we only contract as a company. Our players are veterans. Our two swordsmen alone present a splendid burlesque. They're daring—"

"They're dangerous. They fight like maniacs. And most of your players aren't veterans, they're just old. And I certainly don't need your sour sister as a prompter, I've got a nice little timid one of my own. And Edmund? God, Edmund." He came around the desk, smoothing his mustache with thumb and forefinger. "He's a debauched schoolboy. His lack of professionalism is astounding, especially in light of your own discipline. I can't believe you both trained in the same company."

She kept her voice even. "Edmund is my half brother. His early training was abroad. As you know, he was a child prodigy in England before my father emigrated to Philadelphia. Edmund memorizes with incredible speed. His enunciation is extraordinary and he has a gift—"

"For recitation and histrionic oration, not acting!" Daly shouted. "And you could not sell him to me in a solid gold sack."

She looked down, her cheeks flaming.

"Katie, Katie," he muttered. "I'm sorry. Sorry that you are stuck with such . . ."

Her look challenged him.

"Such obligations," he finished gently. "Couldn't you just send them all the money you're going to make on gate shares?"

"And how much money would that be?"

He rubbed his eyes. He was quiet a long time. "I'm pouring all I have into *Frou-Frou*. I want a smash and I'm going to be running back-to-the-wall to get it. Superb sets, lavish costumes, big cast." He shrugged. "You add it up, Katie."

"I have." Poppy needed a contract and needed it fast. An advance wasn't anywhere in sight in this barren office. She headed toward the door. "I can't afford to leave Poppy."

"You did, once."

She stopped.

He crossed the room and put a hand on her arm. "I can help you do it again."

"Oh, you can?" she said softly.

"I'd like to try. Gossip being as informative as it is unkind, I gained some, well, understanding of the circumstances which forced you back to your father's company a few years ago."

"Three," she said softly, holding her anger. "Three years ago."

"And I could promise you that. . . . Well, you can rest assured you wouldn't face that kind of crisis again." He faced her squarely. "I would make sure of that, Katie."

She was quiet a moment. "Tell me how you would 'make sure.' "

He looked away, tapping his collar points. "K. T. Henslowe, you require a man to be entirely too direct."

"I merely 'require,' " she said, "that his proposition not disgust me. And for the record, Mr. Daly, I do not consider my beautiful daughter a 'circumstance.' "

She lunged for the door but he had covered the doorknob. "Wait."

"For what? Another insult?"

"No," he said quietly. He stood back. "No more."

She angrily jerked the door open.

"Katie, your purse," he said quickly, going to his desk to get it. "Can you tell me where Poppy is playing next?"

"No." She held out her hand for the reticule.

He held on to it. "That small a town, huh? What have they got for period costume? Leggins and a horse blanket?"

"Don't be snide."

"I'm not trying to be. I want you to take the gown."

She looked at him.

"Yes. Juliet's gown," he said.

She ripped her purse from his grasp. "I don't have that much money."

"No, it's a gift. Freely given."

She hesitated. Poppy's stock wardrobe was in tatters.

"It'll help draw," he said. "You know you need it."

"What I need is respect. Please contact me if you ever wish to extend an offer that includes it." She slammed the door on her way out.

The noise reverberated in the high rafters backstage. She saw Edmund jar awake from a standing sleep. Angry, she stalked past him.

He grinned. "I take it things went well."

She ignored his taunt and headed for the dressing room stairs.

"Shall we go, Zemin?" Edmund scooped up the wicker valise. "I'm starved, bloody starved." He opened the door. A blast of cold air caught it and blew it wide. He sniffed theatrically. "Ah, opportunity! 'Who seeks, and will not take when once 'tis offered, shall never find it more.' Remember that at the St. Nicholas, Katie." He stepped out. "Julian's dying to meet you!"

The feeling wasn't mutual. She hated the thought of spending an evening in Edmund's questionable circle of contacts. She hated more the thought of trusting Edmund's judgment, business or personal. He always let her down.

Always.

She went downstairs to get Beth and Lin. After donning a long woolen cape, she gathered Beth in a mound of coverlets. "Let's go," she told Lin.

On the way up the stairs, Katie had her arms full juggling a squirming Beth and the bulky blankets. As they approached the door, she turned to Lin. "Do you suppose Edmund was kind enough to hold his cab for us?"

"Ha. You expect water from the throne?"

"Stone."

"As I said."

Katie shrugged Beth higher on her shoulder. The door was still wide open, pulling a frigid draft through the hall. Stacks of muslin flats rattled in the breeze.

A strong male voice came out of the darkness. "I can get a carriage."

Both women stopped short.

Katie recognized the voice. Looking closely, she discerned a hint of white cuff in the dark corner near the door. The bearded critic stepped out into the light. He was tall, she realized, and he held himself solid, of a piece. A strong, rugged piece.

Fright made her tone severe. "I don't accept help from men I don't know."

He shrugged. "Okay." He put on his hat to leave.

Lin gave Katie a sharp bump with her hip as Beth whimpered from the cold.

"But a simple introduction," Katie added stiffly, "would help matters. I'd appreciate the courtesy of your name."

"You'd appreciate a ride more," he said. His eyes were deep-set and serious. He didn't smile or soften his gaze with friendliness.

"I'm afraid, then," she said, "I must consider you an eavesdropper."

"It's hard not to be," he said, grabbing the door and fighting the wind for control of it. "You people talk loud whether you're on stage or not."

So, she thought, he had overheard her and Edmund talking about going to the St. Nicholas and—What else? Negotiating with Daly, meeting a railroad millionaire, milking the patronage of the man named Julian Gates.

The bearded man stepped outside and the door slammed shut with the force of the wind.

Katie quickly moved forward, juggling Beth, and slid the bolt to lock the door. From outside, the man pushed once, then rattled it hard.

Both women eyed the door. After a moment, it was still.

"Why did you do that?" Lin asked.

"He scares me."

"It was a little scare. Men like to make little scares. This particular man liked getting us a warm cab too. You should have taken it."

"Lin, he was spying on us."

"Spying? Ha. What do you have that's valuable?"

Katie frowned. "I don't know." Beth scrunched her body tight and snuggled deep against Katie's shoulder. She swayed side to side to soothe her. "Maybe Edmund has something valuable."

"All your brother has is trouble," Lin said. "Many troubles. If that's what this man wants, he has found a mothertoad."

"Mother lode."

"As I said."

Katie looked around. "All the stagehands are gone. I'll sneak out the front and get us a ride. Here. Take Beth."

As she shifted her sleepy daughter to Lin's arms, Katie saw a scrap of paper appear beneath the door. It slid slowly across the threshold. She and Lin exchanged wary looks, then Katie picked up the note and read aloud:

"Carriage is waiting. I'm not."

It wasn't signed. She turned it over. It appeared to be the bottom half of an old flier. An advertisement of farms and properties in alphabetical order, all foreclosed for auction. Most of the sites were in Waco County.

Waco County, Texas? The eavesdropper was from Texas?

She turned the note over to study the writing. Hurried but

16

precise. Large, confident letters. He was an impudent sneak, but at least he was a literate one.

"Miss Katie," Lin said. "Can we go?"

A cold draft rushed in as Katie cracked open the door and peeked out onto the landing. He wasn't there. The air crisped her breath white.

She flipped a corner of the blanket over Beth's head as she helped Lin negotiate the metal steps. They pressed down the alley, fighting the frigid wind, and Katie looked both behind and ahead. A cab was waiting at the street, and as promised, he wasn't.

They got in. The vehicle lurched forward and Katie scuffed a nest for her feet in the straw on the floor. The heated brick beneath the straw was still warm. The eavesdropper had done well by them.

Theaters and vaudevilles had emptied their first shows, and the avenue was crowded with slow-moving carriages. It made the short jaunt to the St. Nicholas an inordinately long trip. The driver reined in sharply in front of the hotel, taking a spot vacated by a liveried victoria.

The six-story white marble hotel took up nearly a city block. She hadn't been inside such grand accommodations in years, not since Roddy took her to the—What was the name? A hotel with a two-story fountain in the lobby. Somewhere on the west side of Philadelphia. She looked down at her daughter asleep in her arms. It didn't matter. It was so long ago. She gently settled Beth on the seat next to Lin and got out.

Street noise was deafening. Iron-shod hooves and carriage wheels clattered on the street bricks, and the carriages' themselves creaked as they rumbled past.

Katie handed Lin a coin. "For the driver when you get to the boardinghouse," she said loudly. "I might be late."

"I might wait up," Lin said.

A two-decker red-line omnibus drawn by Clydesdales clanged to a stop beside the cab. As she waved Lin's driver on, she noticed a familiar tall figure about to get off the omnibus.

The bearded Texan paused, spotting her, then swung out. He walked toward her slowly. She took up a handful of skirt, not certain whether she wanted to run or act indignant. He walked right past her, his coat brushing her cape, then stopped abruptly and faced her. He nodded toward the public bus.

"Cheaper," he said.

Shoulders hunched, he trudged up the steps into the warm, glittering lobby of the St. Nicholas.

2

A fashionable crowd milled around the lobby amid plush settees and potted palms. Matt Dennigan dodged protruding bustles and walking sticks as he went in search of a wall register radiating heat.

He tented his hands over his nose and mouth and breathed a pocket of warmth. The open-air omnibus ride had chilled him to the bone. He needed warmer gloves, a heavier coat. He needed the money to buy them.

He stroked a hand down his jaw, smoothing the whiskers and rubbing away the itch. The beard was a nuisance, but the senator was not anxious for him to get rid of it.

"Shave *after* you leave New York," Bill Cahill had said when they had talked backstage at the Daly. "Less chance Julian will recognize you."

"I doubt that Julian Gates could pick me out of a crowd, anyway," Matt had said. "We only met once, face-to-face, in St. Louis."

"Don't push your luck, or mine. Julian's got more private investigators than accountants on his payroll. He's bound to have a likeness of you in a dossier somewhere." The senator had paused. "Probably in his file on Art."

Leave it to Bill to bring up Father, Matt had thought, and in the first five minutes of conversation. "I'm not here to fight my dad's battles, Bill."

"I know," the senator had said. "You're here to fight mine."

Mouth tightened in a grim line, Matt sat in an opulent chair near the hotel coatroom. His feet hurt. He felt as if he'd walked every slab of sidewalk in New York since arriving at Grand Central that afternoon. He'd trekked all the way from the train station to the senator's house, only to find that Bill Cahill had just left for the theater.

"The Senator didn't mention you were coming," the housekeeper had said.

"He didn't know." Bill had sent the train ticket voucher a year earlier, but pride had kept Matt from using it. And pride kept him from asking the housekeeper if he could stay in the senator's nice, warm parlor toasting his feet until Bill returned.

It was a three-mile walk to the Daly. What had galled him was having to buy a ticket when he got there; he used all the money he'd saved on cab fares.

He forgot about the waste of money, though, forgot a lot of things, for a while. K. T. Henslowe came on as Juliet, working body and soul inside the confines of a heavy Renaissance gown, elevating a muddled production and her brother's pretentious Romeo. When she took her life in the last act, she took the audience's fascination with her.

Matt watched her now, crossing the lobby of the St. Nicholas. She no longer looked like a radiant purveyor of fantasies. She was real and weather-nipped, her eyes watery, and she was cloaked in an unadorned black cape.

He tensed when she veered toward him, unbuttoning her cape as she neared. The cape unfurled backward to dramatic effect as she stopped in front of him. "Thank you for getting us a cab."

She turned immediately and continued down the corridor to the cloakroom.

She must have felt guilty about locking him out of the theater, he thought. He didn't blame her for doing it. She'd mistaken him for an unsavory sneak. He'd certainly felt like one. All that skulking around went against the grain. But he'd gotten a few good tidbits of information to pass on to the senator at dinner.

Matt was waist-high in debt to Bill Cahill and he'd be damned if he'd take another nickel without giving something in return. When Bill had told him at the theater that the actor, Edmund Henslowe, had been hobnobbing with Julian Gates all week, Matt had decided to linger and learn more about Julian Gates's new friend.

Crewmen backstage all agreed Edmund was a wastrel, womanizer, and prodigious drunkard. And he had a penchant for exotica.

"What kind of exotica?" Matt had asked a roustabout.

The rowdy had risen on tiptoe and spread his arms in a parody of flight. "Go suck the flute at 13 Pell. You'll find out."

Matt had nodded and switched the conversation to the subject of Katie Henslowe. Unlike her brother she garnered professional respect from all who worked with her, though her personal life was more circumspect. She was no ingenue. She had a daughter and no marriage certificate; the father of the child was a judge from Philadelphia, several years dead.

The two Henslowes were odd contacts for a high-stakes railroad executive like Julian Gates. What use did he have for a down-and-out boor like Edmund?

What use Gates might have for Katie was immediately apparent when Matt saw her emerge from the cloakroom in an understated emerald green gown. He made note of the dress, especially the top of it, the part that wasn't there. Nice swoop.

Real nice swoop.

Other men noticed too, as she crossed the lobby to the front desk. Matt debated following her. He was already late for dinner with the senator, but, hell, a little more close observation couldn't hurt.

He joined her at the front desk. Her expression showed annoyance the moment she saw him, and he guessed she regretted trying to be polite to him.

"Looks like we both have business here," he said, leaning on the counter.

She turned her back on him, leaving him free to study her, the indignant thrust of her shoulders, the fragile trough of her spine. A wisp of dark golden hair had escaped its pin and rested in the curve of her neck.

"I'm here to meet my brother, Edmund Henslowe," she told the desk clerk.

The clerk went off to check the message boxes. She cocked her chin to her shoulder and sent Matt a withering look.

Hazel, he thought. Her eyes were hazel, more green than brown.

"Miss Katie Henslowe?" the clerk asked when he returned. "Mr. Henslowe wishes you to join him in his suite."

She was obviously startled. "His suite? Here?"

"Sixth floor. Number nineteen."

Six nineteen, Matt thought, looking ahead and not at her.

"Thank you." Icy, perfunctory. She was miffed.

The clerk had business at the other end of the long front desk, and they were alone for a moment.

She stood silent awhile, then turned to Matt. "Did you get all that?"

He was cautious. "What?"

"Don't play dumb. It looks too natural on you. Nice piece of news, wasn't it? The fact that my brother has a room here? Makes it seem like he has money, doesn't it? Well, let me assure you, you and whichever of our creditors you're the snoop for. Poppy does *not* have funds to make payments."

Matt played along, glancing around the opulent lobby. "This doesn't exactly look like a place for the destitute."

"I know." She backed down, stiffly. "Just, please, try to understand. My brother is here only to develop resources for the troupe. Now, I'm sure your loan department will be glad to hear that we may have the potential to resume quarterly payments." She paused. "You *are* a bank agent for Philadelphia Savings, aren't you?"

He shook his head.

"New York Fiduciary?"

22

"No."

"You work in the private sector, then, for an individual?"

"You could say that."

She looked away. "It's about Edmund, isn't it?"

"How'd you guess?"

Her glance took in his unfashionable attire and worn shoes. "My brother tends to attract an eclectic and, sometimes, illicit crowd."

"Which one am I? Eclectic or illicit?"

"You're a coward and a spy, and I doubt that you've got enough grapeshot in the bag to so much as fire off your name."

He looked at her for a long time. "Insults like that don't come from a lady."

"No." She held his gaze. "And they don't apply to a gentleman."

"Look, I'm not one of your brother's Jack Nasty lowlifes."

"You're not? And yet you have business here?" She studied him thoughtfully. "Are you meeting the senator then?"

Christ, how'd she know? He felt himself grow stony-faced, trying to keep reaction to a minimum.

"I remember," she went on, "seeing you waylay the distinguished senator backstage, Mr. . . . ?" She waited again for his name.

"Nasty," he said curtly. "Jack Nasty."

"I thought so."

To his surprise, she sidled close and put a hand on his arm. "Sir?" she called to the desk clerk. "My friend here has a request."

Matt tensed. What was she doing?

"Yes, sir?" the clerk asked, returning to them.

"He needs his messages," Katie interjected before Matt could speak.

"Of course." The clerk turned to Matt. "What is the name?"

Damn her.

She smiled prettily at him. "Now, come on. Don't dawdle," she said, as to a child. "You'll make us both late."

He hated being manipulated. He especially hated a woman who did it so well.

She patted his hand. "I know you've had a terrible sore throat." She turned to the clerk. "Maybe if you could just lean close, so he can whisper."

The clerk looked dubious, but obligingly leaned over the counter.

Matt felt pressure rise inside him like steam in a boiler.

"Still hurts?" she asked. "Would it be easier if you just spell it? I'm sure—"

"Dennigan!" The word shot out from between gritted teeth.

The clerk stared, astonished.

Katie removed her hand from his. "See how much better you sound when you try?" she said, then turned to the clerk. "Please check the message box for Mr. Dennigan."

Matt leaned close so no one would see him grab her wrist, grab it hard. "Dennigan," he repeated. "Matt Dennigan."

"Charmed, I'm sure."

She jerked her arm free as the clerk returned. His manner was noticeably more unctuous toward Matt. "Mr. Dennigan? It seems Senator Cahill is waiting dinner for you in the Walker Room."

"The Walker Room," Katie said. "Isn't that the salon for very private dining?"

The clerk nodded again. "Yes, ma'am. Right through the arch and turn left."

Katie looked at Matt. "Well, now, Matt, enjoy your dinner."

She was gracious in triumph, almost sweet, he thought, as she left him. She hurried to the elevator foyer. He stood a long while, watching until the accordion gate of the elevator collapsed sideways to let her on.

She had taken his amateurish game of sleuth and, in one polished play, raised the ante to life-or-death for the senator's investigation. If she dared mention Matt Dennigan and Senator Cahill in the same breath to the cutthroat millionaire she was about to meet, the game was over. Julian Gates would run for cover and retaliate with all the congressional influence—and hired guns—his money could buy.

Jesus Christ.

From the elevator cage, Katie watched Matt Dennigan stalk

past the well-heeled gentry in the lobby and disappear through the arch to the Walker Room. Temper, temper, Mr. Dennigan. She didn't know his purpose, but she did know his name. And she wouldn't hesitate to give it to the authorities if he bothered her, or any member of her family, again.

The ratchet of the elevator echoed from the bowels of the shaft as it rose to the top floor. She stepped off into a mirrored foyer of Grecian urns on tall pedestals. Where in God's name had Edmund got the money to book a suite here? It must be a hundred dollars a week. A steward helped her find suite 19. She made sure he was far down the hall before she knocked and opened the door.

The room was large and dark, smelling of rich walnut trim and hidden dust. Above all hovered a feral sweetness. Edmund's.

One corner of the room was dimly lit. Edmund reclined there in a mound of pillows on a red sofa, as languid as a Shelleyan courting esthetic vision.

On the floor beside him, Zemin sat cooking a bead of opium in the flame of a small, potbellied lamp. The bead was tarry black, stuck to the point of a long needle—a knitting needle flattened at one end and pointed at the other. It's called a yen hock, Edmund had told her a year ago, when she had happened upon him sweating in a darkened room, his eyes intent on the bowl of his pipe as Zemin nimbly plied the needle, rolling the sticky mass to the shape of a cylinder, pressing it into the curl of the bowl, and twisting expertly until the pill was left with a tiny hollow for the passage of air.

Then, as now, Katie tried to avert her gaze, but the sight was mesmerizing.

Edmund stroked a finger along the tortoise-shell shank of the pipe, testing its warmth. His lips closed around the mouthpiece, and he wooed the fume, inhaling long and deep. Then he exhaled slowly, with the reluctance of the practiced.

"Edmund?" she said.

He couldn't answer. He was breathing through his nose to still the reflexive cough. Finally he spoke. "So much disapproval in one word, Katie?" He laid the pipe on a pillow. "You have such vibrant color in your voice. Try it sometime when you're acting."

25

His dreamy tease didn't make her angry. She was ashamed for him and, deep inside, she felt a black clutch of fear. Though normally outsized in manner and presence, her brother lay weak and vulnerable, captive in his pillows. A hungry darkness dulled his face. He was sinking deep into the dream world he craved.

"Astounding visions," he had told her once. "Bright as lightning in my brain. Insight, Katie. It sights me inward. Essential to my art."

Yet he could never remember the insight, only the flash of its existence, like the afterimage of a bright light. Fading. Always fading.

She moved closer to him, and her foot caught the leg of a chair. At the rough scrape, Edmund started violently. His hands trembled, but he did not speak. "Is he all right?" she asked Zemin.

Zemin nodded. "Very sensitive now," he said, concentrating on the opium on the point of the yen hock. The black bead swelled to the size of a chestnut. He struck it against the belly of the lamp, and a thread of steam escaped as a bubble popped. He immediately returned the sticky tar to its cooking flame. It would swell and burst repeatedly until all the moisture was gone.

"Edmund, are you conscious?"

"Supremely conscious of everything." His voice was soft, wispy. "I have saved us, you know. I have done it."

"Done what?"

Across the room, a chair creaked. Her heart jumped. Someone else was in the room.

A voice flowed out of the darkness. "Actually, you are here to meet me, Miss Henslowe."

The voice was smooth and confident, almost liquid. A man approached from out of the shadows cast by the smoke lamp. "I didn't mean to startle you."

"Obviously," she said, heart racing. "That's why you skulk in the dark."

"I don't skulk. I observe." He moved closer and claimed the light, smiling. His elegance struck her immediately. His movements were gracefully defined, his carriage imposing.

"I'm Julian Gates, currently of St. Louis, Missouri." He bowed, and the lamplight glinted on dark hair sprinkled with white and clearly illuminated his face. She saw a hawk's ridge of brow, a straight aristocratic nose, and lips that were surprisingly small and vulnerable-looking. He indicated the tunic-clad Zemin, still bent industriously over Edmund's pipe. "Quite a fascinating process, isn't it?"

"I don't share your vulgar curiosity, Mr. Gates."

"And I don't share your contempt, Miss Henslowe." His tone was arrogant. "Rash judgment is a mistake."

She looked at Edmund, then at the elegant Mr. Gates. "Oh, you're quite right," she said. "It was rash of me to be drawn to this charade in the first place. Good evening to you both." She grabbed a fold of her skirt, shifting it around Zemin, and marched to the door.

"Wait." Edmund rose unsteadily on one elbow. "Katie!"

She opened the door. Hall light flooded the room.

"Miss Henslowe," Julian Gates said, unhurriedly walking toward her.

She ignored him and stepped out into the hall, shutting the door behind her. It thudded loudly to a stop before reaching the frame.

She looked down at the obstruction—a custom-made leather shoe, its polish now bearing a scar.

"Shall we?" the gentleman said, taking her hand as he joined her.

It was not a question.

3

In the hallway Julian Gates pulled white kid gloves from his pocket. "Have you been to the sky parlor on the roof? Should be quite private this time of night. We can discuss the contract there."

"Oh?" Katie said, taking in details of his affluent dress now evident in the hall's better light. His coat was perfectly tailored, its buttons of pearl shell and brass. His silk ascot was drawn through a garnet seal ring. "You obviously believe a woman in my profession can be whisked away to seclusion with a gentleman."

"Miss Henslowe, have I given you reason to doubt my intentions?"

"Of course not. I just want to make sure you have no doubts about mine."

He was clearly annoyed. "Ever the businesswoman, just as Edmund said." He offered his arm. "Let us go down to dinner then. And adequate chaperonage."

She gingerly laid her hand atop his arm, and they walked down the narrow hallway. "How long have you known my brother?"

"Little more than a week. We met the second night of your run at Daly's, at one of those nice places off Sixth Avenue."

"Those places where spoiled sons of rich men get stupid and flush-faced and fall off their chairs?"

"Precisely."

"My brother is not the son of a rich man," she said pointedly.

"No, he's not. Your brother's an artist."

"Is that why you condone his vulgar habit?"

"My dear, I champion vulgarity in no aspect of life, least of all art."

"Well, you certainly seemed fascinated back there in Edmund's room."

"You can't possibly believe I'd care to indulge in a smelly tranquillizer like that. One doesn't reach forty-six in good health without selective self-gratification."

"Good advice, though I'm not half your age."

"Cruel child," he said, though lightly, smiling. Fine creases showed in the corners of his eyes, a welcome sign of flexibility in the strong angles of his face. "Cruel sister too," he added, "to censure the artist's right to use every means possible to summon great visions to enrich his work. If I were the devil's advocate, Miss Henslowe, I would ask whether you're blind to the exotic indulgences of some of our finest artists."

She shrugged. "I know that the writer-philosopher De Quincey was a flagrant opium-eater."

"Coleridge the poet, too, wrote upon wakening from reveries brought on by his laudanum. It's said that he composed *Kubla Khan* in such a dream. And in these very times you have that popular novelist Wilkie Collins."

"He is only rumored to enjoy his opiates."

"Rumor has him downing it by the wineglass."

"It's an anodyne. They say he endures excruciating pain of the eyes and limbs."

" 'They say' one of his daily dosages would kill three men. Yet he writes books with meticulous, intricate plotting. Where are the deleterious effects of his habit?"

"I'm certain it affects his productivity."

"All these artists have produced copious amounts of work, proving the worth of their indulgence."

29

"Surely they would have produced even more if they'd created their own visions instead of dredging them up from a glass of brown tincture."

"Why do you assume the tinctured visions are not their own, drawn from some private well of insight the conscious mind cannot reach?"

She glanced at him from the corner of her eye. "Mr. Gates, you play devil's advocate entirely too well. Are you sure you're not the prelate himself?"

He threw his head back and laughed. "Alas, I lack the powers of the title. I'm merely a student of human nature. Each man makes a pact with his own devil, Miss Henslowe. It's a contract which does not involve the rest of us. We have no control."

Ah, but you are wrong, she thought, wanting to challenge him. Each moment Edmund was on stage, each time they skirted catastrophe, she was involved. Edmund's contract employed all of them. Yet she could not afford to imply that Poppy was pervaded by Edmund's habit, not when she was about to negotiate a paying contract with the stern and stimulating Mr. Gates.

He was obviously a man of power, and quite used to wielding it with women. He watched her now with brown eyes that never wavered, and she knew he was testing her, bathing her with attention that she could accept or reject. She turned to walk away.

"Katie." He caught her arm high above her glove, where the skin was soft.

She whirled with disbelief at his improper touch.

His hand dropped. He stepped away until his back was against the wall, but he held his chin high. "You must forgive me. I saw you perform three times at Daly's. Watched you woo, and wed, and die for love in front of hundreds of people, but really only for me— or so you made me think. It's a common enough fantasy, I suppose."

"Do your fantasies always breed familiarity, Mr. Gates?"

"My fantasies beget business, Katie." He lowered his chin to look at her directly. "Always. And in the case at hand, I need a Shakespearean troupe to open the season at a theater I'm building."

"And where is this theater?"

"In St. Louis."

"You mean—?"

"An opening premiere and extended contract. All traveling and boarding expenses paid, two hundred dollars a night salary for principals, pay for secondaries to be negotiated, and a thirty percent share of gross proceeds to be retained by Poppy. Poppy would be completely responsible for staging, including the auditioning and hiring of resident players. I'll provide an allowance for wardrobe and scenery. And I want two Shakespearean plays, one to be *Romeo and Juliet,* alternating in a four-week run."

A Western premiere, she thought. Expenses paid. Two hundred a night! Was she dreaming? She could hardly breathe, but attempted to cover her excitement with skepticism. "There are many road troupes in the country. And many tried and true stars in New York. Why Poppy?"

"Poppy has expertise in playing to the masses. I want the New Gate Theater to draw beyond city boundaries. You see, my elitist friends will love your highly British enunciation and that heavenly review *The Tribune* gave you last week. And your reckless swordsmen will make the farmers come in for an athletic but enlightening evening. I'll have your innocent Juliet to captivate the men and Edmund's overblown poetry to excite the women. Your handling of rehearsals, set, and staging will prepare my new theater for a resident company. And for all this, I pay less than if I supported two of Broadway's temperamental stars for the duration and had to hire out for production."

She tried to remain calm. "Well planned. You couldn't have gone cheaper if you'd culled the flea market."

"Now, now, my dear. Don't hint for more money. I believe in honesty. You're a company in financial trouble. I'm offering a chance to revive Poppy, and with it, I gather, your father's ambitious dream."

"Edmund prepared you well, didn't he?"

"Your brother and I have dined together a few times. He entertained me with stories about Poppy's illustrious history in folk theater. He told me how your father came here from England, committed to performing the classics with his seven-year-old son, who was . . . How did Edmund put it? 'A recitation impressario extraordinaire.' "

"Edmund is famous for his modesty."

Julian smiled. "Now, let me see. Your father met your mother in Philadelphia at *The Beggar's Opera* on a Tuesday, and they were married after your father played *The School for Scandal* on Saturday."

"Mother was quite struck by him. She was a parson's daughter, very sheltered, and he was a disreputable rascal."

"Good runs to bad, they say."

"She never thought about it that way," Katie said quietly. "She loved him."

"Of course. Sad that she passed on at such a young age." Julian smiled. "That was after the fire, wasn't it?"

Katie nodded once, tense.

"Edmund told me about the fire. What was it, six years ago?"

"Seven." She cleared her throat. "Seven years ago." In Honeyeye, New York. Odd name, but its farmers and smiths were friendly, and its public hall a great barn—

"I take it your sister never appears on stage now?"

"Her leg was broken. The fractures were severe." Katie turned away to pull for the elevator. She held on to the rope. "The surgeon was distant. It was a very small town." A horse stall for a dressing room, a hayloft for their beds—

"A terrible tragedy," he said, then left a silence for her to fill. She didn't. The fire was already too loud in her memory. Sap bursting in the timbers, wind walloping through the hall, and the hiss, the endless hiss of flames supping well.

"A shame," Julian said. "So many a theater's gone to ashes for the tipping of a single lantern."

Edmund, what did you tell him? "My brother obviously found a more than patient listener for supper chat."

"I would have much preferred your company, of course. But you had . . . other commitments."

Her name is Beth, Katie wanted to say. My "commitment's" name is Beth.

The tight whine of a pulley cable signaled the elevator's approach. Had Edmund blathered about Judge Roderick Carding and her year at Newlyn's Aye too? she wondered. She looked at Julian Gates, a man at the peak of maturity and power, a man nearly as old as Roddy was then.

The elevator arrived. Mercifully, Julian took the lead in conversation. It allowed her tumultuous feelings a chance to settle before they strolled through the lobby to supper.

When they approached the high arch that led to the Walker Room, she remembered Matt Dennigan was meeting there with Senator Cahill. The thought was fleeting, though. She had more pressing concerns. Julian bypassed the Walker Room anyway, leading her down a red-carpeted corridor to a small, elegant restaurant furnished for well-heeled clientele.

She tried to relax as she watched the waiter fill her glass with an expensive chardonnay. She didn't like to drink. Apparently neither did Julian, for he waved the bottle away and leaned forward, attentive.

"In keeping with my habit of ungracious questions, I'd like to ask what makes you a man of means, Mr. Gates."

"I build railroads," he said, apparently not disturbed by her question or distrustful tone. "And invest in properties, land, steel, bridges, construction." He shrugged. "Anything that offers a good return."

"Your family is from St. Louis?"

"Not originally, though I've been there so long it seems like home. In St. Louis, civic welfare is a cherished tradition of the privileged class. I'm on many boards—House of Refuge, Orphans' Asylum, the City Mission, Washington University, the Philharmonic. I've been appointed to too many municipal commissions to remember. And I'm renovating an opera house at the same time we're working on the New Gate." He paused, eyebrows raised. "I hope I'm not being immodest. I'm merely trying to pass muster."

She smiled. "Your parents must have been selfless models of charity, to set such an example of public work."

"My family left me quite well-off, of course, but still I've had to work hard to earn the comforts I enjoy."

"With your tendency to rush professionals to contract in secluded corners, I warrant you've earned enemies too."

"I've had a few tussles with old Vanderbilt. Jay Gould and I
have shared board positions—and sometimes divergent views of
how to run a railroad. Any names you recognize there?"

"I am chastened, Mr. Gates. You needn't continue."

He was obviously enjoying himself, though, for he went on.
"Oh, but don't you want to know the runts too? Always nipping at
my heels out there—down-and-out bankers and lawyers. A certain
attorney, Herb Cobb, comes to mind. Malcontents and failures.
There's old Art Dennigan, for one."

Katie masked her recognition of the surname in a long sip of
water.

Julian leaned back, idly toying with his knife. "Now, Dennigan's an example of one end of the business spectrum. A man who
once had a nice rural profession: real estate, livestock, farm goods.
I, on the other hand, am on the board of the Union Pacific, building a transcontinental railroad, a monument to civilization. We
really are on the edge of the frontier out there. I'm afraid you'll find
parts of St. Louis quite wild."

"Regarding transportation for the troupe . . . ," she began.

"Can't we delay those little details? I want Altmann here. He's
my secretary. German. I like Europeans for personal service.
They're so good with detail work, you know. Though from what I
saw tonight, the Orientals are quite fastidious and discreet. At least
Edmund finds them so."

"Edmund quite literally 'found' Zemin wandering the wharf in
Boston. Zemin and his cousin Lin were stowaways." Katie paused.
"Lin is my daughter's nanny."

"A Chinese nanny," he said. "How novel. The Orientals don't
mind short pay, irregular hours, and harsh environs. I'd imagine
Lin feels quite at home in your nomadic situation."

"You're skating perilously close to insult."

"Just toeing the line you drew first in the ice, my dear."

They regarded each other for a long moment, then Julian
reached across the table and laid his fingertips on hers, questioning,
not claiming.

"Business tends to take the charm out of a lovely meal, doesn't it?" he said.

She drew her hand away and placed it in her lap. "I believe it's on personal matters that we have the most potential for conflict."

"I assure you, Katie. We'll come to terms."

4

Ornate booths lined the walls of the Walker Room like stately confessionals. Inside closed curtains, Matt Dennigan and Bill Cahill sat in the glow of a wall-mounted gaslight, finishing their brandy. The portly senator reached into the breast pocket of his jacket for a cigar. "So, you think you can handle a few months as an investigator on my staff?" he asked Matt.

"I don't have any choice. You're calling your loan due next month and I don't have money to pay it."

Bill pulled out a long black cigar. "You think I'm being unreasonable."

Matt looked at him. "I think you're using me."

"Then why did you come to New York?"

"Because I didn't have a free ticket to anywhere else."

"You're as blunt as your father."

"The only similarity between Dad and me is the fact that we're both business failures."

Bill looked down at the cigar he was rolling in his fingertips. "You're not a failure. You were just a little too early for the cattle trade."

"Early? I was too far from a railhead. The Indians niggled me to death. And the price on the hoof in Abilene was puny. I ate dust for five hundred miles and had to sell longhorns for chicken feed."

"Don't be so hard on yourself. The market won't always be bad. Rail lines will eventually get live beef to the packinghouses quicker. Settlers are going to start moving into the territories in droves, building cities, needing meat."

"Populating the Plains is going to take years, even if the Union Pacific and the Central Pacific finish a transcontinental line on schedule."

The senator cut off the tip of his cigar with a precise snip of gold-plated clippers. "You and I and every fencepost between here and San Francisco know that the Transcontinental Railroad will be done faster than anyone thought possible."

"You're just wondering how much fraud, money-skimming, and bad construction it's going to cost along the way, aren't you?"

Bill looked at him a long moment. "I'm ready to dig into a big cesspool of railroad subsidies, Matt. And I don't want a graft artist like Julian getting wind of me."

"Sounds like what you need is an army of auditors going over the records of the Union Pacific. Though you won't find anything there."

"Oh?"

"The creative accounting's being done through their construction company, the Crédit Mobilier."

"I don't need auditors and clerk types. I need a trained legal mind who can pull together hard evidence of fraud and malfeasance of the public trust."

"I'm not a lawyer." Matt's expression was stony. "You know that."

"You were going to be. You were one of my brightest students. Aggressive. A natural prosecutor."

"I was a mean sonofabitch. Everyone hated to see me coming."

"That's because you made mincemeat out of their arguments."

"My brother was good too. But everyone loved to see him coming."

"That's because he didn't challenge anyone on anything. He

37

was a sweet, good-natured soul. And much as I liked him, if I was in trouble, I wouldn't have hired him to represent me on a bet."

"You would have hired him in the firm. You know you would have, if the war hadn't come along."

"I would have hired you both. But the war changed a lot of things. Took Paul. Wounded you." Bill tapped the cigar on the tabletop. "It took something away from you too. Your drive, I think. You lost some of your fire when Paul died. I think it's time you got it back."

"Just because you have someone who needs to be burned?"

"No, dammit." The cigar twitched up and down. "You see how you provoke me? No matter how good Paul was at the books, Matt, the law is made up of people. And people are made of feelings. You know a helluva lot about feelings, don't you?"

"Don't, Bill."

"All I wanted to say is how truly sorry I am about your wife."

Matt downed the rest of his drink.

"It's tragic, how Sarah died," Bill said.

How much did he know? Matt wondered. "I don't want your pity. She's gone. I can't change things now." He raised the glass again to catch the last drop. "Couldn't even change them when she was alive."

Bill studied him for a moment. "Pretty hard man, aren't you?"

Matt looked away. "Getting harder, Bill. God knows, harder every day."

"I could make things easier."

"By giving me an extension on that loan?"

"By hiring you on at the firm. After you finish your degree."

Matt slammed his glass on the table. "I know exactly what you want now—and who put you up to talk about law school. I'm not going to let either one of you jerk me around."

Bill grabbed Matt's arm before he could get up. "You think you *know* so goddamned much. You don't *think* worth jackshit anymore. You just knee-jerk. You're so sure your dad's behind my offer to help you? Well, he's not. As a matter of fact, if he knew I'd loaned you good money to sink into that Texas debacle, he'd skin me alive. I must have been soft in the head. You were goddamned persuasive, I'll give you that much. But I'm not giving anymore. You make your own arrangements to pay back that loan next month."

The senator edged his rotund form out the booth and straightened his lapels.

"Wait a minute." Matt spoke low, so no one would overhear. "What about that job you need done? The one I already started tonight?"

"Tell you the God's honest truth, I don't know if you're the man for it." The senator headed for the door.

"Bill."

He didn't even stop.

Matt pounded his fist against his thigh, cursing his stupidity. His ranch had been auctioned in Texas. He was estranged from his father in St. Louis. And he had just riled the only friend he had in New York. He hesitated a moment, then caught up to the senator. "Just a minute, Bill."

"What?" the senator said, very grim.

"Where you off to?"

"Smoking room."

"Me too."

"You don't smoke."

"I do when you make me mad."

Bill took a deep breath, then gave a grudging nod. "We're going to need a room with a chimney if we have any more of these meetings."

"If you wanted privacy, why are we meeting in Julian Gates's hotel?"

"He wasn't registered here until tonight."

"Maybe he needed to be close to his new pet, Edmund Henslowe. I found out Henslowe has a suite here."

"Then Julian's paying for it because Henslowe's more flat broke than you are."

"Thanks. Comparing me to a seamy thespian."

"You were a thespian once."

"In school. It's not the same."

"I remember there was mud up to the axles the night I came to

39

see your Hamlet. I made it, though." He aimed the cold cigar at Matt. "And you kept forgetting your lines."

"I only wanted the part so they would teach me how to use a two-handed sword."

"Yes, that was a grand fight, that last scene. And I speak as one who was there when I say that young Hamlet severed the spleen of his stepfather the King with enormous passion."

As they passed the hotel's elegant restaurant, Matt saw Katie Henslowe rise from a chair across the room. Beside her was Julian Gates.

Matt stepped up his pace to get down the hall and out of her line of sight.

"What's your hurry?" Bill asked, frowning as he quickened his own pace to keep up.

Matt didn't answer. He hadn't told the senator that Katie Henslowe knew about their meeting. He was going to have to work fast on Julian before the actress—intentionally or unintentionally —gave her new patron a hint of the conspiracy building against him.

The soft pile runners of the corridor led to a dead end. Bill opened the large double doors. A sweet mingled scent of sorghum-laced tobacco and cherrywood pipes wafted toward them. The gentlemen's smoking room was a haven of stamped leather walls and dark wood paneling.

The senator was hailed by constituents at every table. Matt found a padded settee in a corner and waited as Bill made the rounds of his New York electorate. A gregarious and folksy lawyer, Bill was deceptively simple to talk to and sophisticated in his judgment. And very careful. If he had decided to take on a blatant powerbroker and bribe artist like Julian Gates, he had to have solid leads.

Bond fraud, maybe, Matt guessed. The Union Pacific board had been printing new issues of stocks and bonds as if they were penny pamphlets, freely awarding them inside the corporate family. That "family," Matt had heard, included influential congressmen and regulators on the federal railway commission—the commission that was supposed to make sure the Union Pacific adhered to proper standards of construction and money management.

The Union Pacific board never heard a discouraging word from the inspectors monitoring the rails. Never a harsh peep from Congress, which voted government bond subsidies and massive land grants to the two railway companies constructing the great Transcontinental Railroad, the Union Pacific heading west from Omaha and the Central Pacific laying rail east from Sacramento.

Even the press rhapsodized about the great "anvil chorus" ringing over the West. It was the symbol of a modern America—pioneering men battling the elements, snowy summits, flooding plains, and desert dust, all in the name of unity.

Detractors were drowned in the enthusiasm, their warnings about crooked promoters, speculators, and unscrupulous executives who squeezed "juice" between the income and the outgo. Bill Cahill, though, had been listening after all.

Matt watched Bill glad-hand his way closer. The senator carried a paunch big as a bushel basket but he never lumbered. Light on his feet. Perfect for a fighter or a politician. Or both.

Bill finally reached him and sat down, his back to the room.

"Let's lay it out flat," Matt said. "I don't have any money to pay back the loan. All I've got to offer you is my labor."

"I need more than that. I need a man who's going to run this thing mean and smart and so quiet, Julian's not going to know a thing. Most of all, I need a man who's not going to quit on me when things get rough. 'Cause they're going to. And frankly, Matt, I didn't like what I heard in your voice back there at dinner."

"What'd you hear?"

"Defeat. It's something more than the ranch going bust. What else happened in Texas?"

He didn't know about Sarah, Matt thought. That relief oddly heightened his tension. "Nothing that's going to affect the work I'll do for you."

"You think you know what I need?"

"Pretty much. And if it involves the Union Pacific, it'll lead me straight to the Crédit Mobilier and Julian Gates. You read in the papers about their shareholders meeting?"

"Yes, indeed. The company's first year of operation and Mobilier gave a hundred percent return on investment for each share."

"Not bad for a railroad construction company starting from scratch," Matt said, the sarcasm strong.

"Actually, pretty stupid of them to crow about raking in public money and forking it over to private investors."

"Well, what else can they do? They've got too much money to keep. The government gives them a subsidy of sixteen thousand dollars a mile for laying rail on the flats, forty-eight thousand dollars a mile in the mountains. And if the UP's already laid about four hundred miles of rail, that's about six and a half million dollars right there. And that's not counting profits from selling all that land the government gave them. Now, how many acres was it Congress granted to the Union Pacific?"

Bill shook his head and blew out a stream of cigar smoke. "About fourteen million."

"Fourteen million acres of land, a dollar fifty an acre, that's—"

"In the range of twenty million dollars," Bill finished, irritated. "But it's going to take them years to sell all that. They're peddling lots in a flood plain and dust bowl where your only neighbor is a gopher."

"Or a Sioux war party. C'mon, Bill," Matt chided. "Isn't it all prime property when there's iron rail running by?"

Bill didn't answer. Matt knew the senator had voted for passage of the Railroad Act four years earlier, handing over land, mineral rights, timber claims, and bond subsidies to the Union Pacific and the Central Pacific Railroads. "All in all," he said, "a very impressive giveaway of public resources."

Bill scowled. "Don't get smart. I wouldn't vote any differently today. Private industry would never run rail eighteen hundred godforsaken miles across prairie grass and red desert—and bore through a mountain range to boot!—if we weren't dangling awful big carrots on the horizon."

"Then why the change of heart, Bill?"

"What in the hell change are you talking about? I didn't vote for slick promoters and fortune hunters to form a dummy corporation, suck up public money, falsify expenses, and then pocket the difference. And I know where that difference is going. To the men I sit in chambers with every congressional day of my life."

"It's not just your colleagues on the payroll. I know of a railroad commissioner. Some inspectors too."

"Matt, everybody knows but nobody has proof or the backbone to say that the Transcontinental Railroad isn't God's gift to mankind. I'm willing, but I need ammunition." Bill worked the cigar to the other side of his mouth. "You can get it, there in St. Louis. You can nose around land deals the UP's offering, track shareholders' dividends, get a list of contractors who have to pay Julian under the table for contracts. You'll be a free agent investigator on my staff, and you'll be the only man I trust. Except for a police lieutenant in Pennsylvania who's pulling together a personal dossier on Julian for me."

"That's all? Two people?"

"For now."

"Criminy. I'm no detective agency."

Bill poked Matt's shoulder. "And I'm no silver-haired avenger! But I'm sick and tired of sitting across the aisle from senators counting their kickbacks while I get letters from little proprietors in Peehole, Colorado, saying the railroad's going round their town, not through it. And it's all because they didn't pay 'the premium.' The Union Pacific doesn't run the West, and the Crédit Mobilier doesn't run the Senate!"

"You're getting red. People are going to think I'm making you mad."

Bill yanked his vest lower to cover his belly. "Well, that's not a bad idea, for my cover and yours." He puffed on the cigar in agitation, and a stormcloud of smoke rose between them.

"One thing clear," Matt said. "You're not expecting me to deliver the whole damned corporation."

"Just Julian. Of course, when you give him to me, I've got the whole board. They're all dipping into the Crédit Mobilier honeypot. And none of them trusts our man Julian one bit, 'cause he's way out there in St. Louis right on top of granting construction contracts. And everybody knows Julian only looks out for himself. Any friends and votes of confidence he's got, he's bought."

Matt hesitated, then asked, "Has he ever bought your vote, Bill?"

The senator looked at his cigar. "Not lately."

"You get religion?"

"I got tired of seeing a two-faced sonofabitch shave in my mirror." Bill drew a mouthful of smoke and released it slowly. "This is my last term, Matt."

Matt turned the hat in his hand a full circle before he spoke. "Aren't you admitting defeat before the battle?"

"I know Julian and the railroad lobby. This'll be my last battle. But I'm going to leave them bloody enough to draw flies. You can take that to the bank."

Matt cleared his throat. "Speaking of money—"

"I know. You haven't got any." He leaned close, as if making a point, and Matt felt him slip something into his coat pocket. "Just a small advance on the big expenses I'm afraid you're going to rack up."

"How much have you budgeted for this investigation?"

Bill exhaled. "Not much. Your cattle business wasn't my only bad investment over the years."

"It's comforting to know that a smart man like you can make mistakes."

Bill looked at him. "You can't make mistakes anymore, Matt. This case has to be solid."

"With you behind it, it will be."

Bill cleared his throat and raised his chin to free a waddle of skin from his collar. "Let me be honest. You've got to be more or less on your own out there."

"So, I'm an investigator on your staff only as long as I don't get caught? Who am I working for if Julian does catch wind of things?"

"Yourself."

"You mean—"

"He'll think you're trying to bring him down because of what he did to your dad and the family business."

"Me? Avenge my father? Because Julian railroaded him out of business?" Matt shook his head. "No one who really knows me is going to believe that. They'll know I wouldn't feel obligated to do anything for Dad. Dad wouldn't accept it from me anyway. He never needed my help, not once in his life, or he would've asked me before Dennigan Brothers went under."

"You weren't around to give advice or lend a hand. Julian only arrived in St. Louis in '62. You were already stuck in the muck with Grant's campaign."

"He wouldn't have asked me anyway," Matt said. "He would've asked Paul."

"Paul's dead. You can't hold grudges forever."

Matt was silent. What he held for his father wasn't a grudge. It was a shield, deep inside, protecting vital parts. Art Dennigan could cut him to shreds with a word, a look. His father's most benign gestures had an edge of fury; each point of contact was like meeting a razor of pure ice. His father knew, Matt knew. The wrong son had died in the war.

Bill cleared his throat expectantly. "You know, Matt, I don't have money to put you up in a hotel in St. Louis."

Matt shook his head. "You're actually going to force me home, aren't you?"

Bill tapped white ash from his cigar. "Your mother would be thrilled to have you back for a while."

In every letter Matt received, Mother begged him to return. And she promised she would ask no questions about Sarah and the baby. "Just come home," she wrote.

Home. A feeling of dread crept through him. Slowly he put on his hat.

"Matt," Bill said seriously. "It's your house too."

"And how the high-handed hell would you know?" The anger was instant, as if it had been there a long time, waiting. "Have you ever lived under his roof, right under his thumb? You haven't even laid eyes on Dad since before the war. You and Dad and Ulysses S. Grant all scratching bedbug bites in tents up at Springfield."

"Cairo, dammit." The senator's voice suddenly boomed across the room. "Cairo, Illinois! And don't you forget it!"

"I won't!" Matt shouted. He grabbed the cigar dangling at the corner of Bill's mouth.

45

"Christ, Matt," Bill whispered urgently. "Those are a dollar-fifty apiece. Don't—"

Matt threw the stogie to the floor and ground it under his heel.

"Crazy sonofa—!" Bill couldn't restrain himself.

Matt stalked off. He straight-armed the door of the smoking room and it sprang open, nearly hitting a waiter with a drink tray. As he started down the hall, he heard the mumbling of disapproving gentry in the room he had left. The rude display would establish a public breach between the senator and himself. If he could keep Bill Cahill's support secret, he could count on at least one element of surprise against Julian. Julian had not arrived at the top of the elite corps of old-money St. Louisians without a small army of paid operatives. They made sure Julian was never surprised.

They would soon report that Matthew Baylor Dennigan, rendered devoid of property in Tarmay, Texas, was moving to his family's home in Lucas Place, only three city blocks from Greenmore, the Gates's estate.

Matt thumbed his coat collar high as he left the hotel and started the long walk to the train station to get his suitcase. He had money for a ride now, but he also had a slow burn to walk off after the deal he'd just made with a devil of a congressman.

Inside the St. Nicholas, Julian waited near the cloakroom with Katie's wrap. She had stopped at the desk to pen a message to her brother.

As she rounded the corner, he smiled. What superb bearing, he thought. Stage training, of course. She obviously wasn't born to it. She turned her back to him to receive her cloak. How still she stood, as if the simple gesture of robing her were a test of his intentions. She had a healthy distrust. But then, she had been used rather commonly by that judge in Philadelphia. Out of curiosity, he let his hands linger on her shoulders.

"I have a cab waiting," she said stiffly.

All business. A woman after his own heart. He watched as she walked away, passing beneath the gas chandeliers adorning the lobby. The light was crystal-faceted, shimmering on her, illuminating what he already knew. She had bright, bright promise.

46

Julian returned to suite 19 on the sixth floor. He knocked twice, then opened the door. A burnt-sugar haze filled the room. Edmund still lay in a wispy shroud on the sofa.

"Edmund?" Edmund's eyes were open but he seemed not to hear. "Is he conscious?" Julian asked Zemin.

The Chinaman bent, cupping his hand around the flame of the small spirit lamp he had used to cook the opium. He blew out the flame.

"He can hear, but he doesn't listen," Zemin said, opening a wicker box. He began to pack away the layout—pipe, bowl, yen hock, sponge and saucer, and the tiny, coffin-shaped brass box that held the opium pitch. Also inside the wicker case were red fillets of embroidered ribbon, tiny wood figurines on a thong necklace, and bamboo-framed pictures.

"Actually, Zemin, it's you I need to speak with," Julian said.

Zemin nodded. He left the lid of the wicker valise open. He was thin, no taller than a girl, and his plain dark tunic hung to his knees over loose trousers.

"Edmund tells me you have a friend in the freight business in Shanghai."

"Chu King-Sing. He has many ships." Zemin bowed, showing Julian to a seat while he prepared to serve tea.

Julian was quiet as Zemin poured, noting how the Oriental man moved with ritual slowness, as if he were host. Julian sensed the presence of a businessman in the servant and made a note to proceed cautiously.

"I would like to place an order with Mr. King-Sing," he said, accepting his steaming cup.

"Mr. Chu. Last name Chu," Zemin said.

The correction was issued gently, but with the assurance of a man who knew he was in a position to receive as much as he gave.

"How much opium could your friend dock for me in San Francisco?" Julian asked.

"One fune, a hundred fune, a thousand fune. How much do you need?"

Julian paused. A fune was a minuscule measure of Chinese weight. It took about eighty-three fune to make an ounce. That

47

much he had learned consorting with Edmund in that squalid, smoke-filled den beneath 13 Pell. "I need five hundred thousand fune."

The smooth arc of tea entering Zemin's cup halted a moment, then resumed. When the Chinaman looked up, his face was impassive. "Very costly, and very hard to transport."

"It's only about four hundred pounds. Eight fifty-pound flour sacks."

"Ya p'ien is not flour, Mr. Gates. It travels half full in metal cans. Too much heat, it will puff up, spill over."

The little cans, like the brass one Zemin had packed in Edmund's box, were oblong, about five inches in length, two inches wide. Julian knew that one can held four hundred and fifteen fune, about five ounces. They were easy enough to hide.

"I want half the amount in pitch, half in powder. And only best-quality extract."

Zemin bowed his head. "Mr. Chu is very selective, very discreet."

"Good. The cargo has to be at the wharf in San Francisco by mid-March."

"Much too soon."

"I suggest you inquire as to the fastest steamers leaving New York for Singapore. A coastal packet there can run your message to Shanghai in no time."

Zemin shrugged. "Perhaps it can be done. But it is customary to pay for hurry-up." Again he bowed his head, as if in apology. "Chu's policy."

Julian nodded once.

Zemin quickly lowered his eyes and sipped his tea.

Nervous, Julian thought. Zemin was trying to decide how much he'd pay.

Zemin looked up again, focusing on a point beyond Julian's shoulder. "For such a quantity in such a time, it is necessary to pay six thousand dollars."

Excellent starting figure, Julian thought. He had expected higher. He made his outburst severe. "That's entirely too much! Customers only pay eight dollars and a quarter for a five-ounce tin.

48

If I sold all two hundred pounds of the pitch, I'd only make about six thousand."

"You will more than double your money in powder when you dilute it for elixirs," Zemin pointed out.

"Four thousand five hundred," Julian said, "or I consider it hardly worth my while."

Zemin considered that for a while, then calmly poured himself more tea. "Transporting *ya pi'en* is a delicate art."

"It's a perfectly legal import with no restrictions."

"Customs, of course, will charge six dollars a pound tariff. That much *ya pi'en* . . ." He shrugged as if he could not calculate the figure.

Three thousand dollars in import tariffs. "Five thousand dollars, my final offer," Julian said. "But I pay nothing if the customs office finds one fune of *ya pi'en* to tax."

"Do not be concerned. Mr. Chu is very experienced in San Francisco." Zemin paused. "Five thousand, five hundred dollars. My final offer." He bowed. "Agent commission, you understand."

Edmund stirred on the sofa. He tried to rise from the mounded pillows, but sank back as if weighted, his long hair dark with sweat.

The Chinese businessman immediately became an attentive servant, hurrying to Edmund's side with a cup of black tea, placing an arm across Edmund's shoulder to support him.

Julian watched. All the smokers he had observed craved liquid after the pipe. Water, Edmund had warned, would cause nausea, so one should drink only strong tea.

"Sleep now," Zemin said, taking the cup away.

Edmund feebly tried to retrieve the cup.

"No more," Zemin insisted gently.

Edmund noticed Julian's presence. "Ah, you're here." He sat upright, languid and graceless. "Have you talked things over with Zemin?"

"We were just discussing price and delivery," Julian said.

A long moment passed before Edmund spoke again, and Julian watched with curiosity as the actor seemed to put himself in order piece by piece. Edmund's chin jutted forward as he adjusted his collar. "You had a nice talk with Katie?"

49

"Yes. She's very thorough."

"Katie's smart, isn't she?" Edmund ran the fingers of both hands through his hair, then shook his head. The long dark waves hugged his face and fell boyishly along his forehead. "Poppy wouldn't survive without her. She holds the business together. I hold the audiences. We make a good team." He stood and stamped his foot. The pants leg fell free of its cling to his stocking.

"God, I feel wonderful. You should try it sometime, Julian. Stimulates the brain and steadies the nerves. Zemin, the necklace," he said, tugging his cuffs out of his sleeve.

Zemin took the strange necklace of figurines from the teak box. Edmund bent low, and Zemin slipped the necklace over his head.

"What is that?" Julian asked.

"Peach stones. They keep the demons away," Edmund said lightly. "Of course, what they really do is make women lean close, curious about them."

From the box Zemin retrieved an embossed red ribbon and tied it around his master's wrist.

"What is that?"

"Oh, a bit of a charm, I guess you'd call it. One of the eight auspicious signs of Buddha, isn't that right, Zemin? What do I have tonight? The conch shell? The lotus?"

"Wheel," Zemin said.

"Wheel of the law," Edmund said professorially.

Zemin handed his master one of the small pictures framed in split bamboo. Edmund tucked it inside the lapel pocket of his coat.

"And that?" Julian asked.

"A Lohan," Edmund said, getting edgy. "One of the eighteen disciples of Buddha. Something like saints, if you must know."

"What do they protect you from?"

"Great demons!" Edmund said in a theatrical whisper.

Julian played along. "Pray tell what do these demons look like?"

"Like you, Julian. Every one of them. Just like you."

5

Katie went straight home from the St. Nicholas. As the carriage jerked to a stop in front of the boardinghouse on Weehawken, she couldn't stop thinking, *a Western premiere, a Western premiere*. She stepped out into snow flurries and a buffeting wind. Edmund had harvested a winner from his social gambles, a man who could rescue them. Julian's contract meant a reprieve for Poppy and its debts. It meant the possibility of a repertory base for the troupe, a stable livelihood for Peg and Father, a real home for Beth. Upstairs, she tried to rein her excitement as Lin let her in.

"How is she?" Katie asked, taking off her cape and muff.

"Asleep, finally."

Katie walked over to the bed and looked down at her daughter. She had to be cautious. It was too much good fortune for a white knight to appear so suddenly, and in fast friendship with her brother. She knew the association would not survive deep questioning.

Her relationship with the confident millionaire created questions of its own. He had the magnetism of the very monied, and she knew a part of him saw her crudely. She was not virgin territory. Nor was her profession ladylike. She wasn't sure of his expectations, but she knew her smiles must never be inviting, her personality not overly bold or charismatic. She would be careful and capable, qualities a pragmatic businessman like Julian was bound to appreciate.

Beth half woke in a harsh fit of coughing. Katie tucked the blankets around her daughter, watching, waiting to comfort, but Beth sank back to sleep. She was a resilient child. Her energy and curiosity gave each day a sweet center of newness. It was a gift Katie never took for granted. Beth was the deepest, soundest joy of her life.

She's worthy of you, Roddy, she thought. Worthy even without your name, with simply your gentle gray eyes, light hair, and that serious smile. *Roddy*.

Tired, Katie backed to a chair. It was too easy to see his face in memory, to hear his learned, soothing voice. He had been patriarch to Philadelphia's judiciary and a generous patron of the arts. It was he who had paid for a proper coffin in which to rest her mother's consumptive body.

When Katie had lingered after the funeral to watch the listless swing of the gravediggers' shovels, Judge Roderick Carding had lingered too, watching her. She rode home with him in his carriage, to Newlyn's Aye, the Carding manor. It was her first time alone with him. She remembered what stultifying words he had offered. Though he was articulate about life, death drew nothing from him but funereal rhetoric.

"Death is a relief, a time of final rest," he said, his head bent, gaze on the paper lying on his desk. "Your mother's weary search for happiness is done."

She was bold at sixteen, defying death and God and Judge Carding, all powerful, all somehow the same. "Mother was happy the way she was. She didn't want to rest. She had too much to do. He shouldn't have taken her."

The judge lifted his head to look at her, but did not rebuke her.

She sat in his library, surrounded by the antiquities of his family, sedated by the scent of leather-bound books lining three walls. The longer she sat there, the more detached she felt from the worries at hand—how Poppy would get its bookings, which tavern to search for her father, how badly Edmund would maul his cues. With her mother gone, the family had turned to Katie to take charge. Sensible Katie. Dependable Katie.

"Your mother was a wonderful manager," Judge Carding said, completing the bank draft that would keep Poppy solvent through the winter.

Katie nodded, not trusting her voice. She looked around her, at the scrolled shelves filled with books. "Mother didn't trust books. She said truth was in your hands, in what you did, how you acted. She said truth from a book was useless if it stayed in your head, even truth from the Bible."

He put down his pen. "Is that how you feel, Katie?"

It seemed a question from Zeus, from a stern and powerful god judging worthiness in a subject. But she knew he was only a man in his later years, a paternal figure throughout the county. His gaze was so potent, though. He emanated a strange, virile charity.

"I love books," she said, blushing. "I love words, even useless ones."

He was quiet a moment. "Then you may come here and read whenever you like." His face was noble, with a gentle sag around the mouth and eyes set deep beneath gray brows. "I suppose it's as much a waste for knowledge to lie dormant in a case as in one's brain. Perhaps your mother had a point."

"But you are not often here. It would be more pleasant if"—she swallowed hard—"well, if you were. Here."

"Ah." He nodded. After a momentary silence he said, "I'm a widower, as you know. Your company could be construed as—" He paused, smiling. "—somewhat stimulating for me. You do understand."

She nodded.

"You don't." He stood and walked around the desk to perch on one corner.

She dared not look up at him. His nearness was something solid, warm, and ancestral.

"You're younger than my youngest daughter," he said.

"I'm old enough."

"Are you?"

Yes, Roddy.

Old enough to have his child. Young enough to believe he would make provisions for her and the baby. But she had been exiled from Newlyn's Aye upon Roddy's death, and Beth had been born in a mean little roadhouse after a long and difficult labor. So much fever and bleeding. Scarring there, the doctor had warned. That was what she had carried back to Poppy, secret scars and a newborn baby. Penniless too. She had arrived at her father's hostel owing coach fare. He had sacrificed a pint and paid the driver, and was glad to do it, he said. The troupe was dying without her.

Katie felt Lin's tentative touch on her arm, and realized she was bent almost double over her sleeping daughter.

"Sleep now," Lin said. "Worry tomorrow."

Katie rose early the next morning, anxious about the contract that Julian had said would be ready to sign at two. She sent Lin to gather every member of the troupe in the sitting room downstairs. She had told Edmund in a note that she was assembling everyone at ten o'clock. If he personally wanted to make the announcement, he would have to be there.

He wasn't, of course. His nights always stretched into predawn hours.

So, with customary directness as manager of the troupe, she relayed news of Edmund's contact with the distinguished St. Louis businessman. She talked of her preliminary negotiations with Julian Gates for a debut in a first-class theater. Her voice could not hide her excitement when she itemized the generous salary and terms.

"Wait!" The apprentice lead, Tobias, was incredulous. "And all he wants from us is two plays?"

Katie smiled. Tobias was used to a circuit troupe's grueling repertoire. Sometimes Poppy's small cast performed four different productions in a week. "Two plays," she repeated.

Tobias let out a loud cheer. His exuberance loosed the celebratory mood in everyone, and the room came merrily alive. Alleyn, his gray goatee in need of a trim, the whites of his eyes pale yellow, laughed grandly as he gave Katie a crushing hug.

54

"This is it!" he boomed. "This is our chance!"

With effusive la-de-da's, old Marge sang out dancing music and pulled Alleyn into a jig. Marge and her mate, Bester, were original members of the troupe, having come over from England with Alleyn and Edmund more than twenty years before.

Poppy's swordsmen, the immigrant Brandelli brothers, listened intently to their mother's Italian translation of contract terms, then spiritedly joined the dancing.

Only Peg, of course, showed any restraint. She was a year younger than Katie. Her small-featured face had riveting eyes set wide and commanding, sea-crystal blue. Like Edmund's.

She maneuvered around a chair and leaned toward Katie, setting her walking stick between them for balance. "You really should have waited for Edmund," she said loud enough for all to hear. "It's his triumph."

The merriment subsided.

Peg crossed the room, the dip and sway of her gait steadied by her cane.

There was a moment of silence when she left, then Marge blew a raspberry. Everyone burst out laughing, all except Katie. She was worried, not that she hadn't given Edmund his due, but that she had encouraged a premature celebration. The contract had yet to be signed.

Uneasy about Edmund, she sent Lin to the St. Nicholas to remind Zemin in no uncertain terms that he must have Edmund sober for the two o'clock contract meeting.

Lin was gone a long time. It was noon before she returned. She busied herself packing and didn't look Katie in the eye as she told her that snow was falling, the wind was gusting, coaches were slow, and neither Zemin nor Edmund were to be found at the hotel.

"Oh?" Katie stood still, telling herself not to think the worst. "Well, we're supposed to meet Julian in the Tenga Tearoom in two hours. Maybe they left early. It wouldn't be the first time Edmund forgot to pick me up."

"I talked with a maid," Lin said. "They left the hotel about three in the morning. No one has seen them since."

"Maybe you could go check the Tenga for me."

Lin picked up one of Beth's frocks to fold. "I checked. They're not there."

Not there. Katie leaned on the bedpost. "Where could they have gone?"

Lin shrugged and opened the wardrobe, reaching for a hanger. "Where, Lin?"

"I cannot be sure," Lin said, "but Zemin knows a family from Shanghai. On Pell Street, number 13. I think Mr. Edmund makes purchases there."

Purchases. Pray God he hadn't smoked himself into a stupor before she could get there. Katie donned her coat. "If I get him back within the hour, we can still make it."

"But you cannot go there!" Lin said.

"I have to. Legally, Edmund is the chief officer on Poppy's corporation papers. The contract with Julian has to be perfectly legal and binding."

"Miss Katie," Lin said sternly, "this is not a place where ladies go."

"Eight people heard me announce manna from heaven this morning. I will not let them down."

She leaned over to give Beth a quick kiss. Beth held her coat. "Mommy, bring me candy. Two-free-four, this many." Beth held up both hands, fingers flicking for a more impressive count.

"I'll try, darling." Katie opened the door to leave, but Lin stopped her.

"It's in the basement," she said, her voice low. "If they ask you a question, answer '*en she quay.*' They'll let you in."

"*En she quay.* What's it mean?"

"It means you're an opium smoker and they can trust you."

"Splendid," Katie said. Black, bloody splendid.

She walked east, fighting the wind and flurries. She signaled two cabs before one stopped. When she told the driver where she wanted to go, he gave her a wary, wide-eyed look. She settled back in the cracked leather seat, telling herself she would find him in time. She would bring him back, for the sake of the contract. For the shining hope in her father's eyes.

The morning's announcement, she knew, had revived her fa-

56

ther's overwrought dreams of success. But would he understand the need to polish Poppy's tired stock staging of the classics? Her father directed each scene around his beloved Edmund's centerstage orations. "But, Katie," he would say when she suggested new blocking, "don't you see? He has presence! The voice of an oracle! He commands!"

" 'I command her to come to me.' "

"No," Katie said softly.

" 'What is your will, sir that you send for me?' "

The percussive clop of the horse came faster.

" 'Katherine, that cap of yours becomes you not . . .' "

The rollick and rumble of wood wheels on cobblestone was deafening.

" 'Off with that bauble, throw it under foot.' "

"Enough," Katie whispered.

"I will say when enough is enough—"

She covered her ears. "Enough!"

6

Vandals had left their mark on Pell Street. The panes on the street-lamps were shattered. On the deserted street, food scraps and paper litter were fast disappearing under layers of new-falling snow.

"Wait for me," Katie told the driver.

His answer was muffled behind layers of neck scarf. A cold gust whipped up the hem of her long coat and she leaned against the carriage to fight it flat.

She hurried up the sidewalk, avoiding scattered pools of gray water, refuse from a laundry house in the alley beside 13 Pell. She saw a man emerge from the laundry clutching a brown paper bundle under his arm. All she could discern about him was the direction of his stride. He too was headed for 13 Pell, the opium house with a grimy garret and a closed-in porch.

She clutched her coat collar closed and got to the house before him. Running up the steps, she opened the sagging door. The enclosed porch was a welcome windbreak, but she didn't linger. She had to get Edmund to the tearoom by two.

She knocked at the door. No one answered. She grabbed the doorknob; it wouldn't turn.

"Knob's busted," said a man behind her.

She caught her breath, then turned to make sure her recognition of the voice matched the man. Matt Dennigan's chestnut beard was flecked white. Under his arm was the paper-wrapped package from the laundry.

"Mr. Dennigan," she said, projecting calm. "What a surprise. Not a pleasant one, I'm afraid."

His breath hung white in the frigid air. "This is no place for you."

"No, it's not. It is, unfortunately, a place for my brother, though I'm not sure he's here."

"He's here."

"For a man who claims no involvement with Edmund's activities, you seem to be everywhere he is."

He shrugged. The package crackled. "I have a room a couple blocks away. I was picking up my shirts when I saw you. I thought maybe you didn't know what you were doing, coming here. On the other hand—" His smile was humorless. "I thought you might have the same recreational interests as your brother."

"Your conclusion is squalid and insulting," she said.

"More to the point, it had better be incorrect. Get on inside. It's freezing out here."

"You said the doorknob doesn't work."

He reached across her shoulder, placed a hand flat on the door, and shoved. The door swung in and bounced off the wall inside.

They both stepped into a hallway lit by tiny, round-bellied spirit lamps. Matt leaned against the wall, watching her.

She hesitated.

"Are you going down to the basement or not?" he asked.

"Aren't you going?"

"Hadn't planned on it. I don't know the password."

"Then you're not a—you don't—"

"No," he said firmly. "I don't."

She made no move to go.

"You want company," he said.

She stiffened, but answered, "I wouldn't mind."

He led the way down the hall. At the end was a red door. A

59

wicket panel slid open to reveal two dark almond-shaped eyes. She tried Lin's words. *"En she quay."*

"Who *en she quay?"* the man asked.

She hesitated.

The eyes narrowed, then Matt spoke. "Edmund's *en she quay."*

The panel slid shut. She heard a heavy wooden brace hoisted free of its catch.

"I thought you didn't know what to say," she whispered.

"I didn't. I just figured Edmund's a safe name to throw around. He probably sends a lot of business their way."

A Chinese man in a dark tunic opened the door, then bolted it behind them as they descended the rickety staircase. At the bottom, a kerosene lantern hung from the ceiling. The floor was earth, moist.

A twisting black passage lay before them, thick with a basement scent of dank and fecund crevices. A sweet aroma hung in the air too. Opium's musk.

The walls were uncut stone mortared like a carapace, with bulging lines and swells. She wondered what drew Edmund here. It had none of the gaudy brightness and pretentious crowds he loved in clubs and gin palaces. It was a lowly realm that harbored the secrets of its inhabitants—and begat more.

Therein lay the lure for Edmund, she thought. He was an ardent consumer of other people's secrets.

Of course, the man behind her sought his share too. Matt Dennigan spoke and moved with a gravity she found unsettling.

Ahead she saw the yellowish glow of a lantern above a heavy door. At eye level was a narrow slit for viewing; the door opened before Matt knocked. An old Chinese man with a shaven crown and long, graying queue ushered Katie in.

Matt hesitated at the threshold, his body tense, his eyes narrowed.

"What's wrong?" she asked.

"I don't like the smell."

"Of opium?"

"The remembering," he said obliquely, then stalked past her into the small, dark room.

It was warm and smoke-filled. Tiny cooking flames bobbed on spirit lamps. Two platforms ran the length of the room, one above the other.

Patrons lay on the platforms in groups of three or four, gathered around a layout of lamp, sponge, and pipe. Men and women were affixed to one another like puzzle pieces, one's head to another's chest, one's torso pillowed across a leg to reach the flame where the yen hock hovered, bead-tipped, cooking the glistening gum.

Matt stood beside her as she peered into the recesses of the platforms, looking for the long, gaunt form of Edmund. Beside her, the old Chinese looked grim. "You buy," he said, pointing to a far corner blocked off by partitioned walls. Half hidden by the walls was a booth with a small door and a large pay window protected by wooden bars. Inside, two Orientals talked seriously, oblivious to the seamy languor of the devotees outside.

She searched her memory for one of Lin's tutorials. "*Qǐng děng yí-xià,*" she told the old man. A moment, please. She moved on uneasily, past dandies and derelicts intertwined in dreamy recline. All classes came equal to the pipe.

Near the middle of the room, she bent low in order to see beneath the top platform. She spotted her brother's long tousled hair. "Edmund!"

He didn't answer. He was curled on his side, his back to her. "Excuse me," she said to the smokers in Edmund's group as she crawled in to reach him. "Edmund, we've got to go." She grasped his shoulder. "We've got less than an hour until the meeting with Julian. Now get up!"

She jostled him until he could no longer hold his lips to the mouth of the long bamboo pipe. Grunting weakly, he rolled over onto his back, smoke streaming from between his lips. She squinted and waved a hole in the smoke as she shook his arm. "Come on!"

His eyes fixed ceilingward. He did not look at her, did not appear to hear her. She crawled off the platform, tugging at him. He was limp, jelly-jointed. Matt reached in and pulled him close to the edge.

"Edmund!" Frustrated, she rapped him with her reticule. He

did not react. Why wasn't he "very sensitive" as Zemin had explained last night? Zemin. Where was he? She turned to the old Chinese. "Zemin. Where's Zemin?"

The man pointed to the money booth and the two Orientals conversing inside over a sheaf of papers. Katie peered more closely, then walked up to the barred window. She pounded her fist squarely on the counter.

Zemin's animated face froze at the sight of her.

"I would like your help to get Edmund out of this—establishment!" The fury in her voice cut across the opiate drone of the smokers. Talk died. Some rose on elbows or craned their necks to stare at her.

Zemin bobbed an apologetic bow, clearly embarrassed in front of his compatriot. "This is my friend from Shanghai. Mr. Chang."

"Charmed," Katie said with a withering bite.

Chang bowed warily, then helped Zemin fold the parchment papers they'd been discussing. Katie saw that the top sheet was written in Chinese. Zemin tucked the sheaf snugly inside his coat, then hurried out of the booth.

Matt was bent over her brother, examining his eyes, moving his head side to side. Zemin edged in firmly to stop Matt. "Master Edmund," he called with dignity.

"He's going under," Matt said.

Zemin ignored him. "Master Edmund?" He shook Edmund.

Edmund lay staring upward, unresponsive.

"How much did he smoke?" Matt asked.

Zemin was quiet.

"How much?"

Zemin shook his head. "I don't know."

"Too much," Matt said quietly.

Zemin shook Edmund with a sudden urgency that frightened Katie. Edmund remained still. "Master Edmund? How much this time? Too much?" He grabbed Edmund's lapels and tried to jerk him upright. "Too much? Wake up! Zǒu! We stayed too long this time!" Zemin patted Edmund's cheeks and shook him by the shoulders.

Edmund did not react. Katie grabbed his coat. He was limp and open-mouthed, like a bass on a line. He was bloodless pale too, and so deathly still. Fear tingled the length of her spine. "Edmund!" she cried on the verge of screaming.

Matt's harsh command broke her panic. "Stand him up before he's comatose." There wasn't a shred of sympathy in his voice.

Her throat was dry. She hesitated a moment, then touched Zemin's arm. "Let him try, Zemin."

Matt handed her his laundry bundle, then bent over Edmund and slapped his face. Zemin lunged at Matt, and she dropped the bundle and latched on to Zemin. "Give it a chance, Zemin! You couldn't help him. This man can." *She hoped.*

The servant grudgingly gave room. Matt slapped Edmund twice more, then jerked him upright.

Edmund groaned.

"Get him some water," Matt said.

Zemin refused. "No water. He'll throw up."

"We need any response we can get and I don't give a good goddamn how messy it is."

"Get the water, Zemin," Katie said.

Matt held Edmund upright while Zemin got a dipperful of tepid water from a communal bucket. She coaxed her brother to drink. Lax at first, Edmund began to resist.

Matt shook him. "Fight it. Fight something!"

Edmund flailed in an attempt to push Matt away, then he began to heave. Zemin quickly set a basin on the floor, and Matt doubled Edmund to his knees. Edmund heaved again, and Matt stepped back to keep the splash off his shoes.

Feeling the pressure of time, Katie tugged Matt's arm. "I'll go up and make sure the cab's still there."

"Don't bother. Your ride's long gone. The snow's coming down fast now."

She felt physically sick at the realization that there would be no contract signing at two, at any time, that day. The snow would be their excuse, but Edmund was the cause. She watched dejectedly as Matt struggled to right Edmund. "Can you walk?" he asked.

"Walk," Edmund said vaguely, as if it were a word he couldn't recall. Matt pulled him up. Edmund's legs buckled, loose as noodles. Zemin helped catch him, and Matt braced Edmund's arm across his shoulder. They began to drag him out.

Zemin's friend Chang stood at the door as they passed. Chang spoke to Zemin in rapid Chinese. Katie caught a strange word: *băi-fēn-bĭ*.

"*Tài nán,*" Zemin fired back. Too difficult.

She saw the two men exchange angry looks, then Zemin nodded. An agreement? she wondered.

The question was fleeting, though, for as she passed, Chang smiled and bowed and handed her a note. She glanced at it in the dim light of the basement passage.

It was a bill.

The door closed.

The nerve. "Swine!" she yelled, pounding the door. "You—you purveyor!" She was beside herself. "Look what you've done to my brother! And you want me to pay you for it?" She looked at Matt. "Unbelievable!"

"Tear it up," he said, dragging Edmund down the dark, twisting passage.

"What?"

"Tear it up."

"You mean, don't pay it?"

He was nearly out of sight and didn't answer.

"But Edmund owes it," she called.

She could no longer see Matt but she heard him. "Some debts aren't collectible. Now tear it up!"

She couldn't do it. She slipped the bill into her reticule, right beside the scrap of auction flier on which Matt Dennigan had written his note the night before.

A debt was a debt.

She hurried through the dark corridor and caught up with the men, then ran ahead to take the stairs before them. She went out onto the enclosed porch, cracked the door a few inches, and peered out.

The street was already a sea of snow, no boundaries of curb or yard, no beginning or end of purest white.

Matt came up behind her and looked out over her head. "Getting close to a foot deep in spots."

Outside the snow fell silently. "A foot," she repeated as all of her fears amassed into solid weight inside her. A thud sounded behind her. Zemin was having trouble keeping Edmund upright.

"You want to wait out the storm here?" Matt asked.

"Can we?"

He shrugged. "There's no heat. Your brother should be kept warm. He's going to get the shakes."

She faced him. "How do you know? How do you know so much?"

He ignored the question and pushed the door wider, then turned up his collar and fixed his hat tighter on his head. "You're welcome to come to my place. It's not much, but the landlady keeps the coal scuttle full."

She looked at Zemin, struggling with his master, then back at Matt, a man who had secret reasons for following her brother, for meeting a senator, for offering his room.

Help would not come free. For Edmund's sake, though, she had no choice. "Your place."

"Two blocks down," he said, hoisting Edmund's arm across his shoulders again. "Three-story brick house on the corner. The porch sags. Don't fall behind."

She held the door. Matt and Zemin went quickly down the steps with Edmund, his feet dragging. Katie yanked the collar of her coat higher and stepped out into a stinging stream of snowflakes. She saw Matt veer into the alley and followed as quickly as she could past the laundry house. They cut across a backyard littered with rusty staves of old tubs. She was barely able to see through the pelting cloud of white around her. The snow was deep and wet, holding the shape of each footfall. The damp permeated her shoes. After a few minutes, her feet didn't feel the cold. They felt nothing at all.

The farther she walked, the heavier the snow seemed to fall. The three men were nearly out of sight now. Snow crusted her hair and laid a mantle of white on her shoulders. Her eyes were watery, wind-stung. She stopped beside a lamppost to rest for a moment, and the moment grew long. It felt too good, and she forced herself on. Every step was a battle. Her skirt and petticoats leached water from the snow, and the fabric hung heavy as lead around her ankles.

When she could no longer lift her feet, she plowed, snow bunching around her calves. She blinked often to keep the flakes from her lashes. Ahead she saw a dark blur. The wind whirled, dashing crystals into her face. She shielded her eyes and stopped dead still, exhausted. She wanted to sink. She could feel her knees buckling. But she straightened, so he would find her that way, standing on her own two feet.

He was a dark wraith before her, hair plastered to his head, his face miserable with cold. His beard was white. He put one arm around her waist and bent to crook the other arm beneath her knees. He lifted her, wet skirts and all.

He plowed the last half block to the house and maneuvered through the door with her still in his arms. The snow in his beard melted clear and glistening.

"You can put me down," she said.

He didn't answer, didn't stop, but slowly trod the hallway to his room.

7

Matt set her down and closed the door. He knelt at the hearth, blowing on his hands.

"Where's Edmund?" she asked.

He glanced at her as he lit kindling. "A few doors down. Your Chinese is helping him get dry."

"I should help too."

"Can you prop him up and walk him around to keep him awake?"

"No."

"Then you can't help. I'll go down there in a minute. Just let me build the fire. You'll need it." He tipped the scuttle into the grate. Coal tumbled out with a quarry-hard clamor. He straightened and turned to her, dusting off his hands.

She stood by the door looking around the room. Looking, he guessed, for clues to his personality, his intentions. The room was a transient's camp with straight-backed chairs, a musty wool rug, a lamp on a fruit crate, and a wardrobe with broken handles. There were few traces of him there, only a tall suitcase in the corner, packed, and a razor jackknifed over the mirror on the washstand.

It hadn't been hard to get a room close to 13 Pell. With Senator Cahill as a reference, he could have rented anywhere, but he'd wanted to be near the opium den. Its existence ate at him. Like the white dressing gown crumpled in the bottom of the wardrobe after Sarah had left. Like the silence of the house with the baby gone. The more he'd tried to ignore it, the bigger the silence had grown. He'd crashed a chair against a wall to stop it from swallowing him.

It was that way with the opium house. Once he had seen the narrow, ramshackle house, had stood in its hall and smelled the sweet tarry musk that permeated its walls, the house seemed to grow larger, taller, wider, each time he passed it. He had to stop it.

The coal was catching, and warmth drifted outward.

"Will your landlady mind giving up a room for a sick man?" Katie asked.

"She doesn't 'give' anything. She'll probably want a one-night deposit."

"I hope not." She stumbled over her skirts as she walked to the fire. The sopping wet gown and petticoats clung to her legs like bunched rope.

"Don't worry. I can pay for the extra room."

"I cannot accept charity from a man I don't trust."

"That's an uppity posture for a lady who's flat broke."

"Broke? We're about to sign the biggest contract of our career. I'll be able to repay you a room fee and more. Just," she added weakly, "not at the moment."

"This contract. It's with Julian Gates?"

She nodded.

"It wouldn't happen to be taking you to St. Louis, would it?"

She sent him a cautious glance. "The New Gate Theater. Why?"

He shrugged. "Just curious. So, he has a theater now. I wonder why a high and mighty millionaire chose a two-bit circuit troupe like yours?"

"God, you're an arrogant man."

"And you're an intelligent woman. I'm sure you've already asked the question for yourself. I'd be interested in your answer."

Cheeks coloring, she jerked her water-sopped skirts out of her way and moved directly in front of the fire. Matt began to unbutton his snow-dampened shirt.

"What are you doing?"

He jerked the shirttail out of his trousers. "I'm wet." He methodically loosened the long john top from the band of his pants. "I'm cold." He drew the overshirt up and off. "And I need a dry—" He stopped abruptly and looked her up and down, hoping he'd see a bulge beneath her coat. "Where's my laundry?"

She hesitated. "I dropped it."

"Where?"

"In the opium room, when you were helping Edmund."

He slapped the shirt against the chair. "In the opium room?" Damn. "The opium room!"

She seemed taken aback by his vehemence. "I'm—I'm sorry. What were they, shirts? I'll replace them. I promise I'll—"

"Don't you understand?" He shook his head. She didn't. "My name's on it. Printed right on the bottom."

She looked puzzled. "Then won't someone return it to the laundry?"

He tried to calm down. "I don't trust Chang," he said. "I don't trust your servant man, either."

"Zemin? Why? Because he's Oriental?"

"No, because he was too absorbed in his business with Chang to keep track of how many of those tar pills your brother went through."

She glanced at the door. "I should check on him," she said, worried.

"I'll go. Just wait." He heaved his suitcase up onto the bed. He had packed lightly and carefully. No pictures, papers, or memorabilia, nothing to announce who he was, what he did. There was only one item of personal attachment: a Colt .45 revolver. The gun that had seen him through the war. His lucky piece.

He covered the revolver as he pulled out the flannel shirt he needed. "You speak Chinese?" he asked, buttoning the shirt.

"Very little."

"Did you understand anything Chang and Zemin were saying

69

when we were leaving? Pick up any reason why they were mad at each other?"

"I have no idea what the conflict was."

"In a place like that, money's always the conflict."

"You mean, the money Edmund owes Chang?"

"Could be money Chang wants from Zemin. Zemin impresses me as a man who could drive a hard bargain."

"Zemin is absolutely devoted to Edmund, to the point of self-lessness." She looked away. "Usually."

"The deal he was making with Chang must have been a big one to command his attention so long."

"How do you know they made a deal?"

"How do you know they didn't?" He took a dark dinner jacket out of the suitcase and hung it on the back of a chair. "You should change. Put that on and let your gown dry."

She hugged herself. "I'd love to. But I don't have a private room."

"Use mine." He locked his suitcase and pocketed the key. "I'll be down the hall."

As he started across the room, she unwound the strings of her reticule from her wrist. The small purse slipped off her hand and onto the floor, some of its contents scattering onto the hearth rug.

Matt bent to retrieve two coins and a tarnished silver locket. He held up the locket. "You carry a picture of your daughter?"

She nodded.

"May I see?" Without waiting for her answer, he opened it. Two painted miniatures were framed inside. One was of a baby, light-eyed with blondish curls. The other was a patrician man with white hair. "Her grandfather?" he asked.

"Beth's father."

He closed the locket and handed it back. "I'll see to Edmund."

He left her there, staring into the fire.

In Edmund's room, the lamp was turned low. Zemin worked at the fire, preparing coals for the pan of a small iron bed warmer.

Matt self-consciously fingered his beard as he walked in, wishing he had more of a disguise. There was little chance Edmund would recognize him when the troupe got to St. Louis, but Zemin was another matter.

"Zemin?" Edmund called weakly. He lay in bed with knees tucked, arms hugged tight to his chest, shivering. "I need something."

Using a towel to protect his hands, Zemin placed the bed warmer under the covers near Edmund's feet.

"No." Edmund caught Zemin's arm. "I *need* something."

Zemin smoothed the hair from Edmund's forehead. "I don't have our valise."

"Get him up," Matt told Zemin.

"He's tired," Zemin said, wary. "He's sick."

"He's going to get sicker if you don't work that tranquilizer out of his system."

They got Edmund up. Slowly, patiently, they braced his stumbling steps across the room, back and forth, again and again. "Tea, Zemin," Edmund commanded weakly. "I'm so thirsty. Didn't you order my tea?"

Matt halted the forced march. Edmund was able to stand on his own, and he kneaded his face with both hands. "Tea, Zemin. *Chá*, please. I'm so cold." He staggered, struggling for balance.

It wouldn't come, Matt knew, but cold sweats would. Edmund's long hair was already matted flat. It was just the beginning. He caught Edmund before he fell and backed him to the bed.

What would a powerful man like Julian want with a pitiful dissolute like Edmund? From what Matt knew of Julian, the businessman's sole basis for human contact was monetary gain. Julian's "friendship" with Edmund had to be built on a business need then. The logic gave Matt a chill. There was only one product Edmund was uniquely situated to broker.

"The pipe!" Edmund cried. "Zemin, you're hiding it again! I need it!" His voice softened. "Zemin. Just a little medicine then. Please, Zemin."

Always calling for his servant, Matt thought. Zemin was important, more skilled than any valet, more intimate than any friend. He was the apportioner.

"Just a little," Edmund crooned. "A sip. I know. No more. Just

71

a sip of laudanum to quiet the nerves, I promise, that's all. I promise."

I promise. As he helped Zemin get Edmund to bed, Matt remembered promises. Sarah had made them, about laudanum, her Dark Lady. Her curse. Though Edmund preferred the powerful fumes in his pipe, he knew laudanum would serve him in a crisis. It was a tincture of opium, available to all, easy to get. It could alleviate his suffering, give his body what it craved. Overfed on opiates, it expected more. It needed more.

It had been that way with Sarah. She'd always needed more.

He stared out the window at the wind-tossed snow. If he closed his eyes, it would be there, the waiting image, the picture he could not blur. The reddish brown tincture in her Waterford tumbler, and Sarah grasping the glass firmly as a handrail to heaven.

He felt someone staring at him. Zemin stood close.

"My master needs tea," he said. "Where is the kitchen?"

Matt turned from Zemin's scrutiny and went to the door. "Wait here until I talk with the landlady so she won't be surprised."

He crept through the kitchen to the tiny room behind it, near the big wood-burning cookstove. Mrs. Bern lay in bed, snoring.

Matt quietly retraced his steps, then thumped his feet and elbowed the wall as he reentered the kitchen, loudly calling her name.

Mrs. Bern came out in a flash, smoothing her hair and tying her apron. She was a sinewy woman who wore a frown no matter what she was doing. It made her thin face look longer and more careworn. It also made her boarders less likely to ask for anything.

He took his time talking with her. It allowed for better lies. In the end he had negotiated an extra room and an early supper for four on his tab. He made a mental note to get a bigger advance from the senator for expenses.

Mrs. Bern said she'd bring a tray of soup and bread puddings to hold them until the evening meal. "Most of my boarders are still out, snowbound, I guess." Her eyebrows raised suspiciously. "Lucky for you you got the whole place more or less to yourselves. Now, you said a Chinese fellow is going to come get some tea. And what else was that you needed?"

72

"A lady's dressing gown."

"Hmmm."

Matt went back to Edmund's room. The actor was shaking with chills now, and Zemin was anxious to get him hot tea.

"Zemin, I've told Mrs. Bern that Edmund's a missionary with malaria and he brought you back from—"

"China," Zemin said.

"She's very religious. And very suspicious."

"Don't worry," Zemin said on his way out. "I 'Praise Jesus.' "

When Matt entered his own room, he saw Katie wrapped in a blanket and sitting in front of the fire. Her back was to him. Her gown and cotton underskirts were spread out over a chair drying.

He looked at the eyelet-trimmed petticoats, thinking of how long it had been since his bedroom had held pieces of a woman, intimate evidence, soft and lacy. He crossed the room and caught their scent. Rose. Her garments gave a faint fragrance from her clothespress. Or her bathwater.

She remained facing the fire, unmoving. "You didn't knock," she said.

"No, but I walked loud."

"Kind of you."

He couldn't see whether she smiled. He would like to make her smile. Her back was to him. *Trembling in her soft and chilly nest.* Long-buried words of the poet drifted through memory. *Stol'n to this paradise, and so entranced, Porphyro gazed upon her empty dress, and listen'd to her breathing.*

He moved close enough to see her hair piled soft on the blanket, thick rolls of ginger. Hair so unlike Sarah's copper wisps, which crimped tight of their own accord, unruly and ever spry, apt to dance away at his touch.

Katie's hair lay with civility, within his reach. *I will not harm her, by all saints I swear. If one of her soft ringlets I displace, or look with ruffian passion in her face.*

"You're too quiet," she said. "And too close."

He stepped around her to get nearer the crackling fire. "Are you worried about my intentions?"

"I would be, if I knew what they were."

"I've tried to be helpful."

"You have been."

"I've tried to be respectful."

She hesitated, then nodded. "You have."

"What else do you want?"

"I want you to be honest."

He sat on the hearth rug, profile to the fire. The heat hit his cheek like a toasting iron. "In what regard?"

"In regard to Julian Gates. You know him."

"He's a big wig. He throws money around. Lots of people know him."

"And I know you. You're a cowboy in Texas, or maybe a farmer. You lost your land in a winter auction."

He tried to keep his voice even. "Who told you that?"

"Nobody." She threw off a flap of the blanket and reached down for her reticule on the floor. From it she drew a folded slip of paper. He recognized it. It was the scrap he had torn from the auction announcement to write her the note he'd slipped under the backstage door.

"You were careful to tear off the top half," she said, "A through L. That's because your name begins with D, right? You have property that was sold for taxes, or you defaulted on a loan, something like that."

He shrugged, wanting to keep her talking. He needed to know what she'd told Julian. "Is that all you 'know,' what you surmise?"

"You have a relative named Art."

Damn, getting close, and she was watching him carefully.

"I think," she went on, "Art Dennigan's had some difficulty with his business. Land or agriculture, I'm not sure." She paused. "Some difficulty with Julian."

The fire was too hot, and he got up, moving a few feet away. "Julian told you that?"

"Offhand, in conversation." She tilted her head up to look at him. "It wasn't Edmund or me you were interested in following last night, was it?" she said. "It's Julian you're after."

He would have to fall back on the senator's prescient suggestion for cover: revenge of family honor. But first, he had to know: "Did you tell Julian that I was here in New York?"

She stood slowly, the blanket wrapped around her. "No. Should I?"

"No."

"Are you going to kill him?" she asked matter-of-factly.

He was stunned. "What the hell do you think I am?"

She loosed the blanket to reveal what she held in her right hand.

His Colt.

She aimed it dead at his chest. "You tell me."

8

"That's a loaded gun."

"I know," she said.

"I hope you know where the safety is."

"I do. It's off."

Off? Was she crazy? "I locked that suitcase."

"Picking trunk locks is a necessary skill in a road troupe like Poppy. Keys are never around when you need them. You learn to improvise."

"Is that what you call this?" he asked, nodding at the gun. "Improvising?"

"I call it forcing the lie out of the liar. All you have to do is answer a simple question. Why are you stalking Julian Gates?"

"Put the gun down and I'll explain."

"Explain now."

He shifted closer. "I don't think you would shoot me in cold blood."

She coolly extended the weapon. "I could, however, fire out of fear or panic."

"Then you'd have a lot to explain to your rich patron archangel. Getting caught in a flophouse with me." He shook his head. "Embarrassing. Especially since my family's got a long, hard grudgematch against Julian. He might find it odd that you and I were"—he looked at her petticoats sprawled on the chair—"familiar."

She stared at him. "It was a trick, wasn't it? Bringing me here, helping Edmund. You're going to use it against us. Why?"

He took a step toward her, his gaze fixed on her face. "You want to scare me, Katie, or kill me?"

"I want you to stay away from Julian. He's our chance. Our first real chance." She raised the gun, holding it with two hands. The blanket slipped from her shoulders. She wore his formal black coat over a long white chemise. "If you don't, so help me God . . ."

He stopped within easy reach of her. "Do it. Now. Shoot me now, Katie."

She stepped back.

He reached for the gun. "Now!"

Her eyes never left his face as she pulled the trigger.

There was only a click. Her arms dropped to her sides, the revolver dangling from her right hand. "How did you know? How did you know I emptied the chamber?"

"I gambled, knowing the kind of person you are."

"Liar," she said softly. "You don't know me."

"You thank an eavesdropping stranger for getting you a carriage. You dutifully tuck away Chang's bill for Edmund's purchases. You're too damned courteous. And you have a skewed sense of honor. You're too good for this kind of work."

He reached for his gun again, but she pitched it into the blazing hearth.

My Colt.

"You don't know me," she said.

My lucky piece. He grabbed the angle iron and fished frantically atop the coals, trying to hook the trigger guard. She got the poker, though, and clanged it against the iron, knocking him off-line from the target. He cursed her as the Colt slipped deeper between red-hot coals. Holding her off with one arm, he raked vigorously.

An ember flew free of the grate and landed on the rug near her feet. She cried out, backing away, no longer interfering with his effort to save the gun.

"Get it," she said hoarsely as the rug beneath the coal began to smoke.

"Get—it—"

The raw fear in her voice forced him to turn, to forget the gun for a moment. He kicked the coal back onto the hearth bricks with a casual swing of his boot, then glanced at her.

She stood with her back to the wall, the poker still in her hand. She hadn't had presence of mind to use it, he thought, or to see the insignificance of the threat. She had been seeing something else entirely.

Bending to the fire again, he hooked the bent tip of the iron around the trigger guard and pulled the Colt free. He laid it beside the scuttle to cool, hoping it hadn't been damaged.

Still Katie didn't move.

He went to her and took the poker out of her hands, leaning it against the wall. "You're right," he said quietly. "I don't know you."

He was close to her, so close her lips were but a handsbreadth away. Her expression was tense, and yielding, and aware. She knew how close he was too.

As he reached for her, the door swung open wide and a grim Mrs. Bern marched in with a tray. "Looks like I come with the gown just in time," she said disapprovingly as Katie pushed Matt away. "I realize, Mrs. Dennigan, that you two been separated for a while, but I still expect a lady and gentleman to adhere to a Christian decorum during the day in my house."

Matt shot Katie a glance that warned "Mrs. Dennigan" to play along. Katie returned a look that said, "Go to hell."

"Now," Mrs. Bern said, bustling across the room to set the heavy tray on the fruit crate, "that being understood, I want to welcome you. I'm Mrs. Bern. I'm sure Mr. Dennigan's told you about the high standards I set for boarding in my house. Mr. Dennigan told me about your luggage being lost at the station and I'm happy to loan you a dressing gown for the night. And knowing how

78

you got caught in the snow, I went to the trouble of warming up the bread puddings for you." She paused to receive thanks.

"Kind of you, Mrs. Bern," Katie said with lukewarm politeness.

"Like I told your husband, when a boarder comes with superior references from a man like Senator Cahill, I'm happy to go the extra mile for his whole family, sick in-laws included." She shrugged. "It all goes on the bill, anyway."

Matt looked at Katie, sure that she had noted the mention of his patron's name.

Mrs. Bern glanced at the window. "Would you look at that snow. Bad winter ahead." She set out two steaming bowls of soup, two mugs of hot tea, and a napkin-covered basket on the orange crate. "Separation's a sin for a marriage, to my mind. People see they can live apart, they'll forget how to live together. Isn't that what I said, Mr. Dennigan?"

"Yes, you did." He turned to Katie. "Meant to mention that, hon'."

The landlady bustled out. " 'Night, Mrs. Dennigan."

" 'Night."

Katie's farewell was clipped, with a little more spit than was polite.

" 'Hon'?" she said incredulously as Matt shut the door.

He shrugged. "I'm not the actor in this family."

"You are not family. You are not in my script. You are stark raving mad." She whipped her gown off the chair. "And I'm getting out of here."

He caught her arm. "Don't you see I had to do that? Make up lies to cover you and that pipe-sot of a brother down the hall? Are you so selfish that you don't see how I put myself on the line for you two?"

"Oh, you're doing it for us, all right," she said bitterly. "How can you be a hired spy if you act like a good samaritan? Well, Saint Matthew, do accept my thanks for so crudely compromising my reputation just now."

He tried to subdue his anger, but couldn't. "What reputation, Katie?"

Her eyes widened, growing dark and murderously shiny. She lashed out and slapped his cheek.

He released her arm, flinging it away, and she swiftly stepped back. "You cannot hurt me," she said, then her voice grew loud. "I won't let you!"

"Quiet!" He whirled and locked the door. "You're going to get us both thrown out."

"Good! I want to go home!" She strode back toward him and tried to push him away from the door. "I want to see Beth! I want to be with people I know, people I can trust. Unlock it."

He didn't move.

"Unlock it!" She slapped both hands to his chest, attempting to shove him backward. He didn't budge, but grabbed her wrists instead.

"Stop it."

She tried to shake free. "Let me go!"

"Calm down first."

She cried out and struggled harder, on the brink of hysteria. He held tighter as she twisted and squirmed.

"Don't tell me what to do!" she shouted. "Don't hurt m—"

He spun her around, holding her against him, and clamped his hand over her mouth. "Shut up!" He pinned one of her arms, but the other was free, wildly clawing anything in reach. He felt her nails sink into the skin of his neck and tear downward. "Goddammit!" He pushed her away.

She fell against the bed. He lunged for her before she could catch her balance, hooking his arm around her waist and drawing her up onto the high bed with him. The suitcase skidded across the sheets and fell off the other side.

She squirmed to her knees and held desperately to the footpost, but he pulled her back, pinning both hands over her head and straddling her. She started to scream, and he clamped his free hand over her mouth, holding tight so that she could look only at him.

"I'm not going to hurt you." He stared down at her, aware of the tension in every line of her body. "I don't know what kind of men you're used to, but I'm not that kind." He didn't know

80

whether she believed him, and he said it again. "I'm not that kind, Katie."

Her eyes grew wet, an angry, fearful burning of tears. To see that glistening was an act of intimacy, and he looked away. "If I let you go, you have to be quiet. Do you understand?"

She closed her eyes. After a long moment, he felt her body go lax beneath him. He released her hands. His tight grip had left red marks on her wrists.

When he removed his hand from her mouth, she reached up and touched his neck where she had scratched him. Her finger came away bloody.

He got off her, standing beside the bed and wiping away with his hand the blood trickling down his neck.

She sat up abruptly, then climbed over the footpost and jumped to the floor. Jerking her arms from his coat sleeves, she took off the jacket, obviously anxious to get dressed.

She wore a corset over her white chemise, a garment of white linen, gathered at the top. A warm, rolling gather he would remember.

She dressed with tugs and jerky motions like a stiff doll. Or a woman too angry to speak. Her underskirts and gown, still heavy and wet, clung to her legs when she moved. Frustrated, she gathered the skirt to one side and draped the soggy hem over her arm like a toga. She tried to open the door, but the knob wouldn't turn.

"Unlock it," she demanded, breaking the long silence.

"Where are you going?"

"Someplace safe."

"Hope you find it."

He walked to the door, standing close to her as he put the skeleton key in the hole. The latch clacked, and she reached for the knob.

They heard it even before she jerked the door open, noise in the hall. Voices, stumbling steps, bumping against the wall. Someone was leaving.

She ran out in stocking feet. He followed.

Her brother was making his way uncertainly to the front door. He was clammy with sweat and disheveled.

81

Katie quickly followed him, stopping an arm's length away. "Don't do this, Edmund. You're not well enough to go out."

Zemin tried to ease past her, but she caught his arm. "Zemin. Tell Edmund he needs to rest. Put some sense into him."

Zemin bowed apologetically. "Sorry, Miss Katie. We forgot the valise."

"It's at the emporium," Edmund said. "Chang's little emporium. We're going back for a while. The valise has everything, you know. My charms. My Lohans." He turned suddenly, dramatically, to face her. His chin was out, his attitude patrician. "Surely you don't expect me to work without my valise."

He was acting, desperately, Matt thought, and it was costing him. Sweat beaded his upper lip. His eyes were shiny blank beads.

"You're too ill," Katie pleaded, moving closer to him. "You won't be up for the run in Larsen. We leave tomorrow. Remember?"

"Larsen? When we've got a metropolitan premiere planned in St. Louis? Don't be daft, Katie."

"We've committed to the township, Edmund. We've contracted."

He pressed palms to his temples. "Stop it."

"Peg's sent the handbills. Every member of the cast is prepared. Now, please, just rest here, get well. We'll see Julian before we leave for Larsen in the morning."

He suddenly gripped her shoulders and shook her. "Stop it!" he screamed.

Matt lunged for him, but Edmund had already released her.

"Just stop!" he said, holding his head in his hands. "Stop your bloody rescuing!"

Matt pulled Katie back as Edmund paced frantically.

"Do you hear me? Hie thee, nurse Katie!" Edmund's thunderous baritone was weak. "Go and save them all, bright angel. Save Peg the Sad and our broken-down players. Save old Bester when he forgets his lines and fat Marge when she tramples her train. And scavenge costumes for the illiterate swordsmen who shred everything in reach. And Father, dear Father, save him most of all, so that he remains blissful in his ignorance. Rescue *them*, Katie. Fly like an angel, far away. Far away from me!"

Matt felt her stiffen as if slapped. "Please, Edmund." Her tone held a false tranquillity. "It's the contract I want to save. Julian's contract. We have to reschedule the signing. You have to be lucid. You have to be professional. You cannot ruin this chance. My players work hard. They deserve—"

"*Your* players?" Edmund's chuckle roughened into a cough. "Whose players, Katie?" He began to laugh. "Who is executive manager of Populus Felicitas?"

"You have the title on the corporate papers," she said. "I have the responsibilities. That's the only reason I need you there to cosign in front of Julian."

"Ah, now I understand." He wiped away tears of merriment. "Obviously, you don't. You see, I don't need you to cosign, Katie. I already did."

"What?" She tried to lurch forward. Matt tightened his hold on her shoulders. "Don't joke like that!"

"I'm not joking."

"Liar."

"I'm not lying." He started laughing again. "Julian had his secretary up all night writing clauses and making copies. We toasted our partnership sometime in the wee hours and he left. He just left. Then Zemin and I left. To celebrate."

"No," she said, stunned. "That can't be. What were the conditions on travel expense?"

"Oh . . ." He rubbed his temples. "I don't deal in trifles."

"And the thirty percent share of the gate?"

"What?"

"The contract said thirty, didn't it?" Her voice rose in panic. "That's what Julian and I agreed on. Edmund? Two hundred a night for principals, right?"

"God, Katie, let up. He gave me a copy." He clumsily patted his coat. "Oh, hell. It's in the valise. Or did we leave it at the hotel?" He looked at Zemin, who shrugged. Edmund cocked his head, giving Katie a pitying look, then he shrugged too. "It'll turn up."

83

She lunged at him so suddenly, Matt lost his grip on her. She knocked Edmund backward, and he slid to the floor. She fell on him pummeling him, until Matt pulled her off, telling her to let him go.

"Let *me* go!" she screamed, arching away from him. He whirled her around and pinned both arms. She twisted and struggled, but he held on to her.

Breathing fast, shaking, Edmund wiped his brow with his sleeve. "Shrew!" he shouted as Zemin helped him up. "That's what you've always been. Untamed shrew."

Katie froze, fear and anticipation so palpable that Matt knew Edmund had fired a shot point blank in a secret sibling war.

"Yes, Katherine, little shrew, I know who you are," Edmund muttered bitterly. "Sweet Kate. 'Kate of my consolation.' Sly Kate, bowing in my light at the Daly."

Katie pushed away from Matt. "I was Juliet," she whispered, taking a step toward Edmund. "Juliet at the Daly. Not the shrew. I never play Shrew."

"No, no, everywhere, you are Kate. 'Prettiest Kate in Christendom.' Sneakiest Kate. You steal my light on every stage. With Daly. With Julian. But not that day. That day, there was nothing left to light. Remember?"

There was a deadly quiet.

Zemin put himself between Katie and Edmund. "Master Edmund, we go to Chang's now, before you make Miss Katie very mad."

He helped Edmund on with his coat. Edmund bent low like an overgrown boy so that the short servant could button the coat.

Katie jerked open the door. The snow had stopped. Feeble gray light sank into an ocean of white down.

Zemin went out first. Edmund stepped past her without a look, without a word.

She slammed the door shut.

"How was the soup?"

Matt turned instantly at the sound of Mrs. Bern's voice. The old woman stood at the end of the hall, toweling a pot long-since dry, her gray brows arched suspiciously to her hairline.

84

"Too hot," Matt answered. He went over to Katie and took her arm. She was trembling. Inner rage, hidden pain, deep distress, something shaking her from the inside out.

"Still too hot," he said.

9

Back in his room, Katie sat woodenly on the bed. He wanted to hold her. He even took a step closer, but stopped, forcing emotions aside and considering his strategy instead. She was vulnerable now, and a persistent man might find some answers.

Her voice was soft. "You're thinking we would be better off without him, aren't you?"

He didn't answer. He hadn't been thinking about Edmund at all.

"You have to understand," she went on, as if trying to convince herself. "People on the circuit love him, all the folks in town squares and barns and church halls. Poppy comes into town, just another little wren of a road company. Then Edmund prances on with his extravagant gestures and wonderful voice, and the people forget our raggedy costumes, our flimsy props. They love him. We need him."

"Ever think about what you need, Katie?"

She got up, not hiding her nervousness well. Crossing to the makeshift table where Mrs. Bern had laid out the food, she picked up a mug of tea. "It's still warm," she said, and walked on to the fire. She sat, her back to him once more.

He moved the fruit crate table close to the fire and pulled up another chair. "Hungry?" he asked.

She shook her head, holding the warm mug in both hands.

He picked up the blanket from the floor and draped it around her. "I'm starved." He sat across from her and ate, holding the crockery bowl of soup to his chest.

The muffinlike bread puddings were dry and cold. He offered her one from the basket.

She shook her head, then changed her mind and took one, wrapping it in the scrap of auction notice and putting it in her purse. "For Beth," she explained. "I promised her candy when I got back." She looked into the fire. "The afternoon hasn't exactly put a sweet shop in my path."

"Why didn't Beth's father marry you?"

She sipped her tea. "Impudent question."

"I think his was a higher impudence."

She sighed. "He died," she said finally. "But he left me Beth. 'Our indiscretion sometimes serves us well.' "

"Hamlet, act five," he said. "Or is it Katie, act brave?"

He expected anger, but her look held pity. "You obviously have no children," she said, "or you would know how grateful I am to have such a beautiful child."

The conviction in her voice tempted him to be honest in return, but he turned away. "No," he said. "I have no child." He looked toward a dark corner of the room, seeing nothing except the picture his mind set before him. The baby, new and tiny, clean and wrinkled and whimpering with hunger, his weight barely denting the soft pillow on which he lay. How gently he had laid the fragile child beneath Sarah's breast, swollen and dripping its milk. How blankly she had stared ahead, not leaning to the babe, not guiding her nipple to the tiny mouth that stretched wide, searching. She did not notice whether the baby suckled or slept or was spirited away to an Indian wet nurse.

In the end, he had let Samuel be spirited away from himself.

How long now? Three years? Was he three already? What did he look like? What kind of father could not picture his own son?

"How old is your daughter?" he asked.

"Three."

"I would like to see her sometime." *I would like to see my son.*

He grabbed the poker. With fierce stabs he jabbed the ribs of the grate to loosen the gray ash and charred wood.

From the corner of his eye he saw her huddle deeper in the blanket and hook her feet on the chair rung, in case he loosened sparks.

"Tell me why you're so afraid of fire."

"Our hall burned down." Her voice was thin. "The public hall where we were playing a double bill. It was the winter Father added *Much Ado* to the repertoire, and *Taming*—" She stopped.

Taming of the Shrew. "*Untamed Shrew*," Edmund had called her. "Were you hurt?"

"Not a scratch." She was silent a moment. "My sister was the only one hurt. She jumped from a loft. The fall crippled her."

"How'd the fire start?"

"The lamp fell. The oil lamp in my dressing room."

He kept quiet, wanting her to go on. She didn't, and he didn't press her. "How old were you?"

"Thirteen. Peg was twelve." Again she stared into the fire. "I was supposed to be looking after her."

"Who looked after you?"

"Mother, when she wasn't busy. She died when I was sixteen."

"Didn't Edmund help look after you?"

"He was our lead. He was twenty-two, twenty-three, maybe." She spoke slowly, as if the memory was unclear. "He didn't have time for us, except when we had to rehearse new pieces. Father was always adding something new. We were running lines when—" She adjusted the blanket to cover her legs. "When the lamp fell. It was devastating for Peg, for her career. She had a tremendous gift for mimicry and great dramatic range in her voice, just like Edmund. She would have had a brilliant career."

"You're pretty good at praising everyone's talent but your own. It was you they cheered at Daly's."

She looked at him, and he saw irony replace the melancholy of her memories. "I can't feed my daughter and a ten-member troupe on ovations. That's why Julian's contract is so important. If Edmund didn't get the thirty percent, so help me, I'll—" She shook her head. "He ruins everything. Everything."

"Then why not leave him behind when you go to St. Louis?"

"Stupid question. He's family, not an apple you can toss from the bin because it's rotten." She shifted uncomfortably. "Besides, Julian likes him."

"Why?" Matt asked, baiting. "What's Edmund got that Julian wants?"

"I don't know and I don't care." She threw off the blanket and stood. "Maybe Edmund has something *you* want."

"What are you saying?"

"You knew what to do for him at Chang's. You knew how to wake him. You know opium. How? How do you know that?"

He tried to smile at her suspicions, but he couldn't. She thought he was an addict, once or still. He sank down to tend the fire so she would not see his face, the part trapped in Sarah's shadow. "I learned what to do years ago. Someone I knew took laudanum. Sometimes she took too much. She told me once that it was like a lover who never stopped wanting her. The greediest of lovers. It took so much of her, body, mind, and soul."

How could you not know that, Sarah? Couldn't you feel the parts of your body recede, so that when I touched your face, it did not turn to me? When I kissed your lips they were sleeping vessels that did not feel, and when we lay together at night, you willingly opened to me, willingly smiled, but when I reached inside you were gone.

He felt Katie's hand on his shoulder, gentle and real. He had stared too long at the fire.

"Who was she?" Katie asked.

"It doesn't matter. She's dead." He rose slowly.

"Dead? I'm sorry."

Tentative, he touched her cheek. "I'm sorry you and I have so much in common. It makes my job difficult."

She turned her face away from his hand. "What job?"

He was silent. If he was successful, Julian would be ruined. If Julian was ruined, Katie's new life in St. Louis would be too.

"My job is to leave," he said. He cradled her nape beneath her curtain of hair. His hand felt too large for such a delicate place, at rest on fragile cords and teased by tendrils soft and warm. "Can you help me?"

She didn't step away to refuse him, but neither did she turn a nuzzling cheek to his arm to signal willingness. She didn't move at all.

He drew her toward him, anticipating resistance as she neared the invisible divide that held them separate and safe. But she leaned toward him, pliant, as curious as he, and his lips met hers. He measured the breadth and softness and fullness of her mouth in a long kiss, unchastely warm, deeply familiar.

He gathered her body close and felt her stiffen, but he found her lips again and spoke silent reassurance, pulling suppleness from unfirm resolve, nursing her lips apart so he could test the warm depth of her.

She wrenched away with a strange gasp, as if he had torn something from her. It was her taste, he realized, sharper than the tannin bite of tea beneath their tongues. The taste of a carnal promise. He'd found it deep, he'd found it shared.

"Katie." He pressed her quickly, forcing her backward, into motion, into reaction, anything to forestall the caution gripping her, and him.

Her dragging hem made her stumble. Lurching, she grabbed the bedpost. He steadied her from behind with his body, nesting long and close. She stiffened, then pulled herself tight to the pole, away from him, away from the natural fit of their bodies. The warmth of contact lingered, though, and he watched her fight it, hugging the post.

His own warmth was certain and focused, very hard.

"I thought you weren't that kind of man," she said.

He heard no outrage, only uncertainty and an honest longing that surprised him, emboldened him. He tried to kiss her neck. "What kind do you want?"

She slipped down the post and ducked under his arms. "I need a man of stature, unlike you." She backed away from the bed. "A worldly, wonderful man, unlike you."

He advanced slowly.

She flattened against the door, trying the knob. "I need a man who carries all my burdens and doesn't give me more. A solid man, who I can hide behind whenever I wish."

He was closer, and she nervously twisted the knob again.

"I need a man who walks in the garden of a big house," she whispered, turning her face from him, "who can look up at night and tell me the story of every star." She closed her eyes tightly, as if to shut him out. "A man to teach me."

He was too close to shut out. She breathed raggedly, and Matt knew it was himself affecting her, not her memories of another man.

"You know I'm not that kind, Katie."

"Then I don't want you."

"Yes, you do." He lay his cheek against hers, following an instinct for tenderness, an instinct dormant so long that tapping it awakened other feelings. Young ones, yearnings to trust and be trusted.

He pressed against her, hard, to squeeze the feeling out of himself, and out of her. She had looked at him tenderly too, one naked moment that made him realize that a sensual quest had gotten completely out of hand.

"I told you," he said again, for both their sakes, "I'm not that kind."

She pushed him away, crying out angrily and kicking at him. He backed off, and she slid down the door to the floor. She sat, head bowed to her knees.

After a long time, he went down on one knee in front of her. She didn't move. He reached out, then withdrew his hand, waiting until she raised her head.

Her cheeks glistened, wet. "It's just . . . been so long for me."

He got up and turned away, as if honesty so raw was contagious. Not speaking, he put his suitcase on the bed and retrieved shaving soap and brush. Taking the water pitcher from the washstand, he returned to the door. She hadn't moved. He offered her a hand, but she got up by herself, not looking at him. The door creaked sharply behind him.

In the kitchen he set the pitcher on the floor beneath the boiler on the side of the stove. He turned the tap, and steam roiled up as hot water streamed into the pot.

When he got back to his room, she was sitting on the bed. He poured hot water into the basin on the washstand, then stood before the mirror. He could see her behind him, waiting. After spreading out a towel, he soaped his beard, then reached up for the razor hanging over the mirror.

Face foamed white, he tilted his head back, stretching the skin of his neck. The long razor scraped upward in short exact strokes. Russet-colored hair rained onto his towel. Out of the corner of his eye he saw her watching his every move. Skin tingling, he toweled his face, his beard gone. He felt naked.

When he turned, she came forward to see him. Her gaze skirted the line of his bare jaw, then moved inward to his lips. Anxiously she searched his complete face, and he knew she saw a stranger.

He packed his suitcase, throwing in his damp shirt and still-warm revolver.

"Are you going back to Texas?" she asked.

"I'm going home, Katie. To St. Louis."

She repeated it like a pledge. "St. Louis."

He approached her slowly. "Forget my name. Forget the senator. Don't mention me to Julian. Or to Edmund. Or to Zemin." He stood before her.

"That's a lot to forget, Matt. What can I remember?"

He gripped her wrist, and she stiffened, uncertain of his intent as he pulled her arm upward. He pressed her fist to his cheek, stroking it there until her hand opened to trace his shaven face. Her fingers moved across the curve and crevice of his mouth with a gentleness that touched him more deeply than he wanted.

He pulled her hand down and turned away.

"Why?" she asked.

"So you'll know me," he said. "When you're dressed like a princess at Julian's side, you will know *me*." He put on his coat.

"Matt."

He stopped at the door, suitcase in hand.
"I'm not any man's princess."
"A moment ago, I mistook you for mine."
The door screeched closed.

10

March 1868

ST. LOUIS

The Rosewood Hotel in St. Louis was elegant, continental. Service was impeccable. Rooms were tastefully done with canopied beds and scroll-topped chests of drawers.

Each morning, Katie walked the rich cream-and-red carpet of Poppy's new home as if it were an eggshell about to give way. Things were too good to be true.

Even the transit system was painless, just a walk to the corner to one of the city's three horse-drawn railway lines. As she prepared to board one spring morning, Poppy's apprentice lead, Tobias Morse, ran to catch up with her.

"Going in early again?" he asked, taking her arm to help her up. "You were there marking sets until eleven o'clock last night."

Tobias was a strong and stocky man, fair-featured, sensitive of heart, and solid as a stone fence. He would make someone a fine husband, Katie always thought. She had long ago let him know he couldn't be hers.

"You're up early too," she said.

"I want to run drop cues today. Somebody's got to."

"I know. Everything's behind schedule."

She was grateful for his friendship, for his warm hand on her shoulder as he guided her to a window seat. He was a better "uncle" to Beth than Edmund had ever been. A good and kind man, a capable actor. Why Tobias stayed with the troupe was as much a mystery to Katie as how to turn her affection for him to love.

She looked out the open window as the railcar clanged the all-clear at its next stop.

"Pretty day," Tobias said.

"Pretty city." She liked St. Louis. It was a homey metropolis bustling with traffic, commerce, and development. And parks. Beth had bounded out of bed that morning, eager to spend another day in the park chasing pigeons, splashing in the fountains, and watching for squirrels in the big spreading oaks.

"You know," she went on, "Julian told me that St. Louis has eighty-five brickyards just to keep pace with all the construction here. And forty breweries to quench the workingmen's thirst."

Tobias focused beyond her, out the window. "I think Julian's a little too far up the social ladder to know much about a workingman's thirst."

"You don't like him, do you?"

"That's a question we're all dying to ask you."

She wagged her finger at him, a reprimand for nosiness. "Somebody has to work with him, Tobias. He's a businessman. That's all he's interested in."

"Lin will be reassured. She doesn't trust him."

"And when did you start discussing my social life with Lin?"

"When I realized I wouldn't be a part of it," he said, teasing.

She smiled and looked out the window again. "Keep the slings and arrows coming," she said, playing for pity. "I can always use a few more."

"You can use a good rest. Why are your eyes peeled to the sidewalk? Are you looking for someone?"

"Not really." Maybe a tall man with a plainsman's hat pulled low, a man who leaned forward into his stride, challenging anything ahead. He might even have a beard again. It had been so long.

"I'd like to know," Tobias said, drawing her attention back to him, "how you got stuck with all the maintenance and construction details for opening the New Gate."

She paused to choose her words carefully. "Edmund had a hand in negotiations this time." She still hadn't forgiven him for signing the contract, blind, without her. At least the terms had not been as exploitive as she had feared. Julian had kept his word on salary and gate-share figures.

"So now," Tobias said, "in addition to supervising the crew backstage and actors onstage, you're required to hire every ticket taker, punch server, and doorman the New Gate needs to open?"

"It's just one of the extra responsibilities for which Poppy's liable. Julian's contracts have a lot of—" She glimpsed a hatless man whose thick auburn hair needed a trim. She stood, looking back. "—clauses," she finished. The man had spectacles and a soft paunch. Definitely not Matt.

"Who was that?"

She sat quickly, feeling ridiculous. "No one."

He looked at her suspiciously. "Well, this extra show we're supposed to do all of a sudden, that was in a clause somewhere?"

"Yes." In an uncomfortably vague section regarding additional services and performances "as required." They had less than a month to get an unfinished theater ready for a pre-opening benefit performance of *Romeo*, two weeks before the scheduled opening that she and Julian had agreed on. Edmund had been a fool, agreeing to Julian's request for a benefit show not a day after they arrived in St. Louis. And she had been a coward, offering only token protest. She had not wanted to open the door to questions about Poppy's competence. The reward for her acquiescence was a "good girl" smile from Julian that made her feel strangely unclean. The reward for Edmund was immediate guest privileges at Julian's private club.

The situation worsened two days later, though, when Julian unexpectedly arrived at the theater. He found her backstage conferring with a carpenter, and he told her that the members of the

Orphans Board were so excited about the benefit performance, they wanted to take part in it. He had agreed. His friends would only be extras in the Capulet ball scene, he went on as Katie's irritation rose, and they would provide their own costumes. Perhaps Katie could teach them a simple Renaissance dance.

"Perhaps Edmund could," she countered. "If I'm in charge of production, I will not turn my stage into a pony ring for amateurs to parade their finery."

"Your stage, Katie?"

A chill tickled her neck. "I'll be happy to help you hire a separate crew for amateur night."

"I have a crew. I have a troupe. And I have a theater." He paused significantly. "What more do I need, Katie?"

She had no answer. He smiled, satisfied.

"If Edmund helped negotiate you into a mess," Tobias said, calling her back to the present, "he should be there every day helping you get out."

She couldn't help laughing. "Tell me the truth. Do you want Edmund around every day? Telling us how *he* would put together a production three times the size of usual?"

Tobias gave a wild-eyed look of horror.

"You see. Things work out for the best."

"Sometimes."

She knew Tobias was genuinely concerned. Everyone in the cast looked to her for cues of confidence. "Besides," she added, "any mishaps at the benefit show can be corrected in the formal premiere."

"Good plan," he said, but he sounded unconvinced.

Actually, she had grand plans—for magnificent sets, neatly choreographed sword fights, and intriguing interpretation of the Bard. She had made notes on the train trip West, even going so far as to seek her father's support for new ways to enrich their stock staging of *Romeo and Juliet*.

Alleyn's response had been deliberately ambiguous. "See what Edmund thinks," he'd said.

She didn't care what Edmund thought. She had not spoken at length with him since that snowy afternoon, when he'd left Matt's boardinghouse for Chang's den. It didn't matter. She and Edmund had never really been honest with each other. Avoidance was the foundation of their sibling bond. Secrets worked that way, gluing two people together yet holding them apart. It was the only way she could stay with Poppy after she had lied about the fire for Edmund. For her.

"Hey, Miss Melancholy." Tobias interrupted her reverie. "Cheer up. Maybe Edmund won't even make it to the benefit show after all the late nights he's putting in. I see his name in the gossip columns more every day. He's the talk of the town."

"One night, it will happen, Tobias. Edmund won't show, then you can star and present everyone a real Romeo."

"Ah, you're kind, Juliet. But not prescient. That sonofagun always pulls through."

He was right. Edmund's careless overdose at Chang's had been followed by a stubborn, if miserable, recovery. Her brother's current alcoholic sprees were indirectly her fault. She had demanded that Zemin strictly ration Edmund's opium. The ploy had only turned Edmund to whiskey for comfort. Tall waterglasses full of comfort.

The railcar stopped on North Grand. She and Tobias got off. "I hope you've finally got some advance money in the cash box," he said.

"I'm sorry, Tobias, I don't. If you need something, give me a note and I'll see that Julian's accountant gives you a voucher for it."

"Like a kid at boarding school?"

"I know. I'm not happy about it either." Not happy that Edmund had signed without demanding clear wording in the contract about cash advances to sustain the troupe before gate receipts came in.

Julian had advanced plenty of alternatives to cash—train tickets, freight transfers, lodging bills, and meal vouchers. The process was a pain, though. She had tried to speak to Julian about it. He kept putting her off.

She couldn't afford to be pessimistic, she told herself. Julian was truly offering Poppy a chance to turn bad fortune to good. It was up to her to make it work, to create productions so high in quality and innovation that everyone in town took notice.

Even Matt.

Odd, how she'd expected him to emerge from some shadowed corner ever since the troupe's arrival a week before. She knew he was in the city. She had seen his name in the society pages the day they arrived, in a list of the attendees of an elaborate soiree. "Matthew Baylor Dennigan of Lucas Place." He certainly didn't sound like the penniless, transient cowboy who'd gone off the trail in New York.

Here, he had social rank. No wonder he had wanted her to forget his rundown room, his maverick presence as he tracked Julian and Edmund, his secretive ties to Senator Cahill.

Of course, she had forgotten nothing. His nondescript room was a fixture in her memory, and she visited it often. Even now, facing the frenzy of work, she could retreat there and roam, pausing at the bed, the fireplace, the shaving stand, searching for clues to her feelings about Matt.

She did not trust him, yet she wanted to. She wished to see him, but was afraid to. He made her feel physically alive in a way that was hard to control. She could not imagine him taking her arm in innocent friendship, as Tobias did now to help her maneuver past plasterwork rubble in the alley behind the New Gate.

Matt's touch had purpose. It had weight. Whether gentle or crude, questioning or assuming, his touch was a signal to her blood to heat, her heart to race. She had schooled herself not to rise to any man's provocation since Roddy's death.

Matt was not just any man.

She hurried with Tobias through the alley. As he opened the stage door, she heard mewling squeals under the black iron steps. The stray alley hound must have given birth. She'd have to let Beth know.

It was barely past seven-thirty, but already the backstage was filled with a chaotic din. From every direction came hammer blows, saw thrusts, bumps, and thuds, the anxious dissonance of make-ready.

She gathered her skirt tight around her legs and forged a path

99

through the bustle. Rowdies jerked heavy burlap bags of sand across the floor. Grips lowered lines so canvas backdrops could be mounted on the battens.

Pulleys hummed on greased reels, hoisting the backdrop for the Capulet ballroom scene in act two. She watched the cloth wall retract high into the fly gallery, with its painting of russet brown stone and a trompe l'oiel door opening onto a garden. The paint was so fresh, streaks puddled and inched downward the length of the canvas.

"Just a minute!" she called to the prop chief. "The paint's not dry on that drop."

The prop chief shrugged. "Miss Henslowe's orders. What she wants up, goes up."

Peg was steamrolling the production again, Katie thought. Slapdash everything and everyone onto the stage, pack it up, move it on. For once, they didn't have to move on. They had resources. Didn't Peg realize they had a chance to present real theater?

Katie sidestepped the flat of dark, moonlit woods for the balcony scene and shouldered past busy stagehands, seeking her younger sister. Peg was behind the proscenium, leaning on her prompt stool.

Katie interrupted her sister's instructions to a young roustabout with a tap on the shoulder. "Peg?"

Peg turned so abruptly, her walking stick skidded and she had to grab the stool for balance. She covered her awkwardness with a stern look at Katie. "Where've you been?"

"Am I late?"

"The patternmaker's here with samples."

"Which patternmaker?"

"The one from South Seventh."

"Has the man from Steam Forge delivered the ironworks?"

Peg frowned. "What ironworks?"

"It's for an idea I have for act two. If the balcony is partially grillwork, the audience can see Juliet full-length, and Romeo can get achingly close, yet they'll still be separated. It'll add tension."

"It'll add money, time, and trouble."

"We're not paying for sets. Julian is. And isn't trouble what we're paid to handle?"

"Of course. Give me more. It's just what I need."

Peg was more bristly than usual, and Katie guessed the cause. "It's the dinner tonight at Greenmore, isn't it?"

"You know I hate dinner parties. They're nothing but stilted little theatricals with"—she shuddered—"amateurs."

"Julian said it was just a small get-acquainted affair. I think he wants to show off his house and grounds. You'll enjoy it. It'll be good social practice for the big formal gala he's giving us next week."

"Don't remind me," Peg said.

Katie wanted to say more. To tell Peg she should be glad for a reason to wear something other than a simple dark skirt and a baggy matron's blouse, so dowdy for a nineteen-year-old. She needed to pin up the waist-length braid she wore every day too. Peg had beautiful hair, Irish black and shiny. Her face was a pretty oval, but her features always seemed pinched and serious.

"Edmund says that little benefit show will be great advance publicity for us," Peg said.

"If things run well. If not, we make Poppy, and Julian, look ridiculous."

"Fiddlesticks. You've already scaled us back so much, what can go wrong?"

"The drop cues. We haven't tested all the flies. And those wet drops"—Katie gestured toward them—"are going to look like nursery sketches under strong light. And we don't even have enough walk-ons to fill the stage properly. It's like a painting, Peg, you've got to—"

"Hire more supers, stuff them into tights, and dab them around like plants."

"No, no, no!" She lightly hit the stool with her fist. "They need to be active. It's a live tableau. They need rehearsal. We all need more rehearsal."

"What high-minded manure! Absolute manure! Every one of us can say the Shakespeares in our sleep, plus the newest Boucicault and a dozen cozy little melodramas. We're professionals, for God's sake! We can set up in thirty minutes."

"In circus fields or squalid little halls, that's fine. This is different, Peg. Neither you nor Father has grasped that yet."

"Well, poor dolts we," she said, pulling her body up straight. "Is Edmund ignorant too?"

"You know as well as I that Edmund grasps nothing but the limelight."

Peg's cane pounded the floor. "How can you insult him! What nerve! After Edmund stood up for you when Augustin Daly tossed you out the door."

"Tossed me out? What are you talking about?"

"Edmund told me about his New York offer. Daly wanted to contract Edmund for spring, but Edmund wouldn't sign without you. And Daly wouldn't take you on. You were too demanding."

Peg stood so close, Katie could have reached out and shaken her. But Peg was on Edmund's side of the divide. She didn't know of his habit and made light of any dark shadows in his temperament. Edmund inflated his image with tales of great exploits and stardom, just missed. He was Peg's hero. He had carried her out of the burning theater and saved her life.

"I could tell you the truth," Katie said quietly, "but Edmund would only better it with a lie."

Peg looked at her a long time. "Edmund always betters you, Katie." She picked up her prompt book. "Because you never tell me anything."

She brushed past Katie and crossed the stage on slippered feet, each "tump" of the rubber-tipped walking stick a rebuke.

Slowly, Katie made her way to the bannistered stairs that led down to the dressing rooms. Downstairs, future citizens of fair Verona congregated like bees in a comb, picking at tights and twisting wigs as they were fitted for costumes.

Short and round, Mama Brandelli bustled through the crowd with a sewing basket on her arm. She patrolled the costumes, her belly thrust forward and a needle in hand, checking for loose braid on a doublet or a bodice in need of a tuck.

Because Mama Brandelli considered food an essential accessory for a good performance, the wicker basket on her arm was seldom without biscuits, cheese, or sausage.

"Morning, Mama 'Delli," Katie said.

Mama Brandelli stopped her and looked her over, then tweaked her cheek. "Getting skinny, *tesora mia*," she warned. "You work too hard." She rummaged in her basket for a big pastry filled with sausage. "Take this. Help you fill out your gown at the big party."

Katie gave Mama a peck on the cheek and bit into the pastry. She was ravenous.

Coat slung over his shoulder, Matt hurried into the morning room to join his mother for breakfast. He stopped just inside the door.

His father sat reading the newspaper at the small round table by the window. He didn't look up.

"Mother out this morning?" Matt asked cautiously.

Art Dennigan nodded.

Matt donned his coat and slowly fastened every button, a girding ritual. As he watched, his father cracked a new crease in the newspaper. Art Dennigan was broad in frame with a barrel chest and ramrod spine, too big and stiff for the cozy walnut table around which the family took its informal meals.

Matt sat across from him. Eastern light streamed through the bay window that overlooked lily beds and a juniper hedge in need of pruning. The window panes were gray with dirt, and paint curled in dry patches on the sill outside. Simply cleaning the glass would help, Matt had told his mother when he arrived.

"We had to cut back on the house staff again this year," his mother had said, adding, "We won't tell your father I mentioned that."

"We won't tell your father" was the phrase Matt remembered most from his childhood. His well-meaning mother, Hellie, had always stepped into the breech between father and son, protecting a rebellious boy from a patriarch's wrath.

For several minutes the only sound in the small room was the cold plink of their spoons in the egg cups, the rustling of the newspaper. Too much had been kept from his father, Matt thought.

103

They had no moments of connection upon which to build a bridge. Everything had to be volleyed across the chasm.

"Where's Mother off to today?" he asked finally.

"If it's Thursday, she's in the children's ward at the hospital," Art answered without looking at him.

"I think she has a volunteer job for every day of the week."

His father read on, unresponsive.

Matt took a last bite of dry toast, tossed the crust on his plate, and scooted his chair back.

Gray eyebrows arched over half-moon reading glasses. "Busy day ahead?"

"Thought I'd go down to the carriage house and put a saddle on the piebald. Take a ride out Clayton Road."

"Nice acreage out Clayton," Art said.

"I'm just going out for some target practice, with Herb Cobb."

"That's the fourth outing you and Herbert have had this month." Slight interest animated his father's voice. "He's a good, honest attorney. A young lawyer starting out could do a lot worse for a partner than Herb Cobb."

"All we're doing is shooting targets."

Art nodded. "While you're out there, take a ride around the old Merrymill farm. Good price right now."

"I told you. I've got my eye on some land in Texas."

"Money down the hole."

Matt spun and headed for the door.

"Matt!"

Even now, the thunderous force of that voice could stop him cold in his tracks.

"That Texas business sticks in my craw, but I can swallow it. What I can't stomach is the thought of you going to that affair at Greenmore next week. A Dennigan doesn't dignify anything with Julian Gates's stamp on it. You know my position."

Matt didn't turn. "I know a man has to bend sometimes to reach what he wants. I've got my reasons for going."

"They're not good enough!"

I know, Matt thought. *Neither am I.* He put on his hat. "Tell Mother I'll be late tonight."

11

The small get-acquainted supper Katie had expected at Julian's estate, Greenmoore, was actually a formal dinner for twenty. "Just a few supportive patrons and beholden politicians," Julian had whispered offhandedly to her. He sat at the head of the table, a gracious host, elegant in crisp white shirt and black evening jacket with tails. Garrulous Edmund claimed the other end and the lion's share of the champagne. The evening grew raucous with competitive repartee.

Fortunately, that allowed Katie, Peg, and their father to pick politely at their food and not worry about performing socially. Katie was seated beside the police commissioner, Hiram Liggett, a gruff man who had the longest walrus mustache she had ever seen. Peg had drawn a more well-bred companion, the Belgian foreign consul. Alleyn entertained anyone within ear's reach, telling of personal encounters with theater greats he had never met.

Katie was keenly aware that she, indeed the entire Henslowe family, was modestly attired compared to the other guests. Her best green silk had been moiified, but it was stil a season or two behind in fashion, lacking the panel insets and defined bustles of the other ladies. Peg, of course, wasn't worried about fashion. She was watching Katie to find out which of the six forks was for sardines. Katie glanced at another guest for a cue, then nonchalantly picked up the correct fork as she listened to Commissioner Liggett's story of his battle that past winter with the gout. Peg made a comic face of concern.

Katie gave her a warning glance. Peg had been a wicked mimic when they were young. If she got her mocking-face on, the commissioner would find that his gout was the easier misery to bear.

When dinner was done, Julian led the Henslowes on a tour of his mansion, which, he told them, had been recently refurbished. Katie was more amused than impressed by his extravagance. A marquetry floor in the foyer was inlaid with Julian's initials in polished mahogany. Tall windows in the front parlor were hung with ballooning folds of embroidered satin. The music room was rife with caryatid pedestals and Greco-Romanesque pieces. In the ballroom, the chandelier was tiered with delicate incuts and swells, like a hoop skirt scalloped with a thousand lights.

The scent of newness and a taste for excess were everywhere. That was why Julian had found kinship with her brother, Katie thought. At its core, Julian's personality was as showy, as intemperate, as Edmund's.

As they said their goodbyes, Edmund announced he was staying for a late game of billards. Katie wasn't surprised. It had become Edmund's pattern in the past week to stay out late, then rise groggy at two the next afternoon, stop by the theater for an energetic cameo appearance, then whisk himself away for cordials with giggly, well-to-do ladies. He was a social curiosity and much sought-after. "I'm off to sell tickets," he would say airily. Pray God, that was all he was selling.

Julian's coach took Katie, Peg, and Alleyn back to their hotel. The desk clerk at The Rosewood handed Katie a message.

Meet me outside.

M.

Matt. She smiled, then tried to hide it. Her lips wouldn't cooperate. Matt.

She went outside and stood at the top of the steps, which were bustling with people on their way in or out. Not seeing him, she walked down to the sidewalk. Across the street lay the rolling grassy hillocks of the park where Beth played, much of it in darkness now, beyond the streetlamps' reach. She crossed the street to look for him in the protective shadows.

She made him out, not far down a hill, standing with reins in hand, a horse beside him grazing grass. He was watching for her. The moment she appeared, he let the reins trail and strode toward her. He was well dressed, she saw, his hair neatly trimmed. He looked like a gentleman, a gentleman she didn't know.

"Grazing animals are not allowed in the park," she said, before he got too close.

He glanced back at the piebald horse. "Why should you care? You're a newcomer, not a taxpayer."

"I like it here. My daughter likes it here."

"I know. I've seen her."

"Seen her?"

"Playing."

Why had he been watching Beth? "Then why haven't I seen you here before?"

"You've been working. I've been working." An awkward silence fell, then he said, "Let's walk, Katie."

Soft, she thought. His voice was as soft as his last words to her that snowy afternoon in his room. The room lay out there in the darkness ahead of her. The room he had left. "I can't. Not tonight." She moved away and tried to make light. "I see by the papers that you've been busy. Attending parties. Consorting with people of fashion. You obviously found your laundered shirts, or bought new ones."

"I forgot the shirts, until it was too late."

"Too late?"

"The police raided Chang's den. The day after you and I were there."

"Good. An anonymous tip?"

107

"My tip."

She studied him in the darkness. "You hated Chang that much?"

"No. I hate his livelihood and what it does. I hate what he and Edmund and Julian are planning."

"What are they planning?"

"I don't know. But if I understood Chinese, I'd have a clue." She looked away.

"I knew you understood them that day, Katie. You lied to me."

"No. I only picked up a few words Zemin said. One, I asked Lin about later. *Băi-fēn-bĭ.*"

"Well, what's it mean?"

"Percentage."

"Great. What's Zemin wanting a percentage of?"

She shook her head.

"Find out, Katie," he said quietly.

She faced him. "I'm not your snoop. I will not spy for you. Julian is my employer. He's—" She stopped herself. Matt was a man with a home and respected family, a man who had a sense of place and well-being. He wouldn't understand the vivid dream that had risen in her during the hectic months of moving and planning the new shows. A dream of a house, a safe place for Beth to grow up, where friends gathered around a table that was hers, no traveling, no worries about money. A dream that Julian could make real.

"Katie." Matt touched her hand, but she snatched it back, knowing too well that the lightest caress from him could rouse too fierce a need in her. A need she could not fulfill.

He stepped back, as if understanding the danger, her caution. "Katie, you know in your heart that Julian doesn't care about you or Poppy. He cares about money. And he rooks anyone he does business with and leaves them groveling."

"You know Julian hired Poppy because Edmund and Zemin can provide something he needs. You better tell Edmund and Zemin that before they ship in all those little canisters of opium for him. At best, they're going to find themselves in jail."

His voice was even and low, but she saw his hands had curled into fists, and he held his shoulders unnaturally stiff. Was he just trying to frighten her into helping him, or was he truly concerned?

Still, she discounted his warning. If the three men were in league to bring opium to St. Louis, no laws were being broken. The import of opium was legal. Regardless of her own repulsion for the addictive drug, she would not lower herself to spy on her employer because of Matt's suspicions.

"No, Matt, I will not help you." Hurt that this was his only reason for wanting to see her rushed in, and she pushed it back with anger. "And if this was why you wanted to see me, meet me here in the darkness, then—"

"Katie." His voice broke across hers, halting its rising. "There's more. You know that."

"Do I? You didn't even acknowledge that I exist until tonight. And then calling me out in the pitch black. God, you must really fear for your reputation if you can't see an actress in daylight."

He smiled. "You see, you don't know me as well as you think. I have a cousin who's an actress, and I happily call upon her in the daylight." His smile faded. "I see you everywhere, Katie."

A deep note of emotion in his voice stilled her.

"This afternoon," he went on, "you stopped at a patternmaker's on South Seventh." He walked slowly around her. "Yesterday you talked to the owner at St. Louis Steam Forge, 404 South Levee, about novelty ironworks. You also hired a drayman from White & Billingsley to haul costume goods and carpentry supplies."

"Matt."

He stopped in front of her, only inches away. "Two nights last week you worked at the theater very late. Some crewmen were with you, and a stocky man with blond hair. He escorted you to your hotel. I don't know his name."

He waited. The horse's reins jangled in the silence.

"Tobias," she said. "A friend."

He nodded once, searching her face in the darkness, then he touched her cheek.

She caught the vestige of cologne on his hand, sandalwood and wolfsbane, the trace of his dressing table and, somewhere, his room.

Walls close and strange, intimate and unsafe. She turned, unsteady, and started to walk away.

He caught her arm. "I don't like coy games, Katie. And I don't take thoughtless liberties with a woman. I haven't even thought of another woman since New York. I have to see you."

She looked at him, then at the hand on her arm. "You want to use me."

"That's not true."

"You want me to find out what business Edmund and Zemin had with Chang. Isn't the next step, What's Edmund up to with Julian? Isn't that who you really want? Julian?"

He was silent.

"I don't like coy games either, Matt. And I don't like meeting in the dark like a woman ashamed. See me openly or not at all."

She ran out of the shadows and crossed the street. She had nearly reached the circle of light beneath a lamppost when she looked back at the park.

He had mounted and was riding fast toward her. Reaching her he drew up tight, the horse snorting protest. He leaped from the saddle and pulled her fully into the light of the lamp.

His kiss was a fierce search for the passion he had tasted weeks ago. It was there, so instantaneous she felt like a fool, a hypocrite. His embrace was tight, then roaming, forcing a dark warmth to soar upward in her, spreading wings that stretched and strained the sanctity of clothes.

She could not quiet the sounds in her throat. He swallowed, taking them all.

She broke away. He gazed at her, then slowly walked out of the circle of light and mounted in the darkness of the street.

"Lady, take care what you wish. It might come true."

The hard gallop of hooves reverberated in the night.

Julian sat alone in the cavernous Gold Room, waiting for breakfast.

He drew up the chain of his diamond-stud pocket watch. Eight-thirty-two. Two minutes late, and on such a busy day. All the details for the night's gala were hanging over his head.

As he clicked the watch face closed, Drake, his butler, hurried in with the tray. Julian set aside his *Harper's*, his expression disapproving. Drake put the tray across his lap. Julian shook out his initialed linen napkin and waited.

Drake lifted the warming cover from a silver plate, revealing a half-moon omelette, a glistening golden brown sauce trickled over it in a lattice design and with islands of saw-tooth cut strawberries. A decadent whiskied aroma rose, and Julian sniffed discreetly.

"Fine, Drake." The butler nodded and left.

Julian ate slowly, as befit the caliber of the food and the high salary he paid the chef. But after a few bites, he could take no more.

The notes. They were due. Altmann had given him the news last night. Dutiful Altmann, solemn secretary, penny-point account keeper. Altmann had said he would work through the night to consolidate the debt and arrive at a payout schedule. He had requested Julian devote an entire morning to reviewing projects and expenses.

Julian stared blankly ahead. The glass doors of his balcony were open, and he could hear the coo of a pigeon, the pip-tweet of cardinals, the soft *chwirr* of songbirds. Nature's cheerful simpletons. Irritating twits.

He could force extensions from the banks, he thought. He'd have Altmann make account transfers from the holding company. Surely there was a buffer fund in his secret real estate holdings, especially with all those foreclosures and resales last fall of marginal properties. A few in Texas, he remembered. There'd been a Dennigan on the list of ranches in arrears. He'd marked the property for quick foreclosure, knowing it was just a knee-jerk reaction to the name. But any opportunity he had to wound a Dennigan was a good one.

It was old Art's fault. It had been five years since Julian had forced Dennigan Brothers to the auction block, but Art Dennigan remained a royal pain in the neck. The old curmudgeon still had a tiny coterie of the city's old guard on his side, who censured Julian in private affairs at their homes. No one dared censure him in public. He was too powerful. And that was something Art Dennigan just couldn't accept. His son had, though. Obviously a wiser man, one who understood the mutable laws of business, Matt Dennigan had accepted Julian's invitation to tonight's gala. Julian smiled. Art must be near apoplexy.

Julian rang vigorously for Drake. "I assume everything is in order for tonight's affair?" he asked when the butler appeared.

"We'll have to set up at least fifty tables on the terrace, sir." Drake hesitated. "Very large, the crowd."

"The more, the merrier."

"Yes, sir."

"And don't forget to leave a space clear. I told Edmund I want those illiterate Italian fencers of his to give my guests a rousing demonstration. Now, you may call in Altmann for me."

"Very good, sir."

Julian took his place behind the huge French desk that gave the Gold Room its name. Positioned between two windows, its lacquer finish gleamed citron yellow. He tied the sash of his morning coat with deliberate leisure as Altmann came in, burdened with papers. The secretary set a foot-high stack of ledgers and correspondence files on the front of the desk, flipped up his coattails, and sat.

He was noticeably pale and thinner than usual, Julian thought. Still, his jacket buttons shone, his string tie was crisp. There was never a hint of dishabille about Altmann. Even his creases were severe. He was so well trained too, and he was completely trustworthy around money. Like a eunuch, Altmann looked, but had no desire to touch.

Julian sat back in his chair, ready to listen. Altmann pulled the top sheet from the tall stack of papers. As he cleared his throat, Julian said, "You will make this brief? I have to dress for a skeet shoot at the club."

"Brief?" Altmann paled a shade lighter. He made a minute dog-ear on the paper he held, then smoothed it. "If you're going to the club, sir, you will probably see Colonel Wallace. He has written again, about late dividend payments."

"Brig Wallace is a blustery old fool. I can handle him. And I'm sure you can handle a few account transfers to cover notes due."

"Actually, Mr. Gates, I—"

"Good." Julian stood. The meeting was over.

That evening, Katie arrived home from the theater with barely enough time to dress for the gala.

"Mommy!" Beth ran to her and gave her a tackling hug around the legs. "I played with Teddy today!"

Katie bent to give Beth a kiss. "And who's Teddy?"

"My friend." Beth lifted her arms to be picked up.

It had been a long day, with Julian's extravaganza still ahead, and Katie lifted her with a dramatic groan. "A friend from the park?"

Beth locked her legs around her mother's waist. "He pushed me down. I took his ball."

Katie bent her forehead to Beth's. "And did you give the ball back to him?"

Beth's eyes suddenly shifted to something of interest behind Katie, and she propped her chin on Katie's shoulder, mum.

Lin bustled into the room with clothes on her arm. "She threw it in the duckpond."

"Teddy cried," Beth whispered.

Katie snuggled her there, enjoying a moment of peace, grateful to be with someone who wanted nothing more taxing than a hug.

Beth pulled back to show her an invisible spot on her finger. "He bit me."

"Oh." Katie examined the finger closely and kissed it.

"I can play with Teddy tomorrow?"

"If," Katie said, forehead to forehead with Beth, "you don't throw toys in the water. I have to get dressed now. Will you get your treasure box and recite some cards for me?"

Beth nodded and wriggled to get down. Katie let her go, then turned to watch Lin lay out the crimson evening gown Julian had had made for her. Apparently, he had not been pleased to see her twice in the same green gown, in New York and at his dinner party the previous week. His "gift" made it obvious that she would be on display that night, representing the grandeur of the New Gate and the wisdom of his choice of Poppy to inaugurate the theater.

113

She could tell Lin was not happy with the dress. Hurriedly made, it was tight-fitting and risqué in design, with a low-cut bodice. If there had been time, she would have asked Mama Brandelli to move higher the cream-colored lace that edged the neckline. There hadn't been time, though, and she had no choice but to wear the gown. Peg was wearing a dull blue taffeta that Mama Brandelli had quickly refurbished from a costume gown. Katie didn't want Julian's influential guests to see how impoverished Poppy really was.

She kept an eye on her daughter as Lin flicked a buttonhook down the bodice of her day gown. Beth elbow-crawled under the bed and back, pulling out her cigar box of treasures—corn husk dolls, brightly colored bottles, a tiny china dog, and picture cards with nursery rhymes.

"Have you talked with Zemin today?" Katie asked Lin. "I was hoping he would know how sober we can expect Edmund to be tonight."

Beth chanted, cued by her rhyming cards. "One, two, free-four-five, CATching FISHies all aLIVE—"

"Zemin does not confide in me anymore," Lin said as she hung up the gown.

Katie stepped into the new crinoline that had accompanied the dress. Unlike the enormous hoops of a few years earlier, this was flattened in the front, allowing a skirt's fullness to sweep to the sides and back. "Then you don't know whether he's still in contact with Chang in New York?"

"I know he sends letters to Chang," Lin said, disapproving. "Chang is trash. Zemin should be ashamed. Zemin is a good man. He's not a merchant. Merchants are parasites. They take from others and give nothing of value."

Christian schooling had apparently not erased Lin's strong belief in the Confucian social order. But Katie sensed something deeper. "Are you afraid Zemin's going to be a merchant?"

Lin shrugged. "Zemin has secrets now. Zemin and Mister Edmund have secrets."

"—which my FINger did they BITE? Little FINger on the RIGHT—"

114

Katie ducked beneath the crimson gown as Lin held it up, then pulled it down over Katie's body, straightening the small bustle and long satiny train. After Lin had hooked it in back, Katie sat at the vanity. She caught Lin's eye in the mirror. "Tell me about these secrets."

"—Came by a PEDlar, NAME was STOUT, CUT her PET-TIcoats all about—"

Lin began to brush Katie's hair. "On the train, I heard Zemin and Mister Edmund talking about a sea merchant. His name is Chu King-Sing."

"What does he sell?"

"Everything. Everything Mister Edmund likes."

Lord. "I've got to find out what what he and Edmund are up to. Zemin's your only living relative. Surely you can appeal to him to stop this."

"Not anymore. When the Taipings killed the family of Song, Zemin and I had only each other on the road to Shanghai. We shared everything. We survived. The road is different now."

"—beGAN to SHIver, beGAN to SHAKE—"

"He does not walk with me. He walks with Mister Edmund. He walks to hell."

Beth stopped her chant.

Silence filled the room.

Katie could see Beth behind her in the mirror. Her daughter's eyes were large and solemn as she sucked two fingers.

"Go find your picture blocks, Beth," Katie said. The child ran off, and Katie looked at Lin again.

"I'm sorry, Miss Katie." Lin bowed. "I am sorry that it is true."

Katie looked at her own reflection, startled at how pale she was. What was Edmund getting himself into? What deal had he struck with Julian?

She rubbed her hand across her forehead, smoothing away her frown. Whose business was it anyway? Opium was legal. Doctors prescribed opiate solutions right and left. Why shouldn't a man like Julian try it if he wished?

He wouldn't, she realized. He was a man who liked control much too dearly to hand it over to a base extract of poppy. No doubt, as Matt had hinted, he had a business need. And knowing how fond Julian was of excess, it would be big business. Very big business.

"Don't worry, Miss Katie," Lin said, brushing Katie's hair again. "Mister Edmund and Zemin cannot succeed. *Chǐh pāo pú chù hǔo.*"

"What's that mean?"

"Paper cannot wrap up a fire. It means a secret cannot be kept forever."

"That's hardly comforting."

"It is to those with the Five Virtues," Lin said primly.

"I don't have time for a philosophy lesson."

"Why not? Time flies when you have none."

" 'When you're having fun.' "

"As I said."

Katie watched the indefatigable Lin work on her hair, pinning it high and weaving in sprigs of flowers and soft satin ribbons. Lin's eyes were mahogany dark, and her skin held a hue of almond cream, smooth and soft. It was easy to forget how beautiful Lin was; her strong personality overshadowed a delicate, fragile appearance.

"Do you ever think about getting married, Lin?"

"I have no dowry, no family. Who wants a woman of no stature?"

"You have beauty, intelligence, a good education, many skills. You have much stature."

Lin sniffed.

"As a matter of fact," Katie added, "someday you'll be off to a party and I'll have to fix *your* hair."

Lin shook her head and stepped back to admire her work. "You could not do this well."

Katie smiled. "My, aren't we cruel?"

Lin didn't smile. "Maybe you are cruel. I will never go to parties."

"Give me time, Lin. I'll make Poppy a stock company here. No more traveling. We'll buy a house. And Beth will go to school. And we'll hold dinner parties for all our new friends."

"Dreams, dreams." Lin shook her head. "It takes a rich man to pay for a poor woman's dreams."

"Lin."

Subdued, Lin handed her a sheet of paper. "Here. A messenger from Mr. Gates brought this for you."

The guest list. Julian had wanted her to familiarize herself with the names of dignitaries who would be there. She scanned the list quickly, then closed her eyes.

"What's wrong?" Lin asked.

"Nothing."

Nothing but two names. Mr. Matthew Dennigan and Lucy St. Clair. Who was she? An old flame? A convenient companion? Or, just perhaps the reason why she hadn't seen Matt since that night in the park.

12

Julian ascended the orchestra dais to present his four guests of honor. Facing the elegantly dressed guests gathered in the ballroom, he announced, "The Henslowe family players of Populus Felicitas, the New Gate's exciting inaugural company!"

The four Henslowes joined hands and bowed to applause, effusive Edmund and the old patriarch Alleyn at each end, shy Peg and ravishing Katie in the middle.

The daring color of her evening gown suited Katie, Julian thought. Watching her, he was convinced she could affect enough elegance to elevate any show of poor taste. Edmund obviously demanded constant practice of such a gift. The wastrel had been particularly reprehensible at the club that week. He'd actually made innuendos about a unique business venture "I and my good friend Julian" had embarked upon. Julian had cornered him the next day. "One warning is all I give, Edmund. Only one."

The stupid boor hadn't even blinked at the threat, Julian recalled as he held out his arm to Katie to escort her to the dance floor.

Alleyn offered Peg his arm and proudly promenaded her to the nearest tray of drinks. That left the debonair Edmund on the dais without a partner. He made a grand show of looking forlorn. Unmarried ladies giggled behind their fans. One young woman stepped boldly into the cleared space, reached into the cuff of her sleeve, and withdrew a lace hankie.

Julian stretched for a better look. Lucy St. Clair, the red-haired scamp. He might have known. She made a saucy soubrette, pursing rouged lips and blowing a kiss into her handkerchief. She tied the hanky in a knot and tossed it at Edmund's feet.

To everyone's surprise, the handerchief landed with an audible plink. Edmund unwrapped the coin secreted inside and pressed it to his lips, sighing. "Ah, true love!" he exclaimed.

The notion of a bought liaison made matrons mutter and young men laugh. Julian noted that Katie watched critically, though, as if she already knew the end to the scene.

Looking lovestruck, Edmund pocketed the coin and stepped off the platform, one hand to his heart, the other arm swung wide to take dance position with the red-haired maid. Jerking her along in a stumble-footed waltz, he made bombastic declamations of love in badly rhymed poetry.

Aghast, the woman fished his pockets to get her money back.

The crowd laughed and clapped. Julian leaned close to whisper in Katie's ear. "I think Edmund has met his match in scene-stealing."

Katie stepped back to a respectable distance and opened her fan, hiding her decolletage. "That was a clever variation on stock melodrama. She's very accomplished. Who is she?"

"Lucy St. Clair. You might recognize the name."

"Sorry, no."

"St. Clair's her stage name. She's a music hall singer, quite popular and charming. I invite her often. It stirs the ennui of the beau monde."

"I see. Perhaps that's also why my colorful family and I are here tonight. To stir your ennui?"

"Edmund is here for the masses. You are here for me." He smiled as he put his arm snugly around her waist for the dance.

She collapsed her fan and held the beaded stick in her left hand, atop his shoulder.

He gave the fan a wary glance. "I promise not to warrant a blow."

She smiled but held herself stiff and distant, following his lead gracefully but without flair. She seemed nervous, scrutinizing the crowd as he swept her across the dance floor. Who was she looking for? he wondered. Or was she uneasy that everyone was eyeing them? She should be prepared for jealous looks. There were so many eligible young women of good family there that night who wished to be in her place.

He was careful, though, to maintain his bachelorhood. One day he would need to marry a girl of quiet mien and immense dowry, but until then, he would enjoy being the unattainable prize each season in the race for grooms.

"Did you notice what a striking couple Edmund and Lucy make?" he said.

Katie glanced in their direction. "If I were Lucy's escort, I wouldn't think so admiringly of the picture."

"But she's here with a cousin tonight, young Dennigan. I'm surprised he even consented to bring her. His father and I tangled in business once."

"A friendly rivalry?"

"There is no such thing in commerce, my dear. Art Dennigan misplaced his nerve and his market share, and I didn't." He slowed his pace. "He's been somewhat of a recluse ever since." He let his regard of her grow intensely personal. "Some people can not lose gracefully."

She misstepped, and he tightened his arm, drawing her upright. "Are you fatigued?" he asked.

"Hungry, actually," she said, glancing at the buffet table across the room.

They were stopped often by guests as Julian escorted her through the throng. Katie acknowledged introductions with a vague smile, then excused herself when Julian was caught in conversation with an old colonel named Brig Wallace. With each step away from Julian, her heart beat faster, as if she risked being caught.

She had seen Matt. While she danced, she had seen him standing at the terrace doors beyond the buffet. When she reached the tables, she pretended to peruse the elaborately dressed food, the dancing flames beneath a hundred braziers. She opened her fan and stole a look at the French doors that opened onto the garden terrace. He still stood there, in formal coat and silk cravat, surrounded by a boisterous crowd of young men and women.

Smiling, he looked casually beyond his companions toward her. It was a passing glance, yet it fixed her. She felt as if she had lacked substance until that moment, and was now startlingly aware of her own body, the warmth rising to her cheeks. And in that moment she knew he too was completely aware of her, had marked her presence in the ballroom and tracked her every movement.

The distance between them seemed suddenly too small. Milling bodies and trivial conversation provided no buffer. She turned her attention to the safer assault of the table, the heady plume of cooked spice and braised meat, trussed quail, glazed and glistening, medallions of veal simmering in Marsala. She fanned her flushed cheeks, feigning interest.

Two young men came up and jovially vied for the honor of getting her a plate. When they grew subdued, she realized Julian was approaching. And so was Matt.

Julian's cool hand cupped her elbow. "Finding it hard to choose, my dear? When an entrée requires too much thought, one's appetite is probably not as ravenous as it seemed. Allow me to show you the sideboard."

He turned her, and Matt appeared in their path. "Good evening, Mr. Gates."

Katie felt Julian's hand tighten on her elbow. "Please, I am Julian to all my guests."

"I just wanted to thank you for this opportunity to enjoy your hospitality." Matt gestured at the grand display of food. "Your reputation as a generous host is well deserved."

"It's a pleasure to welcome you back to the city, Matt. I imagine much has changed."

Matt was silent a moment. "Much."

Julian cleared his throat. "May I introduce you to Miss Henslowe, one of our talented guests of honor? Katie, this is Matt Dennigan."

Matt held out his hand, but she had to wait for Julian to release his hold on her right arm. He did, and she placed her hand in Matt's. She was relieved that he did no more than lightly squeeze her fingers, then released her.

"My pleasure to meet you, Mr. Dennigan."

"This is a sizable welcome Julian's thrown for you."

"We're honored."

Julian smiled. "A simple affair, really."

"Looks expensive to me," Matt said. "I admire your confidence."

"In what?"

"In the Union Pacific."

There was an audible quieting of the score of people near them. Katie saw old Colonel Wallace edge closer.

"I don't understand," Julian said. He was still smiling, yet Katie detected a strain in his voice.

"Aren't you the one," Matt said, "with a fifteen-thousand-dollar bet that the UP tracklayers will cross the Utah state line before the Central Pacific boys?"

"My friendly wager with Mr. Stanford of the Central Pacific is common knowledge. A promotional aid for both our lines. And frankly, Matt, there's no way I can lose. The Central Pacific has a tortuous section of the summit to cut in the Sierra Nevadas before they can complete the tracks through the mountains. I'm happy to report that the UP is about to reach the summit of the Rockies."

Interested murmurs rose from the crowd.

"That's good news," Matt said absently, surveying the feast. "But I wouldn't count out those Chinese on the Central Pacific. No strikes, no complaints, no drunks, just busy as all get-out, seven days a week. I hear they worked all winter, burrowing under the snow like Eskimos to keep warm. How many days did your boys lose when the blue northers started to blow out there on the Plains?"

"Tracklaying is an engineer's art, not busywork for immigrants. We of the UP are committed to quality. Ideal conditions for spring tracklaying presented themselves just this month. And General Dodge reports we'll average over a mile of track a day, more than four hundred miles for the year."

Polite applause accompanied the little speech.

"A mile a day?" Matt said. "I hear that's just what the CP's Chinese have been laying on the Nevada flatlands."

"But they still have a big gap in the Sierras," Julian pointed out. "Seven miles of solid mountain."

"Didn't you hear? They imported a chemist to mix nitroglycerin right in the summit camp. Blasting oil eight times more powerful than the powder they'd been using. I'd say they're moving right along now. Makes it more of a horse race for your fifteen thousand, doesn't it?"

The crowd hushed. Though he remained stiff and motionless, Julian seemed shaken. "I don't concern myself with animal odds or inconsequentials. And fifteen thousand is, on the whole, a very small wager."

"For you, I imagine it is," Matt said, looking him in the eye. "But you'd be surprised how small things add up."

Katie watched Julian's profile. A vein in his temple throbbed, visibly purple.

Matt turned away and peremptorily tapped a tureen. An attendant responded quickly, filling a China bowl with a creamy potage. As he set the bowl on a tray carried by a uniformed servant, Matt faced Katie again.

"Miss Henslowe," he said, "I'd be honored if you joined me for dinner."

13

Katie could not speak. Not with so many people watching, not with Julian's hand closed tightly around her wrist, hurting.

Matt broke the silence. "Perhaps another time then, Miss Henslowe. Excuse me."

The surrounding crowd released its suspended breath in titillated *Oh's* as he left. Excited rumblings began as Julian pulled her away. She did not dare look back.

A group of older men circled Julian and made forced jokes. "What he said about the CP," one man said. "No more than a snowball's chance, surely." It was obvious they were seeking reassurance. Had they bet with Julian on the UP tracklayers?

Katie remained at Julian's side, inhibiting the men's discussion of business. But to leave quickly would add another delicious tidbit to the gossip mongers' buffet. As Julian confidently assured the men, she risked a casual glance toward the French doors.

Matt stood alone at the threshold, sipping sherry and watching her, obviously untroubled about the embarrassment he had caused. As she watched, Brig Wallace approached him. Deeply furrowed brows gave the old colonel the look of a puzzled pug. He conferred with Matt, and the two drifted outside.

"Excuse me while I see to my sister," she said to Julian after he'd finished his recitation of bolstering facts and figures. She indicated a far wall where Peg stood, barely visible beside ornamental palms, and Julian nodded absently in response.

Katie made her way to the other end of the ballroom where a younger crowd had gathered. There was no lack of gaiety in the group. Edmund was at its center, exchanging repartee with Lucy St. Clair. Katie saw her father, bright-eyed and proud on the periphery of the crowd surrounding his son.

Farther on was Peg. As usual, she had found a place to hide, but her face was not glowering and stoic. Rather, high spots of color bloomed in her cheeks. She was unusually animated, caught in heated conversation with a man whose back was to Katie as she approached.

She swept her skirt against a potted palm to rustle warning of her presence. Peg stopped talking abruptly. In her formal blue gown and with her hair done high, she looked lovely. Katie wondered if the man thought so too. She recognized him as Julian's secretary, Frederick Altmann, the man whose fine continental taste was reflected in his choice of hotel for the troupe. He was severe-looking in gold-rimmed spectacles and an impeccably cut evening coat. His lean cheeks and thin nose had a faint blush. He sipped a near-empty glass of wine, forearm at rest behind his back.

"I'm sorry to interrupt," Katie said.

"Quite all right." Peg turned to Altmann. "We were hoping conversation would drift on to less volatile themes, weren't we, Mr. Altmann? I'm afraid I was boring him with a discussion of the Weimar School and Goethe's Rules for Actors."

"Let us be exact, as the great Goethe would," Altmann said. "I was discussing, you were attacking, vociferously."

"His antiquated frippery calls for an active defense of my principles, sir," she said. "That's all that I gave you."

Katie tried to intervene. "Peg—" she began, but Altmann interrupted.

"I saw your 'principal' at work here and in New York, Miss Henslowe."

My God, Katie thought. He was going to attack Edmund. Peg was already bristling.

"If you'll allow me to be candid," Altmann went on, "I found his a derivative Romeo, flooding the audience with hyperbolic humors until we were adrift on a sea of histrionics. And no boat, Miss Henslowe." He smiled quizzically. "Was that your doing, not requiring a touch of classical restraint to guide the message of the lovestruck? Surely a woman of your intelligence has a higher regard for taste."

"Taste?" Peg echoed.

Katie tried again. "Please . . ."

Peg took a step backward, one hand braced against the wall. "By the gods, sir, you're insulting!"

"No, fräulein, I am arguing. Apparently, to excess." He shook his head and downed the remainder of his drink. "No doubt the consequence of caring too much with the power to change very little," he said pensively. Tilting his head, he looked across the room, fixing his gaze on Julian, who was in the same circle of men. "See how they surround him with questions, how he is looking around, looking for me? The payout schedule. What shall I say this time?" His voice dropped to a murmur. "What shall I say?"

Peg's voice was cold and precise. "You may say you're sorry."

He looked at her, smiling sadly. "Of course, my lady, of course." He took Peg's hand. "My apologies. I beg forgiveness for my tactless nature tonight. I fear my work is too great a strain of late. We must settle on a more soothing subject when next we talk."

He bowed to both women and left.

" 'When next we talk'?" Peg began to pace, her limp pronounced but forgotten. "The absolute nerve!"

"He apologized," Katie said. "Let's get some supper."

"Did you hear what he said about Edmund, and my stage managing?" She glared after Altmann as he made his way through the crowd at the edge of the dance floor.

"Calm down. I'll take you out for some air."

"No!" Peg shrugged off Katie's hand. "I'm going upstairs to the gallery for some privacy." She set off across the ballroom. "No doubt," she said loudly, projecting her voice in Altmann's direction, "I can benefit from the aura of classical restraint in all those depressing Flemish oils!"

The indecorous thuds of her cane were lost in the race of violins in a squealing crescendo. Katie was stunned. It was the first time she had seen her sister walk without self-conscious awareness of her impairment. Mr. Altmann provoked greater emotions than he knew.

Since Julian was still preoccupied with nervous investors, Katie skirted his group and made her way back to the buffet table. She ordered a tray; a servant carried it to the crowded terrace for her. Matt and the colonel were nowhere in sight.

Candle globes lit the dinner clutter atop dozens of lace-topped tables. Katie went down the garden path to a secluded table beside a low-burning torchiere.

The air was cool and bracing after the closeness of the ballroom. Lanky bushes rattled in the breeze, their limbs budding with fresh spring green. She sat facing the garden, seeking its peace.

The quiet was soon broken, however, by scattered pebbles on the path behind her. Rasping skirts swept close, then a bulky matron stepped into the light. She lowered herself to the chair opposite Katie with an anguished crush of organza.

"I hope you don't mind, dear," she said. "So hard to find a clean table."

Katie nodded as she tapped a napkin to her lips, swallowing her mouthful of soup.

A waiter set out her dinner as the officious woman went on. "I so dislike these informal arrangements, don't you? I wish Julian would just invite fifty people for the banquet hall and sit us down, each in our proper place, but no, for him it's something big or nothing at all." The matron raised her lorgnette and leaned back, squinting at Katie. "Oh. You're that actress."

Katie introduced herself.

"I'm Mildred Hartzel Wallace, my dear, of the Virginia Hartzels, originally." She smoothed her crackling skirts and leaned forward, bunching them beneath the table. Necklace loops of yellowing pearls clattered.

"Are you a theater lover, Mrs. Wallace?"

"Frankly, no, dear. But Julian loves the theater and I love the support Julian gives my charities."

"I gather he and his family have been longtime patrons of the arts here."

Mrs. Wallace's heavy-lidded eyes opened wide. "Whatever gave you that impression? Julian's new here, very new. Where his family comes from is a subject of some speculation. I, for one, can't find a soul who went to school with him. Odd, you know, very odd." She frowned at her napkin, as if suspecting a stain. "However, one could not find a more munificent benefactor, as I'm sure you're aware. Cowed us all with his altruism when he first arrived. This town had never seen the like. Galas for the Cultural Friends Society. Banquets for the Provident Association. Opera benefits for the Orphans Board. My personal charity, you know." She paused for comment.

"How gracious of you," Katie murmured.

Mrs. Wallace peered through her lorgnette at an appetizer pie on the end of her fork. "For the life of me I can't tell whether this is veal or crab." She nibbled experimentally. "Of course, it'd be an absolute crime to miss one of his fetes. There's so much to talk about afterwards, you understand."

Katie smiled wanly. "Completely."

"Now, now, my dear." Mrs. Wallace punctuated with her fork. "You must put that little episode at the buffet table out of your mind. People are going to talk behind your back whether you worry or not, so don't worry."

"You do know how to comfort one, Mrs. Wallace."

The old woman smiled, unaware of the sarcasm. "I do advisement for the young ladies in Girls Hall every Wednesday."

Neither woman heard the footsteps of the man behind them. Katie's first warning of his approach was his voice, low and rolling, like a murmur of thunder.

"Sorry to take so long, Katie. I couldn't find your shawl."

She didn't look up as she felt a delicate wool shawl enwrap her shoulders. He touched her arm as he settled it right.

"Good evening, Matthew," Mrs. Wallace said.

"Mrs. Wallace." He took the older woman's hand.

"Seeing you reminds me how much I miss Hellie. I wish she'd come to these affairs."

"Mother's very busy. You know, campaigns, petition drives."

"This suffragette business is consuming her, Matt. It's a disease! And it's left a horrible hole in the Garden Club." Mrs. Wallace leaned toward Katie. "Hellie always organized our Easter Parade, you know. No one got things done better than Hellie. I potted two hundred lilies for her one year, and glad to do it, she's just that inspiring. Such a waste." Mrs. Wallace put down her fork, obviously heartsick. "Dee Dee Schnell did the parade for us last year, did you hear, Matt? Merciful heavens, the snippy little tantrums—"

"Katie and I were going to stroll the gardens," Matt interrupted.

"Now don't be a complete goose, tongues have enough to wag about. Tell me, how's your father?"

"The same. Getting older." Matt paused. "Like all of us."

"You can't insult me, Matthew Baylor Dennigan." Mrs. Wallace jabbed heartily at a medallion of veal. "I knew you in knickers. Rolling barrel hoops through my zinnias with those dirty little street Arabs. Oh, I remember. And you and your big brother horsing around the parlor on cribbage nights. Paul was absolutely stirring with those recitations from Scripture. And you with those magic tricks. You rooked four dimes out of Brig one night, and then only managed to pull a nickel out of his ear."

"I was a much better businessman then."

"You don't need a business, Matthew. You need to be home with Hellie and Art. Don't you agree, Katie?"

Katie kept looking at Mrs. Wallace, aware that Matt watched her intently. "I wouldn't know."

Mrs. Wallace rubbed her arms. "It would be nice if Brig was as thoughtful as you and brought me my wrap. Didn't I see you talking with him?"

"Briefly."

"Well, I'd best find him before his fourth whiskey. His nose turns an awful red."

"Better hurry," Matt said, pulling back her chair.

She waddled off, and Matt sat down.

"We need to talk," he said.

"There's only one thing I want to discuss." She clasped the shawl at her throat and leaned forward. "Whose wrap is this?" she whispered furiously.

"I don't know. It will keep you warm while we walk."

"We are not walking. You're just trying to use me. Treat me like a claim to be jumped in front of hundreds of fine people."

She tried to scoot her chair back, but he swiftly got up and stood behind her, blocking her in.

"Stop it!" She struggled with the chair.

"I merely asked you to dinner in the full light of public approval," he said, his voice low. "I thought that's what you wanted."

"Ha. You wanted Julian for dinner. I was just gravy." She tried again to move the chair, but he held it fast. "You'd already done enough damage starting spurious rumors about his railroad."

His hands grasped her shoulders. She could feel their warmth through the light shawl. "They're facts, not rumors. And it's not 'his' railroad. It's supported by government bonds and run by private crooks."

"You have proof that Julian is a crook?"

He hesitated. "You can help me get more proof."

"*I* can, can I?" She grasped the edge of the table with both hands, threatening to upset it. "If you want a scene, Matt, you'll get one."

She felt his warmth withdrawing as he dropped his hands and stepped back, leaving her free to rise. "All I want, Katie, is a walk."

Defiant, she stood and faced him. "Well, all I want is the truth from you!"

Silent, he backed out of the glow of the torchiere, into the velvet darkness of the garden path. He was leaving.

"I should have known," she called. "There's 'no more truth in thee than in a drawn fox'!"

His voice came out of the night, fading. "Henry the Fifth." There was silence, then faintly, "No. Fourth."

She stood stunned, breathing hard. The flame of the torchiere flickered with each rise of wind.

Sly Falstaff, she thought. He knew his Shakespeare. She gathered the pilfered shawl close, feeling doomed.

14

The garden was silent except for the hiss of her gown as she walked along the winding path. She stopped when she reached a set of wide steps made of stone, wondering which way he'd gone.

"Katie."

His call fell softly, drifting down from above her. Leggy shoots of jasmine teased her sleeve as she climbed the stairs.

At the top lay a pavilion, a vast stone floor under a roof of latticed vine. At the center was a tiered marble fountain, trickling softly.

He stood with one foot on the fountain's lip. She circled nervously to the side opposite him. He leaned in, cupping his hands beneath the gentle stream from a naiad's bowl. "A drink?"

She shook her head.

He drank from dripping hands and flung the excess to the ground. "I should thank you. You and I were 'introduced' tonight." He hunched a shoulder to his chin to dry it. "You never told Julian that we met in New York."

"I owed you that. But I don't owe you anything in this petty game of grudge."

"Investors in the Union Pacific don't consider short payment of dividends a petty game."

"Are you an agent for them?"

"No."

"For whom are you an agent then?"

He didn't answer.

"It's the senator," she said.

He walked around the fountain. "You get another guess because that was a good one."

Uncertain, she backed away, keeping him opposite her. "My guess is that you're really an actor," she said lightly, nervously. "That rude display tonight was a public announcement for every uncertain investor in the crowd. It said: 'See me? I'm the point man for grievances against Julian Gates.' And I think Brig Wallace was your first customer. Did he give you an earful?"

"Katie." His voice was curt, as if she were exasperating him. "All I can tell you is that I need every bit of information I can get on contract services and investment returns. Julian's finances aren't in great shape."

"Where are your eyes, man?" She waved a hand in the direction of the house. "You can't see a glorious, gluttonous abundance in there?"

"Oh, I see all right. Tell me, Katie, has Julian advanced you any cash?"

"He's fulfilling the contract. We want for nothing."

"Has he advanced you cash?"

"We have room, board, transit, workmen—"

"All things he'll be billed for. Even this affair tonight is just one more chain of invoices. He could run up accounts for a year before anyone would think of asking a millionaire embarrassing questions about his debts."

"Stop it," she said, clutching the shawl. She was cold. "You're wrong."

"No." His voice was flat, hard. "I'm being honest with you."

"In that case, tell me plainly: What is it you're trying to get from me?"

"That, lady, is a very bold question." He moved toward her. She moved away, around the fountain.

His pursuit was slow, casual. "I saw you having a nice, private chat with Altmann tonight. Informative?"

She mirrored his pace. "All he talked about was the difficulty of explaining the payout schedule."

"Difficult, indeed, to make up excuses when the investors' accounts have been drained on the boss's orders. Julian always uses other people's money. He does use it to make tempting offers, though, doesn't he?"

"Don't be vulgar."

"Don't be naive." He stopped and perched on the marble rim.

She stood, on guard. Falling water gave an endless rhythm to the stillness, until he broke it. "You don't trust me worth a damn, do you?"

"I don't know you. And despite your spying, you don't know me."

"Well, let me regale you with a little bit about my heritage as regards the illustrious Mr. Gates. We Dennigans dropped down from Canada two generations ago and started as trappers and traders. Over the years, properties accumulated. My dad and my uncle built a business around services, conveyance of claims, commissioning deeds. They called it Dennigan Brothers. They sold little plots of land that people could build a home on, and big commercial stakes down by the river too. Then a flashy Eastern railroad promoter came to town when the War started. Interested in the community, he said as he started handing out money. Julian gave a hundred to an orphanage here, a hundred to a hospital there, all the while buying and selling, but mostly buying." He paused, eyeing her. "Julian loves to acquire."

"No doubt. The urge to possess is common throughout the male species."

He smiled. "Well, Julian tried to talk my dad into a good price on some prime riverfront Dennigan Brothers owned. But Dad didn't want to sell." Matt squinted, as if trying to see something in the dark. "He'd just lost his son in the war. His favorite son. Paul."

He was silent for a moment. "We lost Paul in '61, and Dad

wasn't in a mood to dicker. So Julian went to Dad's partner, my uncle Red. Everyone knew Red Dennigan loved the track. Everyone knew Red Dennigan had gambled away everything he owned except his share in Dennigan Brothers. Julian offered to buy him out, promising him cash on the barrelhead and a big Kentucky horse farm. Uncle Red agreed and Julian paid him off. He even gave him a free ticket to Kentucky, to a lousy little tobacco patch with a training ring, four nags, and a stallion past his prime. Uncle Red died drunk in the barn that winter, all alone. A foaling mare fell on top of him. She couldn't get up. Neither could he."

Matt stood and began to pace alongside the fountain.

"Meantime, my dad was having a hard time with his new high and mighty 'partner.' When Dad wouldn't take a hint about selling big riverfront lots to Julian's holding company, Julian dumped all his shares of Dennigan Brothers on the market at bargain basement prices. Forced my dad into a selling frenzy to survive. He even poured most of Mother's trust fund into keeping Dennigan Brothers afloat. Money down the hole. He went bankrupt. Company assets were auctioned for taxes and Julian got the river frontage he wanted all along at a price he only dreamed of."

"I'm sorry for your family. I'm sorry Julian's such a competitive man."

Matt halted his pacing and faced her. "He's a shark in the food chain, dammit. One bite and you're gone. Edmund doesn't know what he's dealing with. He's got you all in deep water now."

"And only you can see the bottom, Matt?"

"Yes. Maybe." He threw up his hands. "Hell, I don't know." His voice quieted. "I don't know with you, Katie."

"You don't know why I followed you out here?"

"I have an idea why. Maybe it's just a hope."

He walked around the fountain slowly. She allowed him to get so close she could smell the sweet spice of his cologne; almost close enough to feel the warmth of his body. His nearness was tempting. She turned away.

"It doesn't make any difference what I want," she said, "or what you make me feel. We can't see each other."

"Just like that?" He lashed out at the pool of water with a powerful slap that drenched the stone floor between them.

"Matt, don't—"

"Is it just me you don't want to be with, or any man?"

She didn't answer.

"I want to know, dammit!"

She started to leave.

"Katie, wait. I think you care too much what people would say."

She spun to face him, her skirt swaying. "People have already said their worst, when Beth was born. I survived. But I hurt, Matt, so much sometimes, that I questioned the gift of my child, my beautiful child. And that was unfair to her. I will not be unfair to her. Do you understand?"

"Yes. You're fair, all right. But I'm not so sure about the man who fathered your daughter. He was rich, yet he left her nothing?"

"He was . . . remiss."

"Remiss? A jurist who had friends who could discreetly amend a will or enjoin his estate for a small sum to educate his child? Remiss?"

"You're being cruel."

"Me, cruel? I didn't leave you to face scandal alone or mother-hood penniless."

"I was old enough," she said, feeling ancient now. Seventeen. She'd been seventeen when Beth was born.

He moved closer. "How old was he?"

She didn't answer.

"Old enough to feel pride in his virility?"

"Stop it."

"Old enough to look at you fondly, adoringly, treating you like daughter and woman?"

"Stop it!" She covered her ears.

He pulled her hands down. "He was old enough to make arrangements for you and for Beth."

She looked at her hands. He would not let them go. "Maybe," he said, "he was not so much in love with you as with the idea of having you."

She hesitated. "Maybe."

"What was it you loved, Katie?"

When she didn't answer, he shook her once. "What was it you loved?"

"All of it!" She threw off his grasp and pushed him away. "I loved it all! His wisdom, his learning, his experience. I loved his home, Newlyn's Aye." She crossed her arms, hugging herself. "Not the things, just the place of it. A home of one place, always there. Generations of time and family, always there. I was only with him ten months. I was eight months with child when he died. His heart was weak. He died in chambers, far from me. I pictured him lying there in his noble black robe and I was glad I carried his child. She was a part of him. But the day of the funeral she felt so heavy I could hardly walk. She'd become a lead weight, and I tried to hide in my long black crepe. But she was there, swollen large, and all the dignitaries parted around me in the aisle as if I were a rock in a stream. His heirs were furious. They threatened me, but I wouldn't take their money. I wouldn't sign papers absolving him of patrimony. They took me to the train. I left alone. Never so alone," she said with wonder. "Even after Mother died. Never so alone as that."

Matt lifted his arms to embrace her, but she backed away. "No. I stand alone. I'm used to it now."

"You're not used to it. You're afraid."

She stared at him, silent.

"Don't be afraid," he said. "Meet me once. Just once. That's all I ask."

"And if I promise a night to you, what do you promise me?"

"The truth. I cannot lie to you, Katie. I will not marry."

She swallowed with care, as if easing down a sliver of ice. Words came haltingly. "A woman doesn't presume marriage to a man she does not know. It's a foolish thought. And I won't be your fool!"

"No," he said softly. "You won't."

She whipped her skirts out of the way and ran to the steps.

"Wait!"

She held to the limestone wall as she descended, then ran

headlong past the jasmine bush and its scentless limbs. She could not think clearly and took the wrong path.

Foolish woman. Foolish hopes.

Close to tears, she found herself at a side door to the mansion. Out of breath, she ran in and closed the door.

"Can I help you, miss?"

Her heart jumped at the grim voice coming from the hallway behind her. Turning, she saw a black-coated servant approaching. "Can you give me directions to the water closet?" she asked weakly.

He gestured down the corridor.

She walked aimlessly, then paused as she passed a salon. Women's voices and laughter spilled bright as light through the open door.

"—tasteful or not," Katie heard one say, "it's going to be wicked fun now with Julian in it. Do you suppose Lucy could convince Matt to join us?"

"He's ever so clever," said another. "Got the devil's own smile too, and he's not poor, not really. His mother's family was well-off."

"It doesn't matter to me. He's been to every soiree I have in the past month and I'm going to tell Lucy to put a bug in his ear about asking me to the Tucketts' on Saturday."

"Too late, Penelope. The bug in his ear already has a name, and it's not yours."

"Well, I don't care. She's a trollop. And greedy. She's already got Julian slathering over her."

Katie's cheeks warmed to bright pink. She expelled a breath, preparing for a chilly performance entrance, then she heard a sassy rustle of taffeta down the hall. Lucy St. Clair was approaching with a hip-rolling sashay and a glorious smile. She was peach-complexioned and very pretty. Her hair, styled high, was copper red, shiny as the coat of a pampered Irish setter.

She snapped her fan open and gave Katie a conspiratorial wink that bid Katie follow her lead. As she crossed the threshold, she said over her shoulder, "Oh, you *must* tell me what was it like, performing for the Queen of England."

"Well," Katie played along absently as she looked around the Morrocan-style salon, "it was really a royal pain."

Lucy giggled and rushed over to a humorless-looking woman on an ornate divan. "Dee Dee! How are you and what did you think of the skit Edmund and I improvised?"

Dee Dee Schnell gave a smile so thin, her lips didn't part. "Quite original," she said. "But then you always are." A willowy spray of ostrich feathers arched from her mud-colored hair, adding an illusion of height to her squat frame. She had the pinched look of a woman who was having a horrible evening. She turned abruptly to the other three women in the room. "We have to get back, don't we, girls?"

The "girls" loyally followed the bounce of ostrich feathers out the door.

"They hate me," Lucy said airily. She stretched out on a plump divan, revealing white stockings to her knee. "But they can't afford to show it because Julian likes me. All the men like me." She gestured at the door. "Not Dee Dee, though. Poor old stuck-up Dee Dee, waltzing out of here with her bustle twitching like a corn cob's stuck you know where. I know why she's miffed. Julian danced with you. She doesn't like anybody dancing with Julian. Her, with all her money and a face that'd turn buttermilk. And that sly Julian never lets on who he wants. But now we all think he wants you."

Katie sank wearily onto a sofa. "Could we please be introduced before these observations on my social life get lurid?"

"Piffle. We know each other. You saw me play the ballroom and I read your reviews from New York. Ungodly good," Lucy said, openly envious.

"I'm sure you have your share of raves. You're a wonderful mime and a talented comedienne. I only dabble in the comedies. I've never mastered the timing."

"Shoot," Lucy said. "I wouldn't dabble at all if I could round my vowels like you."

No doubt Lucy drew a high salary and large crowds with her musical revues, Katie thought, but she obviously longed for the status accorded a serious dramatic repertoire.

"And Edmund," Lucy went on. "What magnificent feeling, what fire in his voice. He's stupefying, don't you think?"

"Entirely too often."

"He told me he was named after the great Edmund Kean. What about you?"

"Father had outrageous hopes for us all. I was named for Fanny Kemble and her whole talented family. Kemble Thea by birth. K.T."

"That leaves your sister."

"Her namesake is Peg Woofington."

"The Irish comedienne. Your sister doesn't look like the humorous sort."

"Her infirmity gives her little reason to be."

"Oh, but my aunt Hellie says anybody alive can find something to smile about. You just have to see things in the right light."

"My mother said things like that too. And actually believed them."

"Aunt Hellie practically *was* my mother. My dad spent all his time at the office or the horse track. Seems like I spent most of my life at Aunt Hellie's house. Matt and Paul were more like brothers than cousins." Lucy paused. "You met Matt tonight, remember?"

"Oh, yes."

Katie knew she was being watched for signs of compassion or censure, or even mere interest.

"I just hope you don't judge him too hard," Lucy said, "because he'd really be an asset in the play."

"What play?"

"Romeo and Juliet, of course. He'd be a perfect Mercutio. He was a good fencer at the academy and he always did better recitations than Paul. I know I can convince him to take the part."

"Lucy." Katie spoke slowly as apprehension niggled at her. "What are you talking about? All I've agreed to is allowing the Orphans Board members to be the supers for the scene at Capulet's ball. They'll supply their own costumes."

"Yes, I know that," Lucy said, sitting up straight in her excitement. "But I've convinced Julian that he really should be on stage, too, as Tybalt. An abbreviated version, of course. Edmund thought that was a terrific idea, and even suggested that I should play Nurse, what with her comical role and all. But if you don't want me to—"

"I think you should play Juliet," Katie said evenly.

Lucy's eyes widened in disbelief. "What? But that's your part!"

"Not in a farce. Excuse me. I have to speak to Julian."

Katie set such a fast pace, Lucy couldn't keep up and waved her on. The gaslit ballroom was hot and garish. The crowd noise had grown oppressive, decibles added with each new round of champagne glasses. Katie heard a round of cheers erupt on the terrace and headed that way.

"Ah, my fugitive," Julian greeted her as she approached. His manner was joking, unconcerned, but his eyes gave her entire body, from hair to hem, a thorough scrutiny.

"Pray tell me my crime," she said.

"Neglect of your host. Shall we?" He offered his arm. "We have to hurry. Your Italians are about to begin."

She didn't take his arm, but faced him, tilting her chin up so she could look directly into his eyes. "I agreed to allowing your friends appear in one scene in our benefit production. But I hear now you intend on turning the entire performance into a circus."

His eyes narrowed. "I take exception to the word 'circus,' but what is your point?"

She spoke low, so the trembling in her voice would not be apparent. "I will not perform that night. I will premiere formally as we initially agreed. You'll find Lucy to be a capable star for the semiprofessional work you've chosen as the illustrious inaugural for your namesake theater."

"Katie." The one word was a warning. "Defiance is not a trait I find charming in a woman."

"Charm is not a requirement of our contract. Neither am I."

He gave an odd smile. "I see. Well, take my arm like a good guest of honor. You owe me at least the pretense of gracious company after the cost of this tribute to you tonight."

She felt great tension as he escorted her, as if the air were charged by an electrical storm. They walked out onto the terrace where the Brandelli Brothers in Renaissance costume were already clanging swords with abandon.

Bruno, the brawny one, had strength and accuracy. Wiry Gabriel had a shorter reach but greater agility; he kept his older brother off balance and snorting like a bull. Not true fencers, they cared little about proper footwork and minimum movement for greatest gain. They were dramatic athletes and claimed an ever-widening stage.

A tray of champagne glasses was knocked from a waiter's hand as the rampaging Brandellis passed. Katie saw Edmund laughing as he stood on the terrace railing, high above the crowd, holding a lamppost for balance.

Gabriel taunted his raging brother into a lunge that left Bruno open for a faux-mortal wound to the side. The brawny brother fell dead, panting like a hound, and the audience applauded roundly. Gabriel ran over to Julian and, with a bow, extended his sword to his host.

Julian took it, nodding graciously. Without a word, he walked over to Bruno and held out his hand for the loser's sword. Leaning a blade on each shoulder, Julian then casually walked the perimeter of the crowd. He stopped suddenly and waved front-row spectators aside.

"Now there's a likely fellow," he said.

The crowd parted, exposing Matt.

No, Katie thought. No.

Julian sounded jovial but he looked serious. "Lucy has convinced me to recite a modest speech of Tybalt's for our benefit at the New Gate."

"I'm not an actor," Matt said, stepping out into the open.

"Neither am I." Julian ran the edge of one rapier the length of the other. "But anyone can play along for a good cause. You do fence?"

"With foils, and not since the academy."

"Well, the rapier requires a simpler, rougher skill." He offered the grip of the losing sword to Matt. "Perhaps more to your taste."

The insult had barely left Julian's tongue before Matt grabbed the sword. He walked a circle around Julian, then fell back in a semicrouch, left hand held high behind him.

Smiling, Julian took a stance with casual élan. His body alignment was correct, Katie noted, but the placement of his feet was off. Was he really untrained, or just playing the amateur?

Matt tapped Julian's blade sharply, two beats, testing.

Before Julian could respond, Edmund cried from aloft. "What ho!" He jumped down from the railing and strode dramatically into the cleared space. "Gentlemen! Gentlemen!" He waggled a finger. "My not-so-gentle men."

The crowd laughed nervously.

"Why waste good ire?" Edmund said. "Fence on stage, for the orphans! One rousing fight is worth a thousand tickets."

As the muttering spectators watched, Julian lowered his sword. "Edmund makes sense, doesn't he?"

Matt didn't answer. Nor did he look away from Julian.

"Come, Matt, the play's the thing, after all." Julian sent a meaningful glance Katie's way. "Aren't you a sporting man?"

Katie fanned her skirt and rushed forward. "Weapons now, gentlemen," she commanded airily. "There are too many fair ladies awaiting a dance."

Pretty fans fluttered agreement.

Julian laid his sword hilt in Katie's outstretched hand. "Come, Matt. In every battle there comes a moment when a man can trust the honor of an enemy."

"When he's dead," Matt said, lowering his sword at last.

The crowd murmured, aghast.

Only Katie and Matt were close enough to hear Julian's cold reply.

"Precisely."

15

Julian entered the empty lobby of his theater. The voluminous rotunda, newly finished, was dark. "Light the chandeliers," he told Altmann.

Altmann went off in search of a custodian. Frugal Altmann, Julian thought, no doubt worrying about the useless expense of the gas, the waste of time. He would never understand true wealth, the ability to command brilliance.

The lights came up, and Julian blinked in the sudden glare. By the gods, it was beautiful. Rich and Gothic, more stunning than he'd ever imagined. The gleaming floor had a centerpiece mosaic inset with onyx and cut marble. The ribbed dome high above was golden, its pattern as intricate as jewel work. Foiled arcs made bas-relief windows in the wall. Leafy crockets arched out from column cornices like ancient stone hooks.

He strode eagerly into the adjoining esplanade, where mirrored walls shone and he met himself in glorious replication all around the hall. Like a funhouse, he thought, nearly laughing aloud.

Wouldn't the old moneybags back East choke to see him now?

The Goulds, the Vanderbilts, the barons of Wall Street. They had laughed at him, the greedy frogs. He had hated being a little water-skeet in their backyard pond. That was why he had cashed in his coal and ironworks holdings in Pennsylvania to invest in the Union Pacific and other frontier railroads. And the canal. What a loss, but what a vision. A canal across the Isthmus of Panama.

He would rebuild the investment pool and try it again, as sure as he breathed. A man had to leave his name on something that would live after him. It was man's higher duty. Woman's duty was more earthly, to relinquish, to give her name, her heart, her body. And her money. It was usually a man's money in the first place, anyway. Even the Widow Fortney's money had once been her husband's. It was only natural, then, that the Widow's fortune had been returned to a man. Not a husband or son, but a ward, as close and familiar as—

My houseboy.

Her voice cracked through his thoughts, as shrill and annoying as when she'd been alive.

Old woman, get away! Julian waved his hand as if batting a fly and backed away, leaning against a molded arch, watchful. Beside him a small, round-bellied Cupid strained outward. He crooked his finger around its curly head, cupped its perfect pot belly. It was comforting to touch things, nice things. That had always soothed him. When he was a boy he had fingered every piece of silver locked in Widow Fortney's buffet countless times.

Altmann approached, many Altmanns in the mirrors, all sober and reserved.

Julian hurriedly tugged his lapels straight.

"Sir," Altmann said, "perhaps this afternoon we could review the accounts. The situation has grown worse since our brief meeting a week ago. It requires immediate attention."

"Not today."

"Tomorrow then?"

"Altmann, don't nag. I'm busy working on a project with lucrative potential."

"Which project, may I ask?"

145

"You don't have a file on it, Altmann. It's a railroad venture." One that depended, unfortunately, on Edmund Henslowe's exotic circle of contacts. Julian would have preferred getting opium to Sacramento without the help of that treacherous sot, but Edmund had seemed the perfect dupe when they were in New York.

Chin tucked grimly, Julian said, "Let's see how my thespians are getting on in rehearsal."

From the back of the auditorium the people on the lighted stage seemed framed in a distant city. Workers bustled around the rehearsing actors, hammering, slapping paint, scooting walls, rolling columns.

Julian walked down the center aisle of the ornate auditorium, noting the mock-medieval statuary accenting every flange in the walls. And to think that this grandeur would showcase a vulgar actor like Edmund. The toady. Edmund had spotted him from the stage and was applauding his patron's entrance.

Julian smiled as Edmund welcomed him up on the stage. Katie greeted him cordially, correctly, then resumed her rehearsal position. She was a a cool one, Julian thought, the sleeping Juliet, stretched out full and fetchingly. Side-by-side chairs made her funeral bier. She looked like a novitiate, with her hands folded atop each other. Curious, he mused, how she blended the pure and the prurient. Curious too the compelling roll of the drum that had begun in his loins, summoning warmth.

With effort he turned his attention to her sister Peg. She seemed flustered. As he took a seat in the first row and the rehearsal resumed, Julian noticed that Peg glanced often at Altmann, who also sat in the first row, a few seats away. Altmann did seem to be regarding the scene rather critically. Peg also had to keep repeating her stage directions to Edmund. He strayed constantly from his marks beside Juliet's bier, gravitating downstage center, close to the lights, playing full front to the empty house.

Julian had to admit that his pompous attitudes played grandly on the stage. Anguish was loud and hand-wringing, remorse, sad and slump-shouldered.

This is acting, Julian thought, pretending to listen with charm when you are thinking with malice, for if Edmund dared drop one more hint of blackmail around the billiard table, at the club, any-where, he would pay the price. Julian cocked his head thoughtfully. Edmund, Edmund. Someone needs to teach you some subtlety.

The rehearsal ended with Romeo's death, and applause pat-tered from the back of the hall. Lucy St. Clair ran down the aisle, calling, "Bravo, Edmund! Bravo!" She plopped herself down beside Julian, radiant, dreamy-eyed. "Hello, Julian."

He assumed the look in her eyes was love, though his agents could document at least one instance when Edmund had tried to introduce Lucy to the wonders of the pipe.

Altmann had been talking to Peg, and he caught Julian's atten-tion by pointing to his pocket watch. The appointment with the tailor for his Tybalt costume, Julian remembered. Details, details. Business was deadly with them. He smiled. Downright deadly.

Katie watched with relief as Julian and Altmann left, then hurried backstage to see how work was progressing. Lucy followed.

Katie smiled a greeting as she tied a kerchief over her hair. "We're done for now," she said. "You can rehearse with Edmund. How're your lines coming?"

"Rotten. It takes Juliet a hundred words to say a simple little 'Good night.' "

"Well, that's what makes it poetry."

"That's what Matt told me too. Katie." She paused. "I've been wanting to apologize to you for Matt's behavior at Julian's gala last week, but I can't. I'm just glad he's interested in someone. I've dragged him to umpty-one dinner parties in the past three months and haven't managed to pair him up. And it's not like the girls aren't willing, or he's not charming. He's just changed."

"You don't have to explain," Katie said.

"He came back from Texas changed. His wife died, you know."

Shock drained the color from Katie's face. Wife? Matt's words echoed in her mind. *Someone I knew took laudanum . . . Some-times she took too much . . . I will not marry.*

She turned away from Lucy, fiddling with a prop. "I'm sorry," she murmured.

"Sarah ran off with their baby, a little boy, before she died."

A son too. Matt had a son. She felt Lucy's scrutiny and glanced at her. "How old is his son?"

"Must be three or four by now."

Beth's age. "Where does he live?"

Lucy shrugged. "With Sarah's parents probably, but Matt won't talk about it. Uncle Art chews nails over that one. Nothing new. He's been grinding on the Rock of Gibraltar since Matt dropped out of law school. Lord." Lucy rubbed her arms. "Sitting down to dinner across from those two is like eating in an icehouse."

"How does your aunt feel?"

"How would you feel? Your only grandchild. But Aunt Hellie won't push Matt. She knows he'll just leave again."

Katie looked over at Beth playing house by herself behind a canvas flat. "Where would Matt go?"

Lucy suddenly took Katie by the shoulders and faced her. "I don't want you to let him go anywhere."

"Why should I be involved, one way or the other?"

Lucy arched an eyebrow. "Want to try that line again, Katie? Make it believable this time?"

Katie smiled wryly. "Get out there on that stage so I can criticize *your* delivery."

"You'll have to wait. It's late and Edmund and I are rehearsing in private tonight."

"Again?"

Lucy smiled radiantly. "Again."

Peg came up, cane in one hand, promptbook in the other. Lucy turned to her. "You know, your brother is just the most exciting, stimulating man I have ever met."

"Oh, he's our pride and joy," Peg said with a side glance at Katie. "Right, Katie?"

"Oh, joy, all right."

Lucy laughed, walking away. Katie faced Peg, bracing for an argument.

Peg wrinkled her nose. "It was a joke."

A joke? Peg?

Beth ran up. "Can I play with the puppies again, Mommy?"

Beth had spent nearly the whole day under the steps with the alley pups. "No, sweet. Lin just got you cleaned up a little while ago."

Peg gave her niece an exaggerated sniff. "And you smell *so* much better."

"Do not," Beth said.

"More dissension. Just what I need." Peg turned to Katie. "I thought that man would never leave."

"You mean Altmann?" Katie teased.

"No. His Nibs."

Katie agreed. "Julian's a stickler."

"I hope he's not going to come every day. He's full of too many suggestions." She made a prune face, mocking Julian's furrowed-brow expression after the previous day's rehearsal. " 'Might be nice to have real trees for the balcony scene,' " she said with deep voice and high attitude.

Katie smiled.

"And why not add a few children to the ballroom?" Peg switched to mimic a deacon's piety, patting Beth's head. "A good cultural experience for our orphans."

Beth looked up and grinned, delighted, as Katie giggled.

"And why not a real horse for the Prince to ride?" Peg went on. "And a small dog with mange to steal a chop from the feast table. And an ass—"

Katie bent over, laughing harder.

"Yes, a trusty ass to render fine plops amongst the garden trees, making fertile metaphor of love's dearest fruit."

"Peggy!" Katie could hardly speak. "How wicked!"

With a high giggle, Beth joined the merriment. "Wicket!" She wrapped both arms around Peg's legs, imprisoning them. Peg burst out a laugh, then grabbed for a stool. Beth was pulling her off balance.

Katie lurched toward her sister, snagging her around the waist as she teetered forward. Katie tugged backward as a counterweight so Peg wouldn't fall on the child, but Peg had already steadied herself. Katie's fierce pull jerked both sisters off balance. Beth let go and ran free, and Katie landed smack on the floor with her sister on her lap as if they were bobsledding.

Surprise held them breathless a moment, then Peg loosed a peal of laughter that cut across the backstage clamor. Aware of how ridiculous they looked, Katie followed suit. They disentangled themselves and fell back on the floor, siblings stuck in a cycle of contagious squeals.

At last, sides aching, lungs sore, they let the laughter ebb. They lay exhausted and groaning, still prey to latent chuckles.

"Here." Peg rolled to her knees, straightened her maimed leg, and pushed herself upright. "Let me help you up."

Katie sobered suddenly. She had forgotten about Peg's impairment. For a few glorious minutes, she had forgotten guilt and pity and years of chilly affection. "I'm sorry I made you fall," she said.

Peg was still smiling. Her hand remained outstretched. "I don't need your help to fall, Katie. I can do it all by myself."

Katie took her sister's hand. Peg braced herself and pulled. She was strong, stronger than Katie would have imagined.

Holding her hand to her stomach, Peg took a deep breath. "We haven't done that in years."

"You haven't made wicked fun of someone in years."

"Except you," Peg said matter-of-factly. The chasm between them opened again, but not as deep, not half as cold.

Katie shrugged. "I can take it."

"Don't," Peg said. She picked up her cane and promptbook. "And don't treat me like a China doll. Katie?"

"Yes?"

"Can we wait until tomorrow to clean up here? I'd like to leave early tonight."

"Of course. You don't have to ask. I can finish by myself."

Peg turned to leave, then stopped. "I was wondering," she went on hesitantly. "Could Lin come with me to the hotel? I'd like her to fix my hair."

Her hair? Katie thought. A dinner date? What a surprise. She hid a smile. "Beth can stay here with me. Tell Lin to bring her blanket and things up here before you go. Tobias can take you home. He's next door in the workshop."

"What time shall I tell him to come back for you?"

"About nine." Katie raised her eyebrows questioningly. "I noticed you were talking to Mr. Altmann."

Peg shifted and tapped her cane. "He says he has an interesting tract we can discuss. A *Critique of Pure Reason* by a philosopher named Kant. Mr. Altmann says he's having a hard time applying theoretic principles to daily life. I'm not familiar with the work. Are you?"

Katie shook her head, though she had heard of the Kantian study groups in St. Louis. From what she gathered, they were contemptuous of the needs of the flesh and spent exhaustive hours exploring philosophic mysteries. She wondered if Mr. Altmann was out to test the strength of his commitment. "I'm sure discussing things with you will help him," she said.

Peg nodded, barely smiling, and left.

Katie watched her go. Her gait had a relaxed, fluid sway. Was it her imagination, or was Peg's limp less pronounced? No, it was the memory of their laughter, lightening the weight of her guilt and her own fixation on the injury. It was seeing Peg's mimicry again, still there as it had been in the days when she and Peg had run along dirt streets, escaping from Father's lessons in elocution and acrobatics.

After Peg and Lin had left by the backstage door, Katie put Beth's blanket and pillow on the floor in the wings. "Here's your treasure box, sweet."

"But I want to play with the puppies."

"It's too dark outside now. Maybe tomorrow. Wait here while I turn on some lights."

Backstage, she went to the light table near the dressing room steps and opened valves to feed the gas sconces on the backstage walls.

The lamps burned brightly, illuminating the clutter of props and canvas flats, sandbags, L-braces, and fake pilasters. Near the dressing room stairs, however, treacherous shadows remained. She blocked off the top of the stairs with a tall flat so that Beth wouldn't accidentally fall down them.

With everyone gone for the day, Katie knew she'd have to keep a close eye on her daughter. Beth had a habit of hiding in cozy crawl spaces between props.

On her way back to the wings, she stopped, thinking she heard a noise. Footsteps? But whose? The crews had quit at six, and the custodian had left with Julian.

She waited, but heard nothing more, except Beth commanding her dolls in a singsong voice, a tiny sound that carried across the cavernous stage.

Edgy, Katie didn't stray far from the wing where Beth played. She made new notations to the lighting crew about which lamps to kill for the crypt scene, altered the floor marks around the fancy arched doorway of the Capulet hall, and picked up a broom to sweep away the saw chips so the carpenters could start clean tomorrow.

As the broom whisked blond dust into a pile, she heard faint thumping sounds. Did they come from downstairs? Or was it just the back door settling to?

"Beth, come with Mommy. I want to make sure Aunt Peg locked the door."

"Lock the door!" Beth repeated brightly.

"Shhhh!" She held Beth's hand as they walked backstage. Beth's slippers made soft quick pats, announcing their progress.

The door was secure. Katie turned away, puzzled, then nearly jumped in fright as a man said, "I locked it."

She whipped around, then relaxed when she saw Matt step out from behind a canvas flat. "You scared us," she said.

"You scare me, working alone like this." He took off his hat and looked down at Beth. She let go of Katie's hand and sucked her fingers.

Katie's heart beat hard with hope. She had not seen Matt since Julian's party, had not spoken to him since she had left him standing at the fountain in Julian's garden, fleeing his honesty and her own disappointment. His need to destroy Julian had stood like a stone wall between them then, just as her need for security had forced her to reject the little he offered her.

His coming to her now must mean something, though, she thought. He may be there because of Julian again, yet perhaps he had come solely for her. She urged her daughter forward for an introduction.

"Beth, this is Mr. Denni—"

The lights went black.

16

Beth screamed.

Katie stooped to grab her daughter, but only blindly swept the air in front of her. Beth was gone.

Across the backstage, she heard heavy footsteps coming up the stairs from the dressing rooms. An intruder.

"Mommeee!"

"Beth!" Panicked, Katie stumbled forward, knocking into a sharp wood corner and groping among unseen props. Where had Beth run? Ahead or behind?

Just then there was a thunderous crash and a splintering of wood as someone ran into the flat that blocked the top of the stairs.

Beth screamed, then all fell silent.

My baby.

After an endless moment, Katie heard a heart-stopping sob. "Beth!" she called helplessly, holding back tears.

"Katie, here!"

She barely heard Matt calling above the ear-splitting wails of her child. Turning in the direction of his voice, she blindly started toward him. She'd gone a few steps when the back door was hurled open, and light from the alley streamed in. Silhouetted on the threshold was Matt, gun in hand, his arm locked around Beth. "Katie!" he yelled. "Get out of the way!"

She heard labored steps close behind her. Stumbling over a basket, she slipped into a crevice between two tall flats. A man lunged past her toward the open door.

"Beth!" she called. "It's all right! Beth?" The child had stopped crying. Katie climbed out from between the flats. Matt was nowhere in sight.

Too late, she heard a second intruder. She cried out as he grabbed her around the waist from behind. She struggled wildly, until he yanked off her kerchief and grabbed a handful of hair. "Don't fight," he said. "I ain't in the mood." He dragged her roughly to the door.

The man smelled of fish and of dank, swampy ground. Nausea tightened her throat.

"I have a knife," he said, "and your friend has a gun. You make us even." He pulled her into the open on the stoop outside, hooking his forearm around her neck. She felt the flat blade of the knife against her side.

"You shoot, mister," he shouted into the dimly lit alley, "and she bleeds." He started down the stairs with her.

"Let her go!"

Katie saw him out of the corner of her eye, standing alone in the grainy light of a post lamp. His gun was aimed at them. "Release her," Matt said. "You go free."

" 'Free' where?" the thug said. "To hell, looks like."

"You can walk away. I swear, as Devlin's friend. Just let her go and walk away."

"Devlin's no big bosser no more. He's old."

"He's got old friends too. So many friends that they'll slit your slimy throat wherever you try to hide it. All I have to do is ask."

Katie felt the man tense, then he shoved her away. She stumbled forward, trying to reach Matt, the lamppost, anything upright.

Matt's arm encircled her waist, but his eyes never left the

black-garbed man who stood half in shadow, still wielding his knife. "If I ever catch you near her again, you sonofa—"

The man flicked the knife backward, blade between his fingers, and threw it.

Matt fired one quick shot before he dove to the ground, cradling Katie.

The knife glanced off the lamppost. Katie heard the man yelp and she lifted her head in time to see him run headlong down the alley, clutching his arm.

"Are you all right?" Matt asked as he helped her up. Shaken, she nodded, pushing hair out of her eyes. "Where is she? Where's Beth?"

"Under the back steps."

"Mom-meee! Find me!"

Katie ran to the iron stoop and looked under it. Beth sat sucking on a candy stick. Three puppies clambered over her lap, wet-nosed and squealing, desperate for a lick.

Katie choked, holding back a sob. She didn't want Beth to see how scared she had been.

"They want my candy," Beth said with concern. She stuck the candy between her teeth for safe keeping and stretched out both arms to her mother. Katie pulled her from under the steps and hugged her close, sticky mint and all. She hugged so long that Beth squirmed to be free.

"Mommy 'membered," she said, holding out the candy.

"What do you mean?" Katie asked.

Beth pointed to Matt. "He said."

Matt stooped and pulled something from under the steps. It was a sack of peppermint sticks, ravaged by the pups. "You promised to bring her back some candy that day in New York," he said. "Remember?"

No, she hadn't. But he had. He was watching her now, as if he knew that his room would take shape around them like a vessel, and she would be afloat on memory's pool with snow-wet gown and blazing hearth.

"Your gun," she said. "It shoots. I'm glad I didn't damage it."

"This is a new one. The sight melted on the Colt."

"Oh." Her back against the wall, she slid down to the ground, resting her chin on her knees, her hair streaming loose. Beth squatted beside her. Wanting to be helpful, she offered her mommy a bite of candy.

Katie wearily shook her head. "No, sweet."

Beth stretched her arm high over her head to offer the sticky candy to Matt. He knelt down on one knee, gazing at Beth, not answering.

She impatiently flicked the stick right and left, to make it enticing and to get an answer.

He reached out to free a sugar-soaked curl stuck to her cheek. "No, sweet," he said softly.

By nine, the street in front of the New Gate was bustling with curious spectators and police wagons. Backstage, Katie watched a frowning Tobias wend his way past the police officers who milled around, picking over props and pieces of costume.

Lin accompanied Tobias, and Katie saw she was wearing her best skirt. Lin and Tobias? Gone out to supper that night, as Peg had? Had everyone had a grand evening but she? She rubbed her temples. It was the worry, and the questions, and the vicious way Edmund's dressing room had been ransacked. The intruders had destroyed only Edmund's room. What had they been looking for?

"Where is Beth?" Lin asked anxiously.

"She's fine." Katie indicated the blanket and pillow in the wings where Beth slept oblivious to the noise, one hand holding a peppermint stick. Lin hurried over to her.

"How about you?" Tobias asked.

Katie rolled her head slowly, shoulder to shoulder. After falling with Peg and then hitting the ground in a cradle roll with Matt, she was feeling the stiffness. "I could do with a pillow myself."

"Did you check wardrobe?" he asked. "The weapons chest? Has anything been stolen?"

"Nothing we know of."

Lin came back, tsking. "You give her candy? You rot her teeth."

"It was a good option at the time. You'll read all about it in the *Dispatch* tomorrow." She noticed Matt had stopped talking with

157

one of the officers in order to scrutinize Tobias. "Seems that the baker next door has a nephew who's a reporter," she went on, hiding nervousness as Matt approached, "and he got quite a colorful story, with the gunfire and all."

"Gunfire?" Tobias repeated, incredulous. "How in the hell far west are we? Dodge City?"

Matt faced him. "The question is where in the hell were you? Weren't you supposed to make sure Miss Henslowe got home safely?"

Tobias drew himself up straight. He didn't have Matt's height, but he had thick forearms which, at the moment, were drawing tight with the fists he was making. "Whoever you are, my job sure isn't any business of yours." He unbuttoned his cuffs and started to roll up his sleeves.

"Tobias!" Katie stepped between the two men and introduced them. "Matt and I were on the wrong end of a knife-throwing demonstration tonight. I'm afraid it's left us both a little on edge."

"I've heard about you," Tobias said to Matt. "Mercutio versus Tybalt. You're fighting the bloody duel with Julian Gates next Friday."

"It's not a duel," Matt said. "And it's not supposed to get bloody."

"An even-tempered Joe like you?" Tobias said with sarcasm. "Good luck on that score."

"Look. I'm sorry I jumped on you." Matt ran a hand through his hair. "Just hungry for a scapegoat, I guess. Not all rivermen are cutthroats, but I think Katie met the stinking bottom of the barrel tonight."

Surprised by his words, Katie frowned at Matt. He was obviously familiar with the kind of men who had vandalized Edmund's room. And who was this man Devlin, whose name could threaten a thug? Was Matt in league with felons? She hoped not. More, she believed in her heart he was not.

"I'm sorry too," Tobias said, breaking the momentary silence. "Sorry that I followed orders and came back at nine. Looks like you ended up in good hands, though, Katie." He turned to Matt and added, "Hope so."

Lin pulled at Tobias's sleeve. "I want to check Miss Katie's room downstairs."

"I ought to have a look around too," he said.

Katie nodded. "Matt will see me home." She had an urge to keep Beth with her too. Her maternal fears were still reeling from the danger in the alley. But she had to talk with Matt alone.

Inside the hired coach, wood joints creaked. Matt watched Katie in silence. Strands of waist-long hair streamed loose across her front. She seemed weary, undone. Suspicion kept the air between them a thin, crackable shield. "You recognized the man with the knife," she said.

"I had a tip. I knew he came from The Ahmad. It's a place near the river, abandoned buildings and filthy streets, a home for people who don't have one."

"The people who live there are all like him?"

"Not all. Mostly, their livelihood is street selling or thieving off others. You heard Mrs. Wallace talk about the street Arabs I used to run with when I was a boy?"

Katie nodded.

"The thugs you saw tonight are what some of my playmates grew into."

"And Devlin?"

"Dark Irish, older than the rest of us, with a mouth he loved to run. He's the one who christened the slum The Ahmad. Said it sounded like a good exotic place for street Arabs. He had a hungry imagination. I tried to teach him to read once, but he didn't have the patience or the humility to take directions, not from me, not from anybody. But he liked my stories." Matt stared at the dark wall of the coach. "I used to freeze my tail off spinning yarns round Devlin's campfire. I just couldn't leave, not with an audience shivering at every word."

Matt looked down at his thumb, remembering the jagged bite of the tin lid Dev had used, the rush of blood. But it hadn't worked. Boys' blood didn't mix that way.

"Do you still see him?" she asked.

She was worried about the quality of friends he kept. "Dev and I parted company long ago," he said, not entirely lying.

"How did you know there were vandals in the theater tonight? Are you still having me followed?"

"No." He raised the window cover to let in the glow of street-lamps. "I do have one efficient little street Arab who tells me when you're working late. The boy said he saw two rivermen he knew there this afternoon. They were helping your stairbuilders carry material. They obviously came back. Why wasn't the door locked tonight?"

"It was. I checked with Lin. She locked it on her way out with Peg."

"Then the rivermen had the key."

"Who could they get it from? Not Tobias or Peg or me. The custodian?"

"I think they got it from the man who hired them."

"You know who that is?"

"Think, Katie. These men weren't ordinary burglars or vandals. They were searching for something Edmund has, and maybe sending him a message too."

"Why?"

"Edmund's been boasting in high places that he's much more than a thespian under contract. He's Julian's business partner. What if Edmund let loose news that this town's deep-pocket philanthropist is about to set up little opium shops?"

She faced front. "That's ridiculous. Dirty little dens are not Julian's style."

"No. He must have something different planned. But whatever the deal, I'll bet Edmund, or Zemin, has a written record, some correspondence." He paused. "Even I'd be interested in finding that."

She stared at him. "You're asking me to pilfer my brother's belongings, just like those brutes did tonight. You're as unprincipled as they are."

"Probably. All I know is that Julian's got money trouble. He's running up lots of bills and not paying them. He's also been doing some very odd banking. Since last fall, he's applied for small loans at seven nickel-and-dime banks in the Southwest. A man with money gets cash loans from the big boys in New York, Boston. A man in trouble takes tidbits from the back country, trying to hide his tracks. Now I don't know how Edmund and Zemin fit into his plans, but I'd wager Julian's already put money up front to pay for a shipment of what he wants." Matt leaned forward. "You wouldn't know anything about that, would you?"

"What would you do to Edmund, if I did know something?"

"Depends on what Edmund's done wrong, if anything." He shrugged. "He and Zemin might be innocent middlemen." He paused. "But, then, Edmund's not exactly the innocent type."

"I'll talk to him," she began.

"Jesus Christ!" He exploded. "What's it going to take?"

"To get me on your side? A promise. That when you ruin Julian Gates, you won't ruin us. We have to have that premiere. When we came out here, I thought we were on pretty firm ground. But every time I talk to you, I walk away on thin ice."

"Then don't walk away."

He felt her stiffen. "You offer me nothing to make me stay. Not even honesty." She turned her head to gaze at him. "Why did you tell me you have no child?"

He sat back. She knew. Who had told her? Lucy. It had to be Lucy.

"Where's your son, Matt? Why isn't he with you, or living with your mother and father?"

"I support him. I send money."

"Where?"

"Back East. To Sarah's parents. They live near Pittsburgh. They're wealthy. He's better off with them."

"Have you visited?"

He looked out the window.

"But you're his father."

"I'm no one to him. He doesn't know me."

"He knows his father doesn't come."

"Dammit, a father's role is different. I support him. I send money. Even when it's scarce."

She watched him a long time, so long and so closely that he pounded his fist twice on the roof. "Faster!" he yelled to the driver.

"I do not believe you are so cold," she said at last, with the finality of a judge.

He prayed she was right. He no longer knew how cold or warm his heart, how dark or light his life. She had confounded his senses, the certainty of what he saw, so that what had seemed the only right thing to do in the aftermath of Sarah's sordid passing now appeared to be abandonment.

But Samuel would be a far greater responsibility to him than the pretty gray-eyed Beth was to Katie. Samuel would be a constant reminder, a living indictment of a marriage that shouldn't have been.

"You must have loved her once," Katie said. "Even if her habit made you hate her at the end."

He didn't answer.

"Did you? Hate her?"

He slammed his head to the back of the seat. "Yes," he whispered. "Yes, I hated her. She took away the woman I married, the woman I wanted. And I couldn't get her back."

"You told me once that Sarah was very bright. Did she go to college?"

"Katie, don't."

"Matt, please. She was a part of you. Is even still a part of you. I need to know."

In the intermittent light of the streetlamps, he saw her eyes, wide and vulnerable, intent on gleaning clues to his feelings.

"Why do you need to know, Katie?" he said, bargaining. "Do you have some intimate disclosures for me in return?"

She retreated, moving back, out of the play of the light. He couldn't see her face, her beautiful lips and expressive eyes. Dear God. He realized what punishment it would be not to see her face. "Katie."

She remained silent.

"Katie!" He rammed a fist against the wall.

"You want to barter a piece of me for a piece of you," she said. "That's business. Is that what you want for us? A business arrangement?"

"No." He leaned forward and took her hand. "I want to go

162

back, before Sarah, and get back what she took from me. All the warm days and sunshine you take for granted growing up. All the hope. I felt it all in one night when I went to Daly's theater and saw you onstage, full of fire and dreams. I took some of that fire away with me, Katie, but I want more. I need more."

She pulled her hand from his and looked away.

"You need more too," he said. "No matter what you say, I can feel it. You can feel it. It's up to you whether we go on. You want to know about Sarah. I want to know what feeds the fire."

She drew a strand of hair across her cheek and pressed it to her lips. "You first," she whispered.

He stared at her a long moment, then eased back in his seat. "Sarah. God, where do I start? She came from the East, city-bred, idealistic. Got her degree at the University of Pennsylvania and came to Texas to teach reservation kids to read. Her father sent her plenty of money and supplies, making sure she didn't want for anything in little Tarmay, except for a way to reach the children. She would sit them at desks and try to get them to learn a language their parents feared."

"Was she pretty?"

"Beautiful, vibrant, funny. She made the kids laugh. But she couldn't make them read her words. I told her, 'Spell something important to them, something they can't do without, like ga-du—bread—and a-ma—water—and the friendly spirits of the earth, the Nûñnĕ'hï. Sarah spelled book, glass, and Jesus. She had trouble with things like that, simple earthly needs. The grandeur of her mission always got in the way. She was frustrated, and she turned more and more to me. In her frustration, I guess, she agreed to marry me."

He paused, gathering strength to go on.

"I knew she took medicine. She'd had a respiratory condition when she was sixteen and she'd used it ever since. She needed it especially when she found out she was pregnant before the wedding. But everything else was going so well, I didn't care. I borrowed money to buy the ranch. My mother was ecstatic that I was marrying a progressive woman. My father couldn't believe I'd chosen a girl of such good family. Her father's a lawyer."

163

He drew a deep breath. "I was away a lot the first six months, buying up beef. I spent all my savings from my war service. People told me the market was dead, that I'd get more money for a dead longhorn in a hide factory than on the hoof in Abilene. I didn't listen. I wanted to drive my herd across the country and make a killing in the stockyards. Twenty-five hundred steers and an eleven-man crew. I thought I was a king. Ate dust for two months on the Shawnee Trail. Indians threatened to stampede the herd if I didn't pay a fee for crossing their land. Then we lost a hundred head in a ravine when a lightning storm came up one night.

"Finally got to Abilene and the cattle dealer paid me a lot less a head than we'd agreed on. He was being squeezed by the railroad on shipping rates, so he squeezed me. I paid my crew and came back with barely enough to live on. Then I find out that Sarah had run up a lot of bills. Dry goods, the milliner, mail-order catalog. She'd put up gold satin drapes in the living room. Four-room ranch house and we had gold satin drapes. I got mad, she got sorry. Cried and said her daddy would pay all the bills. I told her we wouldn't take his money. We paid our own debts.

"That scared her, not having money, not having her daddy to rely on anymore. After that she stayed in bed a lot. I'd come in for dinner and hear the medicine spoon in her glass. And when she had the baby, she wouldn't hardly look at him, let alone feed him. Hold him." He turned away from Katie. "She never really recovered. Finally, she disappeared one day. Ran home to her folks."

The coach stopped.

"She was gone. My son was gone."

The chassis dipped and sprang back as the driver got down to tend the horse.

Matt got out, then put a hand on each side of the door frame, blocking her in. "You know that Edmund's on his way out of this world too."

She looked down at her hands, twisted tightly in her lap.

"He's hurting," Matt went on, "but it's hard for me to muster much sympathy. He's ruining Lucy. Playing with her affections, making a fool of her. He keeps her out until dawn, stupid sot." He rammed a fist against the coach. "I nearly decked him at the Tuck-etts' Saturday."

Katie lifted her head, facing him.

"I'll talk to Lucy."

"It wouldn't do any good. She's smitten. So help me God, if he drags Lucy down into his smoking pit, I'll kill him."

Katie shook her head. "No, you wouldn't. Because it would only make more misery for you, for me. I don't need any more. Neither do you."

He tilted his head back to look up at the sky. The stars were bright, yet they seemed so small. "God, I don't know how you stand it. Holding out hope, picking up the pieces, waiting for some magical day when they come to their senses." He looked at her again. "How long do you wait, Katie?"

She rose and stood on the step above him. Reaching out, she clasped his head to her bosom. He hugged her around the waist and lifted her, turning slowly once, twice, unwilling to set her down. Her body fit tightly to his embrace, lithe and hungering for tensile motion, tender touch. Her hair fell forward, curtaining him. Her body slid downward, raking vest and watchchain with the round hard buttons of her bodice, yet he would not loosen his hold, even when her feet touched ground.

When they parted at last, the desire had grown so strong, it seemed tangible, alive, lapping at his senses, heightening his aware-ness of her slightest movement, the swing of her hair, her rapid breaths.

She backed away from him, glancing worriedly at the driver tending his horse, at the windows of the hotel where unseen eyes could see lovers kiss.

And she would be his lover. He was as certain of that as of the tension he'd felt in her body, the way she seemed to strain toward him even as she left.

She tucked her hair behind her ear and said farewell hurriedly. Turning, she started up the hotel steps, then stopped, looking back. He knew she was vulnerable tonight. He had lunged forward in the darkness of the theater and embraced her child. She had embraced his confessions in the dark coach. The secrets and the liking had grown too strong. Their words in the garden, denials of affairs or marriage, had no place in the storm gathering around them.

"You know you cannot win," she called.

"Win what?"

"Your duel with Julian next week. Mercutio falls to Tybalt's sword. It's the script we must follow."

"Mercutio dies in a week, not I."

"Still, I pray for your safety."

"Offer not prayers, my lady," he said, serious. "I'm a man in need of dreams. Those 'children of an idle brain,'" he quoted Mercutio, "'begot of nothing but vain fantasy, which is as thin of substance as the air.' Yet I have seen," he added, "the empty air bend a tree, carry a hat, strain a sail full with shape. By such strength, thinnest air is substance without form. Likewise will a dream take substance in an airy word from a beautiful lady."

"Then I shall breathe a dream for thee, good Mercutio."

"Lady, breathe the dream for us both."

17

A grimy street boy showed up at the Dennigans' kitchen door the next morning with a message for Matt. He walked the boy out of earshot of the kitchen help. "What is it, Grub?"

"I was watching in the alley behind the New Gate, keeping an eye on things like you told me. That lady came looking for me this morning."

"Which lady?"

"The one you always ask about—where she goes, who's with her—that one." Grub handed him a small envelope with a wafer seal. "She wanted me to give you this."

Matt tore it open.

Meet me. Once.

Katie.

"Mr. Dennigan?" Grub said. He tugged on Matt's coat. "Can I have my two-cent now? Or are you sending a reply?"

"A reply."
Tonight.

Lin was unusually quiet as she helped Katie dress that night.

It was intuitive, Katie thought. One woman could easily sense another woman's gamble with a man. It was as if desire had fragrance, the telltale scent of hope.

"What time will you be back?" Lin asked finally.

Katie put on her cape and walked to the door. "I don't know."

"Is he a rich man?"

"No. He's not."

"Hmmm." Lin shook her head. "Be careful. It might be love."

Katie tried not to think of love as she stepped into the carriage Matt had sent. She thought instead that she shouldn't be there. What had Matt to offer her? The poetry of a lover too wounded to love again? Secretive schemes and bold challenges? Nothing secure. Nothing of earthly value.

Yet she had been so certain when she wrote the note that he was the only earthly thing she wanted. Simply him, free of his obsessive mission, and herself free of her own frenzied work, then both of them set in the window of a pretty room, a safe place, like cutout dolls the real world could not touch.

But he would touch her. Hold her, teach and explore her. Make feelings live and die inside her. He would make the risk worthwhile.

Terrifying, the risk. Since Beth's birth, she had taken care—scrupulous care—to avoid damaging rumors. She had vowed that she would be a mother of moral principle, that she would never have an affair that would add gossip to her daughter's burden of illegitimacy.

Then she had met Matt again in the park, had felt his intensity without ever touching him, her instincts primed to exquisite awareness of his features and form, the scent and the sound of him.

She'd known that night that her promise not to love had been as ill conceived as her escape into Roddy's world after her mother's death. The long, lonely nights had made her feel good at first, as if she were paying for her crime. Now, though, she felt merely drained. She had emptied the account, but for what? She could no longer remember what she'd done wrong. She had truly needed Roddy, truly loved him as only an untouched girl could.

Her need for Matt, though, was deeper and darker, strung from a hidden knot that tensed and twisted at the thought of him. She had no control of it, as she had no control of him. He would not make her an honorable woman. Honor was something he required her to bring.

The ride was long. She looked out the window as the road became an incline and she was tilted back in the seat. She could see nothing but dark trees lining the way to a crossroads at the top of the hill. The driver pulled to a stop in front of an old frame farmhouse.

From the porch she heard a rusty squawk as someone picked up a lantern. Matt walked the light from the house to the road. After he'd helped her out of the carriage, he talked to the driver. The vehicle left; the sidelight on the jostling carriage grew smaller in the distance.

Katie remained motionless beside him, hesitant now about the rush of intimacy hovering around them.

He held the lantern high and opened the gate, and she forced herself to walk through. She stopped when they were on the porch and sat on the swing.

"We should go in," he said.

"Before we do, I—I have a contact for you. The man shipping the opium for Julian."

"I can wait for that, Katie."

She rocked the swing back and forth. "Whose house is this?"

"The Radenours'. Friends of the family." He set the lantern down and opened the door. "I spent a lot of time out here when I was a boy. Mrs. Radenour lives in town with her son now." He held the door. "We need to go inside."

She waited a moment, then rose. "Yes." She stepped past him into a dim foyer. Matt took her hat and cape and walked her down the hall. They passed rooms modestly furnished and thoroughly cluttered, each smelling musty and also, faintly, of rose cachet that sweetened the air.

They stopped at the door to the dining room. The table was set, candles burned, and laid out on a sideboard was a supper of sliced meat. She turned to him. "I'm sorry. I'm not hungry."

"I'm glad. Because I'm famished." He gathered her in his arms. Urgency drove him. His hands swept the length of her back. She was breathless on an uprolling tide. She grasped the bannister of the stairs behind her, hanging on for balance.

She could not feel the cool railing beneath her hand, could not see truly where she was, where she would be. His nearness rocked all sense of the real and palpable. She felt only the rising of a summer storm, crackling currents and lightning heat, unbearably hot.

He cupped his body to her. Pulling her hand from the bannister, he kissed her wrist as his other hand unbuttoned her dress. He was warm and nimble, opening her. He freed her breast and weighed its warmth in his palm.

She clutched his shirt, tearing at buttons until the linen opened and she could slide her hand across his flesh, warm and tight and aware.

He kissed her hair, her face, her neck, sliding down to the rise of her breast. His mouth enveloped her nipple, peaked and vulnerable, and closed around it with a suckling pull that made her gasp. Her hunger quickened, releasing a tingling balm of wetness. A cry escaped her throat, exhilarant, breathy. She pushed herself away.

She saw the wanting in his eyes, but there was more. There was hope of something, fear of something, feelings that mirrored her own.

He held the cuff of her sleeve. Watching him, she felt a tremulous pull, moist and hot. She backed away, higher on the stairs, so that his grasp of her cuff took the sleeve down, baring her shoulder, her arm. She rose a step higher and half turned so that the dress rolled free of her other shoulder, unclothing her other arm. Unanchored, the dress dropped past her underskirt. She stood in chemise and petticoat, and stepped out of the crumpled shell of her dress. She drew up the chemise to cover her bosom.

He was still holding the sleeve of her emptied dress. He dropped it.

She turned quickly and mounted the stairs. He caught her arm, but she broke away and half ran down the hall, feeling light and warm and free. The room at the end was lit, its four-poster bed made and waiting.

She heard him stop at the door behind her as she wandered the room, touching the quaint quilted throws on the chairs, the embroidered sampler on the pedestal table by the bed. She halted at the window, looking out at the real world, at the pastoral dark and quiet.

"This was my room, when I stayed here," he said, stepping inside.

She sat on the bed to unbutton her shoes. The springs squeaked with each shift of her weight. Shoes off, she got up, smiling nervously, holding the bedpost. "This bed warns of company."

"Not always." He went to the bed and gave the mattress a great tug. The rusty springs squawked, then he dragged the mattress off and onto the floor, blankets and all. He let the bedding drop near the cold hearth. One pillow had fallen free in the move. He picked it up and carefully laid it beside the other on the mattress.

She held still, watching as he undressed.

He finished unbuttoning his shirt, and his skin showed bronze in a long open V. As he pulled the shirt off one arm, she saw a deep scar high on his back. He dropped the shirt on the floor and turned to her. His chest was sun dark, corded hard.

"Are you afraid?" he asked.

Yes.

He misunderstood her silence. "You're afraid that you'll have another child. I can—" He stopped. "I'll try."

She smiled at his words, his honesty. She moved toward him, hesitant with her own truth because she had not spoken it to anyone in the years since Beth's birth. The words could barely be whispered. "I cannot have another child, Matt."

He reached out to caress her cheek, her arm. Slowly he drew her into his embrace. "That knowledge is a terrible gift to a lover. He'll think he's always safe."

"Not always. Once."

He pulled her down to lie on the mattress. Looking into her

eyes he pulled the tie of the drawstring at the waist of her petticoat. She felt the garment loosen with each breath.

His hands lingered at her shoulders, gathering the straps of her chemise, then he slid it down to her waist. Her breasts emerged, flesh pink nipples pinched tight. She heard his breath quicken as he stared at her for a long moment, then he stood abruptly. His trousers slid to the floor.

She looked away.

"I didn't think you would be shy," he said, kneeling beside her.

"One man at work in the dark doesn't make a woman an experienced lover."

"This is not work," he said softly.

She felt him peel the chemise and petticoat down her body, then his fingers hooked in her stockings, drawing them to her ankles and swiftly off her feet.

She tried to rise but he was astraddle her. His weight pushed her back down until he lay hot against her. His kiss roamed deep inside her mouth for response, and she rose against him, losing thought to the feeling of his tongue, slick and searching as it fed her need, making her want more.

He ran his hand the length of her back, cupping the curve of her buttocks, then seeking the tender inner skin of her thighs and the crease where soft curls began. His fingers parted the seam, and she lay still as a doll, tensed to break, straining to feel. The tip of his finger found the place that was swollen, vulnerable. He roamed it delicately, taking measure of its roundness and dainty pulse, and of the cry she tried to hold back.

He parted her legs and entered her slowly, gentling the tight moist path to fit him. His shallow probes pressed suddenly deep, and she shuddered, holding him. Deep again, and her breathing slowed as she waited for powerful movement, for his friction to center the storm deep inside. The storm hit against her, forcing a cry upward. She held it back as the storm's thunder rolled with each thrust of his hips, faster, louder, stronger, until the sky cracked. She cried aloud, and he drove deep, thrusting tight to her, their flesh melding seamless in a moment's stream.

Silence fell, and they did not move in the long, sated stillness. At last Matt felt her hand travel up his back and caress his neck.

He withdrew slowly, watching her. She closed her eyes, as if that could keep her feelings secret. But he knew. He knew how vulnerable and separate his leaving made her. He'd known it even before they lay spent and full, adrift within themselves. He'd known when he entered her what will it would take to leave.

He smoothed a strand of hair from her face, just to have a reason to touch her. She was open to his touch, but he saw uncertainty subtly change her features, like ripples of light on still water.

She turned on her side away from him, nuzzling the pillow, pretending a need for sleep. But how could she feign distance when their closeness hovered perceptibly, rich and secretive in its scent? He stretched alongside her, his weight shifting the mattress downward, toward him. She slid back the crucial few inches until her buttocks lay firm and smooth against his belly. He pulled her into the crook of his groin, embracing her so he could feel the smooth warmth of her skin, feeling like a thief because he took so much from her nearness, all the small graces of a woman, the jonquil-light fragrance behind her ear, the silken fan of her hair, the shape of her breast, white above his arm.

He knew her senses were awake and aware. As he grew fuller, he felt her nipple tighten to his touch. He kissed her shoulder, her neck, the lobe of her ear, waiting for desire to align her and guide him back to the welcoming path, already sleek. She gasped softly at the depth of possession.

He soothed her by slowing the pace, then changed it again, attentive to her pleasure, prolonging the play, his need less urgent than hers. His hands grazed her naked body, learning it, each mound and curve and smooth arc arousing sensitivities until she surrendered a cry, explosive and long.

He stopped, suddenly stunned by the intensity he had wrought, the freedom she allowed. He embraced her shuddering body, holding her gently, harboring her peace. His breath trembled filaments of her hair as she fell asleep in his arms, harboring him.

. . .

Matt awakened to the stealthy shifting of bedclothes.

Katie was easing across the bed, trying to reach the chemise he had tossed at the foot. He lunged up and caught her ankle. She cried out in surprise, then laughed as he pulled her back, wrestling her atop him, holding her there so he could look at her, her eyes vibrant with tease and promise and secrets. He was there, in her eyes.

He kissed her and touched her until she needed him inside her. When she breathed in sharply, as if pained, he stopped. She leaned down to nuzzle a kiss against his mouth. No pain, she assured him, only the discovery of new sensation. She began to move, uncertain of her freedom and his wishes, and too sensitive to hold rhythm. At last, arms enclosing her, he rolled her over, taking the play of thrust and making it serious.

The quiet of the room seemed a shield around them, deflecting the passage of time. She cracked the shield with four words.

"I have to go."

He kissed her and tried to hold her, but she slipped away, lithe and quick. "Katie."

She was already donning her chemise, though, and he got up. He drew back the curtains and opened the window. Crickets chirred loudly. The night air was cool but could not cool him. A grainy aura had begun in the east. Dawn was taking his night, his one night.

They dressed in silence, acquiring a layer of deportment with each garment, until they felt awkward at the loss of nakedness. The sphere of their private joy had broken into separate orbits again.

She sat on the bed to put on her stockings. "Don't you want the name of the contact I have for you?"

He had forgotten. "Yes."

"Edmund and Julian are using a shipper named Chu King-Sing. He's an opium merchant. Lin says his port of choice is San Francisco."

"I'll telegram California tomorrow." He glanced out the window again. "Today, I mean. Katie, listen carefully. I don't want you to make any more inquiries about this. Don't talk to anyone."

She lifted her head in surprise. "What?"

"And don't ask Julian, or any of his vendors or investors, any leading questions."

"I thought you wanted my help."

"Well, I was wrong. I don't want you mixed up in this any more than you are now."

"At this point, I think I'm a little too close to stand clear, don't you?"

He was silent.

"What's wrong?" she asked.

"I'm being followed, by Julian's men."

She didn't move.

"I'm a target now. I don't want you to be."

"A target for what?"

He shrugged off the question. "You're safe tonight. I made sure of that. I spent the afternoon baiting a false trail. But I can't always do that. I can't always keep you safe." He took her in his arms. "You need to know, so you can make a choice."

She leaned back, reaching up to smooth hair from his forehead. "Oh, love." She kissed his brow, his closed eyes, the length of his nose, his waiting lips. "I have no choice."

18

Katie worked at the New Gate each day until evening fell, then anxiously rode the horse-drawn railcars, boarding and reboarding until she reached him, waiting on a dark corner with a borrowed carriage.

Daylight hours teemed with coordination details and production snags. She often found herself asking Peg or Tobias to take charge so that she could leave at dusk. She pleaded exhaustion, knowing it should be true. Her love was too new, though, her private moments with Matt too provocative to allow fatigue.

During the day it took all her control to act normally, to worry about the misspellings on the printed program or the number of braces on the market platform for the fight in act three. She husbanded her energy and emotions for the night, not wasting an ounce of concentration, not even on an irritation as blatant as Edmund.

Her brother's only assistance in preparations came during dance lessons for the high-society volunteers of the Orphans Board. He led giggly ladies and bored gentlemen through the line-walks and circle promenades of a simple Renaissance reel, then left with them for apertifs.

Katie did find herself concentrating on one amateur who came to rehearse. Matt. She watched Tobias coach her lover in stage fighting, in dramatic blade beats and sequenced moves. She kept her distance, feigning disinterest in Matt's athletic stance, his quickness, his prowess. But she knew her feint was unsuccessful, for she herself could feel the glow as awareness of herself, and of him, was heightened and charged.

She sensed Peg's suspicious gaze on her more than once, so she kept contact with Matt to a minimum. Still, when Matt took his leave, she often saw Peg and Tobias exchange looks.

The night before the benefit performance, she confided to Matt her fears about his duel with Julian. "I'm afraid he'll hurt you. On stage, in front of everyone."

"He can't. I hear he's not a very good fencer. Besides, he's not going to lose control in front of all his sophisticated friends. He's getting nervous, that's all. I convinced a few small vendors to press for payment. He's going to have to use up some cash reserves. He's feeling the pressure and that gives me an edge."

"And you think you won't be nervous? Out there in front of a crowd rooting for Julian Gates?"

"Have you forgotten?" He tried to make light. "I'm a man of some thespian experience."

"One amateur play at university doesn't make you an actor."

"Wound me, critic," he said mock-sternly, pulling her close, "and ye shall pay."

"Fortunately for you, I am, at this moment, very rich."

"Not half so rich as I," he whispered.

Julian hooked a finger in the curtain and glanced out the window. Greenmore's neat clipped hedges and grassy rolling acres were gray in the dying light. Dusk. Only a few hours until the show began.

He returned to the mirror and adjusted its cant, then stood back to appraise himself. What a dashing Renaissance man he made. He wore a bloused white shirt with billowy sleeves, the long tail tucked into tight hose of royal blue.

He crooked an arm to receive the sleeve of his doublet. The waist-length vest coat was made of a thick brocade striped in wide silk bands of scarlet and gold. Eye-catching. There was no doubt he would be the most visible person on stage.

His valet held a triangular velvet plastron to his chest and began to lace the doublet across it. For a man not familiar with sixteenth century garb, the fellow worked nimbly, Julian noted, lacing the eyeholes in the doublet with metal-tipped cords. The cords were called "points," Edmund had informed him professorially.

Edmund had offered much useless minutia of theater the past week when all Julian had wanted to know was the color of the doublet Edmund would be wearing. Sky blue, Edmund informed him cheerily. Romeo would be resplendent in sky blue silk.

The dolt. The sweetest triumphs of life depended on the existence of fools like Edmund and prudent men like himself.

He had never been a fool. Indeed, he had always known he walked a higher track. The realization had warmed him like sunlight the day he survived the cave-in. He'd been nine years old, sitting shivering in the number four tunnel, Peady Run portal, Bratton Company Coal, Blacksville, Pennsylvania. It had been his first day working with his daddy, and his last.

Miners moved in and out of the haze like ghosts, a procession of floating lights, the carbide lamps on their tin hats bobbing and weaving. Julian knew that one day a blast of gunpowder would blow a tunnel right through to the realm of Satan, they were all that close to hell.

He hadn't wanted to work in the mine at all, but his daddy had made him. Pulled him out of the one-room school at Mayston, lied about his age. There were three young ones at home to feed. Time for Julian to pull his weight in the Gottswald family, Daddy said. So his mother packed him butter bread and jelly in a dented lunch bucket, and he followed his daddy to work. Down they went, so far down he felt his head get tight from the drop. Then his daddy disappeared down the tunnel to auger a hole for blasting powder.

He never came back out. His daddy fired a charge too close to hell and Satan got wind of him. Roof timbers fell, squashing big John Gottswald like a bug under a shoe.

Julian left for Aliquippa the day of the funeral and begged for work at the richest house in town, the Widow Fortney's. He sent a nickel or two back home to his mother and three sisters, but soon forgot about them. They were colorless ghosts next to the silver trays and gilt-framed portraits. The Widow's declining health and inclining fortune produced an all-consuming plan in him that showed, even as a child, that he was a prudent man.

And look at him now. Julian smiled as he tugged the doublet down around his waist. A man who danced rings around folks of the Widow's ilk.

The valet held up a small triangular shield of royal blue fabric. "The codpiece, sir."

Feet slightly apart, Julian stood while the man laced the codpiece to the legs of his hose. Damn, he thought. So many things on his mind, he couldn't recall the valet's name. The man was new. Julian broke in a new valet at least once a year. He had never been comfortable with the idea of a man who spent his life dressing another man. It seemed an intimate thing to him, and he had changed personal servants as often as he changed mistresses.

There was a timid knock at the door. It had to be Altmann. "Come in."

Altmann entered apologetically, glasses on his nose, holding a sheaf of papers. "I have an invoice, sir, from the tailor?"

"Yes?"

"He's made a mistake, I believe. He's charging you for two costumes when he only made one. I just wanted to confirm this with you before I wrote him a note."

Julian scowled with annoyance. The idiot tailor was supposed to have written two separate bills and sent one personally to Julian. "How many costumes do you see here, Altmann?" He spread his arms wide, indicating the strewn tailor's tissue and hatbox.

"One, sir."

"Obviously, the tailor made a mistake."

"I was just making sure, sir," Altmann said uncomfortably, but

Julian detected a zealous glint in his eye. "There are so many questionable bills, I sometimes wonder where they are all authorized."

The man was getting feistier, Julian thought. No doubt a by-product of invigorating dinner discussions with that opinionated little spitfire, Peg. The relationship would have to be stopped. He crooked a finger and beckoned to Altmann. "Come here."

Altmann strode forward, and Julian leaned close to whisper in his ear. "You are not to discuss even the smallest financial matter in front of the help, do you understand?"

"Sorry, sir." Altmann nodded curtly. "Perhaps then I could have a moment alone with you?"

"Fine." He looked down at the valet, then leaned close to Altmann again. "Just what is the man's name anyway?"

"Norrie," Altmann whispered back.

"Norrie," Julian said aloud, "leave us a moment."

The valet nodded and left. "All right, Altmann," Julian said. He sat, then winced. The codpiece lacing was tight. "The total."

Altmann flicked past three pages and ran his finger down to the bottom. "Four hundred and sixty-seven thousand, two hundred and nine."

Julian struggled to remain seated. "Nearly half a million." How? A mere thousand dollars was a small fortune to a common man, and he had five hundred times that in debt. But then, he was *not* a common man. "These are notes due over the remainder of the year?"

"Due in twelve weeks."

Dear God. Julian laced his fingers. "Extensions?"

"Impossible. The London bank has already imposed a half-percent penalty for gross delay."

"Perhaps if I went personally to London?"

"A costly trip that would appease no one, sir. The British have threatened to correspond with your banks and trusts in New York." Altmann paused. "They probably have done so already."

Julian pounded the arm of the chair with his fist. "How dare they press me to the wall? I have millions in assets."

"What you have, sir, is well over a million dollars in capital assets but not enough revenue to float the accumulated debt."

Julian stood. "I remind you that the Crédit Mobilier just declared first dividends of a hundred percent. One hundred percent!"

Altmann adjusted his spectacles. "As you and all the Crédit's stockholders know, that revenue has certain, well, limitations. It has to be very sensitively accounted for and . . . discreetly disbursed."

Julian scrutinized him. "Altmann, wipe that look of eternal damnation off your face. This is business we're talking about. And you're missing my point. We have a flow of cash. The government subsidizes the Union Pacific for every mile of track laid. Congress also gave us twenty sections of land for each mile, and we're selling it to the farmers and sodbusters for a dollar-fifty an acre and up. We're getting tens of thousands in premiums from towns that want to be on the route. Now, tell me, where's the bond holders' money?"

Altmann checked a paper and began itemizing. "You are aware, of course, that construction costs rose dramatically last year. In the spring we had record floods in western Nebraska. Add to that delay caused by Indian raids all summer. If you'll recall, I summarized Indian losses in a report—"

"I know!" Julian jumped up. "Go on!"

Altmann's paper shook. "Payroll has more than tripled. In northeast Colorado there are now three thousand five hundred graders, with attendant teamsters and mules. We have another three thousand men in the Medicine Bow Mountains cutting wood for ties, plus several thousand—"

"The Central Pacific," Julian interrupted. "How many men do they have?"

"A few Irish bosses and more than ten thousand Chinese."

"Ten thousand diligent, uncomplaining, implacable workhorses. And what's the UP have? Whiskey-lovers, convicted felons, bushwhackers, foreign-speaking immigrants, failed farmers, and runaways."

He looked out the window at the springing green grasses of his estate. "You know what my spies in the CP camps tell me? The Chinese hang in baskets over the Sierra cliffs and chisel the rockface. Chiseling away a mountain, a flake at a time."

"They're a strong and prodigious race."

"They're an odd race. Nothing tempts them. They save every penny so they can go back to China and buy a little farm. Put a tent city of whiskey, women, and faro tables at the end of the line —like the UP has at Cheyenne—and the Chinese wouldn't even go near it."

"To their credit, sir. That's why the CP tracklayers are so close to Reno right now."

"The CP should have been forced to stop at the Nevada line! Congress should have stopped them. By God, we paid dearly for those spineless politicians' support and what did they do? Gave in to Leland Stanford and the CP. Agreed to let them head east as far and as fast as those Chinamen can grade the beds and spike the rails. Every mile of subsidy they get is stolen right out of a UP shareholder's pocket. My pocket!"

Julian was warm, beginning to sweat. A fierce throbbing began in his temple.

You can do better than that, Julian. The Widow's reedy voice flew in his ear. *Now read it again.*

Yes, ma'am, he had always answered, and he would read the poet's words again, with deliberate hesitation. "First, there was Chaos, the vast immeasurable abyss, outrageous as a sea, dark, wasteful, wild." He would read it over and over, until he had phrased her beloved Milton fluidly and her small eyes squeezed closed in satisfaction. She could never see that he was only pretending to be proud of his "new" reading skill, only pretending that he was a poor miner's brat, stumble-tongued before the moralistic frippery of a dead English poet. Oh, he could read. He could read her like a book. Stupid old woman. She was the one who should have been proud. He had used her money well.

"Sir?" Altmann said.

Forcing his concentration back to the present, Julian clasped his hands behind him. "Yes?"

"You know, sir." Altmann took out his handkerchief and mopped his sideburns. "Postponing expenses of any kind would help. I don't think you should start digging the foundation for that pharmaceuticals factory down by the river when—"

"Mister Altmann! I have made and lost more small fortunes in twenty years than you could keep track of in a thousand little lined books. Where do you get the temerity to offer me financial advice?"

Altmann's pale skin flushed red. Still, he straightened. "In that case, there's nothing to do but sell some of your assets, sir, to tide you—"

"I—don't—give—up—anything," Julian said coldly. "Now, get out."

"But—"

"Out!"

The valet, Norrie, came in as a bristling Altmann went out. Julian scrutinized the little man. Had he overheard anything? Doubtful. The man was quiet and obedient, and never asked a blessed question that wasn't related to grooming.

"What about the sleeves?" Julian asked, shaking the billowy folds covering his arms. "What goes here?"

"More lacing, I'm afraid," Norrie said, rummaging in a box for four brocade pieces that matched the doublet. "They wrap around the upper arm and the forearm. Lets the shirt puff out at the elbow and the shoulder." Norrie unenthusiastically reached for another handful of cord points to finish the tedious lacing.

Julian's lax arm jostled with the repetitive motion of the lacing. Tug and cross and loop and tie. Detail after detail, a numbing list. In Sacramento, transport costs and distribution worries. Here, an extemporaneous drama that required precise timing. And a ground-breaking ceremony that week at the site of Gates Pharmaceuticals. Soon, very soon, he would begin to rebuild the fortune no one in St. Louis knew he had lost.

No one except, perhaps, Matt Dennigan. A few days earlier Julian had discovered that he and Matt had been in New York at the same time back in December. Matt had been seen there with Senator Bill Cahill, who was an old family friend of the Dennigans. More importantly, Cahill was an old acquaintance of the Crédit Mobilier's bonus fund. But Julian's New York detective reported that there had been a shouting match and Matt had left the hotel in a fury. Whatever Matt wanted, Bill Cahill wasn't giving.

Matt must have followed Julian and Edmund on one of their

jaunts to Chang's emporium too, for it was there that "M. Dennigan" lost his shirts. The package had been impounded as evidence after a police raid. God bless the efficiency of the police.

And God damn Chang. The enterprising opium dealer had legally witnessed documents for Zemin, including an English-language copy of a letter Zemin had sent to Chu King-Sing: the shipping order for four hundred pounds of *ya p'ien*. And the witnessed letter was now in Edmund's greedy hands.

"It mentions your name, you know," Edmund had said while downing French brandy one night in Julian's den.

"Oh?" Julian had said, pretending calm.

"Yes. It was Zemin's idea to mention you personally instead of that fictitious company you gave us." Edmund drew languidly on one of Julian's imported cigars. "A failsafe, you understand."

"I understand completely. But do you, Edmund?"

Edmund had shifted uneasily, and when he spoke again, his famous voice had become thin. "Your name looks god-awful in Chinese, Julian."

"Chinese? Ah. Your efficient Zemin also made a Chinese copy of the letter? How quaint, Edmund."

"Apparently, full identification is a business requirement of Mr. Chu's that Zemin forgot to mention."

"I understand. Mr. Chu likes to keep a complete record of his customers." Julian had nodded. "Well, let us hope that Chu and I have a long and productive association."

Edmund had smiled, but with uncertainty. "Like ours," he'd said.

Julian had not answered.

He dismissed Norrie, then posed before the mirror. Time for the cap. He donned the blue velvet turban with its band of gold thread. The thick fold of the crown fell to the side. How debonair.

Watching each movement in the mirror, Julian slipped the weapons belt around his waist and buckled it, pulling it tight.

To grievously offend a man, the great Machiavelli taught, one must take his property and his honor. " 'And of the honors that may be taken from a man,' " Julian recited, " 'a woman is the most important.' "

Tonight, fair Juliet. He withdrew his sword and lunged forward in a dramatic stance. I, your dashing Tybalt, will relieve us all of mad Mercutio, that dog of a Dennigan.

Of course, Katie didn't even know yet that she would be called on to play Juliet that night in a production she wanted to boycott. Lucy, however, whose dramatic debut it would have been, was sure to report in soon. Ill. Very ill.

A shame, Julian thought. Lucy had been so pert and plucky only hours ago when she and Edmund were there for lunch.

Bad salmon. Very bad salmon.

19

"Hurry, Lin!" Katie held the padded stomacher against her breasts. "Curtain in thirty minutes."

Behind her, Lin jerked the lacing tight, then ran to the wardrobe for the overgown of Juliet's costume. Only minutes earlier the cast had received word that Lucy St. Clair would be unable to take the stage. She was ill, but not from stage fright. Food poisoning. After the performance Katie would pray for Lucy's survival. At the moment, she was too hard-pressed to be certain of her own.

Buttoning the cuff of the crimson undergown, she quickly stepped into the blue dress Lin held open for her. "Edmund's still not here?"

Lin pulled the gown up. "No."

Bastard. Katie had to hold her tongue. Beth was in the room, playing under the dressing room bench, crooning nonsense words to a doll.

The dressing room door jerked open and Peg peeked in. "For God's sake, can't you hurry? I need help with that herd of amateurs upstairs. Bonkers, the lot of them. Preening for a mirror, whining for a seamstress. One of those cows wants a jelly roll for her nervous stomach. *Her* nervous stomach!"

Katie hurriedly twisted the open front skirt to show the gold brocade panel in the underskirt. "Those people are Edmund's responsibility."

Peg entered the room, cane tapping lightly. "I'm sick and tired of his whole charade too, but we'll have to manage." She straightened the train of her sister's costume. "Now, look. Everything's simplified without Lucy. We're still doing the short version of Romeo, except with our old cast. Masters Gates and Dennigan guest in one scene only, they fight, they die, and we jump to the crypt scene and let Father bring the audience up to date in a centerstage aside. Meanwhile, we've paraded the amateurs at the Capulet ball and everyone's happy."

"Not I," Katie said as Lin's hands raced down the bodice, lacing gold cord across the violet stomacher. "This is nothing but a silly lark for Julian. He's got half the audience going back to his house for a masquerade."

"His Nibs is upstairs right now, the most elegant and loudly striped Tybalt you'll ever see." Peg whacked the door frame with her cane. "He's ordering our stagehands around like they were Greenmore's minions. God in heaven. And me in hell. Nowhere to go but upward, I guess. 'Without haste but without rest,' as Frederick's beloved Goethe says."

"I thought you two were studying Kant," Katie said, watching her sister in the mirror.

"We found *The Metaphysics of Morals* a bit dry, artistically. We preferred a poet."

Katie dipped fingertips in a tin of grease paint. "I see."

"Not what you think you do," Peg retorted, but she was smiling as she closed the door. Katie smiled too, grateful for the friendship she and her sister were gingerly rebuilding.

Working quickly, Katie smoothed the thick white cream across cheeks and forehead, nose and chin, feathering missed spots with practiced massage.

She could see Beth behind her in the mirror, sucking her fingers as she watched her mother's familiar features disappear. Katie grinned and made a clown's face. Beth giggled and hid under the bench again with her dolls and nursery cards.

"I want you to take Beth home as soon as you're done with me," Katie said softly to Lin. She lined her eyes with thick kohl pencil, drawing each orb to an exaggerated point. "Peg can help me get out of costume after the show." She rouged her lips and cheeks, then darkened the lids of her eyes from lashes to brows to offset the ghoulish light of the footlamps. "I want Beth as far from this circus as possible."

Lin nodded as she brushed Katie's hair in long waves down her back. She pinned back the sides and affixed the small crown cap of white satin and blue embroidery. "Beautiful, Miss Katie." Lin smiled at her in the mirror. "Just like New York."

Katie hid her disagreement. It was nothing like New York. There she had performed with professionals in a production meticulously planned. She stood and turned, then stooped low to blow Beth a kiss. " 'Night, sweet."

Katie stepped out into the corridor where walk-ons milled noisily, waiting their cues for the opening act clash in the market square. Capulet soldiers wore royal blue doublets, Montague's had silky amber. The colors alternated in an ever-changing array as the actors bent to button boots, reached up to fluff turbans, or stood with forearms upright so a fellow soldier could lace his doublet sleeve.

Upstairs, Katie couldn't find Matt in the bustling melee backstage. She saw Julian, though, in a doublet of startling scarlet and gold. He was with a dozen ladies from the Orphans Board. Some were young, some were old, and all seemed dependent on Julian's reassuring presence. They sat face-to-face in two rows of benches, uneasily grooming the laps and fronts of their outlandish gowns. Pressed tight as banked cod against the wall were their maids.

On the far side of the hall were the gentlemen partners for the dance. The men stood in a garrulous pack, talking politics as they nervously plucked at sword straps and appraised rival codpieces.

Gathering up her gown, Katie sidestepped a young rowdy dragging a sandbag to the opposite wing, then approached the ladies. She hoped her smile hid her dismay, for the ladies' gowns were awful. Each seemed to be from a different historical period, and some from no recognizable era at all. The possessive Dee Dee Schnell sat closest to Julian. She had unfortunately chosen an Elizabethan gown, whose wide pannier emphasized her hips. She was smiling and nodding at Julian as he spoke, until he rose abruptly to greet Katie.

"Ah, such beauty." He took Katie's hand. " 'She doth teach the torches to burn bright!' Though I fear she hath gone pale at the sight of me in my finery."

Katie realized how strange she must look in her white powder mask and dark kohl brows. "I think it's time for everyone to don their makeup," she said.

The twelve women on the benches stared at her. Dee Dee rose, her chin high. "We do not paint, my dear. We have masks." Her maid stepped forward with a jeweled half-mask on a stick. "So that we may participate with discretion."

Katie turned to Julian. "Do you also fear the taint of your theatrical adventure?"

"I fear nothing tonight," he said, his gaze straying to someone behind her.

Katie turned. It was Matt. He wore one of Poppy's stock costumes, a worn ivory leather doublet with three slashes across the chest to show the bright amber velvet beneath. His hose were dark, his boots brown leather.

Julian spoke smoothly. "I was explaining, Matt, that as guest performers, we will wear masks to avoid confusing the audience."

"I don't think anyone's going to be confused about who's amateur and who's professional," Matt said. "The swords we're using are real and dangerous. For everyone's safety, you and I shouldn't wear masks. They'll limit our vision."

In answer, Julian pulled a scarlet satin mask from his doublet and tied it on. "But I can see you very well indeed."

A chill crept up Katie's spine. When she saw Julian's hand rest on the dagger at his belt, she took a step toward him.

"Julian." She tried to keep her tone low and even. "The knife is a lovely piece, but I thought we sent word that daggers are not part of costuming tonight. No one else will be wearing one."

189

"They should," Julian said, still looking at Matt. "It's a fine ornament. Why the concern? We're all here in the spirit of sport, aren't we?"

"My mistake," Matt said. "I had thought we gathered in the spirit of charity for your orphans."

He took his leave, just as a commotion of scuffling and laughter erupted at the back door. Katie spotted Edmund's long mussed hair and jaunty profile above the crowd. He was still in street clothes. Julian extended his arm to her. "Let's see what all the fun's about, shall we?"

Just inside the door, quivering on a spider web of leashes, were eight nervous greyhounds. Each spindly creature wore part of a costume—a beret, a shoulder cape, baggy doll-size knickers. One dog wore a loosely falling hat with a feather in it. Katie craned forward for a closer look. A Venetian turban? Good God, Edmund.

"Katie!" he exclaimed. "And Julian. That is you, I can tell! Look what I've contracted for us. A little forepiece of animal der-ring-do!" He gestured grandly. "May I introduce Goodman's Grey-hounds?"

Goodman was a porcine man dressed in sour-smelling gabar-dine. Around his neck were jumping hoops, and strapped to his back were three-legged stools nested seat to seat. At his command, a little whippet reared on hind legs, showing a long gathered gown. A Renaissance caul of brightly colored net covered her pointy ears.

Katie stepped forward. "Edmund, you can't—"

"They're perfect!" Edmund pronounced.

"They're Romeo and Juliet," Goodman said with enthusiasm. "She barks it in rhythm, ya see. TA-ta-TA-ta-TA-ta-ta. 'WHERE-fore-ART-thou-RO-me-o.' Then they dance. Up, Toozy!" he com-manded the dog in the turban. The two upright dogs leaned paws on shoulders and turned in a circle with minced steps.

Katie could hardly breathe. She looked at Julian. He wore an expression so tight, she thought he would explode. Edmund, how-ever, was eerily relaxed. The whites of his eyes were red-veined. He had been smoking, numbing himself to the consequences of play-ing his vaunted patron for a fool.

Julian drew himself straighter, his disdain palpable. His blue eyes were malevolent within the red mask.

"It's your show, Edmund." His smile was a cold, humorless curl. "And your chance to show people just what your taste is made of."

Katie saw Edmund's hands tremble before he shored them into the pockets of his coat. He had bluffed too hard. "Keep the dogs outside," he told Goodman. "I'll let you know when we need you."

Julian turned his back and walked away.

"Edmund," Katie began, but he dashed off to the stairwell. He shrugged off his jacket, then snapped his fingers like an imperial prince. "Zemin!" he called down. "Transform me!"

Ten minutes to curtain, Katie thought. Twenty to Romeo's cue. Edmund was playing far too close to the edge that night. She prayed they would not all fall with him.

On stage under hot gaslight chandeliers, feuding Capulets and Montagues clashed in the market square, their faces red, their underarms half-mooned with sweat.

The Brandelli Brothers ran the boards with abandon, and frantic stock players ran headlong off their marks, resuming sword stance in safer quadrants of the stage. Only Tobias, solid and stalwart, held his ground as the Brandellis clamored past.

Katie had assigned Tobias a minor role in every scene. He was there to keep order and avert disaster, if possible.

She edged her way through the actors waiting eagerly in the wings, heading toward Peg. She sat on her stool, prompt book open on her lap. When Katie reached her, she cupped a hand to Katie's ear. "Watch your pacing with Nurse," she whispered.

Tipsy? Katie mouthed. She hadn't seen a sign of Marge all night.

"Reeking," Peg said.

Marge's husband, Bester, was already on stage looking none too steady himself. An old veteran of the theater, he was playing Romeo's young friend Benvolio, wearing a black pageboy wig on his bald head. He strutted left, then right, anxiously stalling. Edmund was late for his cue.

From a backstage corner came frantic scuffling. Katie braced herself as Edmund shoved past her, nearly knocking Peg off her stool.

Handsome Romeo slowed to a walk just before his body emerged on stage in view of the audience.

Poor Bester blanked out on his lines. Edmund could have helped by slowing the pace of Romeo's banter, but Edmund enunciated for himself, never to help another actor.

"Ah!" Bester dramatically raised his index finger. "Ah, but!" He stroked his chin and nodded sagely at Romeo. Putting a hand on his scabbard to keep it from rattling, he strode three contemplative steps upstage, closer to the prompt stool.

" 'One desperate grief—' " Peg whispered.

" 'One desperate grief cures with another's languish,' " Bester proclaimed loudly as he returned centerstage with Edmund.

Bored, Edmund rushed the scene. His rich baritone plowed poetic meter like a corn row. Content meant nothing to him, Katie thought. His words were hollow, aimless. He had wasted his great gift. And, she realized, she had squandered her own, keeping it meek in his shadow.

That was what he had tried to destroy the day of the fire. He had reached in to nip the bloom of her talent before it grew. It must have seemed as simple to him as playing a part. Villainy had been a role like so many others, the words and actions attached to nothing in his heart. His base emotion had been fear, fear that the audience would like her better, fear that the troupe would no longer worship the star when they realized his grand light was but the trick of a tiny flame.

She had been a confident child, but Edmund had crippled all faith in herself that day, twisting her certainty into a grotesque shape that could never unfold as ambition.

Why, then, was it she who had grown stronger, more substantial than he? She who had grown strong enough to pity the straw man?

Slowly, subtly, the burdens of the past were shifting inside her. Success at the Daly had built her confidence. Relocating the troupe had demanded a personal faith, calculated risk, and physical endurance beyond any she had ever shown before.

Loving Matt, though, forced the deepest change, forced her to look into a mirror hidden deep inside. It held reflections of the past she feared, yet when she looked, she did not see an ugly child, a hapless girl. She saw only herself, once young and malleable, now grown and strong. And loved. She was loved.

She hurried through the backstage maze of prop tables and canvas flats, needing to speak to him once more before his scene, fearful of what she could lose.

She passed the Capulet feast table, laden with shiny wax fruits and wooden legs of lamb. She ignored Julian standing nearby in his scarlet mask. He was strangely fond of wearing it, she thought. He had even worn it when he'd strutted on stage before the play began to welcome his friends. It was as if he wanted his generosity, and his elegant costume, noted by all.

Matt stood by himself in the wings, wearing a black satin mask. It seemed as if he'd been waiting for her, so intently was his gaze fastened on her.

She said nothing when she reached him. She did not know how to make light of her deepest worry.

Finally, he spoke, "There are youngsters and rich gentry watching tonight. He won't draw blood."

"Remember that the audience sees only what we let them. It's our job to make spectators unsure of what their senses tell them. Don't make your fight too real."

"I will try." He brought her hand to his lips for a lingering kiss, but she saw his gaze stray warily beyond her.

"Is this kiss to honor me or to insult your rival?"

"My kiss does neither," he said. "Thy hand does the honor."

"Too glib a wit makes too short an affection," she teased.

"Then die, my own wretched wit, die—"

Aghast, she cut him off, her hand over his mouth, all playfulness gone. "Never say such things before you take the stage. Never."

"Door down!" a grip rasped a warning, heeding Peg's signal as he frantically slackened rope.

Juliet's cue was close. She caught up her skirts and ran to her entrance position behind a wing curtain. She felt giddy, as foolish as a girl in love, she thought, smoothing her skirt, securing her cap. Near her, a fancy arched doorway lowered majestically and landed soft as a hat. Two rowdies rushed behind the door and braced it upright. The scene was now the house of Capulet.

Edmund suddenly appeared beside her and caught a fistful of her gown's billowy sleeve. "Katie."

"Later!" she whispered. Nurse and Lady Capulet were already on stage. Her cue was imminent.

He showed her a tiny silver key threaded on a thin silk ribbon. "Hold out your hand," he whispered.

She shook her head furiously as she tugged.

He held fast to the delicate material. His face was unnaturally drawn and zealous. "I need you to hide this."

Was he crazed? She shook her head again.

On stage, Nurse proclaimed loudly, "What, ladybird! God forbid, where's this girl? What, Juliet!"

Juliet's cue!

"Hold out your hand." He pulled at her sleeve as if they had all the time in the world.

Knowing he would tear her sleeve before letting it go, she thrust out her wrist. He slipped the silk ribbon on it. "Remember," he said. "The Eighteenth Lohan. Say it."

Frowning, Nurse walked toward the arched doorway. " 'Where is she, pretty dove?' " she said loudly, fresh out of Shakespeare. " 'Whence comes that sly young dickens?' "

"Say it."

"The Eighteenth Lohan, blast you!"

He released Katie's dress. Instantly she gathered her skirts and ran through the archway, emerging on stage. " 'How now? Who calls?' " she said gaily, hand to her chest as if she were out of breath.

" 'Your lady Mother,' " Nurse said, wagging a finger.

Katie crossed the stage, laughing as she looked back at Nurse. Then she took a deep, controlled breath, expelling her anger with Edmund and throwing it safely distant from her performance.

A seemingly carefree Juliet, she whirled, sliding Edmund's key higher into her cuff. She knew there were dozens of children seated in the gallery, leaning forward, eager to absorb it all. She tried to focus on their quiet neediness.

All she could think of was a whisper. *Remember*.

20

Katie exited. Applause broke out and began to build, but Edmund cut the clapping short. He walked on stage immediately, leading friends and torchbearers to the mask at Capulet hall.

Jealous of her that night, Katie thought, watching from the wings. Or scared. She fingered the ribbon and key Edmund had tied to her wrist. Burlesque dogs, secret keys. Edmund the Obscure was in rare form that evening.

Troubled, she wound through the backstage clutter to the wings opposite for her next entrance. Her father was already there, in the line of jittery ladies and lords of the committee.

Alleyn was regal in a new Capulet robe, coral braided with silver. He smiled cheerfully when he saw her, worry-free. She squeezed his hand and held it as she had often seen her mother do.

Peg was patrolling the amateurs to keep them in entrance order. Belatedly she returned to her stool and checked the promptbook, then wildly signaled the grips on the other side. The backdrop lowered, but it was not the tapestry wall of the Capulets' great hall. It was the cavern of Juliet's crypt.

Peg nearly fell off her stool gesturing the grips to correct the mistake. Quickly, she cued the musicians to take their seats. The maskers, led by Dee Dee Schnell, thought Peg was cuing them. Dee Dee stepped off in a haughty march onto the stage.

"No!" Peg whispered.

One masker turned to hear her better and caught his scabbard on a wing board, tipping the wall behind the feast table. The board and table fell flat with a crash. Startled, the committee ladies on stage began to fan themselves in the excitement. Some of them tried to be helpful and picked up rolling wax apples and the glistening roast pig.

In the wings, Peg mobilized rowdies dressed as serving boys to run onto the stage and repair the damage. Alleyn stalked to centerstage to bombastically welcome his guests and draw attention from the string of catastrophes.

Katie hated taking her mark after such blunders. An audience exposed to reality was an elephant load on the tightrope of fantasy. There was one benefit, though. The small disasters made the amateurs cautious. They quickly fell into line for the dance, arms raised as they had been taught.

Julian was out front, dashing in his costume, wearing a smile that told the audience what a fine piece of fun he was having. He held one end of a silk kerchief and Dee Dee Schnell held the other. From the orchestra pit, violins, mandolin, harpsichord, and flute began as one instrument, and a Renaissance reel lit the air.

Unfortunately, the ill luck did nothing to focus Edmund's performance. He was a preoccupied Romeo, a thoroughly drunk, or drugged, Romeo. He was sluggish responding to Juliet at the masque. Conversely, he was rushed and jittery in the balcony scene.

He nearly knocked over a potted tree in his hurry to scale the trellised balcony. He was turning Romeo's love to farce, Katie thought, struggling to stay in character. He was ruining things. He always did.

" 'Therefore thy kinsmen are no let to me,' " he was saying arrogantly.

" 'If they do see thee they will murder thee,' " she called down, very serious.

" 'Alack, there lies more peril in thine eye than twenty of their swords.' "

His voice carried a sardonic edge, and she hated the falseness of his words. He tried in vain to emulate Romeo's true love, but Edmund had never known love, except love of self. Even brotherly love, God help him, had proved beyond his ken.

She stumbled her lines. " 'I would not—would not for the world they saw thee here.' "

He clung to the trellis like a gigantic, groping fly, climbing toward her. She moved to a far point on the balcony, looking for a way to bury her personal feelings and reclaim Juliet's joy.

Looking across the stage at anything but Edmund, she saw Matt in the wings. She spoke to him.

" 'Thou know'st the mask of night is on my face, Else would a maiden blush bepaint my cheek For that which thou hast heard me speak tonight.' "

Matt pulled off his black mask, watching her.

" 'Dost thou love me?' " she asked him. " 'I know thou wilt say Ay; And I will take thy word: yet, if thou swear'st—' "

" 'Lady,' " Edmund interrupted, cutting short Juliet's classic passage, " 'by yonder blessed moon I swear—' "

She tried to hide her anger as she looked down on him. Pale wastrel's face. Scheming heart she could never trust. It required all her concentration to discipline the pace and keep Juliet radiant through the remainder of Romeo's erratic wooing.

By the time she'd made it through the wedding in Friar Lawrence's cell, she was exhausted by the tension.

Stagehands changed the set to an open Venetian square. On the right was a pillared building fronted with Florentine arches and wide steps. Downstage left, a pavilion platform was braced and weighted. It allowed actors to fence dramatically up the steps of the platform, then fall in mock death over the rail onto hidden burlap pillows. From there, they could secretly make their way off stage.

It was a time of caution on the set. The duel between two obvious adversaries made everyone apprehensive. Katie saw it in the nervous glances of the walk-on swordsmen, who were needed to fill the large stage during the fight scene. She had asked Tobias to join the company of fencers as a secret guardian of fair play. She wanted no bloody missteps in front of the children. Accordingly, she had not allowed the Brandelli Brothers a part in the scene.

Looking around, she saw that the committee ladies and their partners were gone. They had fled the crowded back stage to take comfortable seats in the audience.

"Where's Julian?" she asked Peg.

"Someone said he went out into the alley for air. With all those dogs, I doubt he'll be refreshed. He'd better be back in two minutes or I'll scream."

Alleyn strode grandly to centerstage to shortcut the night's work, setting the scene in which Mercutio would defend Romeo's honor against the aggressive Tybalt, Juliet's cousin.

"Isn't Julian here yet?" Peg whispered as Alleyn neared the end of his makeshift speech. She was obviously frantic at the possibility of yet another missed cue.

"I'll look," Katie said. She headed for the back door, but before she reached it Julian opened it and walked in, masked and ready for the scene.

His doublet looked bulkier, she thought, almost as if he had padded himself against injury. He had lost his mocking smile too. When he passed her as if she weren't there, she followed him uneasily. He spoke to no one in the wings.

On stage, Matt was paired with Bester, the two bantering and walking the square with other Montague friends. Matt spoke slowly but with a convincing bite in Mercutio's taunts. He had natural ability and an appealing roughness, Katie thought. And courage to face tiers full of his antagonist's handpicked audience.

Julian's cue was close. He stood beside Peg, staring at the stage. His cue passed and he did not move.

"Tybalt, you're on!" Peg whispered.

Still he stood there. He squinted, seeming to be looking for someone not there. Peg jostled him. "Get going!"

He sprang forward onto the stage, and his walk-on soldier attendants had to sprint to catch up to him.

On stage, Bester pointed at their approach. " 'By my head, here come the Capulets.' "

Matt's Mercutio was cutting. " 'By my heel, I care not.' "

Julian had a line to deliver, but he missed it. Silent, he walked straight up to Matt. Rattled, Matt stumbled his own line.

Julian offered no words at all. Instead, he dramatically drew his sword—forty lines too early.

Peg paled. "I don't believe it."

Edmund came up beside her, intently eyeing those on stage.

"Edmund, get out there!" She pushed him. "This was your idea. Salvage it!"

With a caution that unnerved Katie, Edmund unbuckled the strap across the hilt of his sword so he could draw it freely. Suddenly he grabbed her wrist, fingering the key. *Remember*. She looked at him. His eyes were glassy as a rabbit's.

He strode stiffly out onto the stage. His entrance drew Julian's attention as obviously as a cape flagged a bull. Sword raised, he charged at Edmund.

The walk-on soldiers surrounding Matt took the charge as the new cue to begin their climactic fight. All drew swords and began to duel with their rehearsed partners.

Within moments the stage was chaos.

Edmund withdrew his sword in time to parry Julian's strike to his left flank, but Julian remained the aggressor. Edmund made an actor's dramatic lunge to Julian's chest, but the thrust was expertly parried, nearly jerking the sword from Edmund's hand. To recover, Edmund ran farther downstage, closer to the lights. Julian followed.

Inexperienced fencers retreated to far corners to beat swords and make fierce noise.

Why was Julian's fury directed at Edmund instead of Matt? Katie wondered. Wasn't it obvious Edmund was only a passable swordsman?

She saw that Matt and Tobias had chosen each other as fight partners in the melee. They frequently locked blades, hilt to hilt, passing messages and keeping watch on the vicious swing of Julian's rapier against Edmund.

In the wings, a dismayed Peg buried her face in Katie's shoulder.

Katie watched Julian wield his rapier with great show and finesse. He had none of the awkwardness he had displayed the night of the party. He no longer even had a slender build.

Oh Lord. His bulk was not padding. Katie pushed Peg away. The man was not Julian!

The red-masked impostor pressed Edmund back toward the footlights, unrelenting, intent on injury.

He was no hired stand-in. He was an assassin, and Edmund was his target. Merciful God. If the audience sensed a real killer on the loose, there would be panic in the aisles.

"Coward in the red mask!" Matt shouted above the clanging swords.

The impostor halted his attack on Edmund to see who had insulted him.

Matt answered with a dramatic display, forcing Tobias backward up the pavilion steps with attacks that stopped just short of their mark.

On the top of the platform, Tobias swung his blade fiercely. Matt parried, then cleanly plunged his sword through the air alongside Tobias. Tobias released a guttural cry and folded forward in mock agony.

In the wings, the prop chief stood ready on a chair, sandbag in hand.

" 'Cowering dog!' " Matt called down to the impostor, withdrawing his sword from Tobias's body. " 'Face now a friend of Montague!' " He pushed Tobias backward over the pavilion railing.

The audience gasped. At the moment Tobias hit the pillows, the prop chief dropped the sandbag and a deep thud shook the floor.

The audience quieted, stunned.

Tobias rolled off the pillows and ducked under a hidden curtain.

In the lull, Edmund took his chance. He sprinted upstage, close to the backdrop, where Bester and the walk-on swordsmen waited helplessly for an end cue.

Up on the platform, Matt ripped off his black mask and taunted the impostor again. " 'Milksop, take off your pretty mask! Your fight is with me! Begone, all others! Clear the square!' "

From the wings, Tobias gestured wildly at the walk-ons to exit the stage immediately.

Bester put his veteran instincts to good use. " 'Let us all depart!' " Hand on his wig, he charged offstage into the wing opposite Katie and Tobias. A stumbling herd of scared soldiers followed.

Edmund tried to fall in with the exiting group, but the red-masked assassin forced him from the herd with a swinging cut to the shoulder.

Edmund cried out as the blade bit into his arm. Holding his arm, he ran panicked toward the pavilion and Matt's protecting sword.

Matt jumped over the bannisters and landed in a crouch in front of the impostor. He lunged forward, but was just out of measure to thrust the point in the assassin's chest.

The assassin jerked back and fell into classic fencing position, wary.

All the while, Edmund crawled toward the wings in what Katie thought was atrocious overacting, until she saw the trail of blood marking his progress.

The audience held an unnatural silence, fascinated by the spectacular effect that allowed Romeo to bleed his way into the wings. When he was nearly off, two Capulet soldiers ran out to help him.

Katie ordered a rowdy to run out into the streets and find a policeman. She told Marge to bring towels to staunch the wound.

"I'm alive," Edmund said, panting as he lay on the floor. "I beat you, bastard. I'm alive."

There was scattered applause for Edmund's dramatic exit, but most of the audience was saving its recognition for the victor of the swordfight intensifying centerstage.

With great foreboding, Katie watched Matt's lonely battle. She was desperate to pull the curtain, but she knew that would not stop the assassin. Worse, it would let the audience know something was amiss, and could well start a stampede for the exits. God forbid a patron—or a child—be hurt in the panic.

The masked assassin announced a swing with a guttural grunt, then feinted low. Matt followed the diagonal arc of the blade and blocked it as the assassin cut down toward his neck.

The parry locked the blades, and the two men wrestled themselves apart. Matt stumbled backward, knocking into the pavilion steps and sprawling across them.

The assassin lunged straight at his chest. Matt rolled off the side of the steps and thrust at the assassin. The agile man twisted hard, and Matt's blade pierced nothing but a quilted doublet.

Rising, Matt attacked again, forcing the assassin to back up the stairs as he deflected the swing. A swift riposte sliced Matt's doublet cleanly across the collarbone. Blood welled through the slit fabric.

Katie gripped Peg's hand, terrified.

Matt staggered. The assassin hailed downward cuts, forcing Matt to keep his sword raised flat above his head. The force of the beating sent a piece of filigree flying from the hilt of Matt's sword.

The assassin ran up the last steps to the platform. When Matt rushed after him, he drew a dagger from his belt and lunged viciously.

Matt twisted away from the knife stroke, but lost his balance and fell against a brace, striking his head.

The assassin charged.

Katie bit back a cry and the audience gasped as one.

Matt grabbed the railing with his free hand to keep from rolling off the platform as the assassin came at him, both weapons aimed low. Using the rail for leverage, Matt lunged upright. He thrust his sword at his enemy's unguarded chest.

The point of the blade rammed home, below the shoulder.

The man gave a gargling howl. With his back to the audience, he dropped his sword and stumbled forward against the railing.

Matt used his foot to tumble the man over.

There was no staged thud this time, only stunned silence.

Breathing hard, Matt straggled to the pavilion stairs and sat, the bannister at his back. Blood glistened at his temple. He bent forward, holding his head.

Sounds of fidgeting began in the audience.

"Quick! Pull the curtain!" Katie told Peg.

Peg tried to give the signal to the stagehands in the opposite wing, but wonderstruck walk-ons were gossiping and blocking the view.

Matt sat unmoving on the platform, head in hands.

Katie grabbed one of the small towels Marge had brought for Edmund and stuffed it in her sleeve.

"He's disoriented out there," Peg said. "We've got to end this."

"Gladly." Katie gathered her skirts and ran out.

The audience settled back with relief as Juliet ran out into the square, seeking her love.

21

Katie swept across the plaza. " 'Mercutio?' " she called. " 'Hast thou seen my cousin Tybalt? I fear he means great harm to my Romeo.' "

Matt raised his head, still holding a hand to his temple. He seemed unable to focus.

She stopped below the steps. " 'Pray, get up and help me find them. I must plead peace between them.' "

" 'Dear lady,' " Matt said raggedly, removing his hand to show the bloodied side of his face. " 'You will find no peace here.' "

Katie's gasp was lost in the audible cry from the crowd. Surely, they could not see the blood was real, she thought, and desperately she kept the ruse afloat. " 'Good Mercutio, my Romeo's friend!' " she cried, running up the steps. " 'Thou art hurt!' " She sat on the step below him and pulled the towel from her sleeve. " 'What happened 'ere I came upon thee?' "

Up close, she would see that the wound was a shallow cut at the hairline, though there was swelling. Relieved, she pressed the towel to his temple. The wound at his shoulder bled through his doublet, but lightly. He was disoriented, not disabled.

" 'Come.' " She tried to urge him to stand. " 'I will see thee to a surgeon.' " All she wanted to do was get him offstage.

He stood and held onto the bannister, unsteady. " 'A moment, sweet lady. Talk to me yet a moment.' "

" 'I will call for help,' " she said, ready to gesture to Tobias to rescue them both. " 'Someone can carry thee.' "

" 'No.' " Matt held to the bannister and took one halting step down. " 'A man walks from his battles. He's carried to his grave.' "

" 'Valiant Mercutio,' " she said in dismay. He hadn't realized the easy escape she had offered. She felt the audience's hunger for an explanation and for news of their hero, Julian. " 'Let us away.' " She urged him down the steps.

" 'Slow, dear lady,' " he said, " 'lest I fall at thy feet, smitten not by love of thee, but by the fury of Tybalt's sword.' "

The wings seemed so distant. " 'What quarrel hadst thou with my kinsman, Tybalt?' "

" 'That he was not Tybalt.' "

Katie knew the audience was confused. " 'What means such nonsense?' " she demanded.

Matt shook his head, unable to fictionalize. " 'He was a murderer sent in Tybalt's clothes wielding Tybalt's sword and a dagger to pierce your Romeo's heart.' "

" 'What evil is this?' " she cried, mirroring the audience's shock. " 'Faith, sir, say you saved my Romeo. Say he is not hurt.' "

" 'He lives, I think. He must. A nick on the arm and he disappeared.' " He looked at her. " 'Now, only I am left for his lady love to claim.' "

Uneasy, she moved downstage, closer to the wings. " 'Did not my Romeo confide in thee? He and I were married in the night by the light of the altar in the good Friar's cell.' "

He raised an arm to wipe the blood from his face. " 'I find that hard to believe. I am overly familiar with Romeo's many loves and his fickleness.' "

She gasped, as did ladies in curtained boxes. " 'You insult me, sir! And him! The friend whom you fought to save.' "

" 'I fought the impostor for you.' "

They were on tenuous ground. She could feel the audience

eagerly lapping at innuendo. " 'Why for me, Mercutio?' " she asked, trying to herd him to the wings.

" 'Because the love Romeo bears for you is a gnat speck in the sky of my own bright affection.' "

" 'Affection for me? Poor Mercutio, you are addled by your trials. The love you bear me must be as dearest friend to your dearest friend, Romeo, for I am his wife.' "

" 'Alas, how wrongly have you married, lady.' " He walked slowly toward her. " 'Chosen a pretty boy of noble family. Left a scarred and gentle warrior of modest means bleeding in the plaza.' "

" 'And where does he present himself, this gentle warrior?' " she asked, hiding confusion in anger. " 'I see none but the rake Mercutio of wicked tongue and fighting temper. Hast thou declared a vow of love for me? Dost thou e'en know how to pronounce the words?' "

" 'God, yes, I know.' " He continued toward her, halting but inches away. " 'I spoke them once to a maid.' "

" 'And what did she?' "

The silence ran long. " 'She died.' "

" 'She died,' " Katie said sadly. " 'But the words did not die. Words survive us all. The honesty of their intent lives on to seed in others. That seed speaks true, even when we do not.' "

" 'Madam.' " He smiled. " 'You speak boldly of my seed when you must know it not.' "

The audience laughed. Cheeks flaming beneath her powder, she tried to catch Peg's eye. Why wasn't she pulling the curtain? Or Father? Damn his worship of improvisational theater. She needed rescue.

Matt suddenly took her arm. " 'I know I am lost,' " he said, " 'for you are already pledged 'til death do you part. In parting then' "—he pulled her closer—" 'I offer a kiss. One felicitous kiss.' "

Curtain. Where was the curtain? " 'Thy kiss must be chaste,' " she said nervously.

He tipped her chin upward. " 'Lady, my kiss must be my kiss.' "

There seemed not a sound in the audience, nor from the wings. As his lips touched hers, the soft shush of curtains began, the heavy drapes drawing to a close. Ladies in their boxes crooked sideways to keep the couple in sight as the stage shrank smaller, slimmer, until the ponderous folds collided in a silent tide of velvet.

He broke their kiss and put his lips to her ear. "Are you all right?"

"No. Are you? Do you need a doctor?"

"No. Did I kill the man?"

"I don't know. I don't care." She led him offstage. "He didn't kill you."

"Or you."

"Me?"

He stopped and faced her. "I have to leave, to make some arrangements," he said hurriedly as her father rushed forward in his Capulet robe. "I'll send word tonight."

"Brilliant!" Alleyn clasped his arms around her. His goatee prickled her cheek. "Both of you, brilliant!" He clapped Matt heartily on the back.

Matt winced, holding a hand to his wounded shoulder. "You're too kind."

"That is what they came to see! Live theater with fire in its belly. That is the genius of Populus Felicitas!"

"It's going to take a genius to end the show," Peg said. "The police are here. Julian straggled in half stripped of his clothes, nursing a bruised jaw. Romeo's got an arm bandage. Mercutio's stolen Juliet. We have an attempted murderer backstage and out-right murder of Shakespeare's plot onstage."

"There's only one thing to do," Katie said absently as she watched Matt slip away. "Bring on the dogs."

Peg didn't argue. She signaled a roustabout. "Go into the alley and tell Goodman that he and his greyhounds are on in five minutes."

"Father." Katie took his arm. "We need you to present a soliloquy in front of the curtain to end the show. Have Capulet lament the fate of the two lovers and then end with the Prince's 'a glooming peace.' Just keep it short and sweet."

Peg directed Alleyn stageward while Katie briefed Tobias about the change in plans. "We'll have a curtain call, a quick one, in a few minutes. Where's Julian?"

"Over there." Tobias gestured toward the dressing room stairs. "He was knocked unconscious. He told the police that someone decked him in the alley. Next thing he knew, he woke up with a few loose teeth and everything gone but his tights and his boots."

"Goodman was out there with his dogs. Surely he saw the impostor attack Julian and take his costume."

"He says he saw the man in stripes go down the alley and fifteen minutes later saw him come back."

Fifteen minutes? Katie thought. "But—"

"Tobias!" Peg called.

As Katie wended her way among nervous supers, reassuring them, she saw Julian near the dressing room stairs. He sat hunched forward, a blanket draped across bare shoulders. His hair was mussed, his face was dirty. His jaw didn't seem to be swollen, but he held a tooth in his hand, and he spat often into a handkerchief as if his mouth were bleeding. He was talking to a policeman.

A bevy of people attended him. Marge had a basin and wet towel for his face. Bester came running up with a nobleman's robe he had grabbed from downstairs.

When Julian stood to don the robe, he saw Katie. He gave a small, wincing smile, seeking sympathy as he slid the scratchy blanket from his shoulders and reached for the robe.

"Out of my way!" a woman demanded in the throng behind Katie. "I know something's wrong! Where's Julian? Where is he?"

Dee Dee Schnell was sidestepping her wide pannier through the crowd. When she broke through the crowd and found herself within a yard of Julian's bare chest, she stopped dead still.

"Heavens," she whispered, and promptly fainted.

Julian's smile broadened. In fact, Katie thought, it was quite broad for a man with a sore jaw. He calmly eased his arms through the slits in the robe. With much adjusting of the folds, during which all could see his paunchless stomach and firm chest, he at last tied the front closed. He glanced at Katie.

"Where is your impostor now, Julian?" she asked pointedly.

He carefully changed the phrasing. "The man who attacked me

209

has been taken to the surgeon, though there is not much hope. It seems Matt wields a deadly sword."

"His sword saved my brother." She turned to the detective sergeant. "Have you identified his attacker?"

The sergeant shook his head as he stood to leave. "A stranger, far as we can tell. And pure lunatic, putting on tights to cut someone down. A man like that's only swinging on one hinge."

"So's the villain who hired him, I suspect," she said, seeking Julian's eye.

"I agree," he said coolly. "It would be wise to investigate anyone who's made outrageous threats against Edmund recently, don't you think so, Sergeant?"

"Good idea, yessir. Start on that first thing tomorrow," the sergeant said, and started toward the door.

No, Katie thought. Everyone knew Matt had lashed out at Edmund in full view of dinner guests last week. But surely no one could suspect Matt of planning tonight's ordeal. She looked at Julian. If ever there was a man capable of twisting logic to his need, he stood before her.

Apprehension grew as she joined the curtain call. Edmund came out with pale face and a bloody bandage on his arm. The audience laughed at the "pretense." Katie could hardly manage a smile. Julian had actually hired someone to kill her brother.

Emotions reeling, she went to her dressing room. She wanted time to think before Peg came to help her undress.

What incredible cunning, she thought. Cruel and bloody mayhem, coldly, precisely planned. She pulled the pins from her cap and lifted it.

And Matt. He had wanted Matt dead too. Her hand was unsteady as she removed makeup with cream and a clean towel.

She heard the thunderous footfalls and noisy babbling of the extras as they came down the stairs to change. The doorknob turned. Peg so soon?

In the mirror, she saw Julian step into the room. "Could I have a moment, Katie?" Not waiting for an answer, he closed the door behind him. She heard him slide the bolt, then he turned to look at her.

She averted her eyes. She felt vulnerable with her hair hanging free, her face newly naked. She folded the towel to keep her hands steady and to tuck Edmund's secret key higher into her sleeve.

He came up behind her, so close she could not see his face in the mirror. She saw only his robed chest and the hand he rested on her shoulder.

"You are not my familiar," she said.

"And you are not my friend. You hurled suspicion at me instead of the sympathy I deserved."

"We both know what you deserve."

"Well then, let me articulate it, to make sure we agree. I deserve unquestioning loyalty, for I am your employer. I deserve respect, for I am a mature man, socially well placed, your better in all esteems. I deserve help in extinguishing Matt Dennigan, for he is a scourge on both our futures. And lastly," he said, letting his hand drift down her arm, "I deserve your affection, for I can give you much in return."

She lurched from her seat, trying to reach the door. He caught her and wrenched her back. Calmly, he posted himself in front of the door.

"You deserve a jail sentence!" she said. "You tried to have my brother killed."

"It was not I. The police will find evidence to that effect."

"You threatened Edmund."

"Not I. I never threaten. I warn, and I promise. Edmund will verify that."

"Will he also verify that you're in the opium business with him?"

He paused. "Edmund makes the most outrageous claims." He moved toward her. "No one in her right mind would believe a word he says."

She spoke quickly. "No one will believe you, either. You made a mistake in the alley tonight."

He stopped.

"Timing, Julian. Your timing was wrong. Goodman said the impostor appeared fifteen minutes after you disappeared in the alley. No actor, let alone an amateur, can cross-lace four sleeve pieces and a plastron in fifteen minutes. By himself? And in the dark, for God's sake? I saw your assassin laced and tied, every last eyehole aligned."

Julian started toward her again.

"Your man was already dressed," she said, backing to the wall. "You had two costumes. Two!"

He grabbed her. She tried to pull away, but he whirled her around and held her tight against him in a strangling hug.

She struggled. "I'll make the police search the alley!"

"Please do. It'll add to my story. They won't find anything different from what I've described." He rubbed his cheek in her hair. "Fifteen minutes. Is that all you have?"

She grew still. "I have instinct to tell me what a vile and offensive piece of work you are."

"I am a formidable piece of work, K.T. Henslowe." His hand moved insolently across her breasts.

With all her energy, she rammed the heel of her shoe onto the top of his foot. He hissed in pain. She shook off his hold and dashed toward the door. He blocked her though, and she retreated to the dressing table, with nowhere else to run. Groping behind her, she picked up her heavy wooden hairbrush.

He tensed, anticipating she would throw it. Instead, she whirled and stabbed at the mirror with the wooden handle. The glass splintered and cracked. He leaped toward her as a shard of silver fell to the tabletop. She grabbed the towel to protect her hand as she picked it up. He was almost upon her when she thrust out at him.

He instantly veered away from the razor-sharp weapon.

Shard extended, she wrapped the towel more securely. Her hand shook.

"Oh, Katie, Katie." With macabre élan, he brought his hands together in a clap. "Bravo, Katie, the perfect wench," he said belittlingly. "A woman of breeding condemns a man's liberties by turning frigid. A woman with no breeding turns hot and wild. Which do you think pleases a man more, Katie?"

Her hold on the mirror blade was shaky. She braced her wrist with her other hand.

212

His expression grew oddly contemplative. "You could please me, you know. It's possible. That's why I've decided to offer you another chance. You're clearly on the wrong side in this affair. But I am forgiving of a woman as long as she learns from her mistake. Some people look on matters of the heart with great emotion. I see them as a matter of accounts. Debit or credit, Katie?"

The door rattled. "Katie!" Tobias called. "Are you all right?"

The bolt clacked sharply as Julian slid it free. He casually opened the door a crack. "A slight accident. You may send for the custodian." He shut the door again.

"Now then," he went on, "to be my consort ensures you, and your daughter, I might add, a life of luxury. Being consort to Matt, you will have a life of denigration and hardship. I'll make certain of that."

He tilted his head down to look directly at her. "Add up the expense of one and the assets of the other and, well, you're a businesswoman. You understand profit and loss. Come see me tomorrow, Katie. No, not tomorrow." He tapped his lip. "Tomorrow you will be very busy. The next day then. I have a proposition that will interest you."

"Why would I be fool enough to come to you?"

"Because you will have need of me." He smiled. "Great need."

He left.

Katie drew in a deep breath, and another, then tossed the piece of glass onto the broken pile on the table. The crash rekindled a cascade of tinkling glass.

Peg jerked the door open. "Good Lord. Are you all right?"

Katie nodded. Peg crossed the room and took her hand. "What happened?"

She shook her head, unwilling to talk.

"What did Julian want?"

"Business," Katie said. "It's just business."

"Looks a little personal to me," Peg said, shoving aside with her foot some broken glass that had fallen to the floor. She began to unbutton Katie's costume. "I assume you'll be seeing your hero 'Mercutio' tonight?"

Katie didn't answer.

"When you do," Peg went on, "tell him we're grateful. He saved Edmund's life and a possible stampede. God knows how wide a swath that lunatic could have cut through the audience if Matt hadn't engaged him."

"Matt's gone now, isn't he?"

"Barely waited for the police to take his statement."

Katie knew he would be on his way to relay news of the attack to one of his trusted contacts. Julian wouldn't have gone to such murderous extremes if he wasn't running scared.

"Peg," she said suddenly, "will you be seeing Altmann tonight?"

Peg was cagey. "I don't know."

Katie turned to face her. "Please, you must. Tell Altmann that I know Julian had two costumes made and I need proof."

"Two?"

"Julian dressed out his impostor beforehand."

"Ridiculous. Why would Julian hire a lookalike to hurt Edmund, his star? Edmund may be a little too flamboyant for him, and sometimes he drinks too much, but that's not grounds for murder."

Katie tamped down her irritation. Peg's misguided faith in Edmund was still solid as a rock. "Just tell Altmann it's important for him to set up a meeting with Matt, secretly, and soon."

"I don't want Frederick involved in this."

"He already is. He's a man of principle tied to a monster with none."

Peg looked thoughtful. "Frederick *is* very unhappy at what he does."

"Of course he is. He has to find a way out. Matt can help him." Katie stepped out of her costume and rummaged the clothing rack for a gown that was dark and inconspicuous.

"I hope we're doing the right thing, Katie. Conspiring against our one and only patron isn't very smart. We're flat broke."

"Hope's the only currency a Henslowe can keep in her pocket anyway."

"I meant to tell you. I'm running a little low on that."

Katie looked at her. Peg wasn't smiling.

214

22

Katie shifted restlessly in the carriage on the drive to the Radenour homestead. Matt met her at the gate, holding a lamp.

She pushed his arm higher so she could see the wound on the right side of his face. The swelling had eased. "Oh, Matt."

He set the lamp down and pulled her into his embrace. She held tighter, tighter.

After a minute he released her, picking up the lantern again and taking her hand. "Come with me." He led her away from the house, down a path into the woods.

"Where are we going?"

"A different way tonight."

The lane was winding, canopied with trees, and bordered by a short rock wall. Twigs cracked beneath their feet. Sounds hung suspended between the trees.

Chilled, she turned up the collar of her dark cloak. "How's Lucy?"

"Food poisoning she'll recover from. She may not recover from missing a chance to play Juliet, though."

Katie was quiet a moment. "Julian did that too?"

He shrugged. "No way to prove it."

"We can prove he hired a man to murder Edmund, if Altmann will help us find out where Julian had the duplicate costume made."

Matt stopped, setting the lamp on the rock wall. "I've been trying to figure out how he's going to link me and Edmund to the assassin he hired."

"There's no way to do that."

"With money, there's always a way. You may not believe this, but I wasn't completely confident how I'd fare tonight. I shipped a box of reports and some affidavits to Bill Cahill yesterday, just in case."

"Have you located Chu King-Sing?"

He shook his head. "Bill was supposed to get in touch with the port authority in San Francisco. I'm expecting a telegram from him tomorrow. Notice whether your brother has freshened his supply lately?"

"Lin thinks so. But she says it came on the train from New York, from Chang."

"Even if Chu's already docked, there hasn't been time to get the drug overland to St. Louis. Something's not right. If Julian wanted opium, he should have shipped it through New York or New Orleans. He wants it off-loaded in California. Why?"

She leaned wearily against his arm. "Why ask? Why can't you call off the investigation? You've done enough. One assassin's sword is enough." She felt his arm curve around her.

"I know. That's why we have to hurry."

As he lifted the lantern, its light revealed deeper woods ahead. "Hurry where?" she asked. "Where are we going?"

"To the chapel."

"Chapel?"

"The Radenours'. It's a private chapel. Mrs. Radenour's son, Cecil, is a magistrate. I asked him to wait for us there."

"For us?"

"I want us to be married, Katie. Tonight."

She finally found her voice. "In the dark?"

He laughed, but his laughter was cut off as she turned away.

No, she thought. Not this way. She didn't want it to be this way. She headed back up the path, toward the house.

He followed, stopping her by taking her arm. "Katie? What's wrong?"

She shook her head, easing from his grasp. "This is wrong."

"You're saying no?"

"I wasn't asked," she said softly.

He set the lantern down once more. Though he was half turned from her, she could see frustration and worry on his face. After a long moment, he looked at her.

"This isn't what I wanted, Katie. Not like this. I didn't think I'd ever want to marry again, but you changed that, that first night we came here together. And then tonight . . ."

He walked over to her and took her hands. "I wanted to wait, to see this thing with Julian through so that we could have a normal courtship, in the light. But I saw that assassin's eyes as he tried to kill me tonight, and I knew I could not wait."

She gently pulled her hands from his. "You're afraid," she said. "Afraid something will happen to you."

His silence was assent.

"You're not doing this for you, are you?" she said. "And you're not doing it for love. It's a charity gesture, for me. And for Beth."

"Dammit, Katie." He whirled away, raking his fingers through his hair. "I don't want to hear your pride talking."

"Pride's the only thing an itinerant actress with an illegitimate child has plenty of."

He strode back to her and took her by the shoulders. His grip was so tight, his look so intense, she knew he wanted to shake her. "You're the one who's scared, aren't you?"

She broke away from him. "I just don't know if I deserve you, if I'm good for you."

"That's not true. You're afraid I would fail you, like I did Sarah."

"No. God, no, Matt. It's just that I've—made mistakes. Mistakes you don't know about."

He shook his head. "What bothers you is my mistake. You're afraid I could abandon you and Beth, like the judge did. Like I did my son." His voice dropped. "I know you're worried about Samuel. You don't think I could love your daughter in place of Samuel."

"You haven't been around her. You don't know her."

"I know that she's a part of you, that she's been loved in your roving camps more than I was in my father's big house. I know that Beth has your beauty, a whole beauty, bedded deep in her heart. As for whether I would be a good father, you're right to beware, Katie." He turned away from her and stared into the woods. "I don't know if I would be a good father. I've never been one."

She came up behind him. "I believe you would be an excellent father for Beth. You're strong and caring and wise, a man who seeks out noble causes. You're a man whose heart needs the smile of a child to lighten it. But the question you must answer is whether I would be a good mother for Samuel."

"No, Katie. Don't."

"I would want our family to be whole. I would want your son in any home we would make. Matt, you know I can have no more children. Your son would be very precious to me."

"No!" He spun around to face her. "Samuel is happy where he is, with Sarah's parents. The Carters are well-off. He's cared for. He's a legacy of Sarah for which they are grateful. I'm not. I tell you honestly, Katie. I cannot live with that legacy."

"Not now, but someday?"

He closed his eyes and shook his head. "It would be unfair to promise you something I cannot give, and I will not be unfair to you, Katie." He jerked the lantern off the wall and started deeper into the woods.

"Where are you going?"

"To tell Cecil he can go home. I made a mistake."

She ran to keep up and followed him to a small stone building with lancet windows and a rustic wooden spire. Without speaking, he held the door for her.

The chancel was tiny, with a center aisle and five benches to each side. In the back, a potbellied stove radiated heat. Beneath a row of coathooks sat Cecil Radenour and a tableful of papers. He stopped writing as they walked in. Cecil was a genial man of plain dress, thinning hair, and expansive sideburns. "I was beginning to think I could finish this whole stack of essays before you got here, Matt. Katie, I take it?" Smiling, he extended his hand to her. "Running late or did the long walk give you both cold feet?"

Matt looked at her.

She was silent.

"Hmmmm." Cecil rocked forward on the balls of his feet, then back. "Well, I'm going to go light some candles." He set off down the aisle. "No matter what we do, we should offer a prayer for Lucy, don't you think?"

From the back of the chapel they watched Cecil light a candle on each side of the chancel railing.

"Is he a minister too?" Katie asked.

Matt shook his head. "He's a teacher at the university. And one of the few male suffragists you'll find west of the Mississippi."

After a long silence she took his arm. "It wouldn't hurt to pray for Lucy."

They stood before the chancel rail and Cecil stood behind it, resting clasped hands on his Bible. He smiled kindly. "Now, then, is this going to be a wedding or a prayer meeting?"

"Neither," Katie said. "I would like you to bear witness for me. To my declaration and--and confession."

"Hmm," Cecil said. "A declaration sounds legal enough for me to handle, but a confession?" He looked suspiciously at Matt.

"We've done each other no wrong," she said quickly. "What I have to confess is a dream. A selfish dream. I dreamed that I would be married in the light of day, before family and friends and all those who've helped me." She was hesitant, self-conscious. "I dreamed that I would, in public, take the arm of this man. That his family and friends would know that he had chosen me without duress, without pity. That I was chosen not because he was fleeing the past but because he was seeking me. It's a woman's dream, a simple thing, but it means much to me."

Cecil nodded. "And what is it you have to declare, Katie?"

She looked at him as if it should be obvious. "A true love for this man, above all others."

"I see." Cecil looked at them both, rocking on his feet again. "Then I think what is called for here is an engagement service, a troth plight I think it was called in the old days. Unfortunately, I don't have a ceremony for that with me, you understand. So you'll have to help me, Katie. Matt, take her hand. Now." He closed his eyes and forged ahead. "Dearly beloved, we are gathered here in the presence of God and man to witness the, hmmm, to acknowledge the love this man and this woman dedicate to each other." He opened his eyes and tilted his head in a questioning look.

Matt nodded.

Cecil went on, speaking thoughtfully. "Now. This love will be sanctified in holy matrimony when the time is appropriate. Is this your promise to each other?"

Matt looked at her. "It is."

"It is," she answered softly.

"Good. This time of waiting will be as important to your marriage as, well, as the budding is to a rose, making all that's beautiful and growing inside unfold over the years in a sacred bloom, always opening. In order to make the wait meaningful, I will ask what each of you wishes the other to learn in this period of engagement. Katie?"

She hesitated.

"No hurry," Cecil said. "Let candor be your guide."

"Well," she said, taking a deep breath, "I'd like him to learn how contrary I am, so he won't overreact when he's expecting agreement. I'd like him to fully understand how maddening my family can be, in case he wishes to nullify our engagement, which he is, of course, free to do for any reason." She looked at him. "Though he must realize such an act would break my heart, force me to function with only a poor remnant of passion, in a state of half-being that is deadly to an actress. To a woman." She had to look away. "I'd like him to know how much happiness his presence gives me, and how forlorn I could become in his absence, so that he learns to use his power kindly on my spirit. I want him to be the strong solace to my sadnesses, the full partner to all my joys. I want—" She stopped, shook her head.

"Amen," Cecil said gently. "Matt?"

He squeezed her hand tight. "What should she learn about me?" he said, looking into the distance. "One thing, I guess, is that

220

I have a temper, but it's quick to rise and quick to fall, and never in my wildest rage would I hurt her, or her child, for I always see her clearly. I can never mistake her for something less. I would never treat her as something less. I would like her to learn to accept my faults, for they're part of who I am, and my judgment, when it's fair. I'd like her to know that she has this power to make me speak from different places in my mind, so that sometimes I say things I haven't thought through, hurtful things, and surprising things sometimes. I like surprising her. I love to hear her laugh. It comes like rain, making me feel thirsty. She feeds my spirit, just standing beside me. I want her with me always, safe with me."

"For now and forever, amen," Cecil said. He cleared his throat and paged through his Bible. "I have a benediction for each of you from Proverbs."

He intoned ancient words of counsel, cadenced with "thee's" and "thine's" and questions of rhetoric that fell like a balm on their raw honesties.

"God speed the moment of marriage," he ended, "when you may be pronounced man and wife."

Matt drew her into an embrace that was warm, all-encompassing.

"How'd I do, you two?" Cecil asked as he snuffed the candles. When they didn't break the kiss to answer, he left them in the dark. "That good."

He was gathering his papers in a satchel when Katie approached to thank him.

"You know, it's just as well," he said. "I brought the marriage certificate but forgot my seal. It's all packed up. I'm leaving tomorrow. I've got a lecture in Chicago."

"I thought your mother could spare some sherry at the house for a toast," Matt said.

"Not for me. I'm going on into town. Besides, I promised your mother I'd pay a visit to Lucy." He buckled his satchel. "Damper the stove. Let's close up." He put on his top hat and locked the chapel doors behind them.

"I'll help you hitch the carriage," Matt said.

Katie went on to the house while the men attended to the

221

horse and carriage. She sat on the porch swing, waiting. The rusty chain creaked a slow, easy rhythm. A bobwhite whistled tentatively for a mate. She saw the lantern appear down the path, then Matt. She took his hand and they went inside, leaving coat and cloak in the hall.

Upstairs, on the pedestal table by the bed, was a tray with two glasses and a decanter of sherry.

He poured their drinks, then tapped her glass with his in a wordless toast. She sipped, savoring the sweetness, but he took the glass from her and began unbuttoning her dress.

She had to use a wet cloth to loosen the bloodied fabric of his shirt. It had stuck to the thin slit the sword had drawn across his chest. Her hands smoothed along the muscles in his back, and her fingers danced across the scar of Vicksburg, deep-creviced behind his shoulder. "It looks so painful."

He drew off his pants. "Easiest pain of the war," he said. "Of every damned thing, the easiest."

She laid her cheek against his back and hugged him. Her nipples tightened, tips hard against his solid warm flesh. She reached around to feel the soft hair of his abdomen, then slid her hand lower, lower. He stood motionless, waiting. Gently, she encircled him, stroking the length of him, hard and swollen and pulsing in rhythm to her touch.

He lay her on the bed, pressing deep inside her. She held him as his lovemaking quickened and grew so stormy, she could no longer stay the path and pace. She fought for breath and thought and a crowning place from which to cry out so he would know he had found her. Reeling, she clung to him, enjoining the tempest, shuddering violently in the wake of its passage.

23

Katie returned to her hotel before dawn, taking the steps at a brisk clip. She let elation escape in one brief whirl of a waltz as she crossed the vacant lobby.

Matt had said she would meet his parents that day. He would announce their engagement to them, then she would tell her family and Poppy.

Betrothed. She could scarcely believe it. And she was not sure she could keep the good news secret from Lin the whole day. Lin was sure to spot excessive contentment in her mistress.

Katie unlocked the door to her suite as quietly as she could, but when the latch clacked closed, Lin came padding out in her white nightdress, long black braid over her shoulder.

"You look worried," Katie said. "Didn't Peg tell you where I'd be?"

Lin nodded. There was a sadness about her, and Katie felt her breath catch. "Beth? Is Beth all right?"

"Yes, yes, Miss Katie. She is fine." Lin turned away.

Katie walked over to her. "Who is not fine?"

Lin took her hand. "Come sit down."

The sun was not far above the horizon when Matt's horse trotted up to the carriage house behind 310 Lucas Place. Seven-thirty, maybe eight, he judged as he dismounted. He'd left his pocket watch at the Radenour house. A wonder he hadn't forgotten something vital. Katie was the only thing on his mind. Remembrance of the night was like a burr on his senses, tingling. She was an intuitive partner, so open in love that he could drown in the gulf of pure feeling, trusting he would not die, for each time he surfaced, she was there, as vulnerable and as invincible as he.

He entered the house through the kitchen. Ravenous, he grabbed bacon and a slice of fresh bread as he ordered breakfast from Cook. He used the back stairs to get to Lucy's room. He knew he'd find his mother there. He was eager to tell her about Katie, eager for them to know each other.

His mother dozed in a chair beside Lucy's four-poster.

Lucy lay half-awake, her copper red hair tangled and wild, one leg stuck out of the covers.

He went over to her and put a hand on her shoulder. "How do you feel?"

She couldn't hold her eyes open. "Rank as a slop mop. Open the curtain. I'm going to get up." She rolled over, groggy, and nuzzled the pillow. "In a minute," she said distantly.

He swagged open the curtains, looking down on part of the front drive. Four horses in harnesses stood there. He couldn't see the wagons they drew. Who would be visiting his father this early?

He went over to waken his mother. She looked fragile in sleep, so unlike the steadfast suffragette who withstood tantrums and roused tempers at the statehouse every year delivering her petitions.

Age had gentled her angular looks. Soft wrinkles pillowed her cheeks and padded the corners of her eyes. She had never been pretty, with her prominent chin and too-broad brow. But she had always been attractive and charming, never lacking in suitors. Why she had chosen a marginally successful land agent like Art Dennigan was a question her friends had asked themselves for thirty-five years.

Her hair was elegantly white now, the lines around her mouth creviced and deep, the worry lines of a peacemaker. How many years of tranquillity had she lost in the war to keep her family together?

He kissed the top of her head and she awakened.

"How are you?" he whispered.

"Stiff." She stretched an arm with deliberate care. "Where were you last night?"

"The Radenours'."

"Cecil stopped by last night and didn't mention a thing to me or his mother."

"I asked him not to. You got my message about the outcome of the fencing match?"

"Oh, yes. Very elucidating. 'I survive.' Period. Not, I was attacked by a human butcher and fought him to the death. Really, Matt. I have to peel potatoes with Cook to get good gossip about you. Looks like you caught a nice blow on the head." She got up to have a look.

"You missed an exciting performance."

"So I hear. But you know your father and I boycott any event with Julian's imprint. Of course, your father was furious when you and Lucy went to Julian's party two weeks ago. Secretly, though, I think he was rather proud that you were so rude you got Julian's goat and a challenge to fight. You men are such boys. I'm so glad I wasn't at the theater last night watching you dance off the point of a sword. Landsakes. No one was sure the fight was real until they saw the police wagons outside. And Dee Dee's maid told Mildred's driver you had a titillating scene with that Juliet, and the driver passed it on to Cook's niece who—"

"Mother, it's a wonder you bother to get a daily newspaper. I do have some good news to tell you that's not on the grapevine or in the paper, so come have breakfast with me."

"I'll be down in a minute. See who's downstairs. I heard wheels in the drive."

He started down the stairs, then slowed when he saw his father step into the foyer, closing the doors to his den. Matt instinctively tensed, on the defense.

Art waited, one hand holding his lapel. "Someone to see you, Matt," he said with cold detachment.

It was a voice of inhuman objectivity and solemn judgment, the voice that had sent Matt fleeing Lucas Place at every opportunity for the warm homestead of the Radenours, or the easy camaraderie of Devlin's street gang. He continued down the stairs cautiously. His father's face was flushed dark, unhealthy-looking. He was livid, and holding it.

Matt opened the doors to the den. Four policemen got up, hats in hand, nods grim. Two took position by the open casement windows, batting down wind-blown chintz. One closed the den doors behind Matt. The fourth officer wore detective sergeant's bars.

Art turned to his son. "The sergeant is interested in your whereabouts last night."

"Why?"

The sergeant ignored his question. "Where were you between, say, 'leven o'clock last night and four this morning?"

"At the Radenours'. I met Cecil out at his mother's place about nine, he left about ten or so. I stayed the night there. I go out to keep an eye on the house for Mrs. Radenour."

"Were you alone?"

Matt hesitated only a moment. "Yes." He would not incriminate Katie or compromise her reputation when their engagement had yet to be announced. Especially when he didn't know the extent of the trouble he felt welling around him, viscid as river muck. "Was it the fencer I fought at the theater? Did he die?"

"No, he's alive," the sergeant said. "It's Edmund Henslowe that's dead."

Edmund. Oh God. Matt thought of Katie, then he stiffened, thinking of himself. "I saved Edmund's life on the stage last night. Why are you questioning me?"

"That sword you used to save him?" The sergeant cleared his throat. "That's the one we found stuck through his heart. You knocked a big piece of filigree off the hilt, remember?"

"I remember," Matt said. "I remember leaving the rapier with my costume in the men's dressing hall of the theater. Anybody could have picked it up."

226

"That's a fact. We understand that. It's just that you threatened to wring Mr. Henslowe's neck last week in front of a dozen people eating their Cornish hens. Why were you so mad at him?"

Matt spoke carefully, aware of the baited question. "I felt Edmund was leading Lucy morally astray."

"In what way, exactly?"

"What 'exactly' do you mean, Sergeant?"

"I mean maybe you didn't want Edmund teaching Lucy to light up an opium pipe like you and he were doing."

Enraged, Matt could barely keep his voice civil. "What the hell are you talking about, me and Edmund?"

"There's a matter of some shirts, Matt. Shirts with your name on them found in a Chinese opium den on Pell Street, New York City. One day last winter. About the same time Edmund Henslowe was frequenting the place."

"Opium?" Art was incredulous. "Our town isn't home to such filthy exotica. You're out of your mind, Sergeant."

"Let's see if I am. Can you explain the shirts and why you were in an opium den, Matt?"

Matt laid a hand on the back of the sofa, just to ensure his steadiness. The muck was shifting.

"Matt," his father said.

Matt turned away. He couldn't reveal the link between Edmund and Julian without compromising the senator's investigation.

"You see," the sergeant went on, after clearing his throat, again in obvious discomfort, "we got some information that your late wife was kind of dependent on opium powder. Laced her laudanum with it. That true?"

Matt felt his father's scrutiny like a candle flame held to his eye. He didn't answer.

"We were thinking you might have picked up the habit from her."

Matt shook his head. "Your thinking's wrong," he said wearily. He ran a hand through his hair. "What else has the bastard trumped up?"

"What bastard?" the sergeant asked.

"The little general who has an army of maggot detectives picking through the refuse heap of a man's life. The little general who can locate a bundle of lost shirts halfway across the country."

Red flared in the sergeant's cheeks. "Mr. Gates was looking into another matter back East, he said, when his specialists came upon your name on a police impoundment list."

"By God, Sergeant," Art exclaimed, "you're telling me Julian Gates is behind this?" For the first time he looked at Matt as if there was a slight chance he might not be guilty. "What more damning evidence could you possibly have against my son, gentlemen?" he demanded, precise and cold.

The sergeant put on a look of reluctance. "Well, the fencer Matt fought last night, he came to early this morning. Confessed it was Matt who hired him for that ruckus last night."

" 'Confessed.' " Matt couldn't help smiling. The situation was hopeless. *Julian, you bastard.*

"The fencer's a bully for hire from Chicago," the sergeant said. "Told us Matt wanted him to get rid of Edmund Henslowe."

"This fencer didn't happen to tell you why he tried to kill me, his supposed employer, did he?"

The sergeant shrugged. "Said he was supposed to turn on you so people wouldn't suspect you set it up. Said *you* tried to kill *him.*"

"I see. Well, he didn't happen to tell you how I knew exactly what Julian's costume would look like so I could have a duplicate made, did he?"

"No," the sergeant said.

"And he didn't mention how I knew Julian would go out for air at the precise moment the impostor needed to change identities with him?"

The sergeant tossed his head, impatient. "Now see here, the investigation's just started."

"Let me give you some free advice, Sergeant. You'd better hurry back to the hospital and talk to that fencer real quick. He's going to die."

"How do you know?"

"Julian's not one to let any man outlive his usefulness."

The sergeant was quiet.

"You might want to see that as personal advice," Matt added.

228

The sergeant looked him in the eye. "We better get you down to the station for a statement."

Matt heard a promise of retribution in his words. The ride was going to be rough.

"Sergeant." Art put his hand on the officer's shoulder, not in friendliness, but to ensure his attention. "I'll have my attorney meet you there."

Two policemen preceded Matt to the door. The third fell in behind him, while the sergeant hung back to talk to Art.

"This all might seem like a peculiar situation to you, Mr. Dennigan, but it's not to me," the sergeant was saying. "In every murder, one man's innocence hangs on another man's lies. Trick is to find out who's deceiving who, you understand."

As he reached the door, Matt turned suddenly and stiff-armed the policeman behind him. He ducked past the startled sergeant and headed for the window.

"Stop him!" the sergeant yelled, regaining his balance.

Matt jumped through the open window and rolled across the juniper hedge. As he'd hoped, three policemen straggled out the window in his wake. He wanted them following him for a while. It would make it harder for the sergeant to draw a bead on him if his own men were in the line of fire.

But the blast of the revolver came straightaway. Lead stung a tree to the right of him. He heard one of the officers behind him slow and mutter "Jesus."

He ran faster, rounding the corner of the house and hurtling breakneck down the hill to the carriage house and his still saddled horse, three men on his tail.

The police revolver fired twice more, resounding like thunder in the morning peace of Lucas Place.

24

The arched ceiling of the auditorium rose cold and high. Katie sat in the front row alone. The stage before her was empty, curtain closed.

From the wings came muted thumps of movement. All of Poppy had straggled there, singly and in groups, unable to grieve properly in their hotel rooms, unable, once they were there, to do nothing. The work went on, half-heartedly, half-guiltily, for any soul who had ever worked with Edmund had wished him a long sojourn in hell.

Katie wasn't sure that's where her brother had gone. She couldn't quite believe that he was gone at all. There was too much of the immortal Puck and prankster about him to believe the stillness of the body that had been heaved into the back of a wagon and taken to the mortuary that morning.

There was no doubting the sword though. It was the one Matt had used. The police had checked with Tobias. They had, in fact, talked with all the cast and crew, except immediate family members. Peg was in bed at the hotel, on the verge of hysteria. Their father was there at the theater, alternating tears and tantrums with each flask. And Katie had been pressed so quickly to take charge and make arrangements, she wouldn't be questioned until the next day. No doubt they thought she was too numb to make sense now anyway.

Julian hadn't come to the theater, but he had sent a note. It had been addressed to Alleyn, but the messenger had delivered it to Katie. She had skimmed it, fearful that if she dwelled on his words, the memory of the scene in her dressing room would rise too strong and make her physically ill. Julian had written little, anyhow. Only that he was distressed by their loss, that they were to come to him immediately for anything they needed, and that he hoped the premiere would go on as scheduled.

Katie leaned her head back. How could Edmund be gone? she wondered. How could he be gone, taking with him a day that should have been one of her happiest? She had a future to plan. What are we to do now, Matt? Why did you run? Why didn't you tell the police we were together?

Tobias appeared in the alcove that led from the stage to the seating floor. "Someone to see you, Katie," he said officially. He pantomimed, Want me to get rid of them?

She shook her head. "No. I'm all right." He left and a white-haired woman came down the remaining alcove steps with a firm hand on the bannister. Katie suddenly realized how dark the area was. "Tobias," she called. "House lights front, please." She felt so heavy. Summoning strength, she gripped the chair arms and pushed herself upright.

The fiftyish-looking woman coming toward her had a vitality she envied that day. She held out a gloved hand. "Miss Henslowe? I'm Hellie Dennigan."

Katie scrutinized Matt's mother as she spoke.

"I've come to convey my sincere condolences on your loss."

Matt had his mother's deep brown eyes.

"I've also come to assure you my son is not responsible for your brother's death."

And direct manner.

"I do not fault your son in this," Katie said.

"Everyone else does, my dear. You and your family were the ones I wanted to reassure most."

Katie nodded once, weary. There was an awkward silence. "How is Lucy faring?" she asked.

"Very fit," Hellie said, then sighed. "Fit enough for another night on the town, it seems."

"Do you know what caused her illness?"

"She and your brother were lunching with Julian and she apparently had some bad salmon."

"No one else was taken ill?"

Hellie shook her head. "Julian sent a note saying he had fired, and fined, his chef for the embarrassment."

"I'm glad Lucy's a sturdy girl."

"Strong, all right, especially in her ways. I raised her to be independent, but I'm afraid she's too free-willed for her own good." Hellie paused. "That's apparently an alluring quality for a certain kind of man."

"Mrs. Dennigan, I know my brother was not the best influence on Lucy. But you don't have to worry anymore, do you?" Katie inhaled carefully, easing air past the hard knot in her throat. "None of us have to worry anymore."

"I'm sorry, dear," Hellie said quietly. "Actually, I came here because Lucy said Matt had approached you at Julian's party. And I had heard that there was, well, a very engaging bit of drama between you two on stage last night, and to be quite frank, Miss Henslowe, I was hoping you would know where my son is right now."

Katie shook her head. "I prayed you would know."

Hellie looked at her a long moment. "Sit down, dear." She eased Katie into the chair, then sat beside her. "I hope you won't mind if I join you. It's not fair, is it? Your loss, my loss. Things were going so well. Not so much between Matt and his father, but with everyone else. Seeing Matt with my friends, hearing them talk about him. It was so good to have him back. He's a good man, Miss Henslowe. People have never made it very easy for him to show it. His father, especially. But Art was surprisingly calm about Matt

232

escaping the police like he did. I think it was a decidedly stupid idea."

"Sometimes the only thing one can do is run."

"I've never known that intense a feeling of entrapment that I could not stand and fight," Hellie said firmly.

Katie looked at Hellie, a strong and confident woman who had spent all her life in the arena of the privileged. "Then you've never been in real trouble, Mrs. Dennigan."

"Matt is, isn't he?" Hellie cleared her throat. "The police said something about shirts left in an opium den in New York. And then there's Sarah, his wife and her tendency to . . ." Her voice trailed off. "Sarah died. I don't know whether Matt too, was—"

"Matt never had an addiction, Mrs. Dennigan. Nor does he now."

Hellie closed her eyes for a moment, grateful. "Hellie. Please call me Hellie." She paused. "If Matt gets in touch with you, I beg you to let me know that he's all right."

"I doubt he can get a message to me. I'm being watched. The police, I think. Maybe Julian's men."

"Julian? What in heaven's name has Matt gotten you involved in?"

"It's not Matt." Katie tried to smile. "It's Edmund." All of them were left swimming in Edmund's wake. Even Julian. It was Edmund's legacy, this big black sea.

"You look so frightened."

"It mustn't show," Katie said, "I can't let it show."

Hellie gathered her close, and Katie felt the sting of tears at her maternal comfort.

"People think grief is for funerals," Hellie said. "Grief is for every time you fight the memory of what you lost. One day you just have to stop fighting and see what's gone in all its glory, in all its weakness. I lost my son, you know, my older son. Angelic boy, Paul. So agreeable. Always ready to do what you wanted. He didn't seem to have wants of his own. That always scared me. Satisfied Art, of course.

"Paul died six years ago. All three of my men went to war in '61. You don't know how terrified I was. Art had a post in Springfield, Illinois. He pulled some strings and arranged for Paul to be sent to a garrison in Cairo, someplace safe, he said. He didn't have many strings left to help Matt. Matt went down the Mississippi under Halleck and spent his first year sending us letters about running reconnaissance and dodging snipers. That first winter in the garrison, Paul caught pneumonia. He died before New Year's, in '61. Art just about died when he heard. Matt kept fighting. Corinth. Vicksburg. Fought under Grant. Art thought Matt would be safe there, the general was such a good friend. But Vicksburg was where Matt was hit in the leg and he kept fighting. A shell exploded beside him. Shrapnel tore into his back."

"I know," Katie said. "It's a terrible scar."

"I wouldn't know," Hellie said. "I've never seen it."

Katie pulled away, but Hellie kept hold of her hand. "You have a little girl, don't you?"

Katie only nodded, unable to speak, to explain.

"It's all right, dear. A mother likes to know certain things about her children no matter how old they are. Not to interfere, you understand. Just to know."

Katie got up. "I didn't want to meet you like this. We wanted to tell you—"

"Hellie!"

A man's voice boomed through the auditorium.

"Art!" Hellie turned in her seat.

Her husband strode quickly down the aisle, braking his descent with his cane and nearly losing the top hat hugged to his chest. He was tall, a robust man with the posture of a flagstaff. His chestnut hair was streaked white and greased flat.

"Lucy told me where you were," he said to his wife, "and I didn't believe her. Here? In this monument to Julian's mendacity? What's gotten into you?"

"You old scold. Dastardly manners. This is a time of mourning for Miss Henslowe. Katie's a friend of Matt's, Art. A good friend."

"My condolences on your brother's passing." Art fiercely scrutinized Katie as he took her hand. "You have to understand that sometimes things happen for the best. From what I hear, he was a miserable soul."

"Art!"

"I'm sorry. I'm no hypocrite. I give no more respect to a man when he's dead than when he's alive."

So this was the unforgiving presence Matt had fought so hard to escape, Katie thought. "That makes you an unusually fair man," she said, "or an unusually cold one. Most people balance their affections with a little regard for circumstance."

Readying a retort, Art jutted his chin high.

"Art. Katie." Hellie started to intercede when a crash in the wings startled them all.

"Get me another bloody chair!" Alleyn yelled. The curtain billowed wildly outward as someone behind searched for the center seam. "I need my peace!" Alleyn cried. "I need peace to think about my boy." He elbowed through the curtain, dragging a straight-backed chair onto the stage.

Bleary-eyed, he tried to focus on the three people in the auditorium. He dragged the chair to the forestage, close to the footlights. "He was my boy!" He stumbled and caught himself. "My dearest boy! Do you hear?" Alleyn called out piteously. "My boy is dead. My boy is dead."

"Mr. and Mrs. Dennigan," Katie said quickly, "I think it would be best if you —"

Her father's booming oration drowned her words. " 'What means these masterless and gory swords to lie discolored by this place of peace? Romeo! O, pale!' " Alleyn groped his way to his seat, genuinely unsteady. " 'And steep'd in blood?—Ah, what an unkind hour is guilty of this lamentable chance!' " He drew from his coat pocket an open flask, the cap loose and clanking on its tether. "Romeo dead." He raised the flask, looking at Katie. "But Juliet lives." A tear rolled down his cheek. "Juliet lives."

He took a long noisy pull on the bottle and worked his lips. "We are doomed, Katie." He rocked the flask in his hand, listening for liquid. It was empty. "He was our light, our brightest hope." He patted the bottle reverently and slipped it back in his pocket. "The fount of a glory we shall never know." He rose and staggered close to the footlights. "No one was his equal. No one!"

He peered over the lights. "You there!" He pointed an imperious, wavering finger at Art. "You, sir! What are you staring at? Have you never seen a father with his heart's blood leached right out of his chest? That is a man without a son, sir. A man without his noble Edmund, grandest of boys, poetic of soul, renowned in his art, an admirable human being, without peer, sir. Without peer."

Alleyn slumped back into the chair, hooking his arm across the back. "We must take him to his public, Katie! We must bury him where we began, in Philadelphia!" He lurched up again. "Where he stepped off the boat reciting Hamlet, my little prodigy, my Edmund. How the papers praised him. How they loved him then." He reached for his flask, upending it, not remembering it was empty. "They would have loved him again. He was on the verge." He staggered into the wings, frowning at his flask. "On the verge."

Katie wasn't sure how long they stood there in silence. "You must excuse my father," she said at last, her voice thin.

Hellie didn't answer. Her face was pinched and tight, and she was looking at her husband. "Sometimes a father has a child who's just a dream," she said. A sheen moistened her eyes. "I can understand that."

Art stepped forward and took his wife's arm. "Hellie." His voice cracked, like ice beginning to thaw. "Let's go."

"A minute," Hellie whispered, pulling a handkerchief from her cuff.

He was clearly uncomfortable at his wife's distress. "You know we have an important dinner guest tonight," he said.

"He's just an old army friend of yours to me." She sniffled, then reached inside the worn leather case she carried. "I want Katie to sign my petition for equality," she said, pulling out a big fountain pen and a ribbon-bound sheaf of papers. "I'm sure she believes women should have equal voting rights. You do, don't you, Katie?"

Katie took the pen, knowing that whether women should and whether they would be enfranchised were two different things. She didn't dare dash Hellie's hopes, though.

The older woman slowly riffled the stiff parchment sheets, passing hundreds of names, until she came to the end. "Here." She pointed, and Katie signed dutifully. Hellie blew her name dry.

"Miss Henslowe." Art reached inside his vest coat and withdrew an envelope. "This telegram came for Matt today. I wouldn't want him coming round the house just yet." He cleared his throat. "Police, you know."

Katie took the telegram, noticing that it had been opened. She tucked it into her pocket, in safekeeping with the key Edmund had given her the night before. "Mr. Dennigan, did Matt tell you anything about the important project he's working on?"

Art cleared his throat and busied himself brushing his top hat and putting it on. "We don't talk much, Miss Henslowe. Hellie?" He held out his arm.

Hellie hesitated. "Come visit, Katie. Bring your little girl."

Art began escorting her up the aisle.

"Beth. Her name is Beth," Katie called, hating the hopefulness in her voice.

Hellie looked back and smiled.

That afternoon, Katie gave in to melancholy. She felt drawn to the hotel suite that had been Edmund's. Zemin did not answer her knock, but the door was unlocked.

The acrid spice of incense wafted around her as she stepped into the room. A dozen candle stubs burned on a low, makeshift altar.

Zemin knelt on the floor before the altar. He was barefoot and his hair was wild and disheveled. The wicker valise that held Edmund's pipe was open beside him.

"Sit down, Miss Katie," he said.

His voice seemed to come from a distance, and she wondered if he had been smoking. She joined him on the floor. On a bed tray in front of them he had arranged small framed Oriental prints in stair-step order, using stacks of books to create an ascending hierarchy. On the pinnacle sat a photograph of Edmund, one she had never seen, taken before he had grown sallow and thin. He was caught in dramatic pose, wickedly handsome even though his costume was paltry, one of Poppy's interchangeable stock robes. He was in his attitude of malediction, arm raised, palm outward, a frown of ferocious intent on his face. She recognized his Hamlet, the tormented Dane, calling down curses on the head of the King who had wronged him.

Around the photograph curled stone necklaces and strips of ribbon embroidered with strange symbols. Between two brass bowls lay Edmund's precious tortoise-shell pipe.

"I washed him before they came for him," Zemin said. "I made him ready."

It was a minute before she could speak. "Thank you."

"They will not dress him properly."

"What do you mean? I thought you already sent them his best suit."

"I did. But will they place a coin beneath his tongue? The spirit world is like the world of men. Comfort must be bought. And his right hand must close around a twig of willow to sweep all demons from his path. In his left hand a handkerchief. Every man on a journey needs a fine handkerchief."

She could see now that Zemin was sober, but that he was suspended above a great depth of grief like a man on a tightrope, alone in the air. She reached into her pocket and withdrew the tiny key Edmund had given her the night before. The ribbon was red, like the ones on the altar. "Do you know what this key fits, Zemin?"

He glanced at the key, at her, then his gaze returned to the candles. "I had wondered where he hid it. I looked for it."

"Does it fit the pipe box?" she asked.

"I have the key for that. Only me. So that Master Edmund would not take *ya p'ien* without my knowledge and my help."

Katie rose in sudden anger. "Why, Zemin? Why did you ever begin to 'help' Edmund in that way?"

"I had to. He was seeking, always seeking, further away from us. You cannot imagine the kinds of things he sought. Lowly people. Dirty people. There is not enough world for a man like Edmund. He asked once about *ya p'ien*. I honored his request. And I knew that it would make him seek closer to home because he would be satisfied exploring the darkness inside. There's much pleasure in that for a man like Edmund. He was a smart man. The mind of a smart man holds many passages."

"Oh, Zemin." She felt deeply weary. "And what do you think he found there?"

"Jewels sometimes, rare things. He would smile. Or great monsters. I could see him pushing them away. Sometimes he screamed. They tried to push him off a cliff into the black sky, he said. Great winged wolves and crawling fish with tiger's fangs. He fought them. Great men have great monsters."

"Zemin, your cure only made him more sick, can't you see that? And I will not let you, or Julian Gates, make more people sick."

Zemin rose and bowed to her. "With all due respect, Miss Katie, this is man's business."

"By God in heaven, it'll be police business!" she shouted. "If you don't help me stop the opium smuggling you and Edmund have begun, I'll—"

He bowed again and held out his hand. "Give me the key. I'll get you the letter."

"What letter?"

"A witnessed copy of the shipment order to Chu King-Sing. The letter incriminates Julian. Edmund told Julian he could purchase it from us at a fair price. The document is in a safety deposit box. That is what the key fits. Only I can open it now. Edmund authorized me, with legal notary."

She frowned, studying him. "Legal notary. Witnessed copies. Edmund must have been thinking with a very clear head the past few months. Funny none of the rest of us picked up on how down-to-earth he'd gotten."

Zemin looked away, uncomfortable. "Edmund relied on me for such things."

"For the idea of blackmail and its execution?"

He did not answer.

"When did you lose respect for him, Zemin?"

He glanced at her, puzzled.

"He is Edmund to you now, not 'master' or 'mister,' your employer."

Zemin's eyes narrowed and his mouth turned down at the corners, as if he were holding back tears. "He was my friend," he said ardently, choking. "Always, my greatest friend. No one else."

239

She was quiet a moment, not remembering a time when Edmund had publicly treated Zemin with the respect due a friend. Slowly, she handed over the key. "Go to the bank tomorrow and bring me the letter."

"What are you going to do with it?"

"I'm not sure yet. I would like you to accompany Father and me on the trip East for Edmund's burial. I'm sure Edmund would have wanted you there."

Zemin nodded.

"We leave the day after tomorrow." She started toward the door, then stopped, remembering the phrase Edmund had made her repeat when he gave her the key. "One last question, Zemin. What is 'the Eighteenth Lohan'?"

Zemin turned to the altar and picked up one of the framed prints, the one on the step below Edmund's photograph. The ink drawing showed an Oriental man riding a tiger.

"It is Po-lo-t'o-she."

"Who?"

"One of the perfect disciples of Buddha. He had mighty power over wild beasts and strength to triumph over evil. Edmund admired him above all others." Zemin paused, then he picked up some slips of paper, each about four inches square. "Here, Miss Katie." He handed them to her. In the middle of each were stamped patches of gold leaf.

"It is joss paper," Zemin said. "It turns to real gold in the spirit world."

He knelt and placed his offering papers in one of the brass bowls. Katie placed hers in another. Solemnly, he lit fire to one and dropped it in his bowl. She did the same to hers.

As the offerings flared, the spice paste smell of the incense nearly overwhelmed her. She had to leave, before grief dropped her to her knees at the altar of her brother.

25

In the hallway Katie saw Lin with a tray of tea. "Is that for Peg?"

"Yes," Lin said, her voice hushed, funereal.

"I'll take it in."

In her room Peg sat in a chair by the window.

Katie set the tray on the bedstand, then crossed to Peg. Her sister's eyes had a burning red rim. Katie put a hand on her shoulder.

Peg looked down and rolled her handkerchief into a tighter ball. "Was everyone at the New Gate today?"

"Most everyone. Some of the supers even dropped by."

"Did Tobias make sure the battens for act two were finished?"

"I don't know. It wasn't a good time to bother him about it, Peg."

"But I told him to last night. When we were standing there watching the doctor bandage Edmund." Her voice trembled. "The doctor said he was fine. It was a surface wound."

"Don't, Peg."

"Nothing serious."

"Don't torture yourself."

"I have to." Peg got up. "I feel like I have to grieve for both of us. You never loved him like I did."

Katie turned to the window. "No, I didn't." She looked out, trying to summon a vision of her brother. She didn't want to see him, though. She didn't want to see him even in memory. "I couldn't love him. Not like you."

"Why?"

"Your tea's getting cold." She closed her eyes, shutting out the sight of Peg, hovering expectantly.

"You have to tell me now." Peg's voice was soft, sure. "Edmund can't lie anymore. Neither can you. You hated him, deep down."

"I couldn't trust him, deep down." *Remember.* "Just leave it at that, Peg."

"No. It was the day of the fire."

"Peg."

"Start it. The day of the fire . . ."

"I told you. I told everyone. The lamp fell. I knocked it over. I'm sorry for that. I've never been so sorry for anything in my whole life." She whirled to face Peg. "Can't you understand that? I'm sorry!"

"I know that, Katie." Soft. Her voice was soft. "I want to know how the lamp fell."

"It just—" She saw it flying across the room, the little dressing room. She heard the glass globe break. "It broke."

"You and Edmund were rehearsing."

She felt the tug of Peg's persistence. It wasn't her voice, her questions. It was her right to know.

"Shrew," Katie said. "Edmund was running me through the lines for *Shrew."* She shook her head. "I kept forgetting."

"Father didn't give you enough time. He switched shows on us. He said the farmers and smiths needed a farce to make them laugh. Hamlet was too gloomy."

"Hamlet was too gloomy," Katie echoed as the strong tide of time tugged her backward. She felt weak, deeply weakened by Edmund's passing, as if she were standing alone in a ring. No one to fight. No chance for her to win.

Peg prompted her. "I wanted to play Katherine, sassy Kate,

untamed shrew. But Father wouldn't let me. I still had to play boys. You were the one growing breasts. You were the one who was thirteen."

"Yes," she whispered. *Quite the young lady.*

"You had a grace that made you seem older when you were on stage. Everyone noticed it. Everyone knew you were going to be a wonderful actress."

Katie nodded woodenly, like a doll, like the soft-bodied doll she had slept with every night. *Younger,* she told Peg silently. *I wanted to be younger, flatter, with nipples small as acorn caps, without the globe that fills a hand.*

"I remember it was cold that day," Peg continued. "Mother put a little iron brazier in your dressing room, didn't she?"

"She brought in hot coals from the cookstove," Katie said distantly, seeing her mother bustle in, her dress a drab wool, her face lined with worries, her smile small and warm. " 'Now, don't let Edmund hog the heat,' she said. 'You dress close to the stove. Don't want my baby catching cold.'

"It never got warm," Katie said, "because it wasn't a room. It was just four blankets hung on lines. Edmund was mad. He said he deserved a theater, not a barn." *I'm wasted here, Katie. You understand that. You've always understood. You listen so well.*

"I think he was a little tipsy that day," Peg said.

Would you like a drink, Katie? It's time you too carried on the inebriate tradition of the Henslowes.

No, Edmund.

You are getting older now. Quite the young lady.

"Drunk or sober," Katie said bitterly, "he was always ordering us around."

"Yes, we had to brush his shoes when he went out, bring his plate when he was hungry, rub his forehead when his head hurt."

"He was mad." She looked out the window again, not at Peg. "Furious. He didn't like my delivery. He wanted Kate's long, devout speech of wifely obedience to Petruchio. I made her too strong." *Kate was his equal. His better.* "Finally, I said we had to stop so I could change for the seven o'clock. He said he wasn't leaving until I did Katherine's lines right. 'Petruchio's Kate, by the end, stands tame,' he said. He had that floating look behind his eyes, you know, like someone else was hiding in his head." *Like none of his actions, his thoughts, even words, would be truly his, truly controlled.*

"He wouldn't leave." She raised her shoulder to her cheek, in a childlike shrug of discomfort. "He just wouldn't leave. I took Katherine's costume out of the trunk. He jerked the dress out of my hands.

" 'Fie, fie, too willful a Kate,' he said. 'Thy husband is thy lord, thy life, thy keeper, thy head, thy sovereign. One that cares for thee and for thy maintenance commits his body to painful labor whilst thou li'st warm at home.'

" 'Is that fair, Katie?' he asked. 'Is it fair that my little sister shares star billing tonight and takes applause which my talent and my experience alone have earned?'

"I told him it was Father's idea for me to debut as the shrew.

"He said, 'Father's desperate. He's been waiting for you to grow womanly enough to take all of Thea's roles. Your mother's a ghastly actress.'

"I nearly hit him. 'Get out!' I yelled.

" 'Not until you convince me Kate can relent. Here.' He picked up the skullcap to Katherine's costume and clapped it on my head. 'Katherine, that cap of yours becomes you not. Off with that bauble, throw it under foot.'

"Time was short. I threw off the cap to get him out of there.

"He came closer and stuck out his foot. 'Katherine, my shoe doth need the brush. Bend to it.'

"I flicked it with my kerchief. 'Enough,' I said.

"He came closer. 'I will say when enough is enough, Katherine. That lamp doth hurt thy lord Petruchio's eyes. Lower it.' "

Katie stopped, staring out the window for a long time, watching her younger self. "I did. I turned down the lamp. Everything shrank. The room got smaller, closer. His voice changed with the light. It got deeper, rippling. It was like a pool. 'Katherine, my collar hath lost its tuck. Come crease it round for me.' "

Peg was still, as if suspended on a ledge.

"I reached up," Katie said softly. "He was so tall. He took my hand. He kissed it."

Peg shook her head wildly. "He was acting. You both were acting."

"He said, 'Katie, Katie, my bonny Katie, prettiest Katie in Christendom, myself am moved to woo thee.' "

"Acting," Peg whispered.

"I felt so odd. 'Those lines are for the play,' " I said.

"He smiled. 'I am no player, bonny Katie. Neither are you.' "

" 'I am your sister,' " I said.

" 'And I your brother, but only by half. Half a brother. Have you never wondered what the other half is made of?' "

Peg stubbornly shook her head again, turning from Katie.

Katie breathed the words. "He said, 'Half is a man, like any other man.' "

"No," Peg said.

"Yes," Katie whispered, staring at her sister. "We worshipped him. He was our idol, wasn't he, Peggy?"

"No," Peg said. "No, no, no." She sank to the floor. "No." She rocked furiously, helplessly. "No."

"Idolatry is a sin," Katie said. "I knew that. I tried to remember that. But he said things. His voice was a river and we were both flowing past something. I was scared. I couldn't move. He opened my dress. He put his hand on my breast. 'Growing up, aren't we, Katie?' he said.

"I shook my head. I was swaying. My knees were buckling. I had no balance. He had to hold me up. I was drowning. I reached out for something, to get away. It was dark. So dark. I leaned away to reach the lamp, to turn it up, to make the light come back so I could see.

" 'No, Katie.' He slapped my hand away. He slapped it hard and it hit the lamp and sent it flying across the room. It hit the floor right beside the brazier. The kerosene burst into flame instantly and I knew it was over. I wasn't going to drown anymore. We were going to burn."

She made her way to the bed, trying to sit on it. Her hand slipped, and she slid stiffly to the floor.

245

Peg crawled over to her. "Katie."

Katie felt her sister prodding, kneading, trying to gather her close. She slipped all the way to the floor, lying on her side, and Peg curved an arm around her. She smoothed her hair. "Katie?"

"I tried to stop it," she said softly. "I threw a pitcher of water on it. But one of the hanging blankets had already caught. I screamed, 'Fire!' over and over. And I heard other people panicking. I knew you were asleep in the loft in the back. I told Edmund to get you. 'Get Peggy!' I shouted. Then I ran to the front of the hall and pulled the fire bell. I pulled and I pulled and everyone was running and screaming and I tried to get back to the dressing room, but the flames were everywhere. I ran outside. Mother and Father were there, looking for us. Edmund was there too, getting people into line for the water buckets. I jerked him out of the line. 'Where's Peggy?' I asked. He just looked at the barn, the barn bellowing smoke, crackling and popping. I pounded him. I screamed at him. 'Help me find her!' He pushed me away."

"No." Peg wept. "No. Not true. Edmund came for me."

"I ran back to the barn. Mother screamed at me. I kept running. I ducked under a stall door. I saw you up there, peeking over the edge of the loft. You'd stopped screaming, you were so scared. You looked so small, Peggy. You were so still, and the flames running everywhere, dancing, always moving. They were starting on the ladder. 'Climb down! Quick!' I yelled at you, it felt like a hundred times. You wouldn't move. 'Come get me, Katie!' That's all you said. 'Come get me.' I couldn't, Peggy. I couldn't. I went to pull over a bale of hay so you could jump. But you jumped. You jumped before I was ready."

"I thought—I thought you were—leaving me," she said. "I couldn't see you. I thought you left me alone—I was at the edge. I wanted to get out. I—just—jumped."

Katie was silent.

"Edmund came then," Peg said. "He came and carried me out."

"Edmund came, because Mother made him. Bester told me afterwards. Father had to practically sit on her to keep her from following me in. She begged Edmund to get us, both of us. Edmund picked you up and passed right by me, never looked back. From

246

that day on, he never really looked at me again. He was your hero. And I didn't mind." She whispered, "I was happy to lose him. It's just that—I lost you too."

Peg was crying again, and Katie lay quiet, emptied. Suddenly she raised herself off Peg's lap. "Am I hurting your leg?"

Peg shook her head emphatically. A tear dropped onto Katie's hand. "I'm so sorry. Your poor leg." She stroked the maimed knee through Peg's skirt.

"It wasn't your fault."

"It was. All our props, gone to ashes. Old trunks of jester bells and fairy robes, harridan rags and good doublets, everything Mother had sewn, was burned. It was my mistake. I turned down the light and couldn't see. I always wanted to tell you that. Never be alone in the dark with Edmund. But I knew he'd never hurt you. He needed you to love him, believe in him. He knew I never would. I could see inside him. In every corner he tried to hide. He drank to make it blurry. He smoked to dream it away. But I knew how small he was. I knew because he had made me small too. He made me so small."

"Oh, God." Peg tried to catch breath to speak. "Oh, God, Katie."

Peg rocked her, rocked them both.

The next morning Katie awoke to Beth's tiny fingers tickling her cheek. "Mommy, wake up now," Beth half whispered. "Let's play."

"Hmmm." Katie gathered her close and tried to catch a few more minutes of rest. She and Peg had talked late into the night, late, long, and hard.

Beth, however, squirmed and rolled, jiggling the bed and jostling her mother until sleep was out of the question. Suddenly, Beth rose straight up out of the covers like a gopher. "Mommy! I see some breakfast! There's jelly." She scampered across the bed and slid off the side in a chute of blankets.

Katie lay still, guessing that Lin had left a tray before she went errand-running in preparation for Katie's trip east for Edmund's burial.

"Coffee, Mommy?"

A cup bottom clinked into a saucer, and Katie rose immediately. She couldn't have Beth pouring hot coffee. She set out biscuits and jelly while Beth went to get her carrying case of picture bricks.

"Which picture are you going to put together this morning?" Katie asked.

"Piggies," Beth said, already poring over one of the twelve puzzle cubes to find a portion of the barnyard pigpen.

"What a smart girl you are," Katie said when Beth completed the picture of a nursing sow and her piglets.

Beth grabbed a brick showing two contented piglets and hid it under the table.

"Oh, no," Katie said. "Now the picture's not finished. Two piggies ran away."

"They're dead," Beth said solemnly.

"I see."

"My daddy is dead."

Katie paused. "Yes."

"Uncle Edmund got dead too. Gone." Beth showed her empty hands. "All gone."

"What's Mother Pig going to do?"

"Be sad."

"Will her piglets ever come back?"

"Look!" Beth ducked under the table. "Here they come. Here they come all the way home!" She completed the picture again.

Katie watched her daughter as Beth fiddled with the blocks. "Mother Pig is lucky," she said. "She's a puzzle. Her pieces can always come back. I could cry a long time, and Aunt Peggy and your grandpa could too, but Uncle Edmund can never come back. Neither can your father."

Beth was quiet a moment, then she scattered the picture bricks. "Do the ducks now," she said impatiently.

By the time Lin returned, they had completed ducks in the pond, horses in the meadow, and Katie was on the floor helping set up a parade of carved animals for Noah's Ark. With Beth in her lap, she leaned back and rolled a stiff shoulder. She felt as if she had already worked a full day.

"Has Tobias already gone to the theater?" she asked Lin.

"No. He's still here."

"Good. Tell him I need him to walk Zemin to the bank, to protect him."

"From what?" Lin asked anxiously.

"It's just a precaution. Zemin is getting a letter for me." She paused. "I'll be going out about sundown, Lin."

"Where?"

"Don't worry. I'll be safe. Please have all my things packed and transferred to the train by tomorrow morning. I may not be home tonight."

"But where will you be?"

Katie nuzzled her chin in Beth's soft curls. "I wish I knew."

26

Katie paced the levee road in front of the wharf. It was nearly sundown.

Where were the children?

She had dressed unobtrusively in a dark skirt, shawl, and plain bonnet. Smoothing her skirt, she felt the reassuring stiffness of the papers in the pocket Lin had quickly stitched inside her petticoat. She was carrying the telegram from Senator Cahill and the blackmail letter Zemin had retrieved from the safety deposit box. Zemin had handed it over with great reluctance that morning.

On the waterfront below the levee, stewards lowered gangways on the decks of paddle steamers. Stevedores yelled warnings as block-and-tackle rigs clanked slowly dockward.

She watched the alleyways and feeder streets that led to the levee road from downtown. At last, a little street Arab appeared at the mouth of an alley. Soon, more appeared, rounding the corner of the brick factory. And more.

Ragged match girls carried empty wooden trays; bootblacks hoisted step cases on leather straps. The flower maids were pale,

German or Northern European, while the girls who peddled fruits and nuts were Italians with eyes as dark as blackthorn.

The raggedy bands had a disquieting similarity, even though their skin ranged from African ebony to Irish porcelain. They were either lean and anxious or cocky and aggressive.

Katie studied each one straggling past. She had hoped to recognize the youngster Matt had employed as a watcher at the theater, but she couldn't pick him out. As the clusters began to thin, she walked across the street and joined the flow of nomadic children.

They seemed divided more by age than race. Younger ones carried remnants of their peddling jobs: newspapers, rags, combs, and needles. The older youths showed no evidence of having worked at anything legitimate that day.

Farther ahead, youths leaned insolently against a derelict brick building. The skinniest of the boys wore the best piece of clothing —a dirty plaid vest with the buttons gone. A tarnished gold chain draped from a safety pin to his watch pocket. The skinny boy suddenly arched away from the wall like a worm unsticking itself. He approached Katie slowly, warily.

She stopped and waited for him.

The boy pointed down the street toward the vacant lots and boarded-up buildings. "If you're lost, ma'am, you're gonna get loster, you keep walking this way." He had blue eyes and a bush of black hair. His accent carried barely a trace of the Emerald Isle from which he, or his parents, had emigrated.

"I need to see Devlin," she said, using the name as confidently as Matt had the night the rivermen had ransacked Edmund's dressing room.

"Who's Devlin?" the boy asked.

"The man with whom I have business to discuss," she said precisely. "Lucrative business."

"Maybe you have some lucre for me."

"Clever boy. But a clever lady doesn't pay until service is rendered."

The boy considered her for a moment, then said, "Follow me." Stiff and nervous, he gave one look behind them and set off, leading the way.

"What's your name?" she asked.

"Andrew."

"I appreciate your help very kindly, Andrew."

His smile was odd. "Think nothing of it."

Dark was descending fast. There were no lampposts, no sidewalks. She stumbled often on debris in the narrow street.

Bedraggled children played raucously in front of the row houses along one side of the street, fighting with sticks and clapping Merry Macs with dirty hands and epithet rhymes. She saw a few lethargic women sitting in doorways, their shoetops drooping, stocking tears visible. Rivermen strolled the street in pairs, scrutinizing the stoops for the best possibilities of the night.

Most of the working children seemed drawn to the other side of the street. Andrew passed four row houses on that side, then slipped through a narrow alleyway beside the fifth. The three-story building had a door set high in the wall. There were no steps, just a pile of rotting railroad ties that could be climbed to the doorway. Andrew scrambled up them and gave the door a boot. It opened onto a dark hallway.

"C'mon," he said.

Katie hesitated, sensing the presence of many young watchers, and maybe some not so young. "I want a lamp, Andrew. It's just a little quirk of mine, light."

He disappeared into the house and was gone for so long, she thought he might have run away. She climbed onto the ties so she could see into the hallway. A hazy light drew near.

Andrew appeared on the threshold of the door and told Katie to move.

"Move *please*," said a professorial voice in the dark hallway behind him.

"Ple-e-e-ease," Andrew said sarcastically as he jumped down onto the ties. A girl appeared behind him. She was dressed in a dark skirt and a shawl like Katie. She stepped down, following Andrew.

"Now, me dear lady," said the unseen man, "we're gonna send me own little sweet pea out in the street with Andrew to make like you're still out there wanderin'. We wanna give those coppers on your tail a good long walk while we talk."

"I didn't know I was being followed," Katie said.

"Lord 'a mercy, who could know? You, with your sweet princess face step-in-hand with a pack of me little homelies."

She untied her bonnet and gave it to the girl who would impersonate her. "I'm sorry if I've done a disservice, Mr. O'Shea, bringing police attention to the house."

"Disservice, she says. More like a flat-out delivery. Now go on with you, Andrew. Hurry."

Katie climbed the pile of railroad ties. Devlin O'Shea hoisted her up and into the hall.

She introduced herself, but Devlin just started down the hall, carrying a wavering candle in a holder. "Don't you think I know that? Why else would I let you in? Now, get a move on, 'fore the candle burns out. You'd break your neck in the dark round here."

Shadows flickered on the door of each room they passed, all of which were crudely boarded shut.

When they reached the stairwell at the end of the long hallway, Devlin pulled a pitch pipe from his pocket and sounded three shrill notes. Magically, the sound of children's laughter and bickering began in the boarded up rooms behind them.

"Disciplined youngsters," she said.

"Them's the ones survive. Now then, missy, before we go any farther, I'd like to discuss price."

"You don't even know what I have to offer."

"Only two things would bring you sightseein' in my neighborhood this fine evenin'. Love or money. And you don't look too promisin' as regards the latter."

"I have something Matt needs. Please. I must see him."

"You gotta pay. This is a house o' business. That's what I teach me kids. They pay me a bit o' room and board, and I pay 'em safekeepin'."

"I'm embarrassed to say I have only carriage fare in my bag." She offered her canvas bag for him to inspect.

He hefted it. "It's pretty heavy."

"Food, Mr. O'Shea. It's the one thing we have plenty of at the hotel. I thought Matt might need it."

Devlin gave her the candle and rummaged in her bag, sniffing loudly and peering beneath the paper. "Sweet Mary. Biscuits and beef?"

"And homemade Italian sausage."

"I take this as a fair barter." He opened a closet door beneath the stairwell and gave four hard knocks on the wall.

Instantly the walls along the hall seemed alive with thumps and stealthy scurrying. Soon, four little heads peered out from the closet dark. One of them was the street boy Katie had used as a messenger. He nodded at her, suspicious.

Devlin handed the boy the treats. "Grub, you take this to Willie's room. Whatever he can't eat can be divided among the girls that's been nursin' him. No cheatin'."

"Aye, sir," Grub said, jostling with the others to leave.

"Are there wall passages to each room?" she asked.

"Some has window entry, some up a vent. Police always try to go straight through the door. I like public servants like that, consistent." He frowned at her. "They've already been here once, you know, lookin' for him."

Did that mean Matt wasn't there now? she wondered.

"This way," Devlin said before she could ask. "Up the stairs. You take the candle. Step only where I do." Each of the board steps had collapsed, though in different places. "'Member this little formula: left-left-right, right-right-left. Reverse it on your way down. It'll save you a bloody shin or a broken leg."

The step remnants felt strong and reinforced, as long as she followed the directions. At ease with the dark, Devlin loped ahead. She passed two landings before reaching the top of the stairs and a door that opened onto a wallpapered room with no furniture. She strolled into the room uneasily. "Devlin?" she whispered.

She was startled when a door-size section of wall swung outward.

Devlin peeked out at her. "Up to the roof with you now."

She edged past him into a tight and crooked stairwell, cupping her hand to guard the candle flame. At the top the door was open.

A draft of river wind snuffed the candle as she stepped out onto the roof.

Above, stars shone in clean, endless space. Around her, though, wire cages, crates, and lean-to's crowded every square inch. Pigeon coops with molty feathers and guano floors made the rooftop earthy as a barnyard.

She wandered recklessly through the clutter, not waiting for Devlin to guide her, not daring to call out for fear Matt wouldn't answer. Matt? Ruffled pigeons gave irritated coos and fluttered from perch to perch as she passed. Pinfeathers drifted through the wire mesh and she batted them away.

Finally she found a straightaway that gave her a clear view to the corner of the rooftop. A man with a telescope stood silhouetted against the sky, peering down toward the streets she had traveled.

She approached him slowly, aware that sudden moves and bursts of emotion were hazardous to a man in his position.

He turned when she reached him, collapsing the scope and slipping it into his pocket, so that his hands were free when he held her. They roamed her back, her sides, anxious and reassuring, then tilted her chin up to align her lips to his, to swallow the taste of her fear, to drown the silent worry pounding in her brain, to engulf her in an embrace that shut out the night. For a moment.

"I wish you hadn't come," he said at last, stroking her hair.

She pressed herself more tightly against him, but he drew back.

"It's not safe here."

"But Andrew is leading the police away."

He gave her a look, oddly like pity. "All right. Devlin's on watch. He'll warn us."

"I brought your telegram from Senator Cahill. Your father gave it to me."

"You met my father?"

"And Hellie."

"Katie, I didn't have a chance to tell her."

"I know. I couldn't either."

He sighed, then asked if Cahill's message said anything about Chu.

"No," she answered. "All the senator found out is that Julian rented a warehouse in Sacramento to store some Oriental antiques."

"We know what's hidden inside the 'antiques,' but Sacramento doesn't make sense. It's the launch terminal for the Central Pacific. Why does Julian need the tracks of a rival railroad? Why warehouse the stuff there, especially if he's got powder for laudanum. I found out that he's ready to start construction on a factory right here on the river. A pharmaceuticals factory. Can you imagine the kind of legal tonics he'll create for the good citizens of St. Louis?"

"Only half of what he's importing is powder. The other half is pitch for smoking, two hundred pounds of each." She patted her skirt. "It's here, all written down in the letter Edmund and Zemin were using to blackmail Julian."

"You brought it with you?"

She nodded triumphantly, but Matt wasn't happy. "Your brother was killed for that letter, Katie."

"But I thought you would need it."

"All I need is to know that you're safe. That's the only comfort you can give me right now."

"Matt, don't. Don't push me away."

His expression told her he would do just that, and she defiantly stepped close, inviting an embrace.

He didn't move.

A cold fear swept her. She drew her shawl tighter.

"I'm poison to you," he said quietly. "Julian's made sure of that. Being together will destroy us both."

"But the letter. It will indict Julian. It will free you."

"It's just another target to cut down, along with its carrier."

"But you can go straight to the police. It'll prove Julian is smuggling."

"Julian will say it proves Edmund Henslowe was a drug-crazed unfortunate who tried to frame a rich man and extort his money. And he will be partially right."

"No."

"The letter is only one tool against him, Katie. He's too accomplished a spider to leave us a big hole. He spins double webs and triple threads, all translucent, hanging in the wind to catch you when you run." He shook his head. "And I have to keep running now, Katie. I miscalculated. I thought he'd run out of money. But he's enterprising. Hiring thugs and paying off lowlifes when the price of a good assassin is too high, Julian did order two costumes, by the way. My man at Greenmore overheard a discussion of it."

"You have an informant there? Is it Altmann?"

"No. Altmann's a loyalist and a loner."

"He's not so alone anymore. Peg and he are close. He's a good man. I know he'll help—"

Suddenly alert, Matt put a finger to his lips to shush her. He listened a moment. All seemed quiet, but the lull fused an urgency in him. "I can't stay in St. Louis. Julian's too friendly with the police commissioner for me to trust my safety in custody. I'm leaving for New York and taking every last scrap of information with me. I'll turn myself in there, after I've met with Bill Cahill. I hope, by then, I can find a way to clear my name."

"But I was with you last night! Tell the police that! Tell them."

"No, love." He stroked her arm. "I would slander you for no good reason."

"But it's the truth."

"It's your word against the evidence Julian's stacked to the contrary." He stepped closer to caress her cheek. "Stay clear of it. And of me."

She breathed a kiss of warmth in his palm. "No."

His hand fell away. "You have to be patient, Katie." He glanced around, his eyes not meeting hers. "I'll be back. We'll start over again then, free and clear."

She looked at him, her gaze steady as a fearsome foreboding, the first intimations of a lifelong pain tingled through her. "Tell me you honestly believe that, Matt—"

Devlin's pitch pipe sounded suddenly, over and over, a shrill warning.

"Oh, no, Zemin's letter," she said, frantically rifling the folds of her petticoat to find the pocket. "Take it! Take bloody wing and fly. Just let me know where you're going."

Matt grabbed her hands and stopped her. Terrified, she stared at him. He had known, she realized. From the moment she stepped on the roof, he had known it was too late, for the letters, for him, for them.

"Listen carefully," he said. "I'll pretend you passed it on to me. But you have to get that letter to Bill Cahill as soon as possible."

The piercing bawl of the pipe died, cut off midcall.

"Get down!" Matt pushed her into a niche between the coops. He drew his gun and clicked the barrel open. "Damn." He clapped it shut. "Empty. Andrew couldn't get ammunition for me today."

Through the open windows of the house, she could hear boot-steps storming the booby-trapped staircase. Curiously, there were no crashing missteps.

"Run before they find you," she whispered.

"Soon."

"They sound like an army! What are you waiting for?"

"There are only two. I saw them from the roof."

She heard them in the narrow stairwell leading up to the roof. "Go!" she begged. "Please go!"

"I don't want to see you again until this thing is settled, no matter what, Katie."

"I love you too, now run!"

He slowly backed away to the edge of the roof, watching the path that wended through the coops and crates. Peering through the mesh of the coop she hid behind, she saw two thugs burst onto the roof. Birds thrashed in their pens, trilling with fright.

Each intruder had a pistol. Matt upended a crate to get their attention, and the noise made them duck and freeze. A moment later they headed cautiously in Matt's direction.

By the time they were clear of the coops, Matt was at the far corner of the roof. When he was sure they could see him, he jumped to the roof of the adjoining row house. The two men scrambled after him.

Hooking her fingers in the wire mesh, Katie drew herself up. He had baited them. He had made sure they would follow him and not find her. But he had waited too long. She walked woodenly to the corner of the roof. The night air was cool and clean; it carried all the urgent scrapes of bootsoles and the panting grunts of the thugs as they chased Matt across the rooftops. They hadn't fired their guns yet. They wanted him alive—or they were afraid of drawing police attention. If they were not police, who else could they be but hunters hired by Julian?

She hunched her shawl higher on her shoulders. She could see Matt silhouetted on the far roof, the last of the row houses. He ran for the roof door which would lead him down into the house. He jerked and wrenched. It would not open. His pursuers were nearly upon him.

They circled him. Caught between two gunsights, Matt had nowhere to run. He dropped his useless revolver.

Katie felt ill as she watched them wrestle him down. She turned away, but then a shot rang out. She jerked around, her hand trembling against her mouth, holding the scream silent. She saw only the two men, then she heard the bullet-weakened lock on the distant door give a splintery wrench. Matt was upright as he disappeared through the roof door with his captors.

Footsteps sounded behind her.

"Ole Julian needs him alive, you know."

It was Devlin, nursing a bruised forearm. She shook her head. "How can you be sure?"

"He needs to know how much dirt Matt has on him so he can sweep it all up. He can't afford to miss one spot right now. Somethin' might grow in it."

"Those roughnecks should have been following your decoy, just like the police did," she said harshly.

"Well," he said, perusing the night sky, "they just weren't hungry enough to take bait. Somebody musta already fed 'em."

She heard wings flapping close to her head. A bird swooped low and lighted on a perch atop the nearest coop.

"Know what this is?" he asked as he reached up and gently corralled the bird.

She shook her head.

"Homin' pigeon." He held the bird against his chest as he loosed the band around its leg.

A boy's voice called from deep in the stairwell. "Devlin?"

"C'mon up, Andrew," Devlin said, his voice strangely flat.

The cocky youth wended his way toward them.

259

"How'd things go?" Devlin asked as he put his pigeon in the coop.

"Lost the coppers easy, up by Kerry Patch."

Devlin smiled as he looked at Andrew. "Found your way back awful quick. Wanted to see the excitement, eh, Andrew? That's a big shortcomin' in a turncoat, having to hurry back and see the excitement."

"What're you talkin' about?" Andrew asked, but his voice cracked.

Dead calm, Devlin scooped a tin cup of birdseed from a canvas sack. "How much those big goons pay you for tellin' them where I was hidin' me friend?"

Andrew propped his fists on his skinny hips. "Just 'cause things go sour, you think it's someone else's fault? You're a desperate old man."

Devlin tapped the cup against the mesh to fill the feeder trough. "It was me cousin Myrtle wanted you here," he said idly. "Me third cousin, once removed. She pleaded with me: 'Dev, straighten him up 'fore he hurts somebody. Andy can be a good boy. So smart,' she said. Oh, you're smart, all right. I betcha feel bloody smart right now, don't you, Andrew Patrick Parker O'Shea?"

He straightened, facing the boy. "Bringin' street work into me house. You gotta good man in bad trouble now with your street work. You even told those filthy buggers how to get up me stairs, didn't you? I'm gonna have to change the formula on account of you. Goddamn no-account you. You're no-house now. See how you like bein' on the street with no house."

"Sorry old bastard," Andrew taunted. "You got no more say on the street than a used-up tom cat."

Devlin dropped the seed cup back in the bag. "What I got on the street is loyalty, Andy. You?"

The boy lifted his chin. "Sure I do."

"Who's friend to a backstabber? 'Nother backstabber, that's all. Those're your only 'friends' now." Devlin neatly rolled the bag shut. "Me, I started me life runnin' with kids, then teachin' 'em, then lookin' out for 'em. I've raised up gentlemen and thieves,

260

booklearners and bricklayers, each one accordin' to how much direction they could swallow. You can't swallow anythin', Andy." Devlin pointed at the boy, punctuating each word with a jab of his index finger. "You're—gonna—starve. *If* I don't have your yellow liver cut out and tossed in the river first."

Andrew took a few steps backward. He twisted a finger in the seam of his pants. "You ain't running cutters. I know everyone out there."

"You don't know the footpads I ran with when I was in knickers. You don't know Razor Bailey. Comin' outta the penitentiary next week. Used to slice the fingers off crooked dealers at me card tables. You know the hatchet man who comes swingin' through Dead Man's Alley sometimes, seems for no reason? He's got reasons. He gets paid for 'em. Hatchet Man's gotta name, Andy, and I know it."

Andrew backed away to the stairs and raced down them. Devlin waited until they couldn't hear the boy's footsteps, then he turned to Katie.

"Well, you gonna sit there all night wool-gatherin'?" he asked irritably.

"It's courage I'm gathering. I'm afraid to ask for your help, Devlin."

"Good. You ain't got enough biscuits to afford me, anyhow." He bent low and squinted, looking for something. "You seen a telescope around here?"

She looked out across the rooftops. "Matt has it."

"Damn. Me best one too."

"I can get it for you," she said.

"How? It'll be at Greenmore soon enough, just like Matt."

"I'm going there."

"There? Tonight?"

"I have to. I'm not going to let him hurt Matt. And he will if we don't do something."

"Listen, missy. Did Matt happen to mention anythin' about steerin' clear of him and his troubles, no matter what? 'Cause if he didn't, I'm about to."

She looked at him. "Save your breath for scaring children." She swept her skirt around the crate and began to leave.

Devlin put a hand on her shoulder. "Whoa. Long as you're headin' into the lion's den, you may as well give your sweet Daniel this." He handed her the message he'd taken from the pigeon. "It's from me friend at Greenmore. He says for Matt to be careful tonight, somethin's up. Ironic, ain't it?"

"Late is what it is." She turned to him suddenly. "Your man at Greenmore, would he be able to help me?"

Devlin shrugged. "Maybe. If you had a plan. And if I sent a note, fresh pigeon. Take about fifteen minutes."

"I think I—" She tried to keep her voice from shaking. "I do have a plan, Devlin."

"Damn." He rubbed his chin. "I was afraid of that." He raised eyes to the sky. "Saint Peter? Keep the gates open late. Got me an angel and she's plottin' a trip home."

27

Walking fast, Devlin led Katie to the waterfront to meet a cab. "Ole Gert's me favorite," he said as they strode along, "the smartest homin' pigeon I got. She'll get your message to Norrie in a spit."

He went on, but Katie was too edgy for small talk. She was keenly aware of time, with half an hour or more already gone. At Devlin's suggestion, she had sent the boy, Grub, to Greenmore with a quick note to let Julian know she would be arriving immediately. How 'immediately'? she had asked Devlin.

"Won't matter," he said. "It's just to distract him from beatin' the bejesus outta Ma—"

The blood drained from her cheeks.

"Lord almighty, girl! Are you gonna turn to mush if he's gotta few bloody bashes?"

She tried to speak and couldn't.

" 'Cause if you are, you're no more good to him than a wet rag, and a wet rag don't stand up to nothin'!"

"I'll be fine," she said.

"Oh, I can see that, missy. Me heart's cool as a clam sittin' on the sideboard waitin' for the pot to boil. I'll tell you right now I'll be cooked if Julian finds out it's me cousin's nephew's boy, Norrie, that's been feedin' Matt the goods. Let's get you in that cab before I feel sorry I let pretty little Gert take off in a storm o' bad luck."

"Please don't worry," she said to Devlin as he closed the carriage door on her.

"I wanna worry," he said. "It's the easiest job o' the evenin'. Godspeed. And Katie." He cleared his throat.

"Yes?"

"Don't forget me telescope."

An hour later Katie was again en route, though not alone this time. Inside the dark carriage Beth played with a music box Katie had brought along. The tinkling song was intermittent as Beth jammed and released the merry-go-round of dancing bears she couldn't see.

Lin sat stiffly across from Katie. "I hope you have not forgotten the Five Virtues."

Oh, Lord. "Give me a minute," Katie said. She was so tired. She'd been rushing like a madwoman to get everyone ready. Explaining the situation to Peg and convincing her to help organize the troupe had taken focused argument and enormous energy. Having to argue then with Lin over Beth's safekeeping had been the topper. Out of time, Katie had finally issued an icy order for Lin to obey, as if Lin were a common housemaid.

Shocked, Lin had stopped packing and frowned at her mistress. "Is it time for your monthly?"

"Lin!"

"Sometimes, I can tell." Lin had coolly resumed packing.

The rift had added tension to an already nerve-wracking ride. It was vital that Lin be in an agreeable mood when Katie left her. To make amends, Katie dutifully tried to recite the Five Virtues of Chinese philosophy.

"Truth is one."

"Of course."

"Purity, wisdom, and . . . wisdom and—" She gave up.

"Propriety and *benevolence*. Benevolence, mistress. Now, I must warn you. Your rich patron is without even one of these virtues.

264

Zemin told me this. He knows him. So you must take this for Beth." Lin handed Katie a small piece of folded paper.

Katie felt its triangular shape. Though she could not see it, she knew the paper was yellow and that inside, a Buddhist spell was written neatly in red ink in Chinese characters.

"A triangle spell?" she said to Lin. "You haven't done one of these in a long time."

"It will protect her," Lin said. "Pin it to her dress."

"You can do that," Katie said, handing it back. "You will be staying with Beth."

Lin sniffed. "This lady may not want me."

" 'This lady' will find you a fascinating person. And," Katie added as the carriage drew to a halt in front of 310 Lucas Place, "she may ask you to sign an important paper, a petition."

A stout housekeeper ushered them up the spiral staircase. Beth pulled free of Katie's hand and raced ahead to the top of the stairs. Katie gathered her skirt higher and ran after her. Nonplussed, the housekeeper stomped faster to stay ahead of Katie.

Only Lin walked with a stately rhythm that paid homage to the once-grand house. Katie knew Lin's precise eye was pinpointing signs of neglect, from cobwebs in the stair rail to water stains snaking down the wall.

Katie caught up with Beth just before the giggling youngster ran through an open door. The housekeeper waddled ahead and announced them.

Katie and Beth passed into a gaslit room cluttered with worktables, books, and Prussian blue prints. Hellie Dennigan sat at a table strewn with fern fronds, feathers, and lace. She wore a work apron over her dressing gown.

"You've caught me at my hobby, I'm afraid," she said, putting aside a glass plate. "Photograms. Sun gardens, some people call them." She gestured at a wall full of blue cyanotype prints bearing ghostly white shadows of dry grasses, arching feathers, and delicate fingers of fern. "I'm delighted you've come to visit," Hellie added, smiling at Beth.

The three-year-old pulled her mother closer to the table and stood on tiptoe to peer over the edge at the colorful collection.

Katie quickly introduced Song Lin as Beth's nanny. "I must beg your pardon for the abruptness and late hour," Katie told Hellie. "But I find myself in desperate need of a safe haven for my daughter."

"For goodness sake," Hellie said. "Sit down, Katie. Tell me what's wrong."

"I cannot. My carriage is waiting. I—" She looked at Beth, and hot tears scalded her eyes. "I have to go."

Hellie handed Beth a little basket of feathers and scrap lace to play with. "Have you seen my son?" Hellie asked anxiously. "Is he well?"

"I'm going to find out," Katie said. "For both of us."

"Perhaps, Katie, this is a matter for the police."

"At some point, it will be. For now, for his own safety, it's a matter for Matt and me. But I can't help him unless I know Beth is protected. You won't let Julian hurt her, will you?" She glanced at her daughter, who had spied something in a corner and was scampering after it.

"Of course not." Hellie took her hands. "She's safe here, Katie. And you must realize there *are* other homes like ours where Julian is not welcome. It's true that a lot of good people toady up to him. But he's made lots of enemies here. He's not all-powerful." She paused. "Though sometimes, I despair. You know the fencer Matt fought? He died today. Without recanting a word of what he said about Matt hiring him to kill your brother."

Katie closed her eyes, gathering resolve. "I have to go."

A clatter rose from the corner. Beth got up, clutching a large toy to her chest. "I can play with this?" she called as she ran to Hellie. "Please?"

It was a pull toy, a brewer's dray with big painted horses hitched to a cast-iron wagon with wheels. Hellie bent down. "It's so dusty," she said sadly, then looked at the hopeful little girl and smiled. "It's been there a long, long time waiting for someone. Yes, Beth, you play with it."

Katie stooped to the floor. "I have to go now, darling." She gave her busy daughter a hug. Beth checked to make sure Lin was

266

near, then absently smacked a kiss on her mother's cheek. Katie rose quickly, tears beginning to stream.

She gave Lin a long hug, then ran to the door. Bracing one hand against the frame, she swallowed a sob and called over her shoulder to Beth, "Be careful with the toy, sweetheart. It belongs to a little boy named Samuel. He's coming to play with it someday."

"Oh, Katie," Hellie whispered.

"He will, Hellie. So help me God."

She ran to the stairs, then stopped short, startled by the presence of Art on the landing. He looked at her sternly, carefully unemotional. She lifted her hem and hurried past him on her way down.

"Miss Henslowe."

The gruff command stopped her cold. She looked up at Matt's father. "I could have helped if he'd asked. You tell him that."

She took the remaining steps at a run.

Chin high as he buttoned his collar, Julian hurried down the hallway toward the Gold Room. His untied cravat flew over his shoulder and his coat was draped over one arm. It had been a hasty toilette, and he had had to dress himself. Damn that Norrie. And with Katie coming, Julian had wanted to look especially elegant. Ah, well. She would have to accept a dashing air of informality. She would accept him in any fashion, of course. She had no choice.

As he strode through the high arched entrance of the Gold Room, he saw that Drake had followed directions. All the wall sconces were lit. On the massive, shellacked desk sat a brandy service and the silver-domed plate. Dependable Drake. He never asked questions, and he always disappeared whenever a young lady arrived late at night unescorted.

He had his coat half on, his tie still undone, when Drake entered. "She's here? Just a moment," Julian said, donning the jacket. He sat at his desk and turned the chair so he faced the window overlooking the garden path. His back was to the room. "Bring her in."

He decided on a pensive pose, propping his chin in the cradle of his thumb and forefinger. After a moment he heard her gown whisk in, a dissonant cascade, fold against fold lapping closer, then silence.

"Miss Henslowe to see you, sir," Drake said.

Julian paused, allowing a silent minute to lapse, then he swiveled around in his chair, slowly, reluctantly, as if there were many more important things on his mind. He eyed her a moment. She didn't flinch. "Her wrap, Drake."

She unbuttoned the collar and winged the cloak out from her shoulders. She was wearing the red gown he'd given her, and despite his pose of uninterest, Julian had to admire her beauty. The gown pinched in at her waist and blossomed upward, holding her breasts in creamy stasis. She wore no gloves, he noticed. It seemed her toilette, too, had been hasty.

She held the cloak on her shoulders a moment longer than necessary. Mocking his own theatrical pause? Nerve, Julian thought. She had it in abundance.

Drake took the cloak. Julian waved him away, then tied his cravat. "Sit down, my dear," he said, indicating a chair in front of his desk. She seated herself. Fixing a ruby pin to the gray silk tie, he gestured at the brandy. "A drink?"

She didn't answer.

"Can't hurt," he said. "You look in need of one." He slipped the cut crystal stopper from the bottle neck, noticing how the tension in the air seemed to magnify small sounds. As he poured, the decanter rapped the rim of her glass with a thunderous clink. "Here you go, my dear." He got up and walked toward her.

When she took the glass, he made sure his fingers brushed hers. She recoiled, nearly spilling the brandy. Not so much nerve after all, he mused. He leaned a hip against the desk and sipped from his own glass. God, how smooth. He hadn't allowed himself a bottle of brandy in years. He'd become too fond of drink when he'd found a cache of Martell in the widow's cellar. Tonight, though, he was due some indulgence. He downed half the brandy in a gulp.

"I thought you would come in black," he said, "in mourning for your brother."

She looked ahead, not at him.

He sipped again. "Perhaps you dress in mourning for yourself. A night with me would kill you, wouldn't it?"

She glanced up. "You don't look that omnipotent."

He smiled. "Good one, Katie."

She looked down at her glass, then took a long swallow. She grimaced and coughed.

"Edmund said you hated liquor. I'm sorry to have brought you so low."

"You regret nothing, least of all murdering my brother."

Her eyes were watery. Surely from the liquor, he thought, and not from grief. Edmund's death had ended a reign of disaster. She should be thankful. "The police know who murdered Edmund," he said.

"I know." She took another swallow and closed her eyes tight against the burn. "I don't want any more." Her hand unsteady, she set the glass on the desk.

"What is it you do want, Katie?"

"For you to let Matt go."

"Ah." He walked around her chair and stopped behind her. "The naked truth, and so quickly." He leaned low so his breath touched her bare shoulder. "Love denudes a woman, no matter how carefully she dresses, or for whom."

"I have the letter, Julian."

Her trump card. The rest of the game was his. "The letter?"

"To Chu King-Sing. The letter my brother was killed for."

"You have it with you?"

"Of course not."

"Wise. I might be inclined to a search."

She stood abruptly, glancing around the room as she walked to the window. "I imagine you're inclined to very little that pleases a woman."

"Katie, Katie, has Matt given you such vast experience to judge other men so harshly?" He downed his drink. "Or perhaps you're just trying to rile me to a rash action, say, by ten-thirty or so?"

She stopped, her face paling.

"The clock is on the mantel," he said helpfully, craning to look past her. "Hmmm. Ten more minutes. Shall we trade insults until then?"

She stood so still, it was as if she feared she would break if she moved. He smiled. "I'm sure you're hoping Norrie will interrupt us soon." He walked back to the desk, his fingers sliding over the silver dome of the covered plate. "However," he went on, pouring himself another drink, "my treasonous little valet won't be of help tonight. Norrie O'Shea has proved himself a quite cowardly spy. He escaped out the window of his room when I burst in on him." Julian lifted the dome from the plate. "His friend didn't fare as well, though."

The homing pigeon lay limp on the plate, neck twisted, dark gray feathers mirrored in the shining silver.

Satisfied by the horror and fear reflected in Katie's eyes, he replaced the cover. "I've always thought of birds as a good-for-nothing branch on nature's family tree. I am impressed with the usefulness of this breed, however." He slid a finger inside his vest pocket and withdrew the slip of paper he had detached from the bird's leg. "I take it Norrie was to somehow help Matt escape the bounty hunters who brought him here. Norrie's specific instructions, though, were to open the front door at ten-thirty"—he glanced at the note—" 'and assist.' Hmmm."

He returned the note to his pocket and looked at Katie. "I've taken the precaution of posting one of those big, efficient bounty hunters outside in the portico and another at the main gate. Wouldn't want them to miss the excitement when the clock strikes the half hour. Who's coming, Katie? Not the police, for they'd only arrest Matt. All your bedraggled players perhaps?"

"Julian . . ." She took a step toward him, obviously struggling for composure. "Let Matt go and I'll tell you where the letter is."

He made a show of glancing at the clock. "Seven minutes." He sipped more brandy. "Heaven knows what Norrie managed to pass on in the few weeks he's been here, but it's all hearsay." Unless, of course, Norrie had been opening mail and copying it. The thought burst like a balloon in his temple, and he tried to shake it off. "Nothing will be corroborated. Altmann is a truly loyal secretary."

She spoke loudly, projecting. "Altmann is an honest man who's appalled by your unethical dealings."

He responded with deliberate calm, forcing aside his own suspicions about Altmann and the many questions he'd asked the past few days. "You can shout all you like. Altmann isn't here tonight. I sent him out. I gave all the house servants the night off too, except Drake and Norrie."

Sneaky little bastard. He could have read any of a score of Julian's communiques to potential investors. Personal, florid invitations to become shareholders in his new pharmaceuticals company, and promises of a phenomenal rate of return for anyone providing immediate capital. He would have promised them the moon if they could come through with cash.

He rubbed his brow with thumb and forefinger, then exerted careful control to set his glass gently on the desk. "You see, Katie, essentially we're alone." He walked slowly toward her. "Except for the two men upstairs, of course. My prisoner and his guard."

She held her ground, not backing away when he stopped within arm's reach of her. "If you don't release Matt within the hour, the letter will be hand-delivered to the police station, so all the officers on the night shift can read about your craving for four hundred pounds of opium. And then you can read about it in the tabloids tomorrow afternoon."

He shrugged. "Who's going to believe the slander of a Chinaman, notarized or not?"

"The letter is in Edmund's handwriting."

"An even more scurrilous source."

"Chang, the opium proprietor, legally witnessed the copying."

"It doesn't matter. Chang is dead. Died in an alley brawl a few days ago. At least, that's what the New York police tell me."

"Chang too?" Her tone was incredulous. "God have mercy, what are you running here? A brokerage for assassins?"

"No, my dear, I'm merely a visionary caught in the constraints of commerce. And I intend to protect my dream."

"You intend to be a parasite, living off addicts like Edmund."

"On the contrary, Edmund and his ilk disgust me. Just as he did

271

you. Tawdry, tawdry man. Though he never did tell me what happened in your dressing room the day of that terrible fire."

How poignant, Julian mused, the sorrow haunting her face. He wished Edmund had divulged that intimate corruption, for he could have used it. Secrets were made for barter and trade. Though now, he had so many to manage.

He pressed the heel of his hand to the throbbing in his head. "Realistically, it would have been better had you lost your family in the fire," he said. "They're such a burden."

She stiffened, her outrage clear in the taut lines of her body. "People do not fit in columns of profit and loss. My family is my home. No matter where I go, I carry them. And they carry me." She looked at him intently. "Who carries you, Julian? Or was your family a burden to be rid of?"

"Dead! All my family, dead. They taught me nothing. I was beyond them. Maybe that's what links us, Katie. You and I never warranted such worthless kin and rank beginnings."

"You're the worthless one." Her words were soft, but well aimed. "Poor, worthless Julian."

He flew at her, clamping down on her arm with a strength he did not want to control. The suddenness startled her, and the pain genuinely scared her. He could see it in her eyes as he bent back her slender wrist, testing the limit. It would be easy. As easy as the fluttery bird, its neck stretched, firm yet delicate.

Summoning control, he hurled her away. She fell to the floor, raking her shoulder against the marble molding of the hearth.

He advanced on her. She struggled to her feet and backed away from him into the hall. "You're too rebellious for me, Katie. There's a place prepared for the rebellious. The great and morbid Milton knew it well. 'A dungeon horrible, on all sides round, as one great furnace flamed; yet from those flames no light, but rather darkness visible.' Where peace and rest can never dwell, Katie. And hope never comes to give you respite."

If I present you with nothing else during your employment in this house, young man, I set before you hope and the possibility of a better life. I embody hope, Julian Gottswald.

He stalked Katie, watching her back down the hall, one hand

to the wall. "Foolish old woman. Only angels embody hope. She was no angel. And neither are you, Katie." His gaze roamed her hair, her face, her lips. Like fruit, he knew, their taste would be moist and sweet. "You scheme. You sin. You reward my enemy with your body."

With three swift steps he caught her and pressed her to the wall. She turned her head, avoiding his eyes. Her lips were parted, and she breathed shallowly, bird-quick. She was frightened.

"I'm afraid it's much safer to be feared than to be loved," he whispered. "You see, 'fear is held together by a dread of punishment which will never abandon you.' Machiavelli. A master. You must read him to me."

The clock in the Gold Room interrupted with a bell-like chime. He felt her body jerk. Half past ten. Farther down the hall, the tallcase clock in the foyer gave a ponderous bong.

He backed away from her. She looked at him, stricken. "Ten-thirty," he said, and smiled.

She picked up her skirts and ran toward the front door. He jogged after her. Reverberations of the chimes died away as she stopped at the door. The pendulum of the tallcase clock tocked in the silence. Again. Again.

Julian unbolted the door and opened it. The burly figure of the bounty hunter patrolled the tile portico. "Everything all right, Raskin?"

"Quiet as a graveyard."

Julian smiled at Katie. "I hope that's not an apt analogy, don't you, my dear?" He closed the door. "I am, by the way, very interested in that slanderous letter your brother wrote. Instinct tells me it's close by, somewhere on your person, in fact. You wouldn't risk coming here without something tangible to trade for your lover's well-being."

He headed down the hall. "Would you like to hear something amusing? Matt told me *he* had the letter." Julian shook his head. "It's important for two people to get their stories straight before they try to negotiate. That's why I never use a partner when the stakes are high. Come, Katie." He started up the curving staircase. "Come up to the gallery. I have quite a rare specimen on display."

273

28

Katie followed Julian up the stairs, her anxiety mounting.

Where were Peg and the others? Strong men like Tobias and the Brandellis, and a crowd of witnesses who could hold Julian accountable for his actions? Had they been stopped at the gate? Couldn't they bluff their way through?

At least they were safe out there. The real danger and blood lust was here, inside.

"This way to the gallery," he said, leading her along the upstairs hall, past giant urns and pretentious statuary. He stopped at the Ionic column facade of the gallery, then waited for her to reach him before opening the double doors. "I am proud to present 'The Fugitive Lover,' a personal work in progress."

Inside, the central chandelier lit a stark, checkerboard floor of glazed marble. Matt sat in the middle on a straight-backed chair. He was blindfolded, his hands tied. His head lolled forward, as if he were unconscious. Dried blood stained one side of his mouth and chin.

She tried to run to him, but Julian grabbed her skirt and yanked her back. She stopped immediately. His hand was within inches of the prop dagger she had hidden with the letter beneath her skirts.

"Don't rush," he said. "He isn't going anywhere. We must proceed with decorum." He pulled her with him to a wall display of ancient weapons. "Let's see. Something of chivalric appeal, I think." He lifted a heavy, crossed-hilt sword from its wall brace and leaned it against his shoulder. "Now, would you like to look at my collection of oils?"

With agonizing slowness Julian strolled the perimeter of the room with her in tow, past dark Flemish portraits of dour lords and pious ladies. She waited tensely for a chance to be at Matt's side, to see how badly he was hurt, to see if he could walk, fight, help them escape. His presence seemed to call to her senses, to anchor them, allowing her to dismiss the feel of Julian's hand, to ignore the armed man watching out the open window at the other end of the room.

When Julian paused before one painting, she tried to wrench away from him. The sword rose immediately to bar her path. "Not yet, Katie." He lowered the blade and hooked the hem of her skirt, lifting it slowly. She jerked the fabric free.

"It's there, isn't it?" he said softly. Then he lifted the sword and drew an imaginary line down between her breasts. "Or here?"

She backed away.

"It would be much tidier for you to give me the letter than for me to start cutting away."

She hesitated.

"You won't get near him until you do."

"Turn around, for decency's sake."

"For my sake, I'd prefer to watch."

She raised one side of her skirt and reached in the pocket of her petticoat. She could not retrieve the dagger; he was staring at her hand as she withdrew the folded paper.

"Matt will hate you for this, you know," he said.

The letter crackled as she clutched it tighter. It was the only solid evidence she had that Edmund and Zemin were minions, not masterminds, of a smuggler's scheme.

"It's too late for second thoughts," Julian said, and snatched the letter from her. "It was too late the moment you entered this house."

She stared helplessly at Matt as Julian scanned the letter. Matt was still a prisoner, and she had just given up the key.

"Quite the opportunist, your clever Zemin," Julian said. "I'll have to repay him for this someday."

"You already have," she said. "Edmund was his best friend. You stole his life. You stole his future."

"Yes, yes, you think I exist in a moral abyss." He smiled, patronizing. "No, dear, I am a moral wonder. I have conquered conscience. It's a squeaking peon to every prince building monuments, an albatross to every dreamer chasing visions. I have no need of a mirror, Katie. I care not what I see." He slipped the letter into a jacket pocket. "Now, what about the second copy? The one in Chinese?"

She was stunned. "What copy?"

He raised his eyebrows. "Zemin holding out on you too? Well, I won't worry. For the moment. Chinese is not exactly the language of legal indictment. Let us continue, Katie."

Their steps echoed in the recesses of the vaulted room. She willed Matt to move, to speak, but he remained unalert. Even when her scratchy silk ceased its swinging hiss, even when she stopped within an arm's length, he was unnaturally still. Julian tapped the sword on the floor in front of her, warning her against any hysteric or loving display.

"Nance!" He called across the room to the armed man. "I thought I told you to leave him functional."

"He should be okay. Playin' dead, maybe." Nance got up. His body was barrel thick, tight as a drum. He used the nose of his rifle to push a battered felt fedora higher on his head. "I didn't do nothin' but bust a rib. Two, maybe. Slowed him down, just like you tole me. Nosebleed come from those Raskin boys." He jerked his head back toward the window. "Something going on out there way down at the end of the drive. Seen a few lights."

"I don't want anyone getting through the gate," Julian said. "Go down and help the Raskins keep an eye on things."

Nance didn't move. "I want to be paid before I go."

"You want to be paid? Here and now before we're done? What put that presumptuous idea in your—" He stopped, turning to frown at Matt.

A taunting smile creased Matt's lips. He raised his head a little. Julian looked livid enough to strike him, but he looked back at Nance instead. "You shouldn't believe the desperate lies of a man in trouble."

"I want my money now," Nance said firmly.

"Look around you! There's enough wealth in this one room alone to pay a hundred thousand like you."

"Maybe." Nance shrugged. "And maybe you're a proud man, too proud to sell off any of your fancy do-dads."

Julian glared at Matt, a promise of retribution for persuading Nance to seek payment. Fumbling with his ascot, he jerked out his ruby pin, then thrust it at Nance. "Turquoise and white enamel with a ruby eye. Collateral enough to hold you?"

"Hell, yeah," Nance said, taking it. He examined it under a globe lamp, then he walked out, chin tucked as he pinned it to his shirtfront.

When he closed the door, Julian exploded in rage. "That's a two-hundred-dollar pin, you sonofabitch! I should have gagged you!" With a vicious kick, he knocked over the chair.

Katie cried out as Matt fell, sprawling free of the chair and hitting the marble floor with a sickening grunt. Julian wrapped an arm around her waist as she lurched forward to help.

Hands tied behind him, Matt rolled over, grimacing, favoring his right side. "Katie?" he said, his voice raspy.

"I have her right here," Julian answered. "Don't worry."

Matt lay still, breathing with slow and shallow care. Controlling the pain of his fractured ribs, Katie thought, and steeling himself for the trouble she had brought him. She knew her presence made him more vulnerable. After a minute he moved, struggling to his knees.

"An appropriate posture," Julian said.

Matt staggered upright, facing them. "Let her go." He lifted his hands to pull off the blindfold, but Julian placed the tip of the sword against his throat, stopping him.

"And what will you give me?" Julian asked, taunting. "The letter? But that's what Katie promised me too. Isn't it, my dear?"

"I'm the one you need details from," Matt said. "The letter's not important."

"Oh, but an hour ago it was your bargaining chip. How quickly a piece of writing changes value in games of intrigue. Your letter is absolutely worthless now, because I have it. Katie kindly lifted her skirt and gave it to me. What I want from you is the name of your boss. You're nothing but a gnat, picking dirt. I want to know who you're working for."

"Lots of people. You're good at making enemies."

"I'm also good at buying friends. And I think one of them's taking my money and stabbing me in the back."

"You ought to know. You're an expert at it yourself."

Julian pushed the swordtip higher, forcing Matt's chin up sharply.

"No," Katie pleaded.

Julian looked at her, then suddenly reached out and seized a handful of her hair. He jerked cruelly, and she cried out. Too late she realized what the sound would mean to Matt in his blindfold. He dodged the blade and lunged blindly toward her.

The blade tip found his stomach and pressed threateningly hard. "Are you going to let me hurt her," Julian said, "or are you going to tell me who you're spying for?"

Matt backed away from the sword. "I'm alone," he said, then added with a smile, "Just a scarred and gentle warrior bleeding in the plaza."

The words triggered Katie's memory of their improvisation as Mercutio and Juliet. What was he trying to say to her?

Matt leaned sharply to the right, as if the pain of his broken rib had intensified. He fell to one knee, then onto his side.

The motion was too choreographed. It was a ruse and he was cuing her to join. "Look at what you've done to him!" she cried, turning on Julian. She pounded wildly at him, hysterical.

As Julian backed away, trying to restrain her, Matt hooked his thumbs in the blindfold and tore it off. He rose, squinting against the light, breathing quickly, harshly.

Julian pushed Katie away and swung the sword up, but Matt rushed at him, head down, and sent them both tumbling to the floor. The sword slid across the marble.

Matt rolled toward it and rose, grimacing. Hands still tied, he clasped the grip of the heavy two-handed weapon, his index finger curled around the crossbar at the hilt.

Julian scrambled up and ran across the room to the weapon wall. As he wrenched another two-handed sword from its rack, Katie took the dagger from her underskirt. Matt might have need of it. She would, surely, if Julian won the fight.

Breathing hard, Julian approached Matt, holding the sword in both hands, weaving figure eights in the air, showing the ease and strength of his hold. "This is a heavy load for a man with cracked ribs," he said. "Pulls the shoulder all the way down the chest, doesn't it? Figure it makes us more evenly matched. I never had instruction when I was young. I had nothing when I was young. And there's no way in hell I'll let you destroy all that I've earned."

Matt's swordtip touched the floor between them, an invitation to fight. "The only thing a thief earns is jail time."

Julian slapped his blade flat against Matt's, and the weapons rose together for the first strike. With a tremendous backswing, Julian arced his blade down, aiming at Matt's right flank. Matt met the strike with a parry, and the searing scrape of blades reverberated in the cavernous room.

Katie could see that the effort cost Matt. Protecting his right side required tension and strength from his injured left.

To her surprise, though, he went on the offensive, swinging up quickly for a downcut at Julian's shoulder. Julian stepped back and raised his sword, blocking the cut and then pushing Matt backward. Matt staggered, letting his sword drag on the floor. Julian strode forward to take advantage, sword poised over one shoulder. Grunting at the painful effort, Matt twisted away from the powerful downstroke, then turned immediately to strike at Julian's unprotected side.

Julian jumped forward into a somersault that saved him, but he lost control of his sword, the weapon dropping to the floor. He scrambled for it and had one hand on the pommel, when Matt's boot smashed down on his hand. Julian recoiled, hissing between his teeth. He got up slowly, Matt's sword inches from his belly.

"Katie," Matt called, breathless, eyes on his enemy. "Cut me loose." With the thin blade of the dagger, she sawed across the rope binding Matt's wrists.

The instant Matt's attention shifted to his hands, Julian darted away to the globe lamp on a stand. He wrenched off the glass protecting the gas flame, crying out at the burn.

The letter! Katie thought. She raced toward Julian, but it was too late. A corner of the paper was already yellow with flame, edges black and curling.

Julian turned to her. "Here, Katie. You can have it back now," he said, and tossed it at her.

The burning paper landed on the floor near her hem. She tried to sweep her skirt out of reach, but she accidentally brushed the flame. The thin, treacherous silk caught quickly. She had escaped seven years ago without a burn. Not so now, she thought, backing away, dragging the licking yellow flame with her. *Not so.*

She screamed, and once she screamed she could not stop. She could not move. She screamed against the sacrifice, screamed as Matt appeared and tore at her gown, ripping it half off her waist, wrenching the smoking cotton petticoats off with it, stomping on the fabric and crushing life from the flame, leaving only dead smoke whorling up to the tiered chandelier.

A voice bellowed from below. "Katie! Keep screaming!"

Tobias?

A crash of glass seemed to shake the house. It came from the room directly below them. The Gold Room, Katie thought, with its glass-doored terrace.

"Help me find you!" Tobias shouted.

"Tobias!" she called. "Upstairs!"

Julian, sword in hand again, had rushed to the window and he seemed mesmerized by whatever he saw outside. She could hear the faint but perceptible noise of a crowd, getting louder. Peg and the others? Advancing up the drive?

"Katie!" Tobias's cry was still downstairs, distant. "Where—"

The loud crack of a rifle cut him off.

Katie's heart stopped.

Smiling, Julian faced her and Matt. "Nance is good with a gun, you know."

Again they heard the crashing of glass downstairs.

"Maybe Nance is good at running like the devil to save his own skin," Matt said. He spoke defiantly, but his expression revealed the strain of the fight, of holding the sword. He let it lower to the floor.

"Tired, Matt?" Julian asked, advancing on him.

Matt gripped the weapon with both hands and grimaced as he raised it.

The gallery doors burst open. "Katie!" Momentum carried Tobias halfway into the room. He was in full costume, bold tights and feathered turban.

He looked at Julian, at Matt, at Katie in her blackened, half-attached gown. Drawing his rapier, he circled the tip in the air as he took a stance beside Matt against Julian. "On guard, you sonofa-bitch."

Julian bent suddenly and sent his sword skidding across the floor. "I'm unarmed. Now get out of here. All of you."

"You don't get out of it that easily," Tobias said. "We're waiting right here until the police come up."

"Police," Matt said, trailing his sword, his left arm pressed against his side.

"Police, Matt," Julian said.

The silence was excruciating and filled with a message Katie did not understand.

"Neither one of us wants you in custody right now," Julian said to Matt. "Police detainment would only interfere with our plans—yours and mine."

With a last hard look at Julian, Matt tossed away his sword. It clamored on the marble. The noise of anxious voices and mass scuffling rose outside the window.

Matt turned to Tobias. "We have to get out of here. Quick."

"I'll give you a hand," Tobias said.

"You've done enough." He clapped Tobias gratefully on the back, then took Katie's hand.

The sounds of people had moved to the foyer.

"Hurry," Matt said as Katie gave Tobias a brief hug.

Matt pulled her away, and she bunched her ruined skirt over one arm, looking back anxiously.

Julian stood in the center of the checkerboard floor, hands clasped behind him, calm and thoughtful. "Servants' stairwell to the right," he said, "all the way at the end of the hall. Run, Katie. Run all the way to the end."

Drake came in with a hasty service of tea for the guests in the library.

"I'll pour," Julian said.

Drake nodded and hurried out.

Julian's attempt at warmth did nothing to ease the strain among his three visitors. Hiram Liggett, the police commissioner, was sleepy and sinking deep into the cushioned chintz sofa. His paunch was considerable; he extended one leg to alleviate pressure under his belt.

A night patrolman named Bohmer was perched stiffly on a straight-backed chair, hat on his knee. He periodically chewed his mustache with his lower lip.

Across from them was Peg Henslowe, looking perfectly at ease in a comfortable wing chair. She was an actress, just like her sister, Julian thought, passing her a steaming cup and saucer. She was outfitted for theatrics in a brocade robe. A Renaissance noblewoman, perhaps Lady Capulet. A costume he, no doubt, had paid for.

Julian remained standing, trying not to pace impatiently. Events that night had drawn far more attention than he liked. And there were arrangements still to be made. He cleared his throat, a signal to get on with it. "Well, then I think we've agreed. I'm withholding trespassing charges against Miss Peg Henslowe and her players. It appears they were fraudulently called to Greenmore by her sister, Katie, who told them I wanted a private performance for guests in the drawing room tonight. Obviously, I had no guests."

Officer Bohmer shifted nervously. "You had a prisoner, sir."

Commissioner Liggett set his teacup on a stand. "Blast it, Julian, why didn't you tell us you were offering a reward? We have a posting procedure and everything. And we get word out to bounty hunters that know better than to bring a city prisoner to a civilian home. What did you say those bounty hunters' names were?"

"Jones."

"Both of 'em?"

"Jones is all I heard."

Commissioner Liggett grunted unhappily and stood. "Officer Bohmer thinks he recognized a river tough hightailing it through your birchwoods with a rifle under his arm. You have an Able Nance here tonight?"

Julian nodded once. "A Mr. Nance arrived with the bounty hunters. Rough-looking fellow. But most of my servants were off for the evening, so I engaged him for security. Matt was, well, quite enraged at being captured. I was just about to send Drake down to the police station with a message, when Miss Katie Henslowe arrived. Apparently, she's hopelessly in love with Matt. Obsessed. She helped him escape."

"How?" Bohmer asked.

"I can't answer that," Julian said. "I was out of the room trying to see what the commotion in the drive was about. I had already sent Mr. Nance down to the gate to investigate."

"You needn't have," Peg said. "Locked iron gates and one snarling bounty hunter were quite enough to keep us out. The bounty hunter's name was Rask—no, *Jones*, you said, wasn't it?" She drilled a look at him. "Was that it, Mr. Gates?"

"Yes," he said quietly.

"No," the stubborn officer said. "I meant *how* did Miss Henslowe know the prisoner was here?"

"I have no idea," Julian said firmly. "Now then, it's very late, we've had a calamitous night, and I think we should all go to bed and deal with details tomorrow. What do you say, Hiram?" He turned to the commissioner.

"Getting back to the whist table sounds like a relief to me. And I was losing." He gestured for Julian to come close as he started toward the door. "You know, on hindsight," he said, only loud enough for Julian to hear, "a lot of people aren't buying that murder charge against Matt. Doesn't make sense. A murderer doesn't blow up at a fool like Edmund in public, get cut up saving his life, then stab him in the dead of night without an alibi. Matt's hotheaded, but he isn't stupid."

"Why are you telling me this?"

Commissioner Liggett tugged his coat down and buttoned it. "No reason. You and me been in and out of business for a few years. Thought you oughtta know." He opened the door and was about to step into the hall, when he glanced back at Julian. "Oh, and that fencer that died at the hospital?"

"Yes?"

"He was Catholic, you know."

"Ah." Julian nodded slightly. "He made confession?"

"Uh-huh."

"In his room."

"Uh-huh."

Someone had overheard the confession. Julian was certain of that. An orderly, a nurse, another lowlife who would need a payoff. The payroll line was growing, and his cash reserves were almost gone. He tried to hide his worry as he turned to Bohmer. "Thank you for coming, Officer. Drake will show you and the commissioner out."

Bohmer rose. "Mind if I look around first?"

Julian shook his head wearily. "Hiram, is that necessary tonight?"

"Well . . ."

Bohmer interrupted. "A lot of broken glass on the other side of the house."

"That block-headed understudy, Tobias Morse, crashed through looking for Miss Henslowe," Julian said. "Apparently he doesn't know how to use a door."

"He was desperately trying to help," Peg said. "We were told Katie was in great danger."

Julian forced himself to look steadily at her. "With a man like Dennigan, it's a reasonable assumption."

"I think Nance took a shot at that Tobias fellow," Bohmer said.

Julian smiled weakly, trying to joke. "That would be enough to make *me* jump through a window."

"Maybe," Bohmer said. "I'd still like to take a look."

"C'mon, Bohmer," the commissioner said. "Leave Julian in peace. He's had enough excitement for one night." He nodded to Peg. "'Night, Miss Henslowe."

Peg got up and righted her cane, preparing to leave.

"Oh, Peg," Julian said. "There are some production items I'd like to go over with you, as long as you're here."

"Of course," she said ingenuously, as if she had not known she would be asked to stay. The commissioner and the officer took their leave, and Julian closed the door. He sat on the sofa, opposite Peg.

She spoke first. "Katie and Matt are engaged to be married, you know."

"Oh?" He was suddenly antsy. He pushed himself up and started to pace. "Then her fiancé is a fugitive, and she is too."

"It's not clear that she helped him escape a lawful custody. I think the police are going to have to investigate more closely. Perhaps apprehend Mr. *Raskin* and question the terms of his employment." She paused. "Do we understand each other?"

He stopped to look at her. "Subtlety is not your forte, is it, Peg?"

"No. I have a message Katie asked me to deliver. First I want to make sure there will be no charges filed against any member of Poppy, including Tobias."

He shook his head, pacing again. "Excluding Tobias. He ruined custom-cut panes."

"He ruined your plans for Matt, whatever they were. Katie wouldn't tell me much. She doesn't want me to have to lie to police. She's funny that way, about being honest."

"Oh, she's a veritable angel, all right." He stopped once more and faced her. "Your angel will be in criminal flight from prosecution aboard the three-twenty to Cincinnati tomorrow afternoon."

Peg's eyes flicked down, and he knew he was right.

"That's the train your brother's casket is on, isn't it? From Cincinnati she can get connections to Philadelphia, New York,

Boston, wherever she and Matt want to go." Wherever Matt intended to meet his protector and boss.

"How did you know which train Edmund's coffin will be on?"

"I told your father I would pay for the tickets. He ordered three, for him, Katie, and Zemin. I'm guessing that Zemin will board as a six-foot Caucasian with chestnut hair. It's my business to know these things. I pay the bills."

She lifted her chin, calm once more. "I know some sawyers and varnishers who renovated the New Gate who might debate that."

"I haven't heard a squawk out of them and I won't. They want my business. Just as you do, Peg. Poppy is dependent on me."

"No, Mr. Gates. We're professionals providing a valuable service according to contract. Dependency is a concept for power-mad employers, or sadists."

"You can be quick, like your sister," he said. "And like your sister, you risk much."

"Our risk was in coming here in the first place. But we are here, and we will premiere in a week, as agreed. You will destroy your theater before it even opens if you fire Poppy now. Further, there's an exigency clause in our contract which allows for change of lead actors."

Julian's lips tightened. She was right about the premiere. His reputation did not need the blow of a possible scandal with Poppy. "What changes are you suggesting?"

"Tobias is an experienced understudy. He'll assume the lead."

"Fine."

"And I will play Juliet."

He stared at her. "You're joking."

"No. I'm Juliet." She rose and started toward the door. Her limp was painlessly fluid and painfully obvious.

"I cannot allow such a breach of contract."

She stopped, glancing back at him. "Let me see if I can paraphrase what Katie told me. She had to talk herself blue just to convince me I could do this. You see, the New Gate's presentation of *Romeo and Juliet* with a strikingly beautiful and talented cripple in the lead role will be reported throughout the country. And you will glean, unrightfully, a reputation for enlightened philanthropy and sympathetic casting. We will restage the production so that I will be sitting most of the time. I guarantee that my impairment will not distract the audience. We will have a comic young nurse, by the way, instead of an old one."

"Lucy St. Clair."

"Of course. You will be hailed for your many innovations, Mr. Gates. I would hate to tell this city's thirty newspapers and periodicals the morning after that you protested violently."

"I applaud your shrewdness, but I cannot allow you to manipulate me this way."

Peg put her hand on the doorknob. "Did I mention that Norrie O'Shea gathered at the gate with us for a while?"

Trump play. His molars pinched the inner membrane of his cheek. "No. I believe you forgot that."

"It was he who told Tobias where in this mausoleum he could find Matt. He who told Tobias to hurry because he was watching through a window and saw you grab my sister and throw—her—to —the—floor." Peg's blue eyes were icy, narrowed.

"I see," Julian said, rubbing his temples. The pain had begun throbbing again. So suddenly this time.

"Norrie is very troubled about his experiences here. He poured out his heart. Frederick joined us too."

Altmann. Double trump.

"Frederick's been in pain for years. He said he can no longer be a criminal accessory. He wants his honor back. He's packing his things."

Personal notes on accounting procedures, no doubt.

"I see," Julian said, so softly he was not sure he could be heard. "Are you finished?"

She opened the door. "The question is, are you?"

He let silence reign a moment, then smiled. "No, my dear. As each one of you will discover."

When she was gone, he quickly wrote down his trip itinerary, then rang for Drake. "Staff is scheduled to return an hour past midnight, correct?" he asked.

287

"Yes, sir."

"Good. You brought my jewelry box?"

Drake put it on the desk. Steps sounded in the hallway, followed by a loud slam of the front door.

Drake cleared his throat. "I believe that was Mr. Altmann leaving, sir. He won't be staying to attend the dinner party tomorrow. I understand the general will be a guest?"

"Cancel it. I won't be here. Now, I believe there are still three more people waiting in the kitchen to see me?"

"Only two, sir."

Damn. He would have to make do.

He descended the cool flagstone steps to the kitchen. Only a wall sconce lit the large room. The soft light bounced clay red off rows of hanging copper pots. At first, he couldn't see them. Cat cautious, the two emerged from the cavelike darkness of the scullery room.

"Sit down," Julian said, pulling up chairs at the plankboard table. He lit a lantern. "Nance said you were specialists. You know your targets."

They nodded, then one asked, "What about the Chinaman?"

"Low priority. If you don't get him, I'll deal with him later. However, under no circumstances may Matt Dennigan and Katie Henslowe survive. If they do, I'll make sure you both become the targets of someone obviously more skilled than you."

"We don't miss," the smaller assassin said, miffed. "And we don't work on threats."

"Or on commission, either, I suppose," Julian said, impatient. "I'm sure you've been talking to Nance. Has he still got my pin or has he already hawked it?"

The big one smiled. "We certainly wouldn't mind some collateral that's reflective of the value of our endeavor."

"Clever man. I can offer you these." He showed them one diamond and pearl earring and one garnet cuff link, telling them they'd get the mates the day of Matt Dennigan's funeral. The diamond necklace and bracelet that matched the earrings would mark Katie's burial.

"You sure they're going to be on the three-twenty tomorrow?" the big one asked, pocketing the jewelry.

"No, but I am sure Katie wants to bury her brother. She's loyal —and predictable—in affairs of family. Follow the coffin," Julian said, "and you'll find Katie."

29

A dray delivered the Mennonite couple to the train station in the soft grayness before dawn. They rode on the back lip of the buckboard, legs dangling. The drayman drew to a halt far beyond the gaslights of the station.

The Mennonite man eased off the lip and landed stiffly, as if the journey had been a long one. He had a honey brown beard and long blondish hair showing below a flat-brimmed hat. He was dressed poorly and plainly, like a country parson.

His wife was hugely pregnant. Her shapeless gray dress had a high waist and she protruded healthily round beneath it, obviously near her time. Her pale face showed a tiredness that was understandable, given her condition. Black hair escaped the brim of her bonnet, framing her face in wispy curls. She sat patiently while her husband put their carpetbags on the ground. There were only two bags, small ones.

The driver hopped down from the spring bench in front. "Lemme help you, sir! Bags all down? Lemme help with the missus, then." He reached up, but the other man stopped him.

"I can handle it, Dev."

As Katie fell forward into his arms, Matt let his right one take most of her weight. Still, he couldn't hide his wince. He landed her clumsily, with a jostle and ungainly hop.

She tried to smile, but she was worried.

"Don't let him help," Devlin teased Katie, "or you'll be carryin' that child down about your knees. Look at him. He tipped a thumb at Matt. "See how his left shoulder sags and his chest curves in? People see him and right away say that's one'a them never-fight Mennonites—or a man with a busted rib."

Gingerly, Matt squared his shoulders. He threw out his chest, slightly. "You hit every loose brick in the street, you know that? Fifty-seven."

"Countin' 'em on me, are you? A crass and ungracious man you've turned into, and me rippin' the very sheets off me only bed to give you comfort. That bindin' job I did gonna hold you?"

A steam whistle blew. The Ohio & Mississippi's six-fifteen to Cincinnati was ready to board.

"It'll hold," Matt said, looking away.

Devlin cleared his throat. "Best get goin'." He gave Katie's hand a squeeze. "Take care of yourself now."

"Wait," Katie whispered as he turned to leave. She reached into Matt's coat pocket and withdrew a polished wood cylinder.

"Me telescope." Devlin took it, shaking his head. "Damned if she's not a woman of her word. Matt me boy, be careful. If ever she promises you a rose garden, clear ground, 'cause it'll be there. Thorns and all." He gave Matt a hard look. "I got the pricklies right now just thinkin' 'bout it. You, Matt?"

Matt resettled his hat brim, disguising a surveying glance of the station grounds. He nodded once.

"Watch your back, m'friend." Devlin climbed onto the driver's seat and snapped the reins.

The predawn breeze was chilly, carrying the burnt-tar tang of a coal-burning engine stoking its furnace. Matt picked up the carpet-bags. He walked slowly, mindful of the exaggerated walk Katie affected. The pregnant cushioning made awkwardness natural. She would carry the padding until Cincinnati. There, she would change her bonnet and, with it, her hair color. His own Arthurian wig and whiskers would come off too. They were made of human hair, authentic-looking and realistically scratchy.

Katie had readied the disguises the previous night, before going to Greenmore, scavenging troupe members' personal costume trunks at the hotel and hiding the bundle for Grub to retrieve later.

Matt had thought the disguises much too elaborate, until now. Two policemen stood on the loading platform of the Ohio & Mississippi and one officer watched the ticket window. Matt kept his face stern, a Mennonite stoic. Inside, though, his nerves were crackling, alert to any sudden movement in the crowd. Katie had told him onlookers would avert their eyes from a woman swollen large with child. She was right. Men especially were too uneasy to look long in their direction, even policemen.

The station was crowded, which meant the coach cars would be full, thirty or forty people per car. Good, Matt thought. Safety in numbers. They queued up with others. Matrons bustled into line, hands on their youngsters' shoulders, guiding them like rudders. Salesmen in rumpled jackets and turned-down collars clutched wide leather cases to their chests.

A bony woman in a faded cotton dress and nappy wool shawl stood outside the line, waiting for a space to step in. Sodbuster's wife, probably, Matt guessed. She had that prairie woman look, squinty and blank, like she was lost in the middle of something. North Platte winters did that to a person.

He moved backward to make room for her to get in line. In doing so he stepped on the crinoline-hoop skirt of the woman behind him. He turned around to apologize.

"That's quite all right," she said, her smile strangely inviting. She was young and pretty, wearing a frilly blue hat with white netting. Primped and powdered, she was testament to the vast social distance between her and the wretched woman standing in front of him.

The steam whistle blew again. Last chance to board. Beside him, he felt Katie tug his coat. "To the left," she said under her breath. "Fifth car from the end."

He looked. A Chinese man in dark tunic and trousers was boarding. Zemin? What in the hell was he doing there? He was supposed to accompany Katie's father on the afternoon three-twenty. He must have found out that Edmund's coffin had been switched to the freight car of the six-fifteen at the last minute. Zemin carried loyal companionship to an extreme, Matt thought. And his presence posed an unexpected danger. Whether or not Zemin carried the Chinese-language copy of the opium order, he was probably being hunted by the bargain-barrel toughs Julian was so fond of hiring.

As their line inched forward, Matt kept his eye on the passengers in Zemin's line. A few had potential to be thugs, men whose faces were rugged, topcoats moth-eaten, and trousers shiny at the knees. There were regular-looking Joes too, in round-crowned hats and plain dark vests. One dandy towered over the others, wearing a stovepipe and patent leather boots. Could be any one or all of them, waiting a chance to jump Zemin somewhere along the three-hundred mile route.

Zemin, of course, wasn't the killer's only target on the six-fifteen. He took Katie's hand and squeezed gently, a sign of caution. She smiled reassurance. He marveled at her gift for empathy, as he had the night before when they lay talking of plans for the journey, of risks and choices. It was as if feelings passed between them on invisible threads, vibrating an inner voice each could hear. He had never felt so close to a woman, to anyone. And he had never feared the possibility of loss so deeply.

He helped her onto a step stool and up to the stairwell of the train. When he gave a last glance to the fifth car from the end, Zemin looked directly at him, acknowledging that he knew they were boarding. The Chinese was obviously attuned to recognizing Katie in costume disguise. Hopefully, he would have enough sense to keep his distance.

In the car padded booths faced one another in sets of two. Katie inched her way down the aisle ahead of him, stopping at the booth where the prairie woman sat hunched in her shawl. Careful of the stomach padding, Katie laboriously scooted in and sat opposite the unresponsive woman.

He took the aisle seat. Adjusting his hat brim low, he scrutinized every man that passed, looking for the bulge of a gun in a pocket or waistband. He felt someone watching him. It was the pretty woman in the frilly blue bonnet; she was across the aisle and one booth back. She smiled, too warmly. He faced front. Why was she playing coy with a dour Mennonite who had a pregnant wife? Maybe just wanting something she couldn't have; some high-class women were like that. But then, why would a well-fixed woman travel coach instead of first-class?

He settled back in his seat, aware of many discomforts—the scratchy beard, the hard seat, the cramped space. Worst of all, though, was the knowledge that he couldn't let down his guard or talk to Katie. Taciturn silence fit both of his roles—Mennonite and fugitive.

"First stop, Salem," the conductor droned, taking their tickets. "Arriving Cincinnati eleven tonight."

Sixteen hours to Ohio. And that was only the first leg of their four-state journey to safety in New York. The train began to roll, gliding slowly to the river. They rode a high, narrow trestle above the brown-bottomed Mississippi. From distant high bluffs, Matt knew, the locomotive would look as small as a millipede walking a line. From where he sat, though, he was in the belly of a great soaring bird, and when they crossed the levee on the Illinois side of the river, he felt free, as if he'd sprouted wings. They were out.

He looked at Katie. She'd closed her eyes and her hand lay on the sterile padding of her pregnancy. She missed her child.

"I've never been away from her so long, so far away," she had said last night as they lay exhausted on a pallet at the safe house Devlin had chosen for them.

"She'll be fine with my mother," Matt had said.

"I know." She'd paused. "Hellie's a wonderful grandmother."

"No."

" 'No' what?"

"I will not bring Samuel here. I told you that. Don't count on that changing."

"Everything changes," she said, getting up and pacing. "People torment you one day, the next day they're dead. They can't hurt you anymore, but they still do."

"Edmund's not tormenting you anymore. You are." He didn't

get up; the pain in his ribs hadn't eased. "And it wasn't a good idea, switching his coffin to the early train. Someone might notice."

"But I have to take care of the transporting, the arrangements. Father's in no shape to handle it. Zemin doesn't have the authority or the presence of mind, staying in his room and lighting candles to worship Edmund. It's up to me. I have to finish it."

"You don't always have to take charge," he said. "Your father's a grown man. Zemin too. Even Poppy can survive without you if you give Peg and Tobias half a chance."

"Surviving and thriving are two different things."

"The first sounds fine to me. Nothing fancy. Just breath left in my body to get back to Texas and buy back my land."

She turned to him. "I was hoping you'd prefer surviving a season as apprentice lead to Tobias."

"Jesus Christ. Acting?"

There was a long silence, then she said, "We're dreaming this, aren't we? Dreaming about living together, putting all the pieces of our lives into a pile and seeing what kind of picture we can make. Can you see a picture, Matt?"

He didn't answer.

"I knew you couldn't." She sat down on the pallet beside him. "You don't like to dream."

"I don't like to be disappointed. And you don't like to let go. You hold on to the past. You hold on to Poppy." He stared up into the darkness. "You hold on to me."

She was silent.

"I'm dangerous for you, Katie. I'm a walking target. We should take two trains, try to meet later."

"No!" She lay down beside him, pulling the blankets up. "No."

He slipped an arm around her. "Please. Stay in St. Louis."

"I have a burial back East. Besides, I can help you. You need me."

"I need you to be safe. Aiding and abetting a fugitive is a serious charge."

"You won't be a fugitive once you see the senator, and once Peg gets Altmann and Norrie together to compare notes. We just need to buy time, Matt, that's all." She kissed him desperately, demandingly. "Time is all we need."

No, love, Matt answered her silently as the train rattled over a rough juncture of rail. They needed Zemin's letter as evidence. They needed to know why Julian had an opium cache in the terminus of the Central Pacific. They needed to find out which of the ordinary-looking people on the train were marching to his orders.

She slept, her head on his shoulder, trusting. The shake of the locomotive lulled him too. He jerked himself awake and caught the prairie woman watching him. She shifted her gaze.

"Heard there was lots of flooding on the Platte," he said.

She didn't answer for a while. "Washed us out."

"Homesteading?"

She looked out the window, as if he were getting too nosy. "Buying."

Most settlers who arrived with no cash and big dreams, Matt knew, took the "long credit" plan set up by the land department of the railroads: ten years to pay, six percent interest. The railroaders' brochures depicted a land of milk and honey, complete with rags to riches anecdotes. What settlers found was arid land, grasshopper plagues, hair-raising storms, and never-ending bills for machinery, livestock, and seed.

The woman said nothing more and was first into the aisle to get off when the train pulled into the waystation at Salem. Vendors walked the loading platform hawking fried fish and breads, meat pies, and sweets. Matt helped Katie down the steps. A bevy of women and children straggled down a path that wound around the south side of the stationhouse to the outbuildings. Men headed for the north side. As Katie joined the south line, Matt looked for Zemin. He saw the top hat dandy from Zemin's car, but Zemin wasn't anywhere in the waystation crowd. Maybe he hadn't gotten off. Matt boarded Zemin's car. It was empty. As he turned back to the steps, he saw the dandy in the tall hat stepping up into the railcar. Matt deliberately collided with him. The dandy pushed him away with a roughness unseemly for an elegant roué.

"Beg pardon," Matt said.

"Pardon granted," the dandy said, irritated. He had meat-chop jowls and a gold-capped tooth. He brushed off his shiny salmon vest as if vermin had touched it.

With conscious effort, Matt looked down and nodded. A Mennonite was peace-loving, unprovocative.

As Matt walked away, the dandy eyed him suspiciously. Matt knew he had just been tested, and he hoped he'd passed. The dandy hadn't. In the scuffle, Matt had bumped against the hard casing of a gun holster strapped to the man's right side. The dandy was a left-handed gunman.

He waited for Katie on the platform, and she asked if he'd seen Zemin. He shook his head. "Maybe next stop," she said.

He thought of the dandy's revolver. "I wouldn't count on it."

The woman in the blue hat sashayed in front of them as they headed back to the train. She dangled her hand for Matt to help her onto the step stool. "Thank you," she said. Matt nodded cautiously. The woman was dressed as richly as the dandy.

He turned to Katie. With a wry look, she extended her arm and dangled her hand as though she were helpless.

The prairie woman was already in her seat. Katie tried to begin a conversation, to no avail. All the information she could elicit was that the woman's name was Mary, she had two sons, and they were home plowing.

Next stop was Vincennes. Most coach passengers broke out biscuits and bacon, or shanks of cold meat wrapped in linen. Matt took Katie into the crowded eatery by the train station for a quick meal. Over in the corner was Mary, treating herself to a big plate of chicken, boiled potatoes, and berry pie.

Through the restaurant window he could see the dandy strolling the length of the train, undoubtedly looking for Zemin. Finally, he leaned against a post in front of his car, picking lint from his top hat and trying to look idle.

To Matt, he looked perturbed. Either Zemin was hiding on another car, or he had left the train at the first stop.

The afternoon trek across southern Indiana stretched into dusk and nightfall. He kept an eye on the lady in the blue hat. She and her cohort were unlikely-looking executioners. It was a quality that no doubt afforded them a nice element of surprise in their work. Matt didn't doze.

The train rolled into the big Cincinnati terminal at eleven-fifteen. The passengers shook off sleepiness and gathered bags. Mary edged into the aisle without saying a word of farewell. As Matt got their bags down from the racks, he saw Katie rub her hands together for warmth. The night air was crisp and chill.

"You have warm gloves?" he asked.

She nodded and reached for one of the carpetbags. Upon opening it, she hesitated. He watched her paw carefully through the vermillion-trimmed waistcoat and the few items of clothing she had packed in the bag.

"Is something wrong?" he asked, very low. The car was still crowded with passengers waiting to debark. The woman in the blue hat stood near the exit; she was gazing intently at them.

"No," Katie said. "For a minute I thought something was missing, but everything seems to be here." She gave him a meaningful look as she put on her gloves.

Someone had gone through the bag. And that someone would now be on the lookout for a woman in a vermillion-trimmed waistcoat making connections to New York.

He didn't say a word as he guided Katie through the aisle and off the train. Their bags must have been rifled when they got off to stretch their legs at Seymour Station just before dusk. Quite a few of the passengers had stayed on board, including the woman in the blue hat.

Matt kept Katie tucked close to him as they negotiated the huge crowd milling around the boarding gates. Vendors patrolled with trays of fried chicken, hot cakes, and coffee. In the terminal, a flash of blue caught his eye. The woman was sitting on a bench across the room. She'd been waiting for them, and got up when she saw them.

Matt tensed as she walked purposefully toward them. He knew Katie was too short to see the woman over the heads of the people

298

around them. "Go check the connections for New York," he said urgently.

She obviously sensed something was wrong. "I'd rather get some air."

"Hurry. Go directly outside. I'll meet you there."

"Take care with our bags, husband," she called with perfect, domestic intimacy as they separated.

He bent down to set the bags at his feet and let his hat fall off. As he retrieved it, he pulled up one trouser leg and slipped his revolver from the elastic bands around his calf. He rose with the wide-brimmed hat hiding the gun.

The woman stopped in front of him. She smiled warmly again, as she had the first time he'd seen her in the boarding line in St. Louis. "I want to apologize for staring at you the whole trip."

He looked at her hands. Out in the open, clutching a small reticule.

"I didn't mean to be rude," she went on. "I was trying to work up the courage to talk to you. You see, my brother ran away some years ago to join a sect like yours. I've not heard from him, and I was wondering . . ."

A ploy?

She smiled again, clearly uncomfortable. "His name is Clay," she said hopefully. "Donald Clay."

Gut instinct told him she was genuine.

"Do you know him?"

She wasn't the killer. *Then who was it?*

"Donald and I grew up in—"

"Sorry, ma'am," Matt interrupted. "Afraid I've never heard of him." He bent quickly, keeping the gun hidden as he opened one of the carpetbags and slipped it in. Straightening, he plopped his hat on his head and grabbed the handles of both bags in one hand. "'Scuse me, please."

Katie.

He wove quickly through the crowd, un-Christianly pushing people out of his way.

Katie.

He saw her dark, encumbered form pass through the main door to the outside. She was following his directions, dammit. She stepped right out into the open.

Katie!

30

Matt burst through the door and onto the brightly lit sidewalk. It was filled with travelers, while cabs and carriages lined the street. Katie was nowhere in sight.

He passed a peanut man squatting beside a black iron brazier. The nutty fragrance of roasting hulls was an unnatural pocket of warmth in a night growing colder.

He couldn't discard his Mennonite character without compromising Katie's. "Wife!" he called sternly. Passersby looked at him strangely, but accepted his haste to get by.

He ducked off the sidewalk and into the street to better see pedestrians ahead. The street was noisy with the clop-clod of horses, the rumble of freight wagons, and the constant chatter of people. He probably wouldn't be able to hear even if Katie returned his call. He hurried ahead, scanning the street, alarmed at the number of well-dressed men wearing top hats.

Katie.

Tinkling music pierced the street noise. The refrain jerked at his instincts like thread looped around a tooth.

The carnival tune came from an alley along the north side of the terminal. Matt retraced a few steps and spotted the battered cap of an organ grinder. Pushing closer he saw the bored man cranking a hurdy-gurdy in the half shadows of the alley, which appeared to cut through to the terminal's loading dock. At his feet a costumed monkey on a long leash did backflips.

And there was Katie, standing with a small group of spectators. He watched her absently reach a hand into a paper cone of peanuts offered by a companion, a woman standing in shadows. He could see a faded print dress and the corner of a wool shawl. Mary.

Shy Mary with no manners, no history, and no answers. Dirt-poor Mary with enough money to buy a big meal and a cone of peanuts. Patient Mary with all the time in the world to watch and wait and search their bags.

"Good wife!" he shouted urgently to get Katie's attention as he shouldered his way through the stream of people on the sidewalk.

She waved him closer, then bent to offer the tiny rhesus monkey a peanut. The monkey climbed onto her arm. Matt reached her as she straightened, telling the organ grinder it was all right.

"We have to go," Matt said harshly.

He saw that Mary had crowded close to Katie. She held peanuts in one hand, and there was no telling what she had in the other. Her arm was folded across her stomach, her hand concealed in the drape of the shawl. Her back was to the alley, an easy escape.

He reached for Katie's arm to pull her away, but the monkey jumped onto his chest, sniffing for peanuts.

People laughed, and the small group's attention shifted solely to him. He didn't even glance at the animal. Instinct warned him to watch Mary instead.

Her hand crooked out from under the shawl; she had a pepper-box revolver aimed dead at Katie.

He desperately jerked forward to put himself in the line of fire, but the monkey with its instinct for food was quicker than the prairie woman's draw.

In a split second, the nervous animal hopped from Matt, to Katie, to the fragrant cone of peanuts in Mary's hand. The paper cone spilled as Mary reacted immediately with disgust. She gave the monkey a vicious whack on the head with the heavy six-barrel pistol.

The monkey screeched in pain and landed on the ground in the midst of scattered peanuts. The crowd panicked at the sight of the revolver.

Matt pushed Katie back and lunged for the gun, grabbing the muzzle and cocking it downward. The shot hit the ground. Against his palm the fat muzzle rotated to align a new cylinder to the strikeplate.

He wrenched the gun out of her hand, but could not keep his grasp on the woman. She broke free and hurled breakneck down the alley, past parked carts and old crates.

After one look back to make sure Katie was all right, Matt ran after the woman. Pain shot through his fractured ribs, and he slowed but did not stop. He would not stop until he found her. He was not sure he could kill a woman, no matter how cold-blooded her aim. He was sure, though, that he could incapacitate her, for Katie's sake, for his own.

He held the pistol nose-down as he jogged painfully past slatted boxes and tumbled bins. The cartmen's alley was dark. The smell of horse dung was strong. He saw the prairie woman slip once. She righted herself, almost at the alley's end, at the dock beside the tracks.

Behind him, the alley walls reverberated the flat-sole sound of men trying to catch up with him to help. From ahead came steam whistle warnings and the chug of an engine beginning to roll.

The woman he pursued didn't hesitate. Once she was in the open she glanced left at the approaching train, then headed straight across the tracks.

The screech of brakes rang out. Skirt dragging, she got clear of the tracks just ahead of the train. But her hem snagged on a nail-head on a crossplate. The sudden jerk pitched her backward and she fell onto the tracks. For the first time, Matt saw human expression light the unrelieved gloom on her face: surprise.

The train couldn't stop.

He closed his eyes and leaned breathless against the building, trying to feel detached from the pain in his side, from the carnage on the tracks. Two strangers ran up to make sure he was all right, then went ahead to get a firsthand look at the grisly scene.

Matt slowly made his way back down the alley, tucking the gun in his belt and covering it with his coat. The pepperbox was an old-style revolver with a cluster of barrels. Unreliable for long-range targets, but for close work, guaranteed deadly. He hoped none of the spectators would think to question why a pacifist Mennonite had run off stalking a woman with her own pistol.

When he reached the street end of the alley he heard jungle screams, the staccato high-pitched squeals from the injured monkey. A crowd had gathered around a cleared space.

Matt picked up his pace when he saw several jaunty top hats in the group. One of them might belong to a dandy with an underarm bulge about the size of a Colt .45.

Katie broke free of the group, hurrying to him and embracing him. Her stomach padding shifted sideways as he held her fiercely. Too close a call this time. Too close.

A policeman approached, and Katie turned away to readjust the pregnant padding. "Evenin', Mr. Smith," the officer said. "People say a crazy woman pulled a gun on your wife here. Atrocious. I was telling your missus you'd better come down to the station and give us a report."

"I'd like to get my wife to the hotel first," Matt said, casually turning "Mrs. Smith" so the officer could take in her fully rounded profile. "I'm sure you understand. It's just down the street."

" 'Course, sir," the policeman said. "Let me get you a cab." He blew his whistle and signaled a vehicle. "Someone said there was a pistol," he added suggestively.

"Probably somewhere in the alley," Matt said, bending down to secure the carpetbag that held his own Colt .44.

The monkey's cries were incessant, a heart-wrenching delirium of pain. The officer tsked once. "Somebody said its jaw got busted. It'll never be able to eat. I better take care of it." The officer slipped the flap on his holster and headed into the crowd.

Katie froze. A shot rang out, and she began to tremble badly. Matt helped her into the carriage.

She stared numbly ahead as the carriage started off. "Mary said she needed help to get her bags." Her voice was tight. "I told her we'd have to wait for you. She said she was in a hurry and she took my arm, saying she wanted to cut through the alley. But the hurdy-gurdy man was there. And she had the peanuts. And he started to play."

"I made a mistake," Matt said. "I didn't realize she was the one."

"She wasn't 'Mary.' She wasn't a farmer's wife. She didn't have sons. She was acting, like we are." She was silent, then burst out, "She was good!"

"Yes, she was. Julian isn't hiring cheap rivermen anymore."

"How many are there?"

"One more that I know of. A fancy dresser in a shiny pink vest. Had a seat in Zemin's car."

"Bartholomew."

"What?"

"That's the name he gave me. He talked to me at the last stop when you went off to look for Zemin."

Matt felt blood drain from his face.

"Did you know Mr. Bartholomew has a gold tooth?" she went on, her voice faint. "On the bottom near the front. He smiles a lot."

A wracking coldness ripped through Matt. Fear. How could he think clearly, react cleanly, when he was so afraid for her safety? The carriage rattled woodenly in the long silence.

"It's not what you imagined, is it, Katie? It's not like a play where we dress up and follow the script, or get prompted from the wings. There's no script. And there's no guarantee that all will end well. You have a child to think of."

"And you don't?"

The carriage dipped as a wheel bounded in and out of a pothole. "We can't travel as a couple now. He'll spot us too easily."

She didn't protest.

"What time does the train leave tomorrow?" he asked.

"Six o'clock. The Atlantic & Great Western line."

Another run at sunrise. "After you're settled in the hotel, I'll go back to the station and get tickets."

"And a freight transfer."

He bit back a curse. "That casket lets Bartholomew track every connection we make, and you know it."

"That casket is my responsibility."

"Dammit, where there's Edmund, there's a killer."

"Where there's Edmund, there's Zemin."

He paused. "You're so sure Zemin didn't get off at another station?"

"I think he's been with Edmund."

"In the freight car? Cold and hungry?"

"Zemin always sacrificed for Edmund. It seemed to suit him. Certainly it suited Edmund. The Chinese tradition is forty-nine days of deepest mourning for a loved one. Zemin has a long time to go."

"You're sure he'll have that second letter with him?"

"The one in Chinese? He couldn't afford to leave it, or himself, within reach of Julian."

Julian was sure to start a smear campaign against Edmund and Zemin as a smoke screen, Matt thought. That letter could turn out to be the only written evidence they had to link Julian to the opium hidden in Sacramento. Why, dammit? Why Sacramento when the market was in San Francisco?

The carriage rocked to a stop. "What a relief to be getting out of here," she said, shifting the padding so she could move more easily. "This carriage absolutely smells."

"Horse manure," he said.

"It does!"

He lifted his shoe. "From the alley."

"Oh."

He scraped his shoe on the front steps of the hotel before they went in. The place was small and not too far from the railway station, and their room was accordingly spare and nondescript. Its only attraction was a gas heater, which Matt lit. Yellow flame tripped across the firing line, and the valves flared. Katie moved close to get warm.

He tore off his hat and the blond wig. "As soon as we change clothes, we change hotels," he said. His scalp itched, and he clawed at it, tousling his hair. He tugged at the edge of the beard and winced.

"Give it a good steady pull," she said, slipping off her bonnet with black wig attached.

Gingerly, he peeled off the blond sideburns and beard, grimacing at the tweak of each hair in his own two-day-old beard. "Damn."

"I put on a lot of cement," she said apologetically. "I didn't know how much you'd sweat."

"Apparently, not enough."

She pulled hairpins, collecting them between her teeth until she could shake her hair free. She sighed with relief and vigorously scratched her head.

After putting on a plain wool jacket and a string tie, he helped Katie, unfastening the buttons on her dress. The bodice slipped free, revealing breasts which seemed swollen, achingly tight to his touch. He knew it was imagination. Her pregnancy was only a plump down pillow shaped inside a girl's cane-hoop crinoline. He used his pocketknife to cut the ties knotted behind Katie's back, and the cushion fell free. She put a hand to the small of her back, which bore the imprint of the knots and the strain of awkward weight.

The gesture reminded him of the months Sarah was pregnant. How she walked, the arch in her back growing sharper with each pound the baby added to her girth. He had tried to massage her back one night. She'd moved away, as if nothing he could do would ever help, the same way Katie moved away from him now.

Her confidence was shaken. The prairie woman had gained her trust with a performance so real and controlled, not even a stage actress had suspected. No doubt Katie's confidence in his judgment had grown wobbly too.

She donned a wide belt and the waist-length jacket with the vermillion trim, then sat before the heater to brush her hair. She leaned to one side, letting the long curtain fall free of her body as she stroked it fluffy and full.

"If something happens to me, Matt," she said, breaking the strained silence, "I hope you'll—well . . ."

"I'll make sure Beth is taken care of."

"I know she's not your responsibility."

"You don't have to believe me. Just understand that if anything happened to you, I would owe her. I would owe her the world."

Katie got up and went to him. She looked very young. "Don't let anything happen."

He embraced her tightly. He could not promise. He could not lie to her. "We've got to go."

Wearily, she put on a small, plain hat. "You think we were followed here?"

He shut the valve on the heater. "I don't want to take that chance."

She reached in the bag and pulled out a pair of reading glasses. "Father's spectacles," she said, fitting the wire rims around her ears. She perched the small round glasses near the tip of her nose. "Do I look like a student on my way east?"

He lifted the frame and set the lenses closer to her eyes. "Not unless you hide your eyes."

"Everything's blurry," she protested.

"Keep it that way. By tomorrow, police and railroad detectives will have copies of a playbill with your face on it. Let's go."

He found a back way out and led her to another small hotel a block away. When they got to their new room, he pulled his revolver from the bag. "Know how to use this?"

She shrugged. "Point and pull."

"More or less. I'll knock three times when I get back. Anyone works the lock without knocking, take aim." He paused. "Better take off the glasses first."

"Matt." She removed the glasses.

He opened the door and waited, but she just shook her head.

The train station was quiet. Broomhandlers were sweeping the throughways. Matt walked in casually, as if he weren't conscious of the half-dozen travelers sitting on benches. None of the men looked like Bartholomew from the back. The hired killer might have changed his clothes but he couldn't change his face. Meaty jowls and a gold tooth.

The elderly ticket agent gave Matt two tickets for the six-oh-five to Columbus and made out a new freight tag. "Want to ship gaskets, you say?" The old man's question bounced around the vast, empty terminal hall.

"No," Matt said, making his grimace a smile. "Let me write it down for you." C-a-s-k-e-t.

"Oh." The old man nodded. "Same price."

Matt pulled his parson's hat low as he left, glancing at the benches. Everyone was looking his way, including a jowly man with a valise open on his knees. Bartholomew.

Senses strained and tingling, Matt walked several blocks in a zigzag pattern until he was sure he wasn't being followed. Then he stopped in a tavern to get a different hat and jacket.

He left his own hat and coat on the coatrack and bought a beer. He planned to take just a few sips, but the brew was yeasty and strong, and he drained the tall mug. The coat he chose from the rack was tight, but that was all right. The round-crown hat didn't fit either.

He took an indirect route back to the hotel and stayed outside in the shadows for a while, observing. The street was empty. It was 2 A.M. He let himself in the back and went up to their room. He knocked three times, but Katie didn't answer. He quickly used the key and threw open the door.

She lay on the bed asleep, the lamp full aglow on the bedstand. She seemed needy in sleep, unarmed, lacking wit or wile or the uncompromising strength of her convictions. Her fragility frightened him.

He blew out the lamp. In the darkness he took off his coat and hat, then pulled the prairie woman's revolver from his belt. In the dim light at the window he checked the chamber. Five shots left. He put the stubby-barrel pepperbox in one of the carpetbags and took his own long-nose Colt from the nightstand.

Quietly, he carried a ladder-back chair to the window. Turning it around he straddled it, leaning his arms on the chair back so he could see the street. Only a few hours till dawn.

Alone with his thoughts, he concentrated on the riddle of Julian's opium in Sacramento. Things just didn't add up. It made sense to hold the powdered drug there until his pharmaceutical factory was up and running in St. Louis. But what about the other two hundred pounds, the gum for smoking? That had to go to a market of people familiar with the ritual. People who knew how to cook it, dehydrate and mold it on the point of a yen hock. The Chinese population in San Francisco had experienced smokers, but it was a low-margin business. Julian was not a nickel-and-dime man.

The bedding shifted behind him. She was awake. The bed creaked, then he heard her stocking feet pad across the floor.

"Somehow, I slipped through your alert sentry defenses," he chided her.

She rested forearms on his shoulders and chin on his head. "Stealthy fellow."

"No. Tired lady." He tipped his head back and kissed her.

"Why aren't you sleeping too?" she asked.

"I've got Sacramento on my mind. I just can't figure out why's he holding it there."

"If it's a warehouse, maybe he's wholesaling it."

"To whom?"

"I don't know," she said sleepily. "Men like Chang."

"Men like Chang." He jumped up, nearly toppling her. "Men like Chang go in and out of Sacramento all the time!"

"You mean laundrymen who peddle opium?"

"No. Caterers who can peddle it."

"I don't understand."

"The Chinese laborers for the Central Pacific don't eat beef and potatoes. In their camps, they have special mess attendants who fix exotic things."

"Like what? Rice?"

"Dried oysters, cuttlefish, abalone, bamboo shoots, salted cabbage."

"Where do they get that stuff?"

"Shipped in from the coast, to Sacramento. That's where a camp agent can pick up supplies for their cooks. And that's how Julian can get opium into every work camp the CP has. The work camps are divided into gangs. Each gang has an agent who collects the gang's pay from the boss and then distributes it. That agent keeps track of how much a Chinese eats, how long he sleeps, how hard he works, how much wages he's due."

"That agent would also run an opium den?"

"The agent wouldn't have to. Life is bleak up there in the mountains. I'd bet lots of workers would accept some pleasure pills for their pipes in lieu of gold coin. It's a captive market. Thousands of men who don't like rotgut whiskey, faro bets, or hot white women. They just keep chipping through solid granite peaks with a pick, some black powder, and a one-horse dumpcart. They're close to finishing thirteen tunnels. When they do, they'll close a seven-mile gap between Sacramento and Reno, link up with tracks on the flatlands, and roll right to the Utah line, collecting government money every mile of the way."

"And if Julian's tranquillizer gets spread around?"

"Productivity slows down, the Union Pacific crosses the Utah line first, and Julian and his friends win the bet."

"A little bit of opium can do all that?"

"It's not just the drug habit, Katie. There'll be deep debts, fast loans, and gambling when opium hits the camps."

"The Chinese are a spiritual people. Maybe they won't let it affect them."

"Put yourself in their place. You're a stoop laborer in a wilderness camp of five hundred men. It's March but you don't see spring. Snow's been falling for two weeks straight. You sleep in a little shanty with a couple dozen others. You never get warm. You shovel rock in your handcart, fill it up, haul it way out on the grade, and dump it. Then you turn around and do it all again, hundreds of times, eight hours a day. And when you go to bed, you know that your crew advanced the tunnel a whopping seven inches.

"Now along comes a man with some sticky black magic and a nice warm pipe. You've got plenty of money saved up, 'cause every month you get thirty dollars in gold, less camp expenses. Are you going to say no to the only chance you have to feel warm for a while? Hell, no."

"Hell's where he's put us right now." She moved closer, looking down at the cold empty street. "Can't sleep. Can't dream."

"I can sleep on the train tomorrow, between stops." It would be

311

safe to doze en route, he figured. Professionals like Bartholomew demanded a clean escape with a clean kill, and a moving train offered only one risky way off. It would be the road stops that would be hair-raising.

"How many more hours on the train?" she asked.

"Thirty-six. We should be in New York by Wednesday evening. I bought first-class. Took most of the money Devlin loaned me. And I still have to send some telegrams first stop we make."

She leaned against the windowsill. "To whom?"

He got up and pulled her away from the window where she was an easy target from the street. "Bill Cahill. And one to the Central Pacific, to Leland Stanford himself maybe. Somebody's got to warn him about what's on the way to his camps."

She leaned against the wall. When he stepped closer, she turned her head away. "You've been drinking."

He knew his breath had the sour-sweet ferment of beer, but he pressed nearer. "Sometimes a man gets thirsty."

"Like my father?"

"No. Like a man. Takes the edge off."

"You feeling well rounded about the edges now?"

"I feel your judgment. And fear like a wall. All the men in your life have let you down. You don't want me to be another one." He stroked her hair. "It's all right. It's all right." She leaned to him. "One beer doesn't make a man a drunk."

"What's it make him?"

"A little less thirsty, for a while." Hand under her chin, he made her look up at him. His kiss was gentle, just a taste of her lips, to make them tense, eager to respond. He kissed again, sucking, knowing she would open to him, draw him in. She rose on tiptoe to press harder. His hand roamed the small of her back and lower, pressing her body tight against his groin.

He felt her hand stroke his belly, then downward, measuring the length and breadth of him. She looked at him, unsure. He laid the revolver on the nightstand, certain.

She climbed onto the bed and kneeled there, undoing the tiny hooks and eyes of her jacket. He stopped her, not wanting either of them vulnerable. After loosening the band of his pants, he lay back, mindful of his sore ribs. She lifted her skirt and draped it over him as she climbed atop. Beneath the gown, his hands caressed her thighs, sliding slowly higher to her undergarment, loose and filmy. He moved it aside, making room, then he entered slowly, sharply aware of her tight and naked warmth.

The darkness hid her expression. She could have been a stranger, except for all that he knew intimately—the sound in her throat when he pushed in, the sudden clutch of her hands, the motion of her hips. She moved uncertainly, frustrated by the prison of their clothes, and he pulled her close, tender.

In need and despair they loved each other, until they met in bliss on a dark height, on a cry of fulfillment, swift and warm.

31

Fifteen minutes late, the six-oh-five to Columbus pulled out of the Cincinnati station.

Matt glanced at Katie in the booth across the aisle. She watched out the window, purposely ignoring fellow passengers, ignoring him.

With her schoolmarmish glasses, timid posture, and mousy mien, she was the antithesis of a poised, confident actress. Gone too was the calm maternity and pious reserve of the Mennonite's wife. Gone was the safety of the night. They were running prey without a clue to where the hunter had set his blind.

He got up to stretch his legs, to check once again for Bartholomew's presence in their car, No. 11, to assure himself that the cool, gold-toothed popinjay was elsewhere. Where, was anybody's guess. He could even have taken a night train to one of the rest stations and be waiting there.

Matt gave up pacing and sat, letting the rock and rattle of the train loosen his tension. Across the aisle, Katie was listening to the talkative matron facing her. The woman had a child, an excitable little girl who was of a middle age. Seven? Ten? Matt realized how little he knew about the ages and actions of children. If he hadn't seen Beth, he wouldn't even know what a three-year-old like Samuel should be doing.

He settled his ill-fitting hat low over his eyes, wondering whether the Carters kept Samuel too much in the nursery. Did they let him run free? Would they teach him the skills a boy needed to know? Take him riding when he was old enough? A boy needed to ride. His father had made sure Matt had a pony by the time he was six. He remembered the first spring his dad took him riding, on Merrymill farmland . . .

Matt woke at the screech of brakes as the train came into Columbus. There would be a wait while passengers boarded from connecting lines for the run to Pittsburgh. It was a busy terminal, bound to have a telegraph office.

He left the car before Katie so he could look around. The day was overcast, trying to warm up and failing. He tugged his coat collar higher. To his left the engine cab was far up the line. Coupled to its coal tender was the luggage car, a boxcar with wide sliding doors on both sides. Handlers were transferring baggage cargo in and out.

Parallel to the train were sidetracks where rolling stock was parked. Matt looked through the coupling gaps between coaches, spotting open boxcars and slatted stock cars. Great hiding places for train jumpers and ambushers.

He took off his hat. It was a signal to Katie: All clear. She disembarked and headed for the terminal, staying close to other passengers. He followed at a distance. She chose a bench near the telegraph cage and opened the book she'd brought. It had a fringed red ribbon for marking her place. She carefully slipped the ribbon through another section of the book; it was a warning of trouble if she let the bookmark dangle free.

He got in line, thinking about the messages he needed to send. One to Bill Cahill urgently requesting a meeting Thursday afternoon at the St. Nicholas; and one to Leland Stanford in San Francisco, advising him to police the CP work camps for opium suppliers. He'd have to sign a false name so Stanford couldn't trace—

Katie stood suddenly, her book closed. The fringed ribbon dangled outside the spine. She was so intent on watching something out on the boarding platform, she didn't even look at Matt to see if he acknowledged her signal. She hurried off in the flow of travelers moving toward the train.

Telegrams would have to wait. She was already out of sight. He tightened his grip on the old carpetbag he carried, put a hand to his too-small hat, and loped through the station like a mannerless country bumpkin, apologizing when his shoulder grazed someone's head and his bag bumped a kneecap. Outside he caught sight of her following a small man in tunic and trousers. Zemin.

Zemin wended his way through the crowd, seeming numb as a somnabulist, unaware of the rude stares of people waiting to board. He hopped off the edge of the wood planking to the roadbed and continued walking.

To Matt's relief, Katie stayed on the platform. She'd be out in the open, a clear target, if she followed Zemin up the line. The Chinese walked slowly past the coach cars, heading for the baggage car.

The whistle blew for boarding, an anxious blast. Matt saw Katie hesitate, then she stepped off the platform and ran after Zemin.

No! Matt jumped down to the gravel roadbed beside the tracks, racing to catch up.

At the coupling platform between two coach cars, Zemin stopped suddenly. When she was almost upon him, he turned around.

He was weeping.

Frightened? Or sorry?

It was a trap.

Matt reached for the Colt under his coat as he ran. Ahead, he saw a flash of white between the train cars. He dived toward Katie, catching her arm and yanking her down as Bartholomew leaned out from the coupling platform, Colt six-shooter in his left hand.

The killer fired high, then corrected immediately and shot low as Matt rolled with Katie. A bullet stung the ground by his ear. He reared up and returned fire. It was a wild shot, the bullet ricocheting off the iron sheeting of the coach car, but it sent Bartholomew into a defensive squat. Matt fired again.

Stationworkers shouted as they closed in on the commotion. Bartholomew ducked back through to the other side of the train and ran off, gravel crunching beneath his feet.

Matt had no time and no breath for words to comfort Katie. The rolling fall had started a throbbing fire in his chest. Someone helped Katie up and asked if she was all right. She adjusted her spectacles and nodded, looking at Matt. A railworker helped him up. Matt bent, giving the pain in his side full attention.

The steam whistle roared, oblivious to all except schedule. An officious conductor pushed impatiently through the crowd. "Every gawker going on that train better be gettin' on that train!" he ordered. "What happened here?"

"Attempt at robb'ry," Matt said quickly, adopting a mongrel Texas accent. He looked at Katie. She was pale and scared. "No need to thank me, ma'am. Just be careful next time and don't follow no strangers."

"I thought I knew the man," she said, numb and distant.

Matt looked around, knowing Zemin had run off at the first shot. "Well, he's long gone. Think he headed for one of those empty sidecars."

"Check every car," the conductor told a stationworker.

"Well, ma'am," Matt went on to Katie, "think you better be gettin' on board yourself if you're gonna make that fun'ral in Pittsburgh. For your aunt, you said?"

"Yes," she said, following his lead.

"Can somebody find my hat?" He looked around. "I gotta be gettin' on too."

The conductor squinted his eyes tight, as if he'd caught a whiff of old herring. "You're not boarding my train with that gun in your hand, mister. You got some explaining to do."

Matt paused only a second. "Whatever you say. I can take a later train. But better let Miss Smith here move on. Shame for her to miss a fun'ral and all. Aunts don't die every day."

The conductor shook his head at the uncouth sentiment and looked at Katie. "I hope, Miss Smith, that you'll see fit not to

317

unduly alarm your fellow passengers. I'm sure this is an isolated incident."

"I'm sure," she whispered. She looked stricken, frightened at going on without him.

The conductor gestured to one of his workers. "Help Miss Smith to her car. Then flag the cab and get rollin'."

Matt avoided her eyes and kept smiling at the conductor. "Here's my gun, sir. I trust you with it. An' I don't trust many," he said as he watched Katie leave. She stumbled once on the gravel.

"I don't want your gun," the conductor said, handing it to a worker and pulling himself up into the first passenger car. "You just stay in the terminal, mister, until the police get here to clear things up."

Katie stepped up into car No. 11, giving him a last glance before disappearing in the vestibule.

The small crowd jostled around Matt. "What's your name?" someone asked.

"Jimmy-Joe Jones," he said, suddenly walking fast as he could toward the boarding platform. A few of the men followed him. He glanced at the man holding his gun; thoughtless bastard was hanging back to show it off to gawkers.

"Where ya from?"

"Tarmay, Texas." The train gave a chug and drive wheels started to roll. Matt stepped up on the platform.

"You a cowboy?"

"Once." The train was pulling away. "No life for a man who doesn't wanna be by his lonesome." The long line of cars rolled past him, picking up speed. "An' I don't ever want that kinda lonesome again."

The last car was in sight, speeding toward him.

"Hey, cowboy—" someone began, but Matt was already trotting alongside the train. Each step sent a stab of pain through his chest. The end of the platform was close. So was the vestibule and grab iron of the last car.

He leaped off the platform, jumping up for the railing of the moving train. Momentum jerked him forward so hard, he lost his footing.

His leg dangled close to the track rail. He bent his knees to keep his feet free of the rolling iron blades. Pulling with all his might, he got a knee on the step as the train rumbled faster, creating more drag.

He lurched up onto the narrow balcony, left arm cradling his side. He collapsed, not caring that he hurt like hell. He was all in one piece. He was on board.

An old man wearing a railroad cap popped his head out the door of the serving car. "Dammit. Another cheatin' train jumper."

Grimacing, Matt reached inside his coat and pulled out his ticket stub. "I paid," he said, panting.

The old man worked his chaw to the other cheek. "You look it, son."

The man dusted him off before he let Matt stretch out on the bench inside the car. As he lay there Matt felt a deep weariness at work on him. It wasn't just his body. His spirit was flagging. The senator and the safety of New York seemed farther away the closer they got. And each day's delay in messaging Leland Stanford was a day gained for Julian and his opium.

When the pain had subsided, Matt slowly made his way forward, through the kitchen car with its hot plates, aproned men, and countless bins, through the cramped and noisy dining cars, the modest parlor car with its cozy interior, and through the passenger cars to No. 11.

He came up behind her. She had her head bowed over her book.

"Excuse me," he said.

At the sound of his voice she looked up so quickly, a lingering tear overflowed the corner of her eye. She wiped away the offending drop as if it were nothing. He knew better. For a few minutes she'd believed he'd abandoned her. He hadn't. He never would.

He took off his hat. "Could we talk a minute?"

She began to rise, but the nosy matron across from her interrupted. "You don't have to, my dear." The woman gave Matt's mussed hair and rock-dusty jacket a dismissive look. "Plain girls can be too easily led. Just because a man asks is no reason to comply."

319

"Madam," he said, dramatically angry, "this girl is my fiancée. And I do not find her plain!"

The matron turned red as rhubarb.

Katie held her smile until they were alone on the lip between cars. The rumble and grate of the train was deafening. She gingerly removed her glasses, pinching the bridge of her nose and squeezing her eyes shut for a moment.

He leaned down close to her ear. "We'll have to change trains at the next terminal, before the railroad puts a detective on us." The scent of rose water was faint in her hair.

She cupped a hand by his ear. "I saw Zemin go under the baggage car. He probably climbed in it from the other side."

If the little turncoat was still on this train, Matt thought, he'd better have the letter.

"I'm sure he was coerced," she added. "He didn't do it on purpose."

But he did it. "We'll check the baggage car when we stop." He put his arm around her. They were approaching the home stretch through Ohio now. They'd pull into Pittsburgh about nine that night.

The door to the coach opened. Matt instantly reached under his coat. With a jolt he realized he had no weapon.

It was the dining car steward. "Careful out here, folks," he said neutrally, but his eyebrows raised at their intimate stance.

"We're on our way to supper," Matt said. The steward nodded and left.

The pepperbox pistol was all he had now. "That pistol I took from Mary," he said. "It's in your bag, isn't it?"

"It's in the bag *you* took."

The one he'd left in the gravel at the Columbus station. Damn. Now he had no gun, not enough money to get one, and nowhere to buy it anyway.

He tried to hide his pessimism as they sat down to dinner, running his fingers through his hair to groom it back. He was presentable, but just. He caught her staring at him.

"It's the first time we've dined together in public like a normal couple," she said.

She sounded so wistful, he ordered a small feast. Soup Italine, baked bass in matelote sauce, Duffield ham, teal duck à la macédoine, and for dessert Neapolitan cake à la Chantilly.

At first, she held herself primly, maintaining her timid disguise. "Forget the eyeglasses," he told her. "We're sitting ducks anyway."

She folded the spectacles and put them in her small purse.

He poured her a full glass of claret. "Drink up. We'll celebrate."

"What?"

"Our anniversary. We've been engaged three days."

"And we're still alive."

He set his glass down. "I wish things were different, Katie. You deserve something different. So much more than this."

"I have all I need," she said, smiling, making light. "Good wine. Fine food. Good company." She paused. "Your company. That's all I need right now, Matt."

They made small talk of large matters, questioning each other about their families, about growing up, compressing years of their lives between the short courses of dinner.

"We're clearing tables now," the steward said at last, unsubtly suggesting they return to their coach. "We've got a little delay coming up in Pittsburgh. A director's car is waiting to link."

"Who's joining the parade?" Matt asked.

"A presidential candidate I'm quite fond of, actually," the steward said. "Ulysses S. Grant. He's a great hero of mine."

The general. "Mine too." *The general here.*

"He's linking up to make a campaign stop in Harrisburg tomorrow," the steward went on. "Maybe you'll get to hear him."

"Maybe so." Maybe the general would get to hear Matt Dennigan. He could tell him how Julian Gates took bribes to award contracts. How he approved construction shortcuts. How he had government money running through the boardroom of the Crédit Mobilier. How he planned to corrupt a hardworking population of immigrants in order to slow down a rival railroad.

Matt would still try to reach Bill Cahill by telegram, but now he had access to an even more influential politician. Grant was a shoo-in for President in November. And he would take office knowing how a rich railroad promoter like Julian Gates used his position to extort bribes and skim money.

He smiled, mentally adding to the list of crimes. Malfeasance of the public trust. Felony avoidance of customs' duties. Interstate black market sale of smuggled goods.

"What's wrong?" Katie asked.

He raised his glass. "We've got him."

32

Drive wheels thundered on the rails. Brakes squealed on every curve. Inside the parlor car, however, all was muted. Long gold fringe swung noiseless from velvet lampshades. Mahogany chairs sank in amber Persian carpet. The ceiling was padded and coffered, stamped with a running Romanesque of the initials JG.

Julian had commissioned the opulent drawing room car from Cornelius Wagner the year before. The cost had been outrageous but worth every penny, Julian thought, walking the length of the car and back.

Snippets of his image paced with him, refractions from mirrors intricately engraved. Fortunately, the acid-etched glass of the windows obscured the passing landscape, for he hated this part of the country. He had been born and raised here. It was a gift to roll blindly, painlessly, past the rugged hillsides of southwest Pennsylvania, not seeing its coal tipples, creeks, and forests.

He couldn't stop pacing. He didn't know whether Matt Dennigan was dead or alive. Worse, he still didn't know who had set Dennigan nipping at him like a dog looking for a tender spot to grab hold.

Somehow, the men in the boardroom at the Crédit Mobilier had gotten wind of Dennigan's challenging questions and invasive detective work. They were all looking westward now, sending little telegrams from New York with mundane questions, letting Julian know he was being watched. Everything that had been under control was falling apart, because of Dennigan.

Julian had left St. Louis on a one o'clock express the same day Dennigan and Katie were supposed to depart on the three-twenty. He had been traveling day and night to get ahead of them, having decided to go to Washington, straight to the politicians' bedsteads to check which side they were sleeping on.

He had friends, friends who owed him. He would meet one particularly powerful one in Pittsburgh. He had offered his private director's car for General Grant's use on a campaign swing through Harrisburg to Washington. It was a gesture of goodwill after having to cancel dinner with Grant when he was in St. Louis. Always a good policy to extend favors to politicians. Every would-be President had to learn that the road to glory was paved with debt.

But Grant wasn't the only person of importance Julian hoped to meet at the next stop. Bartholomew had wired from Ohio. He wanted to meet at the Pittsburgh terminal to renegotiate. Seems he had lost his partner. He hadn't mentioned that the job was done. That meant it probably wasn't.

Julian felt drained, lackluster. He thought about seeing a doctor. Maybe he just needed some jaundice bitters like his mother used to mix. He remembered gathering three kinds of bark for her. Barberry, wasn't it? Prickly ash and ginseng, or was it alkanoke? A new fatigue settled over him, bone-deep. He hadn't thought about his mother in years.

Brakes locked on with a screech. The steward entered. "Pittsburgh, sir. The Atlantic & Great Western is due in soon to meet us. Will you be disembarking until we link?"

Yes, Julian thought. He needed some air, something to clear his head before the meeting with Bartholomew. "When General Grant arrives, get him and his party aboard and comfortable. Tell him I'll be along shortly. A little personal business to take care of."

. . .

"Hurry," Katie whispered to Matt as he squired her down the train steps. "We can catch Zemin in the luggage car."

He gave no indication he had heard. He was tense and grim, scanning the Pittsburgh platform for signs of trouble. It was late, and the station was nearly deserted. She saw scattered men in dark uniforms, station staff, and employees from the adjoining hotel. She held Matt's arm, hard-pressed to keep up as he pulled her forward to the baggage car.

"You folks look anxious to be on your way," said the baggage handler. A smile creased one cheek; the other held a chaw the size of a kiwi. "Lemme get your bags." He slid open the big wooden door to the boxcar. "Phew," he said. "What's that smell?"

Matt held her back, fearing the worst, she thought. "It's all right," she whispered. She recognized the musky sweet smell. Sandalwood incense.

The baggageman hopped up into the car and lit the oil lamp in the drop well overhead. The light cast a yellow glow over the blackness, illuminating portmanteaus and neatly stacked crates.

"Lord, looky here," the man said. Atop one crate near the door, a charred stick was still smoking in an incense holder.

Katie saw the components of a familiar shrine, the one Zemin had erected in his hotel room in St. Louis. There were brass bowls with the cold ash of joss paper and small bamboo-framed pictures, the Lohans, felled like dominos when the train stopped.

In the pile would be a larger photograph, she knew, silver-framed. A handsome actor emoting the tragedy of Hamlet.

As the baggageman began poking suspiciously in the corners of the car for a stowaway, she thought about how she could explain Zemin's presence. Truth was best. Zemin was a loyal family servant severely distressed by the death of his master.

"I see your shoe, mister!" The baggageman tossed aside some string-tied bundles and a leather case. "Better come on out!"

She would even offer to pay any additional fares Zemin might have incurred.

The baggageman froze. "Jesus."

Matt tried to block her view, but she pulled free. She had to see.

The baggageman dragged Zemin's body closer to the door. "Damn if it isn't one of them Celestials," he said.

Zemin's face looked so peaceful, he seemed to be sleeping. But how could he sleep in clothes soaked with his blood? Katie wondered.

"Let's go," Matt said.

She couldn't move.

"Body's warm," the baggageman said. "He hasn't been dead too long."

She started forward, but Matt clamped an arm over her shoulders and forcefully led her away, pushing through the passengers who had gathered to peer at the tragedy.

Matt offered no words of comfort, only urgent speed as he herded her along the boarding platform. They passed onto the loading dock of the terminal, where freightmen rolled dollies through arched loading bays. Matt kept her moving, past the loaders and a service alley. They ran up the steps to the receiving dock at the back of the neighboring hotel.

The long dock was dark. Moonlight showed dozens of milk urns standing like sentinels. Most of the waist-high cans were empty, awaiting refill. Some were full and curdling, a pungent sourness rising from them.

Matt slowed their pace and veered closer to the building, shielding her with his body as they moved along the back wall of the hotel.

"Stay down," he whispered in her ear. "Don't move." He gestured to a light ahead, above the hotel's delivery door. "Maybe we can get in that way."

He continued on a few feet, careful not to disturb the tall tin cans. One milk can would make lots of noise. He stopped and waited, staying still so long she thought she would scream. She knew the reason for his extreme caution. Bartholomew had a gun and he didn't.

The only sounds she could hear were occasional outbursts from the freight workers. They were a few hundred feet away to the left.

To the right, the milk dock ran another hundred feet and

rounded a corner. She heard faint footsteps in the distance, a leisurely pace, someone out taking the air.

Matt took his chance before any pedestrian appeared. He ran up the hotel steps into the light and tested the delivery door. It was locked. He raised a fist to pound on it.

The shot rang out so close, Katie felt as if it had come from directly behind her. The bullet hit Matt in the back below the shoulder. He flattened against the door.

"No!" she screamed, and reached out to topple the metal urn nearest her. Matt slid along the wall to the steps and slumped over the bannister. She swept more and more urns from her path, setting up a loud banging that would not end until she had reached him.

But the next shot was even louder than her diversion.

Hit again, Matt stumbled down the steps. "Katie," he whispered. "Run."

Shouts were raised on the loading dock. Help was coming. She knocked over the last urn between her and Matt. Heavy, it spilled its curdled milk.

Matt was lurching toward her, barely upright, when she heard a tumbling cacophony of milk cans. Their assailant had slipped in the sour milk.

Cursing, Bartholomew rolled into the light, coat white with clotted cream. He rose, revolver in hand, and aimed at her.

Matt dove forward, pushing her down, blanketing her.

She felt him jerk as the shot meant for her hit him.

No.

He went limp.

No.

Suddenly, his body was stripped away and Bartholomew stood over her. He aimed the revolver, point blank.

A shot exploded, but not from his gun.

Bartholomew jerked forward, hit. He stumbled, staying upright, and turned around, astonished. Shots came out of the darkness, flashes of fire she saw and heard, sharp cracks, three of them, then a pause as Bartholomew fell to the ground. Then she heard three more shots, saw Bartholomew's body twitch as he was hit again.

Numbly she waited for the one that would hit her. It never came.

Dockworkers were pounding toward her as she pushed herself up. "Matt?" She could barely whisper. "Matt?" He didn't answer. She gathered him close, as best she could, holding his head in her lap. She smoothed hair back from his forehead. Matt? Her lips moved, but no sound came out. No sound. *Matt.*

From the darkness where the gunfire had flashed, an elegant figure stepped forth. It couldn't be. Julian?

She wiped the tears from her eyes to see better. It was Julian, with his top hat set at an angle and his coat winged back, his hands on his hips. He was showing her: no gun. Seven shots, she remembered each one, but no gun. He came close and extended a hand to help her up.

She held tighter to Matt, rocking him, feeling his blood soak her skirt.

"Miss, you hurt?" a dockworker asked.

She shook her head.

"Is your man there still breathin'?"

She couldn't answer. She didn't know. The worker reached down and pried her arms from Matt. "C'mon now, get up," he said, propping her against the wall, "so's we can see if he needs a doctor. That other fella sure don't."

The crowd around them had grown large. Kitchen servers peeked out the delivery door of the hotel. Bells clamored on the street. Police wagons, she thought. She slid along the wall, edging into the dark, trying to blunt Julian's intense scrutiny of her. Around her, strangers gossiped.

"—an' that dead Chinee was cooking some kind of spell in the baggage car. They found some black magic—"

"—seventeen pictures of Chinese devils, if you can believe it. Seventeen pictures. I watched 'em count 'em."

Eighteen. She didn't have the strength to correct them. There are eighteen Lohans. Disciples of Buddha. They protect the faithful, ensure the peace. The peace.

Police officers broke through the crowd.

"Who shot who?" one of them asked as the others laid a stretcher beside Matt.

"Looks like these two had a shoot-out with the lady in the middle," Julian said, stepping forward. "Of course, I don't know for sure. I was just coming around the corner when I heard all this gunfire. Sounded like a war."

"Sure did," someone in the crowd agreed.

"Clear everyone out of here," the officer said.

Two men heaved Matt onto the stretcher.

Katie looked at Julian. Her eyes were burning. Her voice shook. "You did this."

"What'd you say, ma'am?" An officer leaned closer.

Matt made a sound. A breath, a shaky breath. *Alive.* In an instant she was down on her knees beside him. "Matt?" She laid her cheek to his.

He struggled to speak. "Tal—"

"Don't," she whispered. "Save your strength." She gestured for the policemen to lift the stretcher. Matt grabbed her dress with a fierce burst of strength, then his hand fell limp. She had to lean close to hear him. "Talk—to Grant—Promise—me—"

"I will," she whispered, knowing she would have promised him anything, anything to comfort him. "I will."

"Coming in the ambulance wagon, ma'am?" the officer asked. "The lieutenant over there will want to ask you a few questions on the way."

She was led past Julian, who was talking to the police captain and a rumpled, sleepy-looking lieutenant.

The captain gave her a paternal smile. It was the look men reserved for women of hysterical temperament.

Katie stopped, realizing Julian was already weaving his lies. She was so distraught, she could only whisper. "Mr. Gates is lying, Captain. He had a gun. He fired it seven times."

"I see," the captain said, patronizing.

She glared at Julian, about to say more, but the sleepy lieutenant took her arm. "Better get going to the ambulance, miss."

She shook him off and hurried to catch up with the stretcher bearing Matt. Her feet were leaden, and she had to grasp the rim, holding tight. *I won't let go, Matt. I won't let go.*

She stumbled.

Someone instantly propped a sturdy arm under hers and kept her from falling.

"Thank you," she said to the drowsy-looking lieutenant.

He was surprisingly quick.

33

The hospital corridor had a block tile floor. She paced it off, one square with each step, first white, then green, always looking down so she stepped within the lines. Step on a crack, break your mother's—

"Miss Henslowe?"

Katie looked up. It was the night nun sitting at her desk at the end of the hall.

"Please sit down, dear," the nun said. "You're exhausting me."

Katie sat in one of the straight-backed chairs lining the hospital wall.

Along the facing wall sat Lieutenant Garrick, the police inspector who had accompanied her in the ambulance wagon. He was unassuming in questions, manner, and appearance, as colorless and nondescript as an old blanket. His nose was bulbous and a bourbon-dark flush stained his cheeks.

He said he'd been interrupted at Wednesday night whist with his mother to investigate the sensational triple shooting at the Pittsburgh station. The newspapers were printing extra copies for the morning editions, he'd informed Katie after taking her statement. "Journalists are like flies," he'd added offhandedly. "They carry stink for a living."

"They deliver information the public has a right to know," she had said. "I'd like you to give them my statement, Lieutenant. It's the truth."

"Your truth. I expect Mr. Gates has another."

"Then contact Senator Cahill. Matt sent him a detailed brief about the problems on the Union Pacific."

"I'm not interested in doing a congressman's job, or the railroad commissioner's job. I've got two murders at the railroad station and an escaped prisoner in the operating room. I'd say that's plenty. Wouldn't you?"

She looked across the corridor at Lieutenant Garrick. His eyes flicked away and fixed straight ahead, like those of a military sentinel required to see all without looking at anything.

How much longer? she wondered. The surgeon had said an hour, but already two had passed. *God, help him. Help me.* She pressed the back of her head to the wall, hard, feeling each uneven whorl in the plaster. Garrick mustn't sense how close she was to losing control. Any hint of hysteria would only confirm whatever Julian had told them.

Lieutenant Garrick got up and walked down the corridor to the desk. He came back holding a pillow. He scooted three chairs together beside her and lay the pillow on one. Without a word he took his seat opposite her again.

She took off her hat and slowly reclined on the makeshift bed. The pillow was a luxury after hours trying to rest upright on the train. She felt herself sinking and clasped her hands atop her stomach, a restful pose. Like Juliet in the crypt, waiting a cue to waken from deathless sleep and see her true love.

Thy husband in thy bosom there lies dead.

She curled tightly on her side, strangling fearful cries. The dagger plunged too deep.

Lieutenant Garrick cleared his throat loudly to alert her. There were footsteps. The doctor? She quickly wiped her face on the pillow and got up.

"Miss Henslowe? I'm Dr. Regis." The surgeon crisply unrolled his shirtsleeves. He had thick unruly eyebrows; dark pockets sagged below both eyes. "You do understand how seriously your fiancé was injured."

She couldn't speak. She nodded.

"Frankly, I haven't seen an attack that vicious since the war."

"Is he—will he—?"

"I don't know. A lot is up to him right now. He's got a strong constitution or he wouldn't have made it this far." Dr. Regis ran a finger under his collar to straighten it. "One of the bullets reopened an old wound in his shoulder. A good thing. He still had shrapnel embedded. Bullet stopped there instead of his lung. Other shots hit muscle instead of an organ. Missed his kidney with a centimeter to spare. Luck's been on his side so far."

"Can I see him?"

"You're not immediate family, are you?"

"No, but I'm the one closest to him here, at the moment."

"I'm no sentimentalist, Miss Henslowe. To be blunt, he needs his doctor more than a fiancée right now, and I have very strict policies about patient isolation and hygiene."

She realized how rumpled and unkempt she looked. Her gown was stiff with Matt's blood. "I'm sorry." She tried to smooth her skirt. "I can change."

"No. Let me explain." He slipped on a brown worsted coat. "I'm somewhat of a maverick here. I trained with Dr. Joseph Lister in an accident ward in Glasgow last summer. Since then, I've been charting remarkable rates of recovery with the use of carbolic acid as an antiseptic. And I will not break my rules of hygiene for love or money, Miss Henslowe."

Money. She had forgotten. She was destitute without access to Matt's wallet and the funds Devlin had loaned them.

Dr. Regis tugged his lapels straight. "I think you should find a hotel room in which to compose yourself," he said. "I'll be here all night on call for him."

She turned to leave.

"Miss Henslowe?"

The doctor spoke so sympathetically, she felt a chill of apprehension. "Yes?"

333

"While you're out, wire his immediate family. They do need to be notified, in case they can get here."

She watched him walk away.

"Best be going," Lieutenant Garrick finally said, putting on his hat.

"Am I under arrest, Lieutenant?"

"Not at this moment. There seems to be some question about that aiding and abetting charge. To us, you're a material witness."

"Then I'm free to go?"

He shoved his hands in his coat pockets and rocked up on his toes. "Not at this moment. Captain's waking up a judge right about now to get a court order to keep you in protective custody until we clear this thing up."

"Will the order keep Julian in your jurisdiction too?"

Garrick paused. "I indicated that it should."

"What's that mean?"

"Means Julian Gates is an important man who divvies out lots of campaign contributions. A man with so many favors due is hard to pin down."

"I can pin him down for you, Lieutenant. But I need to see General Grant first."

Garrick gave her a disbelieving look.

"You can take me to him," she said.

"And how do you figure that? The general's conducting business from Mr. Gates's big palace car at the depot tonight."

"At the depot?"

"At the depot. Now, what I can do is help you get some clean clothes."

"I see. I think my bag's—"

"At the depot." He took her arm. "Let's go."

As they rode to the railroad terminal, Katie asked the lieutenant if he'd lived in Pittsburgh long.

"Most of my life. Why?"

"Do you know a family by the name of Carter? He's an attorney. He had a daughter, Sarah. She was in Texas for a while."

"Everybody knows the Carters. They're an old family here. A shame about Sarah. Committed suicide, you know."

Katie closed her eyes briefly. "No, I didn't know."

"Left the baby with her parents and ran off. They found her in a teacher's college in Boston. She hanged herself in a broom closet. Shame."

Katie could only nod.

"A shame about that boy too."

She felt a chill. "He's still alive, isn't he?"

"Far as I know. Mrs. Carter doesn't take him out much. Never did, but especially not since her husband died last year."

It was nearly midnight when they reached the station, but the chatter of newly departed passengers seemed to echo through the high arched dome of the terminal. Katie watched as men in evening dress were ushered out to an opulent director's car parked on a siding. General Ulysses S. Grant was holding court inside.

She knew little about the war hero who had led the Union Army to victory, except that he was enormously popular and certain to take the Republican nomination for President at the convention in May.

Matt had served under him during the war, but had told Katie he was no close friend. "One night," Matt had said, "Grant caught me mumbling Hamlet's 'What a piece of work is a man' speech, trying to stay awake on sentry duty. He said, 'Hamlet's common, son. All that murder and backstabbing. Now, with Coriolanus, you get some good military history with your tragedies. You don't know any Coriolanus for me? Then clam the hell up and hold your post. You got lives at stake.' "

Matt had hoped to extract a promise from Grant, that as President he would appoint an independent commission with power to audit the UP's finances and stop tracklaying until work was redone to specifications.

Katie wasn't sure she could finagle such a promise; she was on a short leash.

She turned to Garrick. "Lieutenant, I hope you were able to make contact with Leland Stanford and the CP."

"We sent some wires. I don't think there's going to be much opium-cooking up in the Sierras. I hear Strobridge, the camp boss, is a tough one to cross. He gets wind that something's going to slow

335

down tracklaying, he'll take care of it like he does everything else. With a pick handle and a lot of bloody heads."

She walked on. "At least it's more humane than using bullets, which is how Julian Gates takes care of things."

"I meant to ask you about the shooting," Garrick said. "You're sure someone fired seven times at that ambusher, Bartholomew?"

"One shot, then two sets of three. To be specific, I told you that it was Julian Gates who fired seven times."

"I remember. You also told me it was pitch dark. You didn't see him shoot at all, did you?"

She didn't answer.

"Better go send your telegram."

He talked to the stationmaster while Katie was in the telegraph office. She wired messages to Peg and to Hellie Dennigan.

"Where can they send a reply to you?" the telegraph operator asked.

"General Hospital, surgery wing," she said, watching Garrick watch her. He didn't trust her to stay in one place.

The stationmaster showed her to a storage room just off his office. The small room held her carpetbag and two old costume trunks she recognized as Zemin's.

"The coffin's in freight holding," the stationmaster said. "You want it to stay here at the depot?"

Garrick nodded. After a pause, he prompted the stationmaster with a nudge in the ribs. The stationmaster reluctantly offered Katie the use of his personal washroom. The two men withdrew, and she closed and locked the door.

Privacy at last. She threw off her coat, pulled a pin from her hair, and picked the locks on Zemin's trunks. She was not the first to search. Bartholomew had been thorough and destructive: Trunk linings were slit, clothes and possessions were a jumble.

She grew pensive, touching Zemin's things. Obviously, he had not planned to return to Poppy after Edmund's burial. Maybe he thought he would live on blackmail money from Julian.

One trunk contained the wicker valise that held the pipe and spirit lamp for smoking. The valise wasn't locked. Zemin had probably opened it to get the Lohans for the shrine. She leafed through stacks of theater bills with Edmund's name and likeness. Surely Zemin wouldn't have hidden the letter in so obvious a place as his luggage. If he had, it was long gone. Who had the letter now?

Not Julian, she suddenly realized, sitting back on her heels. If he did, he would have killed her as well as Bartholomew. He must think *she* had the letter. It gave her a slight edge, but only if she could figure out where Zemin had hidden it.

She stripped in order to wash, then dressed in a plain white blouse and plaid teal skirt. She was pinning up her hair, when there was a knock at the door.

"Miss Henslowe?" Garrick called. "You don't answer in one second, respectfully speaking, I'm busting the door down."

"I'm still here, Lieutenant," she called, finishing her hair. She folded her coat over her arm and opened the door. "You shouldn't worry," she said to Garrick. "I'm not leaving the city without Matt."

"I plan to hold you to that, Miss Henslowe."

"Lieutenant, I'm quite hungry." She avoided his eyes. "Would you mind if I stopped to get something from one of the vendors?"

He scratched behind his ear awhile, as if the decision were a major one. "All right," he said finally.

They walked out toward the loading platform. Few vendors were left. Two sleepy boys sat against the wall, elbows propped on a switchman's lantern filled with hardtack candy.

At the south end of the platform, closest to Julian's director's car, a young black woman walked slowly, holding a wooden tray of hotcakes going cold. She stopped when she saw Katie looking at her.

Katie clasped her hands in front of her. "I lost my reticule somewhere on the milk dock behind the hotel. Could I go look for it?"

Garrick reached inside his coat. "This it?" He dangled the beaded bag.

"Yes," she said, disappointed. The purse was useless. It held handkerchiefs and hairpins, no cash or coins.

"Better check to see if somebody took your money," he said.

Suspicious, she reached inside the bag, feeling a coin at the bottom. She withdrew a silver dollar and looked at Garrick.

He avoided her gaze. "Go on. Get your hotcake."

She walked toward the vendor, glancing back once. Garrick was watching her. As the black woman searched her apron pocket for change, Katie looked again at Garrick. He was walking across the wide expanse of the terminal, heading for the freight office. His back was to her. He was giving her her chance.

She grabbed up her skirt and ran the length of the platform to the ramp leading to Julian's car.

"Miss! Your change!" she heard the black girl call.

Katie leaped up the steps of the car and yanked open the door of the vestibule.

Two dozen men stood enjoying their gin and port amid the glitter of mirrored glass and the warmth of marquetry walls. The men's baritone rumble faded, glasses stopped clinking, as they caught sight of her. Cigar smoke wafted past her on the draft of the open door.

An alarmed steward shouldered past the guests, inadvertently spilling the drink of a pudgy young man standing close to Katie. The steward whipped out a linen for the dampened guest. "Madam, this is a private car," the steward said to her as he dabbed apologetically at the jacket. "You must leave."

"I have to speak to General Grant," she said evenly. "It's a matter of great emergency."

"But, madam—"

"I have a crucial message from a friend of the general. This friend is very ill. The surgeon says he may not—" Her mouth was dry. "He's very ill. Do you understand?"

"No," the steward said. "Though I sympathize, you are not permitted here."

The pudgy young man intervened. "Let's let the general decide if it's a message he wants to hear. A visit from a mysterious young lady might add a spot of color to my book." He turned to her. "James Harrison Wilson, madam, erstwhile author engaged to compile the campaign biography of Ulysses S. Grant. And may I say the material up to now has been high, dry, and depressingly political."

"Katie Henslowe." She took the arm he offered, and he led her past flush-faced men in plush, cushioned chairs.

She held herself cool, distant, until a group of standing men parted, revealing a short bearded man sitting on a brocade divan.

The general.

Sharing the divan and holding a tall whiskey was the group's elegant and urbane host.

Julian Gates.

34

Julian rose, his smile reptile slim. "How nice to see you, Katie."

She did not respond, but held herself perfectly still.

The general put his drink on a table and stood to take her hand. "Miss Henslowe."

He hadn't waited for an introduction, she thought. He'd been briefed.

The general's clasp was not warm, not cool; it was careful. He was a guarded man, compactly built, solid in appearance and demeanor. His clothes were well cut. His eyes were bloodshot and liquidy bright. She wondered how much he'd been drinking.

"I've been sent by one of the men who served under you, General. Matt Dennigan."

"I heard about his misfortune tonight. How is he?"

She felt Julian's scrutiny, but kept her gaze on the general. "Matt is—not well."

"Sorry to hear that. I just had dinner with his dad a few days ago. Passing through St. Louis, you know. My wife's family lives there. Always like to stop by to see Art."

"Reliving the war years with old Dennigan, I imagine?" Julian said, but Katie noticed his smile had become strained.

"That," Grant said enigmatically, "and catching up on the present." He leaned down to get his glass. "You can be sure I'll offer a prayer for Matt, Miss Henslowe. He was a courageous soldier. Could always count on him to lead the charge. He was a good shot too."

"I'd prefer you didn't put your praise in the past tense, General. It makes me very nervous."

"Apologies," he said.

"All I ask in penance is thirty minutes of your time in private."

"This is not the time or place to harangue the general on a matter best left to the police," Julian said.

She ignored him. "It's a matter of gross mismanagement of taxpayers' money by the Union Pacific," she told the general. "Gross negligence in construction and bribery of government inspectors. Soon it may be a matter of criminal profiteering from the sale of a poisonous drug."

The room went quiet. Julian cleared his throat and gave the general a significant look. Grant smoothed his mustache and took Julian's cue. "Perhaps we can talk another time, when you're not so overwrought."

She fought down her anger and frustration, but some spilled out anyway. "Peculiar, isn't it?" she said. "When a man like yourself speaks with conviction, he's called a leader. When a woman speaks with conviction, she's overwrought. That's not very logical. Is it men's intuition?"

A murmur ran through the crowd and on its heels, a sprinkling of nervous laughter. Wilson the writer broke in quickly. "Gentlemen! It's high time we adjourned to the Park Hotel so you all can get a bite to eat."

"So you can jot down notes!" someone rejoined.

Wilson grinned and looked at the general. He wasn't amused.

Immediately, guests began to abandon their glasses and call for their hats. The car steward looked crestfallen as the men exited noisily. Julian stood in the vestibule and shook hands in apologetic farewell.

341

Grant stiffly took Katie aside. "Miss Henslowe, let me be frank. I resent and deplore the power of destructive rumor. I've seen it destroy troops and long-range projects. And it can destroy a campaign."

"Perhaps what you really resent is the truth."

"If a soldier of mine gave me backlash like yours, he'd be up for disciplinary action."

"I didn't think you required military obedience from voters, General."

His eyebrows drew together in a grim scowl, and he dug inside his coat for a cigar. It was thick, dark, and aromatic. "There's more at stake here than a vote, isn't there, Miss Henslowe?"

"Matt and I are desperate," she said softly.

The general looked at her a long time. "The war taught me a lot." He bit the end off his cigar and spat it into his hand. "Taught me that desperate soldiers are the hardest to beat. They aren't fighting to win. They're fighting like hell just to stay alive. That right?"

She nodded and pressed her lips together.

He looked down at his hand, rolling the cigar in his fingers. "Well, I wonder if Matt mentioned any particular counselor he would have me consult in this matter."

"Yes," she said, unable to hide her hopefulness. "Senator Bill Cahill, sir. Please."

He lifted his gaze to her. "Art Dennigan insisted I talk with Bill too."

She'd been right then, she thought. Matt's father had read the senator's telegram before giving it to her that day at the New Gate. "I would trust Matt's father, General. Art Dennigan is a man of principle."

"Unfortunately, politics runs on only ten percent principle any given moment in Congress. It's ninety percent compromise and smoke screen. That means odds are always against men like Art and Matt."

Her hope began to sputter. "I don't understand."

"I'm an unabashed believer in the transcontinental railroad,

Miss Henslowe. It's not a luxury, it's a necessity. This country can't be completely united without it."

"But surely it can be done with quality workmanship at a reasonable profit. Do you call the Crédit Mobilier's first year dividend of one hundred percent reasonable? That's a definite red flag."

"Or a red herring. Good business is good business. And business is a tonic in this country. It tastes bad sometimes." He looked across the room at Julian. "But it's good for us."

"General!" Wilson called from the vestibule. "You coming?"

"Coming." Grant tried to step past Katie, but she took his arm. "You must help," she said. "Matt believes in you."

"So do Julian and men like him. A President governs the whole for the good of each part, not vice versa." He gave her a curt nod and strode to the door where Julian stood waiting.

Julian patted the general's back and tilted his head in Katie's direction. "Parting is not always sweet sorrow, is it?" he said conspiratorially.

Katie walked toward them. "Fain would I have thee remember."

Grant turned, curious.

" 'Many great men have flattered the people who ne'er loved them.' "

"That's a goodbye?" Julian said, shaking Grant's hand.

"No, Julian," Grant said pensively. "That's *Coriolanus. The Tragedy of Coriolanus.*" He wiggled the cigar at Wilson; the writer drew out a match pouch to light it. The other three stood silent, watching as Grant puffed the dark stogie to life.

Julian seemed uneasy. "Well, it'll be a tragedy if we don't get some rest tonight. We pull out in the morning on the nine-fifty-five."

With an exhale like a sigh, the general blew a stream of smoke. "Thank you anyway, Julian, but I won't need your car tomorrow. I've decided to stay on another day."

"I can easily change my schedule," Julian said. "We can leave Friday. You can—"

"No, thanks."

"But—"

"No, Julian. Thanks." He pulled the door shut as he left.

"No." Julian repeated the word softly. He grimaced and pressed fingertips to his temple.

The steward straightened a tray of hock and claret. "I'll call a porter to finish servicing the car, sir."

"No," Julian said, looking at Katie. "Leave," he told the steward.

Katie tried to follow the steward out, but Julian stopped her by saying her name in an eerily calm voice. "We haven't discussed terms," he said, "for the valuable item you have for sale."

She turned to him, and the door clicked shut as the steward left her alone with Julian.

"I spared you, Katie," Julian went on. "I didn't have to. I wanted to."

"Spared?" she whispered. "Spared me what? Dearest God." Tears pooled in her eyes. "Spared me to see Matt so hurt, so . . ."

"Dying," Julian said. "Finally. Matt's dying."

"Stop it! I will not let him!"

"You cannot stop it." He moved toward her. "We have no power over life except to discontinue it. Love conquers nothing but the dullness of life." He was close to her. "Love is the little frill we tack on to our existence. A frill on a dead man is wasted trimming. I deplore waste, Katie."

He reached for her, but she knocked his hand away.

"You're angry with yourself, aren't you?" he went on, unperturbed. "Because you believed the promise. I promise people success and security and they follow like lambs. Edmund believed. You believed, you so blindly that you could not admit the paradox: a seedy actor like Edmund as partner to a man of impeccable taste."

"There was no paradox," she said. "You're as seedy, as hopeless, as doomed as Edmund."

He smiled, though not with his usual confidence. "You're mistaken, Katie."

"No, I'm not. But you're a liar, Julian. You lie to yourself. You told me once that you don't need a mirror, that you don't care what you see. You care, Julian. You care for your very life, because it would kill you to truly see yourself, to strip away the lies and glitter and fine clothes, the veneer around a rotted log, dead in a forest of living things."

"You act as if this is your stage, Katie."

"Oh, no. I act as if it is yours." She looked around, gesturing with one arm. "I know because it has so many mirrors. Everywhere mirrors, reflecting one another, not you." She crossed to the far end of the car near the sleeping berth. "But here's one by itself. Come look, Julian."

He didn't move. "You look first, Katie. You first, and I'll tell you what you see."

She stepped hesitantly in front of the full-length dressing mirror.

"You see a woman who has not slept well, if at all, in three long nights. She is tired of the chase, tired of not knowing who will step out of the dark to fire at her, or at one she cherishes. A lover. A child."

She turned to look at him.

"I see a woman horrified," he went on quietly. "A woman who will give me the letter in exchange for her child's safety."

Katie was silent for a moment, weighing his threat, her own ability to bargain when she had nothing.

"I don't have the letter, Julian."

He frowned, obviously trying to judge whether she told the truth.

"And you don't have it either. Zemin hid it well."

"He was a wily Celestial."

"No. He was a highly intelligent man. Smarter than your Mr. Bartholomew. Smarter than me. He knew I would have no failsafe if he gave me both letters. As it is, you'll never know where the Chinese letter may turn up. Must make you very nervous."

"I don't get nervous, Katie." He shrugged casually, slipping his hands into his pants pockets. "I get new ideas."

She tried to open the vestibule door behind her, but it was locked. She backed against the door as Julian stepped closer.

"Your smart Chinese," he said. "I expressly forbade him to use any written communiques with my name in them. I don't like anything written down. Even something as small as that bill for the

345

duplicate costume. It made Altmann question me. Now the police will question the tailor and I will have to stuff more money in his mouth. And Norrie, Lord knows what all he's got to sell. It never seems to end, Katie." His right hand clenched strangely in his pocket. He was holding something. "Where will it end?"

"What do you expect from men whose loyalty you have to buy?" she said quickly, hoping he would not draw out a weapon. "Loyalty is given freely, when you earn it. You have no one loyal to you, Julian? No one? Not even your family?"

He was close, his profile reflected in the mirror. "They're all dead and gone."

"You're still here, Julian. And you must take your turn. Face the looking glass. I'll tell you what you see."

"No."

"You'll see a man who is rich and handsome."

He turned slightly to the mirror, his distrust apparent.

"Though his beauty is brittle as glass," she continued, "and his wealth spread thin as ice."

Chin out, he faced the mirror fully, denying her challenge.

"A man surrounded by people who care about the things he owns. A man without a soul on earth who cares about him. A man alone, without even one imperfect relative to madden his emotions or gladden his heart. He's the man made of things, and they will all be taken away. When everything is gone, he will disappear. Look, Julian. See the invisible man who glitters."

He looked for a long time, then said, "I see nothing, Katie." His voice was plaintive. "Nothing at all." He took his hand from his pocket. His thumb rested on a piece of curved metal. A short tube protruded between his first and second fingers.

"But," he whispered, "do you know what is worse? I *feel* nothing, Katie." He pushed the strange weapon to her ribs. "Nothing at all."

35

The door rattled as someone outside tried the latch.

Julian jerked Katie away from the door. He heard a set of keys jangle. The steward? Dolt.

Julian slipped the small gun back into his pants pocket just as the door opened. A middle-aged man in a poorly fitting suit stepped in. "Knew I'd catch up with you, Miss Henslowe."

"Lieutenant Garrick," she said, her voice shaky.

Garrick moved closer, placing his stocky body between her and Julian. "The steward here is going to escort you to the stationmaster's office," he said as he tossed the key ring to the worried steward on the tracks. "You stay there. I need to speak with Mr. Gates."

He flashed Julian a look, not confrontational, Julian thought, but very careful. Julian was surprised to feel prickling along the top of his spine. He kept his hand in his pocket.

"Be careful, Lieutenant," Katie said. "He's got a g—"

"Grand place here, I know. Now go," Garrick said sternly, nearly pushing her out the door.

Julian studied the lieutenant as he closed the door and turned to face him. Undistinguished man, rumpled face, starched collar.

Garrick removed his hat. The too-tight band had left a ridge in his greased hair. Julian relaxed. He took the expansive wing-back chair and motioned for the lieutenant to sit in the ladder-back Queen Anne opposite.

Garrick tossed his hat on the Queen Anne and remained standing, feet slightly apart.

"What brings you so rudely to my door, Lieutenant?"

"Looking for Miss Henslowe, sir. She's a witness in my custody. She slipped away."

"She does seem like an escape artist at times, as I'm sure you've heard from the St. Louis police."

The lieutenant nodded. "We've been in touch, yes, sir."

Unease raised the hair on his nape. Julian smoothed the back of his head with his hand. "I had understood from the captain that I wouldn't be bothered with questions until morning. I'm entertaining guests."

"Your guests left."

There was a long silence.

Garrick clasped his hands behind his back. "Didn't think you'd want to be bothered in the morning, what with you scheduled to pull out on the nine-fifty-five and all. It's still the nine-fifty-five?"

Julian crossed his legs. "Make this quick. I'm already late to join the general's dinner party."

"You own a gun, Mr. Gates?"

"Several, most of them antiques hanging on a wall five hundred miles away."

"Carrying any with you right now?"

"One. In my toiletries bag." He gestured toward the narrow doors that hid the sleeping compartment. "Look if you like."

Garrick glanced toward the doors, then asked, "What kind of gun is it?"

"Small revolver."

"Five or six shot?"

Julian pressed the heel of his hands to his forehead. "I don't know, Lieutenant. I dislike firearms. I'm a terrible marksman. I only carry it for personal security. Now, I'm awfully fatigued. I'm sure you understand."

348

The lieutenant didn't move. "Miss Henslowe heard seven shots."

Julian frowned as if puzzled. "I don't understand your dilemma."

"Miss Henslowe distinctly heard seven shots come out of the dark and kill the man who ambushed Mr. Dennigan. Now, I collect guns for a hobby, Mr. Gates, and I only know of one gun that has a seven-shot chamber."

"Perhaps there were two guns in the dark. Or two men. Or three, for God's sake."

"Thought of that, sir," Garrick said obligingly. He paced slowly. "Also thought of a new contraption a friend out Chicago way wrote to me about. It's an assassin's gun, a little palm pistol. They call it a lemon-squeezer." Garrick opened one hand and traced the shape on his palm. "No bigger around than a lemon, about as flat as a snuff tin. Has a three-inch barrel and a little lever that rests here under your thumb. Only part visible is the barrel poking out between your fingers."

"Intriguing," Julian said dryly, shifting in his seat, seemingly bored. He felt the lemon-squeezer glide deeper into his pants pocket.

"Exactly seven shots in the chamber, small caliber," Garrick said. "Doctors found four small-caliber bullets in the body of the ambusher. You know what that means."

"What?"

"The guy had to be a terrible marksman. He missed three at close range."

Julian rose slowly from the chair.

"Or maybe he was nervous," Garrick said, "coming upon something he didn't expect. Taking advantage of the situation, if you know what I mean."

"This has all been elucidating. Perhaps your men will find your little tweezer—"

"Squeezer, sir."

"*Squeez*-er at the scene of the crime."

"They've looked. Nothing turned up. I didn't think it would. It's an expensive bit of mechanics. For specialized work, close-in and sneaky. You understand."

Julian was silent.

"Man gets himself a real unique toy like that, he'd want to hold on to it, don't you think?"

"Lieutenant, what I think has no bearing on what you do, else you would have exercised good manners and left immediately upon apprehending Miss Henslowe."

"I didn't apprehend her. She's not under arrest."

"When I left St. Louis, she was known to be aiding and abetting a fugitive."

"Not anymore. Police dropped the murder charge against Matt Dennigan."

"Oh?" He breathed deeply for control. "Why?"

"Telegram didn't say. I wired back some questions." He shrugged. "Maybe I'll find out in the morning."

"Maybe." Julian walked stiffly to the door to usher him out. "Now if you'll excuse me."

Garrick picked up his hat from the chair and sat down. He pulled a tablet from his coat and fished his vest pocket for a pencil. The nib was clean and newly sharpened. "Seeing as how the captain asked me not to bother you with anything so disturbing as a search tonight, I thought I could get some background information. Just a little personal history. You were born and raised in these parts, weren't you?"

There it was, Julian thought. The first whiff of blackmail. He cautiously took a chair far from the lieutenant. "Yes."

"Any place in particular?"

"Near Aliquippa."

"What town?"

"I answered Aliquippa. You may write down Aliquippa."

"Parents?"

"They're dead."

"Any brothers or sisters?"

"No."

"Father's name?"

Julian rubbed his brow. "John."

"Mother's name?"

"Mirta."

"Last name?"

Julian glared. "Gates."

Garrick scribbled a moment. "Father's occupation?"

"My father owned dry goods stores."

"You work there growing up?"

"I went off to school at an early age."

"Must have finished early too. Bought a little ironworks company over at Weirton when you were just eighteen, I believe."

"How do you know that, Lieutenant?"

"Old newspaper clippings." Garrick looked up at him. "My mother saves them. She grew up about twenty miles outside of Aliquippa. She knew lots of the little towns around there. Mining towns like Blacksville, places like that."

"Well, I never knew any Garricks."

"Her maiden name was Fortney. My mother is a Fortney."

Fortney. Julian swallowed to coat his dry throat. "Fortney."

"Pretty well-known name around Aliquippa back in those days. I'm sure you heard of it."

Julian said nothing. He did not even move.

"My mother had an aunt who lived in Aliquippa," Garrick went on. "A rich widow woman name of Emma Fortney. People thought she was touched in the head. She let her house go to hell and wouldn't hardly spend a cent of the money her husband left her. He owned a line of dry goods stores. Maybe your dad knew him."

Julian shook his head slowly.

"Now, my mother thought Aunt Emma was a fine person, just a little too high-minded and bullheaded for a Christian woman, Mother says. Aunt Emma had been a missionary once and she was always taking in housekids to teach them things, polish their upbringing, support their education. Couple of the girls went on to teaching college. One of the boys went to seminary. She took in a boy from up Blacksville there at the last, my mother said. A Gottswald boy. Family was dirt poor. His dad was a coal miner."

Julian couldn't stand the silence. He got up to walk around. A mirror flashed at him in passing. He retreated out of range.

"My mother met the Gottswald boy once," Garrick continued.

"Julian was his name. Like yours. Mom didn't like this Julian much. Said he slunk around. Said Aunt Emma had him writing all her letters, her eyesight was getting so bad. All she could do was sign things. Julian handled all her papers. And Julian was the only beneficiary in her will when she died. Some people thought that was peculiar. Some people thought that was a crime."

"Lieutenant."

Garrick waited.

"Lieutenant, I have important people to see. Are you finished?" *Are you finished polishing the silver, Julian? Then come read to me. Start in "Book Eleven," where the archangel shows Adam the fate of mankind after The Fall.*

"Immediately a place before his eyes appear'd, sad, noisome, dark; a Lazar-house it seem'd, wherein were laid numbers of all diseased, all maladies of ghastly Spasm, or racking torture, qualms of heart-sick Agony, all feverous kinds, Convulsions . . ." He hated how she sat with her eyes closed, nodding, stopping him if he missed one ulcerous pestilence in the list of man's woes. *"Dire was the tossing,"* her reedy voice would chime in, *"deep the groans—"*

"Mr. Gates?"

The lieutenant's voice was loud. Julian turned abruptly. "Yes? What?"

"I said I'm done for tonight."

For tonight.

Garrick tucked his tablet in his pocket and put on his hat. "See you in the morning." Julian watched him cross to the door, mirrors on each side reflecting segments of his stocky frame so that there were many determined lieutenants who gathered as one in the vestibule.

"Lieutenant Garrick?" Julian said. "Isn't there something you want from me?"

"Just the truth, Mr. Gates." Garrick smiled. "All a policeman ever needs."

He left, and Julian leaned wearily against the wall.

Suddenly the door wrenched open again, and Garrick popped his head in. "Now, a visit to my mother might be nice. She doesn't

352

get to talk with folks from around home too often. She's bedridden now. Ailing bad."

He was in no hurry. He had a captive audience.

"My mom, she went to work as a draper right after my dad died. Twenty years, up and down ladders, treadling that big sewing machine. I helped out some, but I had my own family and she understood. Too understanding at times. Never did contest that will. The lawyer she tried to hire advised her against taking it to court. I finally did a little investigating. Do you know that lawyer'd been bought off?" The lieutenant shook his head in wonder. "That boy Julian. From the get-go, stacking the deck. 'Night, sir."

From where she waited by the telegraph cage, Katie watched Garrick leave the director's car. He walked straight to her, and they were quiet for a moment. Finally she took his hand and turned it palm up. "The hotcake seller just stopped by." She tipped a stream of coins into his hand. "Gave me change. Said if she took money that wasn't due her, she couldn't sleep easy tonight."

Garrick nodded toward the director's car. "Shame more businessmen don't have street ethics."

"I'm glad you came in when you did, but really, I wouldn't have minded seeing you earlier."

"Sorry. It was a hard thing to judge. All I could see were your shadows moving across the room. But I hung close to the car after I saw Grant leave. He was puffing like a steam engine. Think you lit a fire there."

"I hope so. Did you get Julian's gun?"

He shook his head. "Too risky for a man like myself who needs to keep the job he's got. Gates is a setup artist. If I had wrestled him down to look for that palm pistol, he would have twisted the story and had me in jail for planting the gun on him."

"At least now we know that he doesn't have the letter. But where could Zemin have put it? Matt said that if we could translate it and show it to Leland Stanford, the CP would take Julian's hide to court and scrape it dry."

"Your young man doesn't mince words. I like that."

She held her jaw tight a moment. "He's fought too far and too hard to lose now."

"Don't go soft on me. He hasn't lost yet. Sent one of my men to the hospital to check. Things are the same. No better, no worse."

"I'm going back there tonight. I'm going to stay with him."

"Doctor said no."

"The doctor said immediate family excepted.. Matt's son will be with me. He has to see his son."

"I don't think that's a good idea."

"Can't you understand? Matt has a son who needs him."

Garrick kneaded his face with both hands. "Lord, I'm tired."

"Don't you have children?"

"Four. I have four. And I hope I get home by dawn to see them."

"Can you at least tell me where the Carters live?"

"A few miles north of town."

"Could you, maybe, go with me to help explain? It's so late, they're going to think it's peculiar for a stranger to approach them about this."

"And they'll be right." He studied her. "Ah, cheese'n'crust." He took her arm and led her outside to a police carriage. "Old folks don't sleep regular hours anyway. Mrs. Carter probably catnaps all day. Stays up late. My mother's that way. Mrs. Carter must be up in her seventies now."

"How old is your mother?"

"Sixty-two. Her fingers are all twisted up with arthritis now, but she can still hold a mean hand of whist."

"Does she win?"

"All too often. She's a patient player. She's always telling me, 'Wait for the right card. It'll turn up if you can just stay in the game.'" Garrick gave the horse a tap on the rump and the carriage started off.

"You ever see this boy of Matt's?" he asked over the clatter of the wheels.

"No, but I have a three-year-old. It's not hard to spot another child of the same age and ability."

"Wait a minute. Didn't Matt tell you?"

"Tell me what?"

The carriage slowed. "Samuel doesn't have all his abilities."

36

Katie followed the elderly nursemaid down the hall. "Oh, he has his stubborn times, but he's mostly very good," the nursemaid said, opening a door. "Imbeciles are, you know."

Katie hesitated at the threshold, frightened to cross it. She felt as if she could no longer see ahead. The dream that had guided her was fading. She had carried it deep in her heart like a secret family portrait painted in colors too bright; used it like a beacon to lead her beyond fear of Julian, the prospect of death, even beyond the threat of losing Matt. She had sketched Samuel into the picture for balance, to compensate for her barrenness, to show Matt she could love his child—and so that Matt would feel constrained to love hers. Selfish. She had been selfish, and so insecure about marrying Matt, about deserving him. Samuel had become a symbol of her commitment, and his. She had not really thought about Samuel as a person. She had not really thought about Samuel at all.

The portly nursemaid lit a lamp and waddled to the wardrobe to sort through knickers and day clothes. The nursery was a bare room. The only toy was a rocking horse with its mane picked clean.

The light did not waken Samuel. He lay on his stomach with

one hand hanging off the edge of the low bed. She could not see his face.

"Samuel?" Nurse called in a high, babyish voice. "Get up, dearie. A nice lady's going to take you for a ride. She wants you to see your daddy before he—" She caught herself and didn't look at Katie, who still stood outside the door.

Samuel stirred. He rolled over, eyes closed, and began to suck his fingers, two fingers, like Beth. Just like Beth. Katie crossed the threshold and sat down on the bed, jostling the child gently. "Samuel?"

He awakened slowly, his limbs slack. Hiding his eyes from the light, he sat up. He was small for three and a half. He had handsome features, wide-set, deep brown eyes, and thick chestnut-colored hair. His expression, though, was strangely withdrawn. He did not react quickly to the presence of a stranger at his side, but with great deliberation slid feet-first off the bed. When he ran to his nursemaid, she saw he had a stiff, flat-footed gait, like a two-year-old's.

Nurse tugged off his nightgown and began to dress him. Samuel stared blankly ahead. Katie couldn't tell whether his lack of interest was due to a deprived intellect or a shield for his emotions. Nurse dressed him with a joyless efficiency.

"What do the doctors say about his disabilities?" Katie asked.

"Mrs. Carter don't have to take him to doctors." The nursemaid sniffed. "I take care of him. He don't hardly get sick, neither."

"How limited is he? Can he speak?"

"Sure. Says Nanny, that's me. Hungry. Bye-bye. Birdie. Things like that. And he's trained to the toilet, I want you to know."

"He can't be too backward in his development. What's he call his grandmother?"

"Nothing. He don't see her much. She's always out and about, especially since Mr. Carter passed on. It was him, you know, who liked to visit Samuel. Always came up to the nursery after supper to hold his grandbaby. Just sat and rocked him and looked out the window. Looking for Sarah, I figure. Wondering where his little girl went. She was high-strung, that girl, like her mother. Too smart, that Sarah. Too spoiled. I oughtta know. I was the one put on her first diaper right here in this room."

Nurse shook her head as she bent down to get his shoes. "And I'm too old to raise another one. Mrs. Carter's just going to have to face it. Put Samuel in a home or get a younger girl to help me." She pulled Samuel up onto her ample lap and shoved a shoe on his foot. "No two ways about it, she's going to have to spend some money on him instead of on all those window trimmings and fancy dresses. So much taffeta whisking the hall anymore you can't hear the creak of an old lady's bones in this house, mine nor hers. And her just out of mourning. Take a look at her when you go down. This hour of the night and she's sitting in the parlor in her finery, writing grand letters to old beaus. She should start getting her affairs in order, I say. She's got a poor little imbecile to think of."

"Don't call him an imbecile."

"He don't understand one way or another." The nursemaid gave him a little push toward Katie. "All done." Samuel ran a few steps, then stopped. He stood there waiting for something, a sign, a word, a shove in the right direction.

"Where are his toys?" Katie asked wearily.

"Think he's got a ball around here somewhere. Mrs. Carter put all Sarah's old things up in a cupboard for safekeeping. He couldn't play nice with them."

Katie stooped low, sitting on her heels. Samuel watched her. When she smiled he smiled back, shyly. He was shy, she thought. He had expression, feeling. His eyes never left her. She clapped her hands three times. "Pat-a-cake?"

Samuel held up his hands and waited. Nurse came along and knocked his hands together.

"Those are Samuel's hands," Katie said, controlling her anger. "Those are his hands, fine hands." She tapped the tip of his nose. "And Samuel's nose. A fine nose."

He touched his nose. "Nose," he said softly.

"I know a poem you'd like." She tapped his nose gently as she chanted a verse from Beth's rhyming cards. " 'Nose, nose, jolly red nose; and what gave thee that jolly red nose? Nutmegs.' " She pointed to his eyes. " 'And cinnamon.' " She stretched out his arm.

" 'And spices and cloves.' " She danced fingers through his hair. " 'And they gave thee that jolly red nose.' "

He smiled, listening and watching so intensely that drool overran the corner of his mouth.

"Samuel, wipe off," Nurse said irritably. Samuel buried his mouth in his sleeve, but his gaze was still so fixed on Katie, he blinked as if she were too bright a light.

Nurse packed a bag with a change of clothes and carried him downstairs to the parlor where Lieutenant Garrick waited with Mrs. Carter. Samuel's grandmother wore an ingratiating smile and thick white facial powder that made her wrinkles dry, sarcophagal.

"Samuel's ready, ma'am," Nurse said.

Mrs. Carter didn't look at the child. "Wait a minute," she told Katie. "I have something to return to Matthew." Skirt whisking, Mrs. Carter went to her polished desk and ran a finger along a row of cubbyholes, all neatly labeled. "Sixty-three, sixty-four, ah, here we are. Eighteen sixty-five." She withdrew a bundle of letters and took one from the bottom. "It's the one Matt wrote us from Texas. There are lots of things I don't have to keep, now that Mr. Carter has passed on."

Lieutenant Garrick chatted with Mrs. Carter while they took their leave, allowing Katie time to scan the letter. The Matt who'd written it had been young and hurt, his tone so tight that something seemed ready to burst between the lines. Sarah had just run away, and he was trying to prepare the Carters for the grandchild they would see.

"Sarah said she has written frankly to you in the year since Samuel was born. Sarah has also told me weekly to expect a visit from President Lincoln who would offer felicitations on our son's birth . . . Samuel was born a month too early. He suffered convulsions. His limbs stretched rigid. We feared daily for his survival. Then the trembling began. I never saw such tremors in a full-grown man let alone a being of five pounds. Gradually, the tremors lessened, but he was a jittery baby in the early months, alarmed by the slightest touch, a sudden sound. The wet nurse swaddled him so he would feel all of one piece as he fed from her. Sarah refused him her milk. His physical progress has been slow . . . I am sending money for Samuel and Sarah. I know it is not enough. Sarah will tell you too. It has never been enough . . ."

Katie looked at the child who awkwardly walked the room, touching adornments, absorbing the feel of soft cushions, tickling fringe, polished wood. He went all around the room touching, seeking, then started over again. Katie put herself in his path, stooping low to look in his eyes. He touched her buttons. He touched her chin. He touched her cheek. His finger slid in the wet track her tears had left.

"Ouch," he said softly.

"Yes," she whispered, gathering him up.

The carriage ride back to town seemed endless. The first leg of a long journey was always so, Katie thought, as she rested her chin on Samuel's head. He slept in her arms, a lax weight. His muscles lacked tension. He wasn't solid.

Lieutenant Garrick cleared his throat. "Mrs. Carter tell you the boy has a bad heart?"

Katie shook her head.

"Didn't think she did."

"It doesn't matter." She held him tighter, trying to gather him all of one piece as the wet nurse had, as she had tried to pull Edmund together in the opium den when his limbs hung like jelly.

"Sarah's need was Samuel's need," she said.

"What?"

"Laudanum." Her voice was weak. She had no energy left. "The drug is everywhere, not just in Chang's den in New York or in Julian's black market in California. It's in nerve tonics and elixirs. Who hasn't been given Godfrey's Cordial as a child? Or Mother Bailey's Quieting Syrup? Even paregoric is nothing but a camphorated tincture from the poppy."

"Now my wife, Jane, swears by paregoric for the colic. Used it on all four of our boys. They're healthy as horses."

She looked down at Samuel. "Then you're very lucky, aren't you, Lieutenant?"

He was quiet a long while. "Think Samuel's going to get lucky?"

"Maybe. I don't know. He hasn't had a chance to frolic and

play and grow. I never knew how privileged my daughter's upbringing has been. Always on the road, pulled hither and yon, but it was
always stimulating and she's surrounded by people who care. Sarah
probably thought she was doing Samuel a service returning him to
the security of her parents."

"I don't think Sarah knew what she was doing at all. She was a
talker and a charmer, but she didn't have much sense."

"Like Edmund." Katie hugged Samuel.

"Sometimes, I don't know if people lose their sense in drink
and drugs, or whether they didn't have it to begin with. That
Chinese friend of yours, he had sense enough for two people. Wish
we knew where he hid that letter."

"Your men searched the baggage car?"

"Thoroughly. Delayed that train for two hours."

"And Zemin's things?"

"Took his bags apart. Someone had already torn into them. We
even pried apart every one of those flimsy little Oriental picture
frames."

"Seventeen of them, your men said? There were only seventeen?"

"Yep. Didn't find anything. Even had the morgue go through
every article the dead men had on them. Searched the Chinese
man's body and the killer's."

She thought about the articles of the dead and how important
they were to a man like Zemin. Unfortunately, he would not be
buried as Edmund would be, with the fine handkerchief Zemin had
provided for the journey, and the money beneath his tongue, and
the worldly possessions he cherished lying nearby.

The things he cherished. "Lieutenant," she said suddenly, "did
you search Edmund's things too?"

"You mean in the casket? It's still at the station. The crate was
all nailed shut. Nobody stuffed anything in there."

"Not while it was on the train. But I think Zemin sent accessories to the mortuary in St. Louis, things Edmund needed. Maybe
too, something Edmund could protect."

"What do you mean? What kind of accessories?"

She tried not to envision Edmund's pale form in its still, satin

360

bed as she spoke softly from memory. "In Edmund's right hand a twig of willow 'to sweep all demons from his path.' In his pocket a silken handkerchief, for 'every man on a journey needs a fine handkerchief.' And somewhere near him, I think, you'll find his protector, The Eighteenth Lohan."

"What's that?"

"The framed print that's missing. The Eighteenth Lohan is a great man riding a tiger. A man with strength to triumph over evil."

"I see." Garrick nodded skeptically. "Myself, I'm a man of lesser idols. All I ever pray for is hard evidence and a jail sentence."

"Just check, Lieutenant."

He got off at the train station. "You don't mind if we open the casket without a family member there?"

"No," she said, looking away. "I don't want to see him yet. I'm sorry."

Garrick found a driver to take her on to the hospital.

She held Samuel's hand so he could jump the tile squares on the way to Matt's ward. Samuel's balance was uncertain when he hopped ahead on his own, but he never gave up.

She met Dr. Regis in the hall, and as she'd expected, he protested her plan to stay with Matt.

"But this is his son," she said. "I want Matt to know that Samuel's here."

"Matt doesn't know anything right now. He's unconscious."

"Then what harm can I do?"

The doctor looked at Samuel and shook his head. "I don't know. But people with good intentions often hurt more than they help. You realize Matt doesn't need any more pain right now."

"And I don't need a lecture. I understand the chance I'm taking."

"You do, do you?" He frowned fiercely, colliding his bushy brows. "You know him that well, do you?"

"I know he trusts me. And I trust him to fight. He won't give up. We're too close. We've come too far."

The doctor rubbed his eyes, seemingly wearied by what he saw in her face, or heard in her voice. "Stay the night," he said. "In the morning, you take the boy and go home."

"But that's only a few hours. What if Matt doesn't wake up to see him by then?"

The doctor didn't say anything. She understood: Then Matt would never see him.

37

Cane in hand, Julian left the late room of the White Lion Hotel. He hated to lean, but he needed support. The distasteful encounter with the police lieutenant had provoked a craving for strong drink and light company. The fellowship, though, had not been as friendly as he'd expected.

Conversation had halted longer than was polite when he'd joined General Grant's party in the private dinner room. False smiles had ringed the table as he was greeted, seated, and immersed in stilted conversation on insignificant matters.

He'd filled his glass often to offset the feeling that Grant was waiting for him to leave again. Finally, the general stopped twirling his cold cigar stub and adjourned everyone to the late room, where they all began talking nomination strategy for the convention. Julian was stuck talking with Wilson, the campaign biographer, who wryly recalled a friend's account of an evening with the opium pipe. "Very romantic. He left with the rise of dawn and vomited all the way home."

Julian decided then to leave. He swerved slightly as he entered the lobby, but the cane steadied him, and he stopped. A new

Currier & Ives print had been added to the White Lion's ongoing collection. Another sentimental scene of home and hearth, he thought, farm life at its rosiest. America had grown entirely too nostalgic since the end of the war, longing for peaceful illustrations of family reunions and rural simplicity. Everywhere one looked were paintings and lithographs of friendly little houses, rolling hills, and good country folk amidst their fowl and fat cows. Ice pond scenes for winter, cornhusking for fall, picnics with linen tablecloths for summer. His mother had never owned a linen tablecloth. He had never been on a picnic as a boy. Impossible to create nostalgia for things that never were. He continued on across the lobby.

" 'Evening, Mr. Gates."

Lieutenant Garrick sat on an ottoman, idly crimping the corners of a telegram. He got up when Julian halted abruptly, a few feet away. "Pretty prints, aren't they?"

"You don't strike me as the kind of person who cares much for art," Julian said.

"Oh, but I like those. My mother was raised on a farm, you know."

"I hate farms." *I hate hearing about your mother.*

"Not an easy life. But my mother, she was always one for rationalizing. Things could have been worse, she says. Could have been as bad as for the Gottswald family I was telling you about. Father got killed in the mines. Mother and three girls tried to make a go of it back there in the hollow. But the boy stopped sending them money after he got the Widow's inheritance. A bad winter came up. The mother died of pleurisy before the second snow. The three sisters moved into the mine camp in town. The youngest girl had rickets pretty bad and she died when the scarlet fever went around. The next one had three babies in three years. The oldest sister ran away, looking for her brother. Makes you wonder if she ever came across him, doesn't it?"

What was her name, Julian wondered, the oldest one? Surely he could remember. Jane. Plain Jane, he used to call her.

"Got an interesting telegram from St. Louis," Garrick said.

Julian started walking again. Jane hadn't really been plain, he thought. She'd had fair skin and merry eyes. Very thin. All of them, very thin.

Lieutenant Garrick followed him. "You've been charged with a crime, Mr. Gates."

Julian stumbled and caught himself, stamping the cane firm to the floor. "A crime?"

"Destruction of private property." Garrick cleared his throat. "Seems you killed a pigeon."

Julian turned to look at him. "Surely you're not serious."

"A certain Mr. Devlin O'Shea pressed the complaint and wants to sue for redress and damages."

"Well, I don't know how I'll be able to sleep tonight," Julian said, mock-contrite. "I'll have to wire my attorney first thing in the morning."

Garrick pulled an envelope from his coat. "Good idea." He opened the flap and slid out a letter. Unfolding it, he held it so Julian could see. "Fascinating, the way they write. Like pictures."

Like needle-leaf flowers, triangle-topped trees, and tiny black storm slashes, Julian thought. Hundreds of them. God, what a secretive, uncivilized language Chinese was. Still, it was decipherable. Someone would find words there. He frowned in concentration. What did his name look like in Chinese?

"I'll be on my way to Washington soon," Garrick went on. "I'll need help to get this translated. I know a senator, Bill Cahill. I think he can make the right contacts."

Cahill. Was Cahill behind all this? Julian stared at the lieutenant, trying to judge how much he should offer him. But Julian couldn't concentrate. He couldn't calculate a figure. So many things running together. Must be the whiskey. He tried to stall. "This letter, where did you get it, Lieutenant?"

"Edmund Henslowe gave it to me."

Edmund? Liar! Devious liar! Julian's vision blurred. The lieutenant's face grew pinched, long, and tight; the eyes were small, bird-sharp. Like a shadow, she hovered in front of him. Julian flitted his fingers through the haze, but the Widow's bird eyes only grew more distinct. He waved an arm, but the vision was undisturbed, ungodly pale, though her eyes were still blue and fully open, as they'd been when he had removed the pillow he'd used to suffocate her. Open and astonished, as if she had never guessed his thoughts. He'd been there four years. Didn't she know him after so long?

He stumbled backward. The lieutenant didn't move, but the Widow loomed closer. *Read, Julian. "Book Eleven, after The Fall."*

He pivoted on the cane and walked stiff-legged across the lobby, barely allowing the porter time to open the door to the outside. Julian ran down the steps to the street, out to the middle of the street where it was dark, where he could not see her.

Too late he realized that the coach driver, the four horses in harness, could not see him either.

Katie entered the room quietly. Matt lay unconscious on the bed.

Samuel hopped the tile squares from the hallway into the room with resounding thuds and high energy.

A nun brought in a floor pallet for Samuel. Katie rummaged in his bag for the rubber ball she had insisted his nursemaid find before they left the Carters'.

While the nun straightened Matt's covers and laid the back of her hand to his cheek, Katie sat primly on a straight-backed chair. As soon as the nun closed the door, though, she moved the chair close to the bed. She lay her fingers to his lips; his breath glanced off her skin. She touched his cheek, his forehead. Feverish. Live heat.

"Matt." He could not hear her, of course. She held his hand, stroking his skin, wishing he would waken to her touch. She held to him a long time, feeling a strange, vague anger. It was possible he would leave her. After all the threats they had faced since their escape from Julian's gallery, after she had delivered his message to Grant and enlisted the help of a good policeman, Matt might yet leave her.

"Finish it," she pleaded. "Stay and finish it."

There's so much to gain, Matt. Your father's pride, your son's love. You cannot leave Samuel in that house. He's a sweet and gentle child. Every small ability he harbors is vital to him. Each will be diminished by those grim, unloving women. They are limited people.

I am limited too. I don't think I have enough strength left to dream for both of us. I know it's not the dreaming you hate, it's the disappointment. But disenchantment doesn't come from dreaming. It comes from giving up. Hope has no end until we kill it ourselves. I'm so tired. It's your turn, Matt. Your turn to dream.

He seemed barely to breathe.

She rested her head on the mattress. Across the room Samuel chased the ball. When he grew tired, he climbed up on Katie's lap and sucked his fingers. When his eyes closed, she allowed hers to also.

She slept, exhausted. When she woke, dawn lit the room and fingers tickled in her hair. Samuel sat on the bed, trying to remove the small wooden comb from her hair. She gently caught his hand, then looked to Matt. He was still unconscious, still clammy with fever.

Lifting Samuel from the bed, she held him on her hip as she poured fresh water in the basin. She dipped in a cloth, and Samuel leaned down happily to finger-play in the water. She glanced at the bed and caught her breath.

Matt was staring at them.

Matt. She turned to him, still holding Samuel.

Matt's expression was one of pain, more than physical pain. "You should've—listened—to me—"

"You should've told me the truth," she said.

"Would it—have made—a difference?"

She looked at Samuel as he clapped wet hands together. "No."

He grimaced, or was it a smile? "Didn't—think so." He was drifting off. She went to the bedside. "Stay awake, Matt," she pleaded softly. "Let Samuel see you."

Matt couldn't hold his head straight. He lay his cheek to the pillow and closed his eyes. She sat Samuel on the bed. "Talk to him, Samuel," she said. "Talk to your father."

The boy crept close to his father's shoulder. He studied Matt a moment, then solemnly placed his index finger on his father's nose.

"Nose, nose." He spoke as softly and seriously as Katie. He looked up at her. "Jolly red nose."

"Yes," she whispered. He remembered. "That's right. What else?"

"Nutmeg," he whispered. Gently he touched Matt's eyelid. With a wary squint, Matt opened one eye.

Samuel had heard it once, Katie thought, and he remembered.

He took his father's arm and tried to lift it, grunting with the effort. " 'Ci'manen,' " Samuel said, and waited. " 'Ci'manen,' " he commanded, louder. Matt could not raise his arm.

" 'Spices and . . .'?" Katie prompted hopefully.

" 'Clove!' " Samuel leaned on his father's chest to tickle fingers in his hair. Matt inhaled sharply at the pressure, and Katie jerked Samuel away. Scared, Samuel sucked two fingers.

She stroked his hair, urging him to finish. "And that gives thee . . . ?"

Samuel sucked silently.

Matt slowly raised his hand. He whispered, " 'And that—gives thee—?' "

Samuel took his fingers out of his mouth and leaned down low enough for Matt to touch his nose. " 'Jolly red nose,' " he said.

Matt's hand strayed to his son's hair.

"He's a fine boy," Katie said.

Matt nodded.

"He has a good mind."

Matt was motionless. Sleep, or a deep weariness, was overtaking him.

"He just has much to learn."

"Like father," he whispered, "like son." He drifted off.

She picked up the boy and held him close. "Oh, Samuel," she whispered. "Oh, Samuel." She hugged him tightly and set off in a whirl, dipping and swaying, not stopping until the child's giggles filled the room and spilled over into the hall.

She took him out of the room to find some breakfast. Not far down the hall, Lieutenant Garrick sat alone on a chair. He stood when he saw her. " 'Morning."

"Did you come for me?" she asked brightly. "Am I in trouble after all?"

"No. I found the Chu King-Sing letter, just where you said."

Her mood turned sober. "Edmund came through. Too late, though, for him."

"Death redeems us all, or so I've been told." He nodded in the direction of the private room behind him. "I'm here to question Mr. Gates, if he ever gets coherent."

"Julian's ill? What happened?"

"He had an accident. A four-in-hand ran him over last night. Crushed his pelvis. Doctor think's he's got a skull fracture too. They gave him enough morphine to hold a mule and he's still moaning. Delirious."

"Has anyone been notified?"

Garrick took his seat again, staring straight ahead, a grim watcher. "He doesn't have any loved ones."

Two days later Matt's parents were due to arrive with Lin and Beth. Katie was so anxious she traipsed up and down the corridor, waiting. She tried not to pass Julian's room; his groans seeped tortured and fearful beneath the door. Lieutenant Garrick seemed unaffected. He also seemed to be on twenty-four-hour guard.

"Mommm-eeee!" Beth's call was unmistakable. Katie spotted Beth and Lin far down the hall and ran all the way to meet them.

"Mommy!" Beth jumped up into her arms. "I found you!"

Katie kissed her and squeezed her tight. "I missed you, Beth. I missed you so much."

"Mommy, I saw a num."

"Nun, darling."

"I saw a man be sick on the floor. It smells." She pointed back the way she had come. "Right back there."

"Beth," Lin said in a tone that warned against details. Lin's eyes were red-rimmed; she was dressed in mourning white.

"You've been to the mortuary?" Katie asked. "I didn't want to make arrangements for him until you got here."

Lin nodded. "I have asked that Zemin rest beside Edmund."

"Of course. How's Father?"

369

Lin searched for an appropriate word. "Incapacitated. He will not be on stage for the premiere."

Beth wiggled to get down, and Katie let her go. "Poor Father."

"Poor Poppy. Paying for all that Scotch whiskey. Mr. Altmann wants to put your father on an allowance, founder or not."

"I take it Altmann has taken a look at our books?"

"Mr. Altmann is your new business manager. He is also an investor."

"Investing in what?"

"The theater Miss Lucy St. Clair is buying. She convinced some of her music hall patrons to be partners in a little theater a block from the New Gate."

"It's the Shakespeare, isn't it? Lucy loves it."

"Oh, yes. She is wonderful, such a funny Nurse. I watch her in rehearsals with Tobias."

"And how many dinners out have you had with good Tobias while I've been gone?"

Lin gave her a scolding glance. "None. There is no time. Everyone is too crazy to eat. The premiere is tomorrow. I am heartsick to miss it. Tobias is a star, for the first time, a star."

"And what about Peg? Is she nervous?"

"Yes. And excited. And glowing. And beautiful. Such a beautiful Juliet. You would be so happy for her, Miss Katie."

"I want more than that. I want to be jealous of her."

"Well, she exhibits better diction than you," Lin teased. "But her words do not shine yet. Not like yours."

Katie hugged her. "I missed you and your unbiased, expert opinions."

Hellie and Art appeared with the doctor. Lin went on down the hall toward Matt's room to corral Beth.

Hellie put down her leather bag and embraced Katie. Art stood stoically, hands gripping his lapels, his shoulders curled forward. He looked ashen, hollow-cheeked. He turned to speak further with Dr. Regis while Hellie talked to Katie.

"The doctor says Matt's just about out of the woods and getting stronger by the hour." Hellie smiled. "No doubt a tribute to his nurse." She glanced quickly to see if Art was watching her, then whispered, "Ever since the telegram arrived, Art's hardly spoken. He can't eat. He's terrified." She turned to her husband and took his arm. "I was wondering if you had asked the doctor about Julian's condition yet?"

"Mr. Gates is not in good shape," Dr. Regis said. "His bones will knit over time. I don't think he'll ever walk free of pain again. He's certainly not as lucky as Matt."

"I could give a gnat's wrap about Julian Gates," Art said, but his words lacked vigor. Something had been sapped from him. "I want to see my son."

"Fifteen minutes," the doctor said. "Your son, but my patient." Dr. Regis took his leave of them at the door to Matt's room.

Matt lay fevered but awake. In the corner Beth sat on the floor rolling the ball to Samuel while Lin watched. Hellie went to Matt and embraced him. When she straightened, her gaze strayed to Samuel and she smiled wistfully at him.

Matt grabbed the edge of the bed and tried to pull himself up.

"Matt, let me help," Hellie said.

"No. I can do it."

"Art, help him."

"Mother." Matt set his teeth, trying to manage the pain. Hellie stood back, and he tried again, rolling slightly to one side. His forearm trembled with the effort to pull.

Art stepped up to the side of the bed and put out his hand. "Son?"

Nearly exhausted, Matt grabbed his father's hand to keep from falling back. Art pulled him closer and put an arm around him to keep him upright. Matt fell forward against his father's chest.

The women instinctively turned away. Katie took Hellie's hand as the older woman drew a handkerchief from her sleeve. She was quiet a long while, holding the cloth over her eyes. When she spoke, her voice was unsteady. "I'm ready to meet my grandson now."

"Matt told you about Samuel?"

"Yes. Long ago. I couldn't make him change his mind and bring Samuel home. You changed his mind. You changed many things."

Beth jumped up and tugged on Hellie's skirt. "Hellie, this is Samuel. We're playing."

Samuel scrambled up and held on to Hellie's skirt, just like Beth.

"Hello, Samuel," Hellie said, smiling down at him.

"Give Samuel his toy now," Beth said.

Hellie reached into her bag. "I've been saving this for you, Samuel." She pulled out the brewer's dray with its carved horses and wooden barrels. "Beth reminded me to bring it for you."

Samuel stared open-mouthed at the toy as she set it on the floor, then he looked at her. "It's for you, sweetie," she said. "It's for my Samuel." She reached out with her handkerchief and wiped the drool from his chin.

"Samuel!" Beth said. "You're letting out your spit."

Samuel quickly clamped his mouth closed.

"Say thank you to Hellie and we can play store," Beth said.

Samuel plopped down and pulled the polished wagon toward him. "Fank you, Hellie."

"Grandma," Hellie whispered, sitting on the floor beside him. "I'm your grandmother." She combed the hair from his eyes with her fingers, then straightened his collar. As he studied all the parts of his new toy, she smoothed her hand down his back.

Matt watched her, then looked at his father. "I shouldn't have kept him away from her."

"You didn't. You were keeping him away from me."

Matt glanced away.

"Nothing else you could've done," Art said. "Like father, like son. I know that."

"You know that." Matt's expression held feelings too painful for Katie to see, and she stepped out into the hall.

A few doors down, Lieutenant Garrick was still sitting outside Julian's room, stone-faced, looking straight ahead.

As she watched, a nun bustled past the lieutenant and into Julian's room. She emerged a short time later and spoke briefly to the lieutenant. He nodded. She walked down the hall and returned with the doctor and a litter borne by two orderlies.

Garrick got up, draped his rumpled coat over his arm, and put on his hat. He turned to face Katie and nodded grimly.

The watch was over.

Chilled, she rubbed her arms as she went back into Matt's room. It was noisy. The children and Lin were laughing as Hellie and Art talked low with each other.

Katie sat beside Matt. She said nothing for a long while, only touching his arm to assure herself of his solid warmth, his alertness to her, to every live thing around him.

"What's wrong?" he asked.

"Julian."

"He's dead?"

She nodded.

"Dead," he repeated. "But it's not finished, is it?"

"Senator Cahill is on his way from New York. He says with your reports, he can build a roasting spit for the Crédit Mobilier by summer. And there's a reporter from the *New York Herald* waiting until you're strong enough for an interview. The paper's going to send him to the end of the line on the UP to critique railroad construction."

"Tell him I can see him tomorrow," Matt said.

"I will not. You're crazy."

"No, practical. We can't afford to let the momentum die."

Dr. Regis stepped in. "Visiting's over. I want to turn this back into a hospital room for a while. You can come back this afternoon."

As everyone took their leave, Samuel and Beth began running down the hall. The chasing game grew giggly and loud.

"Stop that!" Dr. Regis shouted. "Someone corral those kids!"

Art turned to the cavorting toddlers. "Samuel! Beth!" His voice was ferocious, and the children froze.

He walked over to them and scooped up a small hand from each, as if they were game birds felled by a shot.

Beth pulled away and looked up at him. "You yelled at us."

He kept his hand extended. "How else were you going to hear me?"

Suspicious, she ignored his hand and looked over at Samuel.

He sucked two fingers. She promptly did the same, holding out her other hand to him.

He dropped Art's hand and took hers.

Art followed the subdued youngsters down the hall. Exchanging smiles, Lin and Hellie followed him.

"I'd like a minute alone with Matt," Katie told Dr. Regis.

"A minute." He left.

She closed the door and sat on the bed. "Are you tired?"

He pulled her close and held her head to his chest. "Exhausted."

"I wanted to talk about home."

"Whose home?"

"Ours. Beth wanted to know where we're going to live."

"And you didn't want to tell her about Texas?"

"How did you know I wanted to talk about Texas?"

"I could see it in your face the night I mentioned it in Devlin's safe house."

"That was a few days and hundreds of miles ago. How did you know I would bring it up now?"

"I don't know." He shrugged. "I just knew you'd be worried."

"About what?"

"The future. You always worry about the future. It's a habit."

"You shouldn't know my habits so well before we're married." She kissed him lightly. "You'll get bored."

"Oh, there are lots of things I don't know," he said, teasing. "Like what we're going to live on."

"My theater work." She hesitated. "And, maybe, your law degree?"

"I'm sorry," she went on when he didn't respond. "I know you haven't wanted to think about that."

"I've thought about a lot. About all the claims there'll be against the UP, from little sodbusters and big shareholders alike. I'd like to prosecute those claims."

"You would?" She looked at him, frowning. "I don't know about that."

"What's wrong?"

374

"Crusaders make impassioned lovers, but impractical husbands."

"Actresses make impassioned lovers, but impractical wives."

"Well met."

"No, well matched."

"Concede the game. We have work to do."

"Katie?"

"Hmm?"

He cupped the back of her head, guiding her lips to his. "This is not work."

Thank You Notes

To Nita Taublib, Elizabeth Barrett, and Carolyn Nichols for editorial guidance.

To Deborah Roffino, Nancy Hageman, Liz Lynch, Cheryl Wolfe, Judy Cuevas, and Ronnie Londner for helpful reading, critiquing, and special research.

To Tim McNamara and Therald Todd for details of theater.

To Jonathon Nelson and Sam Boldrick for details of trains.

To Heather and Sean for loving care of a writing mom.

To Pete and Nancy for books, stories, and beginnings.

To Wayne, for all the rest.